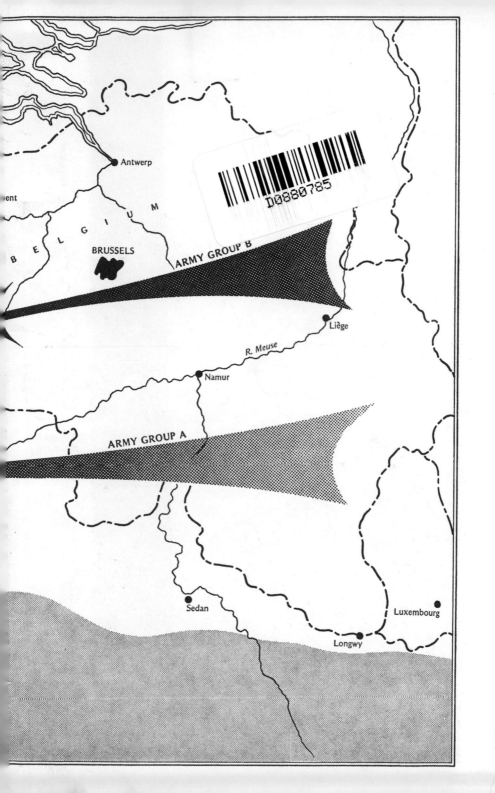

Antwerp

BELGIUM

BRUSSELS

ARMY GROUP B

Liège

R. Meuse

Namur

ARMY GROUP A

Sedan

Longwy

Luxembourg

RIDE OUT THE STORM

Also by John Harris

NOVELS

The Lonely Voyage
Hallelujah Corner
The Sea Shall Not Have Them
The Claws of Mercy
Getaway
The Sleeping Mountain
The Road to the Coast
Sunset at Sheba
Covenant with Death
The Spring of Malice
The Unforgiving Wind
Vardy
The Cross of Lazzaro
The Old Trade of Killing
Light Cavalry Action
Right of Reply
The Mercenaries
The Courtney Entry
The Mustering of the Hawks
A Kind of Courage
Smiling Willie and the Tiger

HISTORY

The Somme: Death of a Generation
The Big Slump
Farewell to the Don (as editor)
The Gallant Six Hundred
The Indian Mutiny

FOR YOUNGER READERS

The Wonderful Ice Cream
The Sword of General Frapp
Sir Sam and the Dragon
Sam and the Kite
A Matter of Luck
The Fledglings
The Professionals
A Tale of a Tail

JOHN HARRIS

RIDE OUT THE STORM

A novel of Dunkirk

 MASON / CHARTER

NEW YORK 1976

5-7-76

First published in the U.S. by Mason/Charter
Publishers, Inc., 641 Lexington Ave., N.Y.C.

First printing, February, 1976

ISBN 0–88405–144–7

CONTENTS

We shall . . . ride out the storm of war and outlive the menace of tyranny . . . That is the resolve of HM Government . . . That is the will of Parliament and the nation . . . we shall not flag or fail . . . We shall fight on the seas and oceans . . . we shall fight on the beaches, we shall fight on the landing grounds, we shall fight in the fields and in the streets, we shall fight in the hills, we shall never surrender . . .

Winston Churchill, 4 June, 1940

AUTHOR'S NOTE

Since this book is based firmly on fact, I have read everything possible on the subject by historians and by the soldiers who where there. I am particularly indebted to three books: Gun-Buster's *Return Via Dunkirk* (Hodder and Stoughton, 1940), Sir Basil Bartlett's *My First War* (Chatto and Windus, 1940), and David Divine's detailed and authoritative *The Nine Days of Dunkirk* (Faber, 1969). I also owe a great deal to those men who agreed to go through the whole thing again with me in their homes, producing old maps and photographs and digging into their memories for modest accounts of how it had seemed to them. Like most old soldiers they were very casual about it, and for the most part seemed to consider only that it had been 'a bit dodgy'.

SUNDAY, 26 MAY

Dunkirk!

There were nine days of Dunkirk and in the early afternoon of the first of those nine days, 26 May, 1940, well aware that his country was on the threshold of one of the greatest crises in her history, Alban Kitchener Tremenheere was walking through the flat streets of Littlehampton in Sussex towards his lodgings. He was none too sober and felt in the sort of devilish mood that had more than once in his lifetime got him into trouble. Indifferent as always to other people's opinions, he was convinced that before long he was going to be dead, dying, or at the very least a slave of the Greater German Reich, and was therefore determined, even if no one else was, that he was going to have some fun before the chopper fell.

For eight months since the war had started the previous year there had been no fighting and, with most of the casualties coming from road accidents, he had lulled himself into believing the war wasn't as bad as people had led him to expect. He had not been alone in his view, of course, because the whole country had felt the same and even the Prime Minister had said that, like an old soldier, the war would eventually fade away to nothing as the Germans became convinced they couldn't win.

Hitler had changed all that. With a vengeance. Invading Denmark and Norway, he had flung aside with contemptuous ease the scratch British and French force that had gone to the rescue, and then in the darkness of the morning of 10 May the blitzkrieg which had devastated Poland the previous year had begun to sweep across Holland, Belgium and Northern France against

soldiers who had spent the period of the Phoney War painstakingly building up the traditional forces of 1918. By 20 May it
had reached the sea to split the allied armies in two and the
British, still expecting to fight according to the gentlemanly rules
of earlier wars, had suddenly found themselves dealing with situ-
ations which had not even come within the scope of their imagination.

By 26 May – *that* Sunday morning – the disaster had reached
such proportions that the Secretary of State for War had sent a
telegram to Lord Gort, the commander of the British Expeditionary Force in France, announcing bluntly that there was no longer
any course open to him but to fall back upon the coast. It was
out of date and quite superfluous because by that time, together
with the remnants of the Belgian army and the French First and
Seventh Armies, the B.E.F. was penned in a tongue of land no
more than 40 miles deep and the same distance wide with, on
the east, a highly dangerous indentation. Lord Gort, despite
a V.C., three D.S.O.s, an M.C. and a Guardsman's instinct for
obedience, had decided he must disobey his French superiors'
orders to smash his way through the Germans to the armies in the
south in order to close the dangerous gap opening to the east, and
was in effect already doing what he was now being instructed to do.

None of these details was known to Tremenheere, of course.
But, though the newspapers – making much of the self-sacrificial
bombing attacks by brave young British airmen in out-dated
machines – would only admit that the situation was 'grave', it
required no particular intelligence to grasp what was happening.
The Channel coast of France was ablaze and the whole of the
B.E.F., sent to the Continent with such high hopes the previous
autumn, was in danger of being captured. In London, instead of
being concerned with victory, thoughts were suddenly dwelling
on the possibility of defeat and, though an attempt was still being
made to keep open the Channel ports for the struggling army,
one after the other they were falling to the Germans. Calais alone
had held out – to hold the right flank of the beleaguered B.E.F. –
but by this time it was clear that when that evacuation by
sea which was already uneasily being mentioned in high places
became a fact, there would be only one usable port left – Dunkirk.

As he had sat on a box on the deck of the motor launch,
Athelstan, on which he was employed as the hired hand, Tremen-

heere had stared at the heavy print of the Sunday newspapers with a sense of growing horror. He was a sturdy black-haired man whose speech still retained the burr of the Roseland peninsula south of Truro where in the last days of 1917, having got a girl into trouble, he had decided it might be a good idea to give up fishing and join the navy. By the time he found himself home again, his problem had been solved by the girl marrying the man for whom he'd worked a twenty-five-foot lugger, but his father, an unforgiving elder of the Baptist Church, had nevertheless cocked a thumb as he'd opened the door and spoken only two words in greeting – 'Keep going'.

It hadn't particularly worried Tremenheere because by then there had been another girl in Portsmouth and he did just what his father advised and returned to make an honest woman of her. At the age of nineteen he'd been a handsome young man with heavy brows that collided in the middle to give him the look of a good-humoured satyr; but he'd always liked his beer too much, and, three years to the day after he'd led her from the altar surrounded by none-too-sober relatives, his new wife had abandoned him like a parcel left on a bus, for a sergeant in the Royal Marines.

Despite the sergeant of Marines and the fact that he'd fought for jobs all through the thirties, Tremenheere had never once ceased to believe in the British Empire and the nobility of British arms. He'd been raised on pictures of men standing on hilltops, holding flags in heroic attitudes, and nothing had ever destroyed his faith. Now, in the general confusion of defeat and dismay, he wasn't so sure. The headlines that morning had been like mourning bands and there had been pictures of Cabinet Ministers crossing Whitehall for Downing Street, grim-faced with a sense of destiny and despair. The reports from Germany had claimed enormous successes, and hastily-drawn maps had shown a situation that was already out-of-date as events moved faster than the newspapers could co-ordinate them.

Hardly aware of the slow clang of church bells over the still air, Tremenheere had stared at the stories, sucking his empty pipe, startled at the frightening speed with which disasters seemed to be following each other. It had seemed impossible that the British Army was being defeated in France by the men they'd licked so completely only twenty years before. For months everyone had been wanting something to happen and, now that it had, events were crowding one upon another with an intensity that was terrifying. Moving restlessly on his box, he had suddenly felt badly in need of a drink. Climbing ashore from the dinghy, he'd walked to his local, aware of an uncomfortable feeling that somewhere something was terribly wrong, and as he had seen the barman waiting for his order, somehow it hadn't seemed to be a day for a pint of mild.

'Give us a rum, me dear,' he'd said briskly. 'A bloody big one!'

Now, several rums later, he was heading towards his official residence, Thirteen, Osborne Road, with a view to sleeping it off.

Number Thirteen was a small detached house that contained a kitchen-living room, a sitting room that was never used, and three bedrooms, one of which was Tremenheere's, one his landlady's, and one her fifteen-year-old son's. When he arrived, his landlady, Mrs. Noone, after a morning at church, was belatedly making the beds and, as the door slammed, she appeared at the top of the stairs and stared suspiciously down at Tremenheere.

'What are you doing here?' she demanded.

It was by no means an unusual question because during normal summers he was often away with *Athelstan* and they saw each other only when he appeared to bring washing and collect clean clothes. She was three years younger than he was and had been widowed since 1930, but she'd not yet lost her good looks and between them for some time had been growing an awareness of each other that had gradually become the size of a house.

He stared up at her, then he grinned and started to march up the stairs towards her. She moved back as he reached the top step. 'What do you want?' she demanded.

'You know damn' well what I want, Nellie Noone,' he said.

'No, I don't.'

But she did and they both knew she did because he'd caught her eyes on him more than once, speculative and thoughtful.

'There's a war on, me dear,' he pointed out. 'And before long we'll all be dead. So we'd be daft to waste what time we've got left, wouldn't we?'

'I don't know what you're talking about, I'm sure.'

But she moved back again in front of him until she was inside the bedroom.

'We might not be allowed to, if them Nazis win,' he pointed out.

'Might not be allowed to *what*?'

'You know damn' well what.'

She caught the gleam in his eye and, as he made a grab for her, she shrieked and scuttled round the end of the bed. 'You randy old donkey,' she said.

He grinned and, jumping on the bed, boots and all, ran across it to trap her by the wardrobe.

'You've been drinking.'

'Makes a man eager.'

She pushed his hands away but, as he pulled her to the bed, her struggles grew less convincing. 'I've been a widow for nine years,' she said, her voice coming in harsh little gasps as she wriggled beneath him, her legs waving. 'What'll the neighbours say? What'll happen if Teddy comes home from Sunday School?'

Tremenheere kicked the door shut. 'That'll stop him,' he said.

As Alban Kitchener Tremenheere and Nell Noone happily slept off their passion clutched in each other's arms in the afternoon sun at Littlehampton, in Dover harbour nearly a hundred miles to the east, Kenneth Harry Pepper was watching a party of naval armourers fitting an ancient Lewis gun on the stern of the naval auxiliary *Daisy. Daisy* had originally been a Suffolk trawler working out of Lowestoft but the coming of the petrol engine had long since swept away her sails and now, with a topped mast and a little cabin built round the wheel, she was an ugly bald-headed vessel. Because she was solid, roomy and reliable, however, she'd recently come under naval orders, her duties to carry stores, messages and personnel to more noble ships. And since it was intended that she should, if necessary, carry them as far as the Goodwins to the north where the German hit-and-run raiders sometimes struck, she'd become entitled to a gun.

The fact that the Lewis had been rejected by everyone else as useless made no difference to Kenny Pepper. It was a gun. With a gun you could shoot Germans, and it was Kenny's dearest wish to shoot a German. He was still only fifteen and knew nothing of war beyond what he read in boys' magazines.

'How do you fire it, Sy?' he asked.

Simon Brundrett, the ship's engineer who doubled as cook, and had been considered by the navy to be the only man likely to be capable of firing the gun, pushed him away. 'You're too young to worry about that,' he said. 'You got to be a bit older for this lark.'

'You can be *too* bloody old,' Kenny said.

His eagerness to see the gun was placing him in the way of the working party, and the petty-officer in charge turned.

'Do you mind?' he said pointedly, and Brundrett gave Kenny a shove. 'Go on, kid,' he said. 'Fuck off!'

The obscenity didn't worry Kenny. Although he was only fifteen he heard it hundreds of times every day. *Daisy*'s crew were a rough lot and the Williams brothers, who ran her, a vulgar, bawdy, cheerful pair who used the word as naturally as drawing breath.

'Fuck off yourself,' Kenny retorted.

Brundrett scowled. 'You shouldn't be here. *Daisy*'s a naval auxiliary now and there won't be no room for kids.'

Kenny stared about him frustratedly. Surrounded by the backdrop of the high chalk cliffs with the ancient castle nearly four hundred feet above the town, the old Cinque Port was crammed with shipping. In the main harbour there were between forty and fifty mooring buoys all occupied by ships taking on stores. Some of the ships had been damaged trying to bring soldiers out of Ostend, Boulogne and Calais, and workmen were already at work aboard them with acetylene welders. On one of the buoys an oil tanker was berthed; on one side of her a destroyer was re-fuelling while on the other was an oil-burning cross-channel steamer and several pleasure boats.

Kenny knew what was going on across the Channel. He'd even heard that the Germans would soon start erecting guns at Calais to shell Dover, and it seemed to him that it wouldn't make much difference whether he were killed at sea or within half a mile of the shabby house he called home.

'I'm not scared,' he said loudly. Nor was he, because he wasn't close enough to the hospital ship across the harbour to see the frightful work the war had done on some of the men being lifted off, and the magazines he read showed conflict only in terms of glory in which none of the heroes ever seemed to get very much hurt.

He glanced again at the ships about him, aware of anger and shame. The naval armourers had almost finished now and were applying grease to the ancient gun. Privately, they'd long since decided that, with its smooth barrel, worn breech block and battered pans, anybody who could get it to fire more than a couple of rounds without it jamming was not just a good gunner, he was a bloody miracle.

Kenny stared at them for a moment, aware of a strange excitement. To hell with Brundrett, he decided. If *Daisy* went out of the harbour, he was going with her.

He glanced aft. Brundrett was bent over the gun with the naval men and there was no sign of Gilbert Williams or his brother, Ernie. So, lifting the hatch of the forepeak, he dropped quickly down among the anchor chain and the new rope that was stored there, and made himself comfortable.

'They'll need everybody they can get,' he said aloud.

Unknown to Kenny Pepper, the same view exactly was held by the vice-admiral in command at Dover.

He was a man of medium size, quiet, and so unemotional he was considered by some to be rather a cold fish. Before the war he'd been regarded as a failure because, having disagreed with his last chief, he'd thrown up his appointment and had been on the retired list when the demands of the time and his unquestioned ability had brought him back. Appointed to Dover, he'd reported a devastating neglect and said coldly that the place had gone to seed, with the harbour silted up, the facilities inadequate, and the defences and communications deplorable.

His face was grave as he went about his work. The British Government had been faced with the hardest of decisions in the last few days but for the first time, under its dynamic new leader, Churchill, it was dithering no longer. Already there was a new confidence about the signals coming from London, and even the propaganda hand-outs seemed to be recognizing that the British people had sufficient intelligence to face facts. The battle in France was finally being spoken of as a major disaster and the government was at last accepting its responsibilities.

Naval headquarters were set up in deep galleries hewn by French prisoners during the Napoleonic Wars, in the cliffs below Dover Castle. The admiral's office ended in an embrasure at the cliff face and small rooms nearby housed his secretary, flag lieutenant, chief of staff, and the staff itself. The large room beyond, which had once been used to hold an auxiliary electric plant was known as the Dynamo Room.

On that early Sunday morning, as Kenny Pepper made his decision, these offices were full of grim-faced men trying to bring some order out of the chaos. As the situation across the Channel had begun to develop, thoughts had turned naturally to removing the allied troops as the Royal Navy had done in countless earlier campaigns, from one point of contact to another. Up to four days ago nobody had been considering a panic evacuation, and Lord Gort had given instructions to his staff only to get rid of the 'useless mouths' of the army who filled the ground between his fighting regiments and the coast. Now, however, with the distant rumble of gunfire audible from Calais, the men in those offices at Dover all knew that this plan had already been terminated.

'We can no longer expect an orderly evacuation,' the admiral commented dryly. 'We must plan for emergencies. What ships are available?'

The chief of staff began to turn over papers and no one spoke because they all knew there were already less than there had been.

'*Keith* and *Vimy* both hit at Boulogne,' the chief of staff was saying. 'Both captains killed. *Venetia* hit. We don't know yet about damage. On the other hand, *Vimiera* brought out one thousand four hundred, which seems pretty good considering all cargo handling's ceased. The French lost *Orage*, *Frondeur* and *Chacal*, with *Fougueux* damaged.'

The admiral's face was expressionless. His experience of war went back to 1903 and he was not the type to be dismayed by losses. 'And at Calais?' he asked.

The chief of staff frowned. 'At Calais,' he said, 'we lost *Wessex*, with *Vimiera* and *Burza* damaged.'

The admiral studied the papers in front of him. His chief problem at that moment was to secure the area through which the merchantmen moving across the Channel to evacuate the troops would pass. It was going to be difficult because the Germans could already bring guns to bear on a lot of it, and they had light craft operating from Flushing, while he only had a bare flotilla of destroyers to guard the east, cover the routes, establish a protective counter-bombardment and anti-aircraft protection, and sweep the approach channels and the area round Dunkirk itself.

'Isn't *Vital* at Portsmouth?' he asked.

'Yes, sir. Undergoing repairs.'

The admiral nodded. 'Draft a signal,' he said. 'We'll need her.'

As the admiral's signal started on its way, *Vital* was already struggling to get to sea, and her officers, aware of what was coming and conscious that perhaps it was their last chance for a drink, were toasting their chances in the wardroom. Nothing official had been said, and though the newspapers were still admitting nothing beyond the fact that a battle was being fought in France, in Portsmouth, with its antennae reaching out to the Admiralty, it was well known that the British army had suffered a major defeat and was now waiting for the navy to lift it off, as it had at the Dardanelles and a dozen similiar operations before.

Vital was small, weighing only just over 1,000 tons, and her armament consisted of four 4-inch guns and six torpedo tubes. She was supposed to be capable of thirty-nine knots but could do only thirty-two because she was long past her prime, and she had just returned from an up-Channel escort voyage limping badly with condenser trouble.

What was of more importance to Paymaster Sub-Lieutenant James Barry Hatton, however, was that she was thin-skinned, and not even on her bridge, where it was his duty to station himself, was there much in the way of protection.

Hatton glanced round him at the rest of the men in the wardroom – the captain, Lieutenant-Commander Neville George Hough – pronounced Huff – the torpedo officer, the navigating officer, the gunnery officer and all the others. They were all regulars except the navigating officer – who wore the twisted braid of the Reserve and came from the Merchant Service – and Hatton was the only man among them who'd not previously followed the sea for a living.

At that moment the chief engineer was making his report to the captain. Despite the gin in his hand it was urgent and forceful. 'We've fixed the condenser, sir,' he was saying, 'but there's a bearing that's running warm that we ought to look at. If it got really hot, we'd have to stop engines.'

Hatton studied the chief, a square, hairy Scot called Mac-Gillicuddy who'd come up from the ranks. His speech was thick and at meals the way he held his knife and fork wasn't the way

Hatton had been taught. Hough seemed indifferent to such faults, however, and Hatton knew it was because the chief, whatever else he might lack, had a thorough knowledge of his job.

Which was something Hatton did not posses.

Before the war he'd worked for the *Kent Messenger* at Dover but, with an adoring girl friend on *The East Kent News* who had a flat, and well-organized to avoid too much work, he'd been stupid enough to throw it all up for a job on a big and bouncy national in London where, in September, 1939, everything had suddenly come to a full stop, and Hatton had found himself without a job.

For a grim fortnight he'd allowed himself to be employed by the Greater London Air Raid Precautions Authority as a telephonist, sitting in a cellar at Islington reading paperbacks, and it was his loathing for the job rather than any sense of patriotism which had driven him to the navy recruiting office to insist that they take him under their wing. With the background of a minor public school and a father who was a Church of England parson, he'd done a quick trip in an armed merchant cruiser before being given a commission as a captain's secretary. He'd now been in *Vital* for a matter of one week, still conscious of being an amateur in a wardroom full of professionals.

He glanced towards the captain again. Hough was having to make his decision and he did so without any trace of being aware of the responsibility it entailed.

'I think we'll have to chance it, Chief,' he was saying. 'I've just been warned there are a few soldiers in a bit of trouble near Dunkirk and that we might be needed.'

The chief engineer nodded, downed his gin and disappeared, and Hough turned back to the others. Hatton watched him, his mind full of envy. Very early in his sea-going career he'd decided to write a vast novel about the navy which would expose all the time wasted on parade grounds learning to salute properly, present arms and come to a halt without falling over himself. In recent weeks, however, he'd taken to thinking about it again and was slowly beginning to see that those early weeks had done more than that. They'd taught him instant obedience and – in action with the enemy, he suspected – the habit of not discussing everything first was what won a battle. When the time for action came, he imagined, life or death would depend on one thing only – the decision of Neville George Hough, who, despite his youth, had been trained ever since school to know exactly what the navy expected of him.

As he thought about it, Sub-Lieutenant Hatton realized that within a matter of days – perhaps even hours – he was going to have to face up to the climax of his life, and he wondered if he'd been good enough in terms of honesty and decency to fit him for the demands it might make. He had a feeling he ought to be communing with some inner spirit, steeling himself for the ordeal he knew was about to come. But, try as he might, that Sunday afternoon, the only thing that would come into his mind was the memory of the shabby way he'd treated Nora Hart when he'd left Dover that spring morning in 1939 to catch the train that took him to London. He wondered uneasily if she'd ever forgiven him and, suddenly, unexpectedly, if she were still in Dover.

While Sub-Lieutenant Hatton struggled with his conscience and his memories in Portsmouth, a man, who, in effect, was his counterpart on the opposite side was staring at a dead man near Asquellines in France. To Walter Boner Scharroo, of Milwaukee, Wisconsin, U.S.A., it had seemed at first to be a privileged position to be accompanying the German land forces as a representative of United Associated Press. Now, wracked by weariness, his face burnt bright-red by the sun, he wasn't so sure.

Attached to a propaganda company hitched to a reconnaissance squadron, he'd considered himself a very lucky man. It was not the practice to allow foreign correspondents to be so far up at the front, but Walter Boner Scharroo had a cousin with the ear of the German Propaganda Minister himself and he was following close behind the spearheads of the German army.

He had got the job not only because his cousin knew Goebbels but also because he spoke German like a native. His father had been a Belgian from Kontrijk who'd emigrated to America. His mother's name had not been Boner but Böner, and she'd come from Hamburg. Because she was the dominant member of the family and his father had died young, they'd spoken German in the home rather than Flemish or French or even English, and he'd associated with German-Americans rather than any other ethnic group.

Uninvolved, untouched by emotion, he'd found the speed and efficiency of the Germans incredible. This, he'd felt, was how the Americans would do the job. Hitler's war machine worked on oiled wheels. The French machine, rusted and neglected, had fallen apart at the first sign of strain, and their defeat was caused less by the weight of German arms than by the moral degradation of a nation long since undermined by her out-dated political system, and years of distrust and contempt for governmental authority.

He'd followed the panzer tracks through the Ardennes, and for a fortnight now had watched the dusty streams of defeated French soldiers heading heavy-footed to imprisonment. He'd firmly expected the same thing to happen with the British, but somehow in the north things had been different. The Dutch and Belgians had resisted fiercely, opening their dykes and flooding their land before the panzers, and jolting in his little Opel, his mouth parched, his eyes gritty with the dust from the thundering wheels of the Führer's mechanical might, Scharroo had felt the first twinges of uneasiness about Germany. In the eyes of the man in Berlin, victory would not stop in France, and he tried to imagine what it would be like to see these grey uniformed jack-booted figures strutting through Milwaukee.

Suddenly the column halted – so abruptly he almost ran into the lorry in front. As he slammed on the brakes, he saw soldiers jumping out of the back and waving him away, and almost at once he heard the tearing sound of a Schmeisser machine gun, like the ripping of cloth.

Leaving the car with its rear tucked into a hedge, he began to run down the lane in the heat of the afternoon sun. From up ahead there was another spattering of fire but the Germans seemed untroubled by it and were standing behind their vehicles, sticking helmeted heads out in the hope of seeing where it came from.

'*Was ist denn da drüben los?*' he asked. 'What's all the fuss?'

The young German in front of him was leaning against the tailboard of a lorry, a young blond god with two days' growth of beard on his cheeks, his clothes layered with white dust.

'The Tommies,' he said. 'We'll soon polish them off.'

He was eating from a mess-tin full of cherries he and his friends had rifled from an orchard in one of the hot little valleys behind them. His face was brown and his teeth were white like his eyes with the brilliant whiteness of youth.

Like the young German, Scharroo didn't expect the resistance to last long. The advance had gone exactly according to plan. They'd known all the way just where the dumps of petrol and water would be, where the food would be, where to obtain the local maps, the condition of the roads, and how many refugees there were in front. It had been a triumph of organization, though Scharroo realized it probably involved some treachery too.

While he waited, he heard the harsh grate of a radio and the shrilling of whistles. Almost immediately, another spattering of firing broke out and this time he knew it was not German. Then he heard the thump of a gun, and the screech of a shell whistling overhead and decided it was time to head for the ditch. Several of the Germans went with him, but most of them stayed where they were, merely ducking their heads and laughing at their friends' nervousness. Up ahead he heard a muffled explosion and saw a column of smoke rise into the air.

'They've hit one of the lorries,' someone said – indignantly, as though the enemy weren't playing the game – then Scharroo saw men running forward, their equipment bouncing on their backs, among them the blond young god, still cramming cherries into his mouth as he ran.

The firing ahead was growing stronger now and a sergeant came running along the column, shouting, 'Get those lorries away! Get them away!'

The drivers ran to the cabs, and the vehicles started to back and fill as they turned in the narrow road. For a moment there were all the signs of panic and Scharroo saw another lorry burst into flames and the driver running from it, beating with his hands at the flames springing from his jacket. Other vehicles – lorries, scout cars, motor cycles – came through the smoke, and the men who had moved forward so arrogantly appeared to be having second thoughts about their invincibility.

The lorries had vanished behind a bend in the road now, with the exception of two up ahead, which were slewed slant-wise across the tarmacadam – one of them in the hedge. They were burning furiously, and suddenly the air seemed full of flying pieces of metal as Scharroo crawled back to where he'd left his car. The din was terrific with the chatter of machine guns and the steady pop-pop of rifles, and above it the thump of the hidden gun ahead.

Gingerly raising his head, Scharroo saw two or three figures lying in the dust, one of them without a leg and apparently trying to bite the ground in its agony. The chattering of the guns went on and he saw leaves drifting down through the sunlight as they were snipped from the branches above his head. Nearby an officer, his head well down, was shouting into a radio microphone, and just alongside Scharroo a sergeant was cursing furiously in steady gusts at the men ahead.

It seemed humiliating to crouch there in the afternoon sun and Scharroo was beginning to think they'd be there for the night when he heard the roar of engines and the clatter of tank tracks.

'Here are the panzers,' the sergeant yelled, his grin reappearing.

The tanks rumbled round the corner where the lorries had vanished, the grey snouts of the guns poking forward, and the sergeant went wriggling along the ditch to where they waited. The tank commander seemed to be trying to pin-point his enemy and Scharroo saw the gun swing. The crash of the shot jarred his teeth and made him jump, and lifting his head, he saw it had torn aside part of the hedge.

Then the second tank fired, the hedge burst into flames, and the Germans jumped from the ditch and began to run. The rattle of machine pistols and tommy guns started again. Then it was all over and everything was silent except for the crackle of flames and the distant drone of an aeroplane high overhead. The officer was walking forward now, his pistol in his hand, and Scharroo saw the sergeant shove a man in khaki uniform through the hedge. He fell on his knees in the ditch, then rose slowly, his hands in the air. Several more men followed and stood in a group in the dusty road, their hands on their heads.

The Germans were surrounding the Englishmen now, their grins reappearing, their confidence returned. One of them gestured derisively at the weary captives and at the still shapes sprawled under the hedge, and there was a gust of laughter. There was something cold-hearted in it that chilled Scharroo. Even in war there seemed room for compassion and he suddenly had a feeling that these ardent young Nazis had had it drilled out of them, as efficiency had been drilled in.

The officer was telling off three men to escort the English soldiers to the rear now and the sergeant was moving among the German dead, getting their names from their identity discs.

'Four,' he annouced.

'Leave 'em,' the officer ordered. 'And get the wounded sent to the rear. It's time we moved on.'

Shouts sent the soldiers running back to the lorries. Scharroo followed them, but the front of his Opel was crushed, as though one of the tanks had caught it as it had turned. The lorries were beginning to move again now, stirring the dust in the afternoon sunlight, and as they jerked forward they crossed a trail of blood where one of the wounded had dragged himself from the road to safety.

The Englishmen were stumbling to the rear now, pushed into line by their guards, and the German dead had been laid in a neat row at the side of the road for the labour battalions following behind to collect. As he passed them, Scharroo noticed that one had golden hair and that his mouth was stained with the red juice of cherries.

While Scharroo was still staring at the dead German, Lieutenant Basil Allerton, temporarily attached to the Field Security Branch of Intelligence in the Third Division of the B.E.F., found himself near the village of St. André just to the north of Armentières. After nine months on active service during which the war had seemed only a bore, he was beginning to wake up to the fact that it was instead a dead weight of disaster.

When the German attack had started, with the magnolias out and the fields showing green with new corn, he and his unit had moved into Belgium with the rest of the British army, only to move all the way back again very soon afterwards and a great deal faster. The rumours that the Belgians were cracking had seemed to be well and truly borne out when, as the frontier guards had started evacuating themselves as forcefully as the civilian population, they had very swiftly been joined by a large proportion of the Belgian army, some of them apparently getting into their stride so fast they hadn't even stopped to put on their boots.

Far from being a real warrior, before the war Allerton had

taken a dilettante interest in poetry and intellectual plays, but because it had become the fashionable thing to do after Munich, he'd joined a territorial unit and as a result, rather to his surprise, had found himself in France.

Disliking the discomfort of the infantry, he'd found himself a comfortable niche with Divisional Intelligence and had worked through the bitter winter in Caepinghem, a small town near Lille, his office a crowded flat in a tenement block. With the baker and the milkman calling it had been pleasantly domestic, and Allerton's work had seemed chiefly to consist of marking all the brothels on a map because V.D. was increasing – a fact which the padres blamed on bad morale and Allerton more realistically on bad luck – keeping an eye open for gun-runners along the Belgian border, and giving to regiments newly arrived from England lectures on security which they promptly ignored. His staff had consisted of a sergeant, a corporal and twelve men, all territorials who were supposed to have been picked for the job because they were better educated than their friends. In fact, they were self-important, given to reading clever books that had no meaning, and considered themselves far too intelligent to go on parade. Allerton was easy-going with them, however, and, convinced that soldiering was not a job for adults, had allowed them to put up two stripes at night to impress their French lady friends, while he spent most of his time teaching a willing girl with a flat in the Grande Place how to speak English with the aid of an ancient phrase book which contained such gems as 'Why will you not kiss Mary? Because she is smoking and I am wearing a celluloid collar.'

He had had a low opinion of Hitler and an even lower one of the French. They had been gloomy and suffered from a tremendous envy for British phlegm – what they called *Le sang-froid habituel*, which Allerton translated in its turn as 'Their permanent bloody colds'. The notices on the walls, *Nous vaincrons parce que nous sommes les plus forts!* had seemed spiritless, and he had been well aware that the common poilu endured the British only because the Germans were several degrees worse. Since every vice imaginable had seemed to be practised in the brothels that were Allerton's concern, he had long suspected that the people who ran them would sell their country as quickly as they sold their bodies and when the Germans had crossed the border he had not been surprised to notice that their attitude was not the old-fashioned *Ils ne passeront pas*, but 'Good God, already?'

To his surprise the British army seemed to be fighting well and its generals were keeping their heads, but they had been moving south-west for days now, sometimes waiting for hours in five-mile queues of traffic under the cold moon until someone cleared a cross-roads. Every village was buzzing with rumours and there were said to be parachutists round every corner and fifth columnists in every bar.

Suddenly the war had become a holocaust such as Allerton could never have dreamed up even at his most imaginative. Everyone in France was terrified, everyone was exhausted and bewildered, and everyone seemed to be drunk – and he knew by now that it was because they were expecting defeat. Apart from making sure he emerged with a whole skin, he still wasn't sure what his own attitude ought to be. As an intellectual, he felt he ought to have one, but 'glory' was a word that never seemed to cross the minds of the troops these days. His men still carried their football boots and clever books, but Allerton himself had long since decided that the selection of intellectual literature he'd brought to France, to give himself the detached and mildly bored air he admired, had become surprisingly trivial and he had thrown it all away. There seemed no place for such things in a situation where units were lost, telephone communications were broken and soldiers were taking to their own two feet because trucks failed to appear to pick them up.

As they approached St. André there was a smell of summer in the air, a rich scent of blossom and young fruit, and the church bells were ringing as the old women from the farm cottages emerged in their black clothes for mass. Built on the curve of a small hill, surrounded by woods and near a river, by a miracle the place had so far not been touched, and after bombed Armentières with its mutilated dead, the red-tiled cottages ahead looked like a different world from the one they'd been living in for over a fortnight now.

Allerton was just looking forward to a halt and to drawing the clean air of the village into his lungs when he noticed his men pointing. Then, from the south, across their path towards Calais, he saw a heart-rending tide of refugees coming round the curve of the hill which had concealed them until the last moment, a vast black-clad column of people filling the streets and eddying into gardens and alleys like water from a burst dam.

They were Belgians and border French driven west by the fighting as their parents had been driven twenty-five years before, and within moments they'd swamped the column Allerton was with, and the trucks had to halt short of the cross-roads in the centre of the village as the wave of misery lapped round them.

Some of the refugees were carrying a single blanket tied bandolier-fashion over the shoulder – all they'd saved of their worldy possessions – but some had still not yet been able to throw off the habits of a lifetime, and women struggled along in smart hats, fur coats, and dainty shoes that crippled their feet. They had no idea where to go or where to get information where to go, and their faces were distorted with terror.

Short of food and sleep, they were far too frightened to stop – women with sore feet carrying exhausted children, old, and sick, all moving like frightened cattle. An old man was wheeling his equally ancient wife in a wheelbarrow and a group of women were pushing perambulators piled high with household goods. One of them suckled an infant as she trudged by, while a second child, not more than six years old, had harnessed itself to the perambulator and plodded forward like a small beast of burden. An overloaded farm cart, carrying a brass bedstead and a dozen old people, came to a halt on the rise to the cross-roads, and as the way ahead cleared, the ancient animal between the shafts hadn't the strength to start it again. In the gutter an old man had collapsed with fatigue and lay with his back against a suitcase. The two women who bent over him had faces that were taut with vexation, as though they were wishing he would die so they could continue. A child that had lost its parents was screaming with terror, and an elderly woman sat sobbing while her husband massaged her numbed feet and legs.

There were thousands and thousands of them, all pressing against the military vehicles. Then Allerton noticed a Fieseler recce plane hovering over the village, humming like a dragonfly in the blue sky, and with a sudden horrified awareness of what was going to happen, he set his men to digging slit trenches in a field alongside. They were none too willing, but they were philosophical and still managed to laugh. Then a Heinkel roared over the village just above the church spire, lifting above the trees to the west. They heard the whistle as the bomb came down but it fell in the next street and Allerton's batman, a cheerful idiot in spectacles called Rice, yelled out, 'Foul! Send him off, ref!'

As the Heinkel disappeared and there were no more bombs, Allerton decided the single missile was all they need expect. He was just watching a mechanized regiment of French cuirassiers, hurrying past him in their four-seater cars and motor-cycle combinations to force their way through to the bridge, when the Stukas arrived, ten thousand feet up, bunched together in the shape of an arrowhead. Even as he saw them the point of the arrow seemed to wobble and the refugees started to run.

The sky came alive with bursting shells as the leading plane did a half-roll and went into a dive. It came down at a terrific speed, piercing the air with a maniac scream so that on a simple impulse they all hurled themselves down to hug the earth. No one spoke because they were all of the opinion that they'd been singled out individually for destruction, that nothing on God's earth could stop the diving plane. As the first group of bombs landed, Allerton saw the ground heave among the clouds of yellow and grey smoke, like the sea in a heavy swell. Almost immediately a second plane came down, followed by a third and a fourth, and he felt the ground thumping him in the chest as it leapt under the concussion. There was a roar nearby as a house collapsed in a great billow of dust, and children started to scream as walls fell flat and tiles flew through the air, slicing viciously at living flesh through clouds of smoke that were lit with tongues of red flame.

The horror seemed to go on for hours, while they clawed at the earth, their mouths hanging open, their eyes blinking at every scattering of debris and pulverized earth. Dimly through the din, they could hear the incoherent cries of women and the shrill agony of a wounded horse. The last salvo of bombs burst only a few yards away. Then, as suddenly as it had begun, the world was full of a silence which, after the din, seemed uncanny and Allerton and his men lifted their heads, breathing painfully and still trembling.

St. André seemed to have been blown off the face of the

earth. It was now nothing but scree slopes of rubble, and the air was filled with wailing in a strange rising and falling cadence that was broken almost immediately by the shouts of stretcher-bearers among the broken walls as soldiers ran from hiding places to do what they could for the injured.

The old man who'd been sprawling against the suitcase was dead now, his face the colour of grey mud splashed with red, and there was no sign of the two women. A French soldier, half-buried by cascading bricks, waited in silent agony, his black hair dull with dust, only the slow clawing of his fingers showing that he was still alive. Nearby, an old woman lay on her back in the gutter, staring at the sky, one shoe missing, her toes sticking through a hole in a black woollen stocking.

The schoolroom had been hit and from the rubble a sickening stench of blood filled the air. Alongside, indifferent, the un-wounded gathered their senses and, brushing off the dust that covered their clothes, began to push past in dumb panic, ignoring the injured in their determination to escape. An old woman, her face bone-white and covered with blood, held a dead baby in her arms and shook her fist at the sky. By an iron calvary three small girls were praying on their knees, their hands clasped fiercely together. In an emergency where children were born, lost and killed by the wayside, no one took any notice. When someone yelled 'Gas!' and everyone started stampeding again, Allerton looked helplessly on, knowing it was nothing but panic or the work of a fifth columnist.

To some of the German pilots, like Major Karl Schmesser, of *3. Sturzkampfflugzeuggeschwader (Kurt Wolff St.G.1)*, the job they were having to do was distasteful. Schmesser believed in the Nazi Party because it had done things for Germany which ten years before he wouldn't have believed possible, but he was by no means a heartless man and the policy of machine-gunning refugees and dive-bombing defenceless soldiers was one he hated. On others, like Leutnant Alfred Stoos, the fighting had had a different effect. Far from affecting his morale it excited him like a drug. Ten years younger than Schmesser, he was a tough young fanatic who felt no qualms of squeamishness, and he'd taken to the job without turning a hair.

That morning, however, in his self-confidence he'd allowed

himself to be caught off guard by three Hurricanes which had turned up from nowhere and shot his machine out of the sky. With his oil tank holed and his instruments and radio shattered, he'd only just managed to escape with his life, but such was his moral toughness he was mentally untouched, his only wish to get back into the air at once.

Unfortunately, however, the speed of the advance had left them without machines to replace the ones that had been lost and the mechanics were having to perform miracles of repair. They'd started at Gütersloh in Germany and moved from airfield to airfield until they were now at Outreux, south of Guise. They'd moved so fast they had few creature comforts left and were living in tents and flying from bumpy grass fields. The *Flughafenbetriebskompanie*, which flew in their supplies of fuel, bombs and ammunition in Ju.52s, had been bombed by the French in one of the few successful missions they'd carried out, so that spares were suddenly hard to come by.

Stoos stared at the cranked-winged aeroplane he'd brought back, with its spatted wheels and Jumo engine. The *Junkers Flugzeug- und Motorenwerke*, he sometimes thought, might have done better for him. Because it had hitherto been employed only against undefended targets he'd felt the Stuka was better than it was but in the last week he'd discovered how wrong he could be.

His hand moved across the hole the British bullets had torn in the swastika painted on the tail surface. There were more holes in the fuselage, one, it seemed, in each circle of the number, D/6980.

'How long?' he demanded.

Oberfeldwebel Hamcke, in charge of the tented hanger, slapped to attention. 'A long time, Herr Leutnant. We can't perform miracles.'

'You'd better try!'

Hamcke watched the officer as he stamped away. '*Sondermeldung*,' he said. '*Leutnant Stoos ist angekommen!* Special announcement: Leutnant Stoos is here! The last of the warriors! The trouble with that one is that he can feel his Knight's Cross at his throat and it bothers him.'

Stoos had accepted Hamcke's information with bad grace and now he went to see Schmesser to demand a replacement. 'I can't sit on my backside, Herr Major,' he complained, 'until someone in the rear echelon wakes up to the fact that there's a war on. Why can't I have Fink's machine? He's not as experienced as I am.'

'And never will be if we take him off flying every time anyone gets shot up,' Schmesser said.

'Schlegel's then, Herr Major! I could do more damage than he could.'

Schmesser stared at Stoos, suddenly disliking him. The boy seemed to delight in killing. 'Schlegel's reliable,' he said shortly.

Stoos stamped back to the makeshift hangar where the mechanics were working over his machine. If D/6980 wasn't in the air again quickly, he decided, somebody was going to suffer, because he'd heard that army units were already pushing east along the coast from Calais.

They certainly were – among them Leutnant Heinrich-Robert Hinze, before the war a teacher of mathematics in the *Schieffers-wegakademie* in Hanover.

Hinze was no Nazi. He wasn't even a soldier, but he had been on the reserve when the Führer had gone into Poland, and as Alfred Stoos was working off steam at Outreux, he was placidly jogging along beside the driver in an Opel staff car in front of his battery. He was an inoffensive-looking man with pale hair and eyes and no ambition for glory whatsoever. All he wanted was to return to Hanover and his wife and two children, and go on teaching mathematics.

His fellow officers regarded him something of an oddity because he spent his spare time doing maths problems for pleasure, didn't join in their drinking and had little interest in ultimate victory. Nevertheless, they also regarded him with a certain amount of awe because he was clear-headed and never got excited. He was not given to self-analysis and introspection and knew little about ballistics or the stresses inside a gun beyond what the figures told him, but he seemed to control his spotter and his director and rangefinder with great skill, and his team, with their clinometer and range-to-elevation and deflection instruments, were highly skilled despite Heinrich-Robert Hinze's prim old-maidish looks. He rarely smiled, and was just about as different from Alfred Stoos as it was possible to be, but, because he so regularly and with such ease hit his targets, he was known to the battery as Bob the Nailer. He was now moving up under instructions from Army Group A to set up his guns as far forward as possible to cover the approaches to the coastal ports.

Not far to the south, Major Hans-Joachim Horndorff von Bülowius, of the *Spezialdienstabteilung* of the 8th Panzer Division, was impatiently waiting outside Eblinghem. British resistance was hardening and it was essential for specialized assault units like Horndorff's to bring everything possible to bear on it.

Sitting with his head out of the turret of his 40-ton PzKpfw4 tank, Horndorff stared upwards as a squadron of Dorniers passed overhead. He was blazingly angry. It was quite obvious that the tanks should still be moving ahead but forty-eight hours before, all forward movement had been stopped except for local actions and he was still carrying out minor repairs and waiting for instructions to move on again.

Just old enough to feel the humiliation of 1918, he had no quarrel with the French or the English and little love for the Nazis, but he had to admit that Hitler had done more for Germany than all the democratic talkers in the Reich for twenty years. He'd joined the army in 1931, because the Horndorffs had always joined the army, and when the Wehrmacht had followed Hitler, Jocho Horndorff hadn't questioned it because his loyalty belonged not to the political head of the state but to his commander-in-chief. With the rapid expansion that had followed he had come into his own, because the hard core of regulars had been given increased responsibility and now he was a major at thirty and had a strong suspicion that before the war was over he'd be at least a colonel.

It was what he'd trained for all his life, and his body under his dusty clothes was as hard as steel : Man for man, he considered himself a match for anyone, either in combat or in bed. There was a girl who lived at Koblenz, as fair and handsome as he was, whom he'd intended to marry the previous September. Because of the war, he'd put it off and it hadn't pleased either of them very much because they'd been sleeping together for six months and their parents were good Rhineland Catholics, stiff in their attitudes to sexual freedom. On his first leave early in the year the wedding had had to be put off again because of the

death of his father, and it had been put off a third time because
of *Operation Sichelschnitt*, the advance into the Ardennes and
through the Low Countries and France. The campaign was going
so well now, however, Horndorff had little doubt that he'd be
back home again before the summer was out to make everything
right.

He was still thinking about the future when a scout car came
up alongside and an officer stood up in the back.

'We're moving?' Horndorff said.

'Yes.'

'Why in God's name did they stop us?'

'Because the spearheads have had fifty per cent losses – battle
and wear and tear – and they're afraid of losing more in the
flooded areas up by the Aa Canal.'

Horndorff made a derisive gesture. 'The attack's lost momen-
tum,' he said. 'We could have collared the whole of the B.E.F.'

The officer in the car shrugged. 'It's over now, anyway. First
Panzers are on the coast, Second at Arnecke, and Sixth and
Eighth near Hazebrouck. Twentieth Motorized are near Cassel
and the Hoth Group's trying to cut the Tommies off at
Armentières. You're to head towards Vitry. Lorried infantry and
tanks up there seem to be in trouble.'

Horndorff reached for his microphone, and an hour later Vitry
lay just in front of him over the brow of the hill. He could see
houses and the spire of the church and, as he glanced at his map,
he saw that it was on a cross-roads, with one route leading
directly north where the Tommies were trying to withdraw to the
coast, the other east where they were still trying to scuttle back
from their fatuous adventure into Belgium.

Something seemed to have gone wrong at Vitry, however,
because in the open area in front he could see columns of smoke
crawling skywards like black treacle and burning tanks and several
tiny figures running back, their clothing on fire. As he watched,
a rising pall told him another tank had been hit, but he was quite
calm as he passed the word to the rear, giving the proper co-
ordinates and calling for help from the Luftwaffe. Horndorff was
a regular soldier, not a death or glory boy, and it wasn't his
job to get his tanks knocked out to capture a wretched little
village.

Those Stukas that Horndorff was calling up were to have a profound effect on the life of nineteen-year-old Marie-Josephine Berthelot.

Although her home was at Saméaon far to the east, at that moment Marie-Josephine was in Bout-Dassons just to the west of where Horndorff waited. The last fortnight had been a nightmare of noise, smoke and terror, and she was wishing she hadn't quarrelled with her family before she'd left Saméaon. Her parents had been unable to appreciate that the world had moved on from the days when a girl accepted without question whomever they put forward for a husband and, as she was a teacher of English, not a peasant, the quarrel had been going on for weeks.

'I will not marry Monsieur Ambry,' she announced flatly. 'He is a dirty old man and I shall be leaving home.' She'd put on her best cream coat and, without saying goodbye, had left at once for Esuires near Lille to stay with her friend, Isobelle Lemaître, until the storm had blown over. Her resistance had slowly weakened as the days had passed, however, and she had been almost prepared to go home when the first bomb had dropped.

On the night of 9 May they'd heard anti-aircraft guns and seen searchlights, and it had been reported that there was an air raid to the north-east. The following day they'd heard that the very thing they'd all been dreading had happened – the Germans had attacked.

From that moment, they'd seen aeroplanes all the time – none of them ever French, British or Belgian – and then the refugees had started. Finally there'd been French soldiers, and when they'd asked how things were going, the men had replied quite simply : 'The Germans are coming!' It had shocked Marie-Josephine to life at last. Esuires was no place for her.

She'd packed her belongings and gone to the bus-stop to go home. But suddenly there were no buses heading east and, deciding to head for relatives who kept a café at Vitry, she'd borrowed a few francs from Isobelle and taken the bus north instead. Vitry was full of refugees and when she arrived she learned that her parents were dead. The farm had been on the direct route of the Panzers and the place had been razed to the ground. The news had shocked her but, because she was of hard-headed northern French stock, she'd dried her tears and accepted the fact that she was on her own.

The news that came in now was that the Belgians were collapsing and that Queen Wilhelmina of Holland was in England, and from then on the air was filled with noise and she'd soon found she could distinguish between bombs and anti-aircraft fire. The refugees had continued to pour past, ancient carriages driven by ancient coachmen and ancient cars with solid tyres and acetylene lamps, dusty from years of lying unused in country garages; priests, frantic women with children, farmers trying vainly to drive their stock. They were followed by soldiers in lorries with buckled mudguards, their faces stubbled and grimy. The rumours they spread that half the refugees were really spies or enemy agents were so widely believed that many refused to help them.

It had seemed to be time to move further west and she'd just set off towards the bus-stop when the German aeroplanes arrived. She had stood, shocked and uncertain what to do, until a French soldier, diving at her, had knocked her flying into the ditch and she'd lain there with all the breath knocked out of her body, the man's heavy frame across her in a way that might have terrified her if she hadn't been already frightened out of her wits.

She lay with her arms over her head, her ears assailed by the shriek and clang of explosions, her eyes full of flashing light. Her body seemed to be lifted from the ground in a serious of jerks as the explosions occurred, and she was deafened, half-blinded and stupefied by the clamour, trying instinctively to claw herself under the ground away from the showers of stones, rubble, splintered wood and flying fragments of glass and pulverized soil.

As the ringing in her head died and she became aware that the din had stopped, she rose to her knees, her hair matted with dirt, her face caked with it, spitting it from her tongue as she tried to draw breath in what seemed an airless vacuum. The man who'd flung her down had already disappeared, running down the village street, and then she realized she could hear the crackling of flames and the high thin sound of someone crying.

She decided she'd better go back to the café to clean up, but it was only when she was on top of it that she realized it wasn't there any more and that the screaming she could hear came from her aunt who was sitting by the roadside, her clothes blasted from her body. Her face was black with soot, her open wailing mouth a round pink hole, and one eye hung out on her cheek like a bloody ping-pong ball. Of her uncle there was no sign.

The British soldiers reached the village with their guns as her aunt died the following afternoon. They'd fought all the way back from Belgium and they were grimy, stinking and struggling under the dead weight of weariness. No one welcomed them because they'd soon learned that soldiers brought bombers, and Marie-Josephine spent a whole day and night in a cellar, shivering, hungry and frightened, her mind revolving again and again round the question, 'Where shall I go now?' The only other relation she knew of was an aunt in La Panne on the Belgian coast.

As she'd set off again, the road, its borders green with the first colours of spring, was already crammed with demoralized and distressed humanity toiling in the sunshine. In the distance the horizon was shrouded with smoke clouds from burning villages, and to the south she could hear the continuous rumble of guns, bombs and aircraft. In the fields beyond the cross-roads there were dead cattle and broken trees.

Just ahead of her a woman was pushing a perambulator full of small children like pink baby mice in a nest. Alongside the woman a man stumbled along, bent under a load of bedding and blankets, and a sorry-looking mule trudged head-down between the shafts of a broken cart whose wheels shrieked for lack of grease.

They'd not gone more than half a mile beyond Bout-Dassons when a man just ahead turned and glanced up at the sky. His expression changed as he pointed and, swinging round, she saw the glint of sun on metal wings over Vitry where half a dozen aeroplanes nosed into a dive. Horrified, she heard the distant scream of the sirens and recognized them as dive-bombers, the symbol of treachery and mutilation; then the column broke like chaff before a wind. The man with the blankets headed for the ditch but the woman with the perambulator was running ahead in a wild erratic scamper, the perambulator bouncing and rocking on the rough surface of the road. As the bullets passed her, chirping in a high strange note as they whined away, Marie-Josephine saw one of the children fall out of the perambulator and lie on its back, screaming. The woman didn't seem to notice in her panic and went on running, then Marie-Josephine saw her stagger and her knees go limp almost as if they'd turned to rubber. Her hands dropped limply and the perambulator went rolling on by itself, curving slowly off the crown of the road towards the ditch. As it disappeared the woman stared after it, her hands at her side, her knees gradually giving way, then she collapsed in a puff of dust, and Marie-Josephine started running.

The man with the pile of blankets was there first. He appeared from the ditch, a sturdy working man in a cap and a ragged jacket, who scooped up the fallen child as he went. He arrived by his wife at the same time as Marie-Josephine and, as he turned her over, her head fell back and Marie-Josephine saw there were small welling patches of blood all over her clothing. The man was sobbing as Marie-Josephine turned to the ditch where the perambulator had disappeared.

It lay on its side and as she stopped on the road above it, she saw there were splintered holes in its side. The amount of blood turned her stomach over and she swung away abruptly and vomited weakly into the grass.

As the Stukas lifted into the sky again, Major Karl Schmesser was frowning deeply. The army was pleased with the confusion and dismay that was being spread by the policy of attacking the roads, but to Schmesser it seemed like sheer slaughter and, try as he might, he couldn't fit it into the rules of civilized warfare. Holding the Stuka in a nose-up attitude he was narrow-eyed with self-disgust and decided that perhaps he should let Stoos fly after all, because this was the sort of work he was fitted for.

He glanced across at Schlegel and then at Fink climbing on his left. What Stoos said was quite true, he had to admit, but, though he had no great hopes of Fink ever becoming a successful pilot, it was Schmesser's job to try to make him one. He swallowed, suddenly hating Stoos' ardour, hating himself and the job he'd had to do, even for a moment conscious of doubts in the infallibility of German leadership.

As he was trying to thrust his thoughts aside, Unteroffizier Roehme, his gunner, banged him on the shoulder.

'*Achtung*,' he shouted. '*Achtung, Spitfeuer!*'

Unteroffizier Roehme was making the mistake many German airmen made, because there were no Spitfires in France and the machine diving from the sun was a Hurricane.

Its pilot, Flying Officer Rupert Arthur Rokesby Conybeare, was just twenty and looked sixteen. He was round-faced with smooth cheeks, his hair so pale as to make him anonymous. He didn't drink and didn't smoke and the only thing about him that indicated his dedication were the faint dark lines below his eyes which showed how tired he was.

He'd been in France since September the previous year, and he'd been flying in action on and off ever since. When he'd gone on leave at Christmas he'd already had five German aircraft to his credit and had hoped to be able to cut a dash with the girls in his home town of Harrogate in Yorkshire. Unfortunately, the girls in Harrogate had looked at his childish features and refused to take him seriously, and he'd returned to France aware of something his father had once said about the previous war – that England didn't seem like home any more.

He'd added another two German machines to his score in the early days of the year and then, on 10 May, had been dragged out of bed after a noisy night when guns had been firing along the frontier to the east. 'Wing's in one hell of a stew,' he was told. 'The balloon's gone up at last!'

They'd been expecting it a long time and for the most part the R.A.F. was going to have to commit suicide with machines which were as out of date as the bow and arrow – '*Ganz ohne Bedeutung*' – quite negligible – they'd once been contemptuously called by a captured Nazi pilot.

There had been so many plots it had been hard to know which one to head for. Nevertheless, four more Germans had fallen to earth before Conybeare's guns. Two others had limped home damaged, and he knew very well that more than one gunner would never pull a trigger again.

The day he bumped into Major Schmesser's Stukas they had been ordered to patrol Lille at 10,000 feet but they hadn't been there more than ten minutes when they were warned of activity near Courtrai had swung north-east. Five minutes later, Conybeare had seen forty Dorniers in close formation and above them squadron after squadron of 110s stepped up to 18,000 feet.

He lost the other Hurricanes as they went into the attack so he selected one of the 110s and dived on it. Pieces flew from the German machine at once and flames leapt from the engines, and he just had time to see it go down into a vertical dive when he heard a crash behind him and swerved to see another 110 coming at him. His engine started to smoke and a large hole appeared in his port wing and it was as he began to fall from the sky that the Stukas led by Major Schmesser were just pulling out of their dive. Conybeare's machine was in no condition to get involved in another fight, but as the Stukas – always regarded as the fighter pilot's dream target – lifted in front of him he couldn't resist having a go.

His first burst killed Schmesser immediately and tore the arm off Unteroffizier Roehme, and his second killed Leutnant Fink. As Fink's machine rolled over, Conybeare's engine stopped and he could hear only the sound of the wind rushing past the open cockpit. Guessing at his speed because the indicator wasn't registering, he chose a field, pumped his flaps down and went in with his wheels up. As the machine bounced and bucketed across the field in a cloud of dust and flying clods of earth, he thought it was going to turn over but eventually the tail fell back with a thump and everything was silent.

As he recovered his wits, his head throbbing from a welt over the eye, he saw wisps of smoke rising from the cockpit and, hauling himself on to the wing, he began to run. The bang blew him head over heels and, as he lifted his head, he realized he'd lost his eyebrows and that the bruise on his head was throbbing appallingly.

Rattling in his fifteen-hundredweight open truck towards Villers-sur-Grandie in the lowering sunshine, Leading Aircraftsman George Reardon was well aware of the time element involved. He had a matter of an hour and a half to get there, pick up Flying Officer Conybeare, and start back again.

He knew the road well because the squadron had had a forward landing field ten miles outside the village during the winter, but at Richepanne he ran into a French mechanized column entirely without march discipline which was pushing everything else off the road. Among the vehicles were a few infantrymen, dirty and unshaven, bits of wet cigarette hanging from their mouths, who seemed indifferent and philosophical, so that the

British military policeman trying to sort out the confusion seemed incredibly smart by comparison.

'You can't go this way,' he said. 'Jerry's got the road to Villers taped. You'll have to go round by Girency.'

As he set off again, swinging right towards Girency, Reardon noticed a solitary figure walking towards him. It was a British soldier, dressed in immaculate khaki, which was a sight in itself just then. He wore his full equipment but carried no rifle.

Reardon pulled to a stop. 'Where are you heading, mate?' he asked.

The soldier, a slight fair man with spectacles, frowned, as though he weren't sure.

'West,' he said.

'I should head north,' Reardon said. 'You on your own?'

'Yes. I was with 3 M.U., R.A.S.C. We were sent to do a job in Suchez.' The soldier gave a shy smile. 'The Germans dropped some bombs, though, and when I came out of the shelter the lorry had gone.'

'You walked from Suchez?'

'I'm used to walking. I was a Scoutmaster before the war.'

'Where's your rifle?'

'It was in the lorry.'

'If I were you,' Reardon said, 'I'd find another. You might need it. And you'd better step out. Jerry's not far away. I'll be back before long. I'll look out for you. My name's Reardon.'

'Mine's Sievewright. Clarence Sievewright.'

It suited him, too, Reardon thought as he put the truck in gear.

A few miles further along the road, Reardon began to pass soldiers trudging back, their heads down, their bodies bowed with weariness, and among them now were some in British battle-dress.

'All right up front?' he asked.

'At the moment,' he was told. 'But it don't pay to sing and play the piano much.'

At Vanchette, three miles short of Villers, the soldiers moving back had disappeared and the roads had emptied, and he was surprised when a tall figure in khaki stepped out of a hedge and put up a hand.

'Hold it, mon,' it said. 'You cannae go doon there.'

Reardon frowned. 'I've got to. One of our pilots was shot down near Villers. He's waiting there.'

'Well, me, John Gow, of the Coldstream Guards, is telling you that you cannae.'

'I've got to.'

'Listen, mon –' Gow was a tall sullen sliver of a man with white skin and white eyebrows, and a nose and cheeks that were burned red by the sun ' – y'oughta know that when the Guards say you cannae get through, you cannae get through. Our lot's behind yon hedge there and I've been put here to stop anything coming up.'

Reardon looked Gow up and down. He was not very old but behind him there were nearly three hundred years of discipline and pride. Reardon had once been on an aerodrome at the beginning of the war when a battalion of Grenadiers had arrived in the neighbourhood and, because they had to show the rest of the Services that they were something special, they'd taken over the parade ground twice a week to perform the ritual saraband the army called foot drill. The high screech of the officers and N.C.O.s and the stiff puppet-like turnings and stampings had seemed a little stupid at first to men trained in the free-and-easy atmosphere of a technical outfit, but, as they'd watched they'd realized that these tall ramrod-straight men who wore their hats over the noses to force their heads up possessed something that made them envious that they didn't possess it, too.

'O.K., Gow.' He admitted defeat. 'I got it.'

'I am no' "Gow",' the Guardsman said coldly. He touched his sleeve. '*I* am "Lance-Corporal Gow" and you address me as such.'

Reardon gestured. 'Wrap it up, mate,' he said. 'I'm here to pick up my officer, not stand about arguing.'

Gow stared at him with bright icy eyes then he pointed. 'You'll have to go by Banfort. And just look out. We've been expecting yon bastards down by here for the last hour.' His bony white face cracked into what by a vast stretch of imagination might have been called a smile. 'And they'll get a gey fine surprise, mon, when they arrive. We found a convoy of abandoned R.A.S.C. lorries and they were full o' land mines.'

The hum of engines came even as he spoke, and as Gow trotted off, his boots heavy on the road, Reardon became aware that he was right under the Germans' noses and that the chances of Flying Officer Conybeare being picked up were growing slimmer all the time.

He'd just backed the truck into a gateway when the Germans turned the corner, two scout cars mounted with machine guns, two motor-cycle combinations and three lorryloads of troops. The blast of fire from the Guardsmen hit them just as their wheels detonated the row of land mines.

One of the motor-cycle combinations and one of the scout cars disintegrated, their crews hurled through the air like limp bags of bleeding straw. The other motor-cycle combination and the other scout car curved into the ditch, their crews already dead or dying. Behind them, the driver of the first lorry was hit in the chest and throat and died at the wheel, and the men in the back bolted for the ditches, several of them going over like shot rabbits before the Guardsmen's fire. Out of sight, they brought their weapons to bear, and Reardon had just swung from the gateway and moved the gear lever into neutral on the way to second for a quick getaway, when a burst from a machine gun caught him in the shoulders and neck, shredding his windpipe, in bubbling gouts of blood. The truck slowed down as his foot slipped off the accelerator, and rolled gently towards the side of the road where it came to a stop, its wheels against the verge. The last thing Reardon thought about as the light went out of the day was that Flying Officer Conybeare was going to be lucky if he didn't end up in a prisoner of war camp.

Baudain was a deserted village with a single street of one-storey houses. From the huddle of bricks where he crouched, Corporal Gustave Chouteau, of the 121st Regiment of Infantry in the 25th Division of the French Seventh Army, studied his officer. Captain Deshayes was an overweight reservist who owned a packing business in Limoges, and Chouteau knew perfectly well that if the Germans came he wouldn't be over-anxious to die. He had a solid bank account, a string of young children and a wife whose family owned a department store in Clermont-Ferrand.

Life or death was a matter of supreme indifference to Corporal Chouteau. He had no bank account, no wife and no children. All he possessed to make him different from his fellow men was a period of service in the Foreign Legion that had left him with a face deeply lined by the African sun. His return to civilian life and the Reserve had not been happy because he'd noticed something very different about the France he'd left some years before : Everyone had suddenly seemed to be afraid of the Germans, a result, as Chouteau well knew, of twenty years of Ministers who took more notice of their mistresses than they did of their constituents, and of the nerveless ruling of the same old gang who changed positions in the government as though they were playing musical chairs.

Chouteau glanced again at Deshayes. He was standing in front of the major, Soustelle de Louis. Soustelle was a regular soldier, thin, spare and greying, who in Germany would have been at least a colonel but in the weariness that had gripped France since 1918 had remained only a major while lesser men with better connections rose over his head.

'Command reports that lorried troops are heading this way,' he was telling Deshayes. 'They've been turned aside near Vanchette and they're trying to feel their way round. We must stop them.'

Deshayes was nodding but Chouteau noticed that he'd gone pale and was chewing at his lip.

'Your men are in position?' Soustelle asked.

'Yes, Major.'

'I hope you have some good ones,' Soustelle said, and Chouteau knew exactly what he meant. In spirit most of the soldiers around him were like Deshayes, boys newly called to the colours or middle-aged men with families and good jobs who were unlikely to consider dying before their children and their wives. Pacard, sitting behind the Hotchkiss, was a baker by trade; Angelet, on his right, a mere youth who'd been an assistant in the millinery department of a Marseilles store. Favre was a journalist from one of the weird little magazines the capital had always managed to throw up, given to Leftist politics and considering himself a cut above his fellow soldiers; and Burnecker, a big talker and a better boaster, was a fascist if ever there were one.

The afternoon passed slowly and Chouteau was beginning to wonder whether he could persuade Deshayes to send someone to the village to find some beer when he heard the sound of Soustelle's car and the screech of brakes.

'They are here,' he announced cheerfully, his thin face alight
with optimism.

He moved along the line with Deshayes who was licking his
lips nervously. As he stopped at Chouteau's position, he glanced
along the barrel of the gun where Pacard crouched.

'Good,' he said, 'Good!' Then he saw the pale-blue and white
ribbon that Chouteau wore on his breast, a relic of the campaigns
in North Africa. 'At least, you know *your* job, *mon vieux*,' he
grinned.

As he vanished, Favre began muttering. 'Old fool,' he said.
'Who wants to sacrifice his life these days? It's out of date.'

'Especially against the Germans,' Burnecker added. 'He
belongs to the past.'

'So will you, my friend,' Chouteau said quietly, 'if you don't
shut up.'

He turned his back on them contemptuously. 'Observe,' he said,
pointing. 'You will see dust over the hedges there. That, I suspect,
my friends, is the enemy.'

He glanced to right and left where other outposts were dug in
under the hedges, then Soustelle came back with Deshayes.
'Don't fire, *mon vieux*,' he said to Chouteau, 'until I give the
signal.'

Chouteau nodded, and they went on waiting, aware of the
distant sound of lorry engines and the singing of the birds among
the houses about them. Somewhere in the distance, they could
hear the dull rumble of artillery and somewhere overhead the
drone of a flight of aeroplanes. Chouteau didn't look up. He had
his eye firmly fixed on the moving cloud of dust.

'Sight on that corner there,' he told the others. 'It's two
hundred and twenty yards away. I measured it this morning. At
that range, even you lot ought to be able to hit something.'

He was already aware of Pacard glancing towards the rear, of
Favre muttering with Burnecker, and Angelet whispering to
himself. But Soustelle was standing just behind them now, quivering like an excited terrier at a rat-hole. Alongside him, Deshayes
crouched behind a stone wall, keeping his head well down already, Chouteau noticed.

The dust cloud came nearer and Chouteau saw that it was
slowing. As the first lorry came in sight, Soustelle lifted his
revolver. The lorries drew nearer and Chouteau became con-

scious of his own breathing and of Angelet praying in a high feminine voice. The birds seemed louder than ever in the stillness.

'Come on, you old fool,' Favre whispered. 'Give the signal!'

As he spoke, there was a crackle of firing from the hedge on his right that was taken up immediately from the post on his left.

Soustelle was still standing with his pistol in the air to give the signal and Chouteau saw his face go red with fury. Then Pacard's Hotchkiss started rattling and Burnecker's weapon exploded close to his ear and he gripped his rifle and joined in.

Favre began to sob and Chouteau swung backhanded at him. Then a blast of Schmeisser bullets rattled and clinked against the brickwork above their heads and as Chouteau glanced back he saw Soustelle's right leg buckle, then he pitched forward on his face, his helmet rolling off so that his thin grey hair moved in the breeze that stirred the dust.

The Schmeisser fire was rattling all round them now and they could hear bullets whining and cracking overhead. The Hotchkiss stopped and, as he reached out to jerk at the cocking handle, Pacard somersaulted backwards to sprawl among the scattered bricks. Chouteau swore and hammered at the breech to remove the damaged round that had jammed it.

'That's it!' Burnecker said. 'Deshayes has hopped it! He's got Soustelle on his back and he's putting on a hero act! I bet he doesn't come back! *C'en est fait!* It's finished!'

Turning his head, Chouteau saw men running bent-double across the fields, then another burst of fire rattled against the bricks and Burnecker disappeared over a low wall behind them, his booted feet sticking up in the air. Favre stood up, his mouth hanging open, and began to run, throwing down his rifle as he went. Angelet was still whimpering and praying but he was also still firing. Chouteau got the machine gun going again and the Schmeisser fire stopped.

But then he realized that the men on the left were also moving back across the fields, running for the trees, and that from among the forty or fifty men in the buildings around there was only an odd rifle still firing. Gradually even these stopped as the stouter-hearted men realized their numbers had dwindled to nothing and they were isolated, then Chouteau saw men standing up around him among the scattered walls, bewildered and frightened, wondering if they, too, shouldn't join the rush for safety.

Then, over on the right, out of one of the windows, he saw a white sheet appear on the end of a rifle and begin to wag frantically. He glanced at Angelet. The boy was scrabbling among the bricks for Pacard's ammunition pouches, sobbing and whimpering as his grimy fingers pawed over the dead man.

He slapped the boy's shoulder. 'Do *you* want to surrender, too, *mon brave*?' he asked.

'No.' Angelet's lip was quivering and there were tears in his eyes but he shook his head. 'I'll stay if you want me to.'

Chouteau grinned at him. 'There comes a time,' he said, 'when death and glory begin to lose their point.' He slapped the boy's shoulder and jerked his head to the rear. 'It's time for *Système D.*'

'*Système D?*'

'*Débrouillez-vous!*' Chouteau said. 'Fend for yourself.'

Not only Private Angelet, of the 121st Regiment of Infantry, was worried about his future. So was Private Elijah Noble, of the 5th Field Company Workshops of the Royal Army Ordnance Corps who, one way and another, was suddenly having quite a war.

When the despatch rider had come through the trees, weaving in and out and ducking his head to avoid low branches, Private Noble had been counting his spoil. Called up not long before under the new Enlistment Act to become a National Serviceman, Private Noble – wrongly named, if ever a man was – had long since decided that the wisest soldiers were those who were near enough to a battle to be able to pick up a little reflected glory but far enough away to be safe. His skill had always lain in knowing how to make a comfortable bed from chicken wire, what to barter for eggs and how much to pay for *vin rouge*. He knew the best brothels and called the local *maire* by his first name, and he had a nice little racket going in changing francs into pounds when his friends went on leave and vice versa when they returned. The life, even if it were dead boring, was also dead profitable.

Brought up in the East End of London by a father with a sharp eye for the main chance, his school years had been spent mostly in playing truant while his mother had fought off the school attendance officer, and he had passed most of his time watching the little cheats his father had worked so that it was small wonder he'd found it easy to follow the same bent. It had come as a shock when the letter announcing his call-up had arrived and his first instinct had been to bolt. His father had jeered at him. 'Garn, Lije,' he'd said. 'You'd be in dead trouble if you did and you can make money in the army as well as you can out of it.'

Noble had soon discovered the truth of his father's words. Crown and anchor had emptied the pockets of less quick-witted men and when he'd taken over the job of one of the transport drivers, his future was assured. He'd known all the people in Shrewsbury, where his unit was stationed, who could use a joint of army meat, and all the publicans who'd swop a bottle of whisky for a few bags of army coal.

Since he hadn't really taken to the dung-coloured spud sack rough-hewn by a one-armed tinsmith with which the army had replaced the Jimmy Cagney jacket he'd been in the habit of wearing, he'd taken it to a tailor and had it so fined off he could hardly lift his arms. He'd gone through the usual dodges of reporting sick to avoid church parades and fatigues and had not been in the slightest alarmed when his unit had moved to Dover Castle. Unfortunately he hadn't been quick enough to catch on that he was going to France and before he knew where he was he'd found himself at the other side of the Channel.

Which was a bastard. Because until that moment he'd hardly known where France was and hadn't been interested enough to find out. The French language seemed to consist of talking down your nose and waving your arms about and, as for the Nazis, they were obviously a rotten lot while Hitler was just dead common.

He'd looked up as the despatch rider had passed him.

'What's the buzz, *mon fils*?' he'd asked.

'The front's given way at Cambrai,' the despatch rider had said.

'That's a long way from here.'

'Not the way the Germans are moving.'

'Where are they?' Noble asked, pushing forward a packet of fiddled fags.

The despatch rider had taken one of the fags and stuck it behind his ear under his helmet. 'All over the shop. The whole bloody front's moving back!'

As he'd kicked his machine to life again and roared off, Noble had stared after him, his eyes thoughtful. If the army was in retreat, he'd decided, there'd be barrowloads of cameras, field-glasses, tennis rackets and golf clubs lying around loose, because the winter had been so quiet everyone had imported something from England to make for comfort, and he'd lit a bent cigarette and walked slowly towards the 15-cwt van he drove. If he'd got to wade in tyrant's blood he might just as well turn it to his advantage before he joined the waltz.

Now he wasn't so sure. He'd collected an excellent assortment of abandoned weapons, field-glasses and typewriters, but south of Tournai he'd been startled to see British troops setting fire to the stores they'd laboriously collected during the winter months, and it had suddenly made him feel nervous. As a city boy, apart from Cockney nerve, he hadn't much he could offer in a situation that seemed to present certain difficulties. The army had merely showed him how to do pointless things with a rifle he'd been care-ful never to do since, and now somebody had taken a diabolical liberty with his safety.

In fact, he'd barely started.

By dark that night the whole front was alight with bursting bombs and shells. Two big fires were blazing, one in a petrol dump so that the smoke ascended in great rolling billows and, in the sky above, an incredible display of tracer shells had made weird designs through which an occasional rocket burst into a ball of brilliantly-coloured flares. Among them were Very lights and all too often the white rockets which by this time he'd learned the Germans fired to indicate a success.

Somehow it didn't look right even to Noble.

He'd slept in the van again and again, scrounging a cup of tea here and a bully beef sandwich there, spinning a yarn about looking for his adjutant to anyone who asked, but then the army had stopped and dug in again, setting up their Brens and the few mortars they possessed and Noble had seen Heinkels, Dorniers and Stukas in dozens. The only British machines he'd seen had been ancient Battles getting the chop one after the other with monotonous regularity, and once at a first-aid post he'd heard a bitter Lysander gunner, his tunic torn from top to bottom by bullets, complaining about the politicians sending him up in a machine whose only noteworthy characteristic was that it looked as though it had its wings on backwards.

He had found it wise to continue at full speed, but near Seclin he had been caught up in a flood of retreating Frenchmen, a double row of horse-drawn vehicles and a double row of motor-ized vehicles – four lines altogether – that had forced him into the fields. He didn't argue. They didn't look the sort of men you could argue with. The drivers were unshaven, their clothes muddy, and there were no officers or N.C.O.s. As they had passed they had managed embarrassed smiles that had sent a cold chill through Noble's heart. This wasn't just a quick nip back to re-form, he decided. It was a rout.

As they turned the corner, one of the tanks, an ancient Model R35 which they used for training purposes, brushed against the last of the stragglers. A man screamed and fell and Noble's eyes started out of his head as he saw how the treads had crushed his leg to pulp. A few of the soldiers stopped but the tank didn't even pause, its tracks clawing a deep gouge in the turf, and as the rest of them pushed past, indifferent to the screams of the injured man, Noble started up the 15-cwt and began to bounce across the fields, his stomach heaving.

Though he'd not worried at the time, he realized now that those sensitive antennae of his which warned him of danger had told him when he'd first arrived in France that something was wrong. The French had seemed slack and listless, and their officers had a habit of collecting bunches of flowers which they gave to their red-faced British liaison officers to carry. Noble hadn't much time for officers of any nationality, but he'd sud-denly found that when it came to comparison with the French he was prepared to stand up and defend his own with his dying breath. They were all bastards but, as bastards went, they weren't *bad* bastards. And the British soldiers at least looked clean which to the dandified Noble with his soaped trouser-creases and for-bidden pencil-line moustache, was important.

As the long day's fighting died and the rifle fire began to fade he managed to attach himself to a field company of Royal Engineers he found in a group of trees on the side of a low hill. They were all tired, dusty and hungry and were glad to hide their vehicles away from the dive-bombers that had harassed them continuously for days. There was an observation balloon hanging on the horizon in the east, but it was far enough away not to worry him, and the woods were full of diagonal stripes of sunshine. The men were brewing tea on small fires, and the cooks, white aprons over their battledress, were bent over petrol cookers. After the adventures of the last week, the wood had for Noble the comfortable feeling of home and he dug into the back of the 15-cwt and produced his haversack. There was a bottle of cognac in there with a box of cigars, and he decided he might as well make a pig of himself.

The observation balloon that Noble had noticed was over Lanselles ten miles away, but it was high enough to be able to cover a lot of country, and it was with the high-powered 10 × 60 Zeiss binoculars on his chest that Leutnant Dieter Steinhoff, of the 3rd *Fesselballonkompanie* of the Engineers, first saw the drifting yellow cloud. He studied it for a moment, then he nudged his companion, Unteroffizier Distl, and pointed.

'Tommy column,' he said.

The dust was hanging over a road that led up the side of the only hill for miles around and on top of the hill was a small clump of trees, unexpected in that bare landscape. Steinhoff noted down the co-ordinates and map references, then, passing the slip of paper to Distl, he lifted the glasses again to watch.

'*Alle Mann auf Gefechtsstationen,*' he grinned. 'All hands to battle stations.'

The bang of the first shell made Noble jump. It came like the crack of doom and was enough to galvanize the dead, and in the split second before he realized what had happened, it was as though he were watching a Disney cartoon. Mugs of tea and dixies of food seemed to hang motionless in the air as everyone dived for cover, then a soldier started screaming in a harsh nerve-racking wail of agony.

'Shrapnel,' someone yelled. 'Shrapnel! Take cover!'

It was Noble's first experience of violent death and as he cowered under a lorry he was so gripped by the horror he couldn't keep his head down. Flinching and whimpering, he saw men running about covered with blood, their clothes torn by the flying fragments of metal. Every now and then shrapnel balls clattered like football rattles against the lorries and he saw men rolling in the grass with their faces and legs slashed. A young soldier no more than eighteen was running as fast as he could, and as he passed, there was a flash above the trees and the boy's face changed. Noble knew he was already dead, though he went on running until he crashed into a bush and hung there suspended, the back of his head and neck covered with blood, his limbs draped bonelessly among the sagging foliage.

'Spread out! Spread out!' an officer was shouting, then there was another flash and something like a football flew past Noble. There was a heavy thump as it struck the metal side of the lorry and, as he lifted his eyes again, he saw it was the officer's head. It had left a dent marked with a thick paste of blood before bouncing off again into the grass.

The vehicles were like sieves now, and he could see tanks spouting petrol.

'Put them fags out,' a sergeant yelled in a hoarse voice. 'Put 'em out, I said!'

But one of the men running for his life plunged unseeingly through one of the many small fires that had been lit and Noble saw a piece of burning stick go flying before his boots. It landed underneath the lorry that stood alongside his own truck, and both vehicles went up with a 'whoomph' into a high pyre of flame.

As a unit the group of engineers had ceased to exist. Most of their transport had vanished and many of the men. What were left of them were running and staggering and crawling over the slope of the hill and flinging themselves down in the grass on the dead ground at the far side where a few men had set up a field ambulance. As the shelling stopped a major appeared, white-faced and angry.

'Bloody poor show,' he was saying. 'Bloody poor show! Get the chaps together! Find out how many we've got!'

A sergeant was holding a water bottle for a man lying under a blanket and the smell of death made Noble feel sick. Nearby two officers, one of them reading instructions from a thick book, were bending over a man on a trestle table, sponging with cotton wool that was rapidly becoming soggy from the blood that dripped into the pulpy earth. It dawned on Noble that they were amputating a limb and the very amateurishness of it made him want to cry. He'd never thought of death in this way, his only experience of dying the occasions in the East London streets where the mourners got together afterwards with the tongue sandwiches and the beer and port.

Then the major started to sniff the air. 'Tanks about,' he said. 'I can smell 'em.'

Noble's nostrils twitched. He could smell nothing but burning and blood and the stink of fear. He was terrified of tanks and the idea of being caught and crushed by the monster 40-tonners the Germans were supposed to have, reduced his bowels to water.

The day was silent now and over the country sounds – a dog barking, a cow mooing as though in pain, a lark singing in the clear air – he could hear the distant thud of guns and then the short sharp sound of a machine gun firing.

The cigars in the haversack forgotten, Noble lit a cigarette with a shaking hand and stood lost and bewildered. He'd never been so afraid in his life and, because he'd never felt any pride in his own unit and didn't belong to this one, he felt completely rudderless. The need to get back to his own unit had become desperately important; above all else he needed the comforting sound of an N.C.O.'s harsh voice telling him what to do.

By midnight that Sunday, a lot of other people were also beginning to see things differently.

At Dover the signal had long since been made that the evacuation of the British Expeditionary Force – an operation called *Dynamo* after the room where it had been conceived – was to commence. As H.M.S. *Vital* with Barry Hatton on board, was approaching Dover, the admiral received a signal from London which informed him that the plan was to be implemented with the greatest vigour with a view to lifting 45,000 men within two days. 'After which,' the signal continued, 'it is probable that evacuation will be terminated by enemy action.'

It provided grim news but the admiral could only suppose that the men in London were aware of what was happening. By this time Dunkirk was a place of horror. The waterworks and mains had been destroyed and already the brackish water from the flooding of the lowlands was seeping into the wells. Burning warehouses lit up the white column of the lighthouse and wrecked cranes, while, endlessly since dark, the thunder of the bombs and the flash of their explosions had punctuated the increasing destruction.

The admiral rose and moved to the window. He could hear the noise of battle from the office as he turned and glanced at the officers waiting by the desk.

'I see no alternative but to use the beaches,' he said. 'What do we have?'

'The motor-boats of Ramsgate Contraband Control, drifters and small craft of this base,' the staff officer, operations, said. 'Together with four Belgian passenger launches and the ships' boats themselves.'

'Signal Admiralty for reinforcements.'

'They're probably on their way already, sir. Small Vessels Pool's been collecting them for some time. I gather they have a lot near Westminster Pier.' The S.O.O. glanced at the list in his hand. 'Officers have also been sent to the principal yachting centres, *King Alfred*'s been asked to send trainee seamen, and flag officer, London, and the commander-in-chief, Plymouth, and a few others have also been asked to help, as well as a few individual yachtsmen who've already volunteered.' The S.O.O. glanced at the list again. 'The harbour here's full, and cross-channel steamers, coasters and barges are gathering in the Downs. Ramsgate's filling up from the Thames and further north, and they're on their way from every other port where they've got any.'

The admiral nodded. He wasn't given to using a lot of unnecessary words. He took the slip of paper the flag lieutenant passed to him.

'This the total of men lifted?'

'Up to midnight, sir. Nearly 28,000.'

The admiral looked up, his narrow face keen. 'A not unreasonable start,' he said. 'Considering they're expecting only 45,000 in two days.'

Nor was it. And now Alban Kitchener Tremenheere was ready to help. Not from any feeling of heroism or because he considered it his duty, but because it was as far as he could get from Nell Noone.

As he made his few preparations, on board *Vital* – now edging alongside a tanker at Dover where *Daisy* also lay – Sub-Lieutenant Hatton was trying to screw his courage to the pitch he felt sure it ought to be screwed. Walter Boner Scharroo was walking stolidly north because the Germans had left him behind and it seemed the only thing to do. Lieutenant Allerton was also heading north. He hadn't a map and didn't particularly want one; the situation seemed so horrifying he wouldn't have dared look at it. Hans-Joachim Horndorff was still waiting outside Vitry, and Marie-Josephine Berthelot, recovering a little now, was stumbling along without any sense of direction. Major Karl Schmesser and his gunner, Unteroffizier Roehme, or what was left of them, were still in the smoking remains of their aeroplane. The man who'd shot them down, Flying Officer Conybeare had abandoned hope of rescue because Leading Aircraftsman Reardon, who was to have picked him up, was lying in a ditch near Vanchette. Corporal Chouteau and Private Angelet were also tramping silently through the darkness, Chouteau's face grim, Private Angelet whimpering soundlessly to himself. Captain Deshayes had long since given himself up while Favre, dressed in civilian clothes he'd found, was heading for Paris. Lije Noble was lying behind the wood ten miles from Lanselles, still shuddering with fear, and Lance-Corporal Gow of the Coldstream Guards, that tall expressionless man with the bone-white skin and the gingery Highland hair, had reached the line of the River Lys.

MONDAY, 27 MAY

At dawn on 27 May, just as England was beginning to stir, German panzers were rattling north in a vast pincer movement. They were already too late, because there was still a gap ten miles wide through which the French and the British were streaming at full speed. In the west, however, the Germans were still moving along the coast and Leutnant Heinrich-Robert Hinze, in his curiously impassive, mandarin manner, was preparing himself for more shooting.

Long before Calais had fallen, the outposts had been called in, the office equipment loaded into trucks, blankets rolled and the cookhouse piled into the mess waggon, with the contents of the first-aid post and the medical stores, and the battery was on its way towards Dunkirk.

The presence of men like Hinze was confusing the position for the planners at Dover. Because of the shellfire and the increasing attacks of the Luftwaffe, ships were being forced to turn back and the signals that were dropping one after another on to the staff communications officer's desk made it brutally clear that the short route to Dunkirk could not be used during daylight.

'There are two other possible routes,' the staff navigation officer was saying. 'Route Y – eighty-seven miles long – runs to a point off Ostend and comes in west through the Zuydecoote Pass. Route X – fifty-five miles long – cuts across the Ruytingen Bank to a point between Gravelines and Dunkirk. There are minefields.'

The admiral chewed at the earpiece of his spectacles. 'Route Y. Is *that* mined?'

'It might be, sir. We don't know yet.'

'We must take the risk.' The admiral glanced at the staff officer, operations. 'Signal the personnel ships and the hospital carriers to stand by. We'll try to sweep Route Y ahead of them.' He turned to the communications officer. 'In the meantime, tell Fighter Command we shall need a heavy increase in patrols over the area. The Germans are still concentrating on the Belgians, and we might just get away with it for a while.'

Sub-Lieutenant Hatton certainly hoped so.

That Monday morning the quays in Dover harbour seemed very inadequate and, save for the cross-Channel station, the port quite unsuited for the heavy work with which it was now involved. It had been designed chiefly as an anchorage for the old Channel Fleet, yet at the eight berths at the Admiralty Pier Hatton could see as many as eighteen or twenty ships moored in trots two and three deep. As the tender from *Vital* headed towards the small boat stage, a hospital ship on the inside berth was unloading into a row of ambulances, and khaki-clad figures were moving ashore from other ships in a way that indicated sheer exhaustion. As he watched, one of the ships pulled out again, in tow behind a tug, and headed for the refuelling basin, and another tug began to butt at a ship whose white paintwork forward of the bridge was scorched in a great black scar with steelwork wrenched back like the lid of a sardine tin.

Aware of a tremendous excitement underlaid with a sense of dread and a fear of defeat, Hatton stared up at the cliffs and the crooked old houses, and once more wondered if Nora Hart was still working in the town. He hadn't really missed her when he'd moved to London but now, for all that he was aware of the notorious sentimentaliy of sailors, contacting her again seemed a project eminently worth pursuing; especially with defeat and possibly death somewhere in the offing.

He was so busy with his own thoughts, he jumped when Hough spoke to him. 'I'm going up to naval headquarters with the pilot,' he said over his shoulder. 'You'd better come too. We might have to get everything down in writing.'

'Very good, sir.' Hatton felt privileged to be called upon, aware that not very long before he'd been an insignificant reporter and that now he was involved in history, like it or not.

Every vehicle in the dock area seemed to be spoken for, so Hough set off briskly on foot, followed by Hatton and the navigating officer. They managed to hire a taxi at the gate where people were walking their dogs in the sunshine, much as though it were still peacetime.

At naval headquarters, Hough went alone for his orders, and when the navigating officer also disappeared Hatton was left outside in the corridor, twiddling his fingers in boredom. There was a public telephone near the door which the ratings used and out of sheer nostalgia he looked in the directory to see if Nora Hart's name was still in it. It was, and impulsively he pushed two pennies into the slot and tried it.

'Who?' she said when he told her his name.

'Barry Hatton. Surely you remember me?' He felt faintly hurt that she hadn't recalled him at once.

'Oh!' Her voice seemed distant and didn't show much enthusiasm. 'What are you doing back here?'

Because he couldn't tell her, there was a long awkward pause, then she went on with no more interest than a nervous curate passing the time of day at a sticky garden party. 'Are you here long?'

'Don't think so.'

'Oh, well!' She sounded relieved. 'You'll have to come round some time.'

She slammed the receiver down too sharply for his self-esteem and he stared at the telephone, wondering where his charm had gone. Perhaps it was as well he was going across the Channel.

There was a lieutenant at a table further along the corridor frowning at papers. He looked tired and, seeking information, Hatton approached him cautiously. 'What's happening?' he asked.

The lieutenant looked up. He didn't seem to resent Hatton, though his eyes flickered to the wavy ring on his sleeve. 'You going across?' he asked.

'I suppose so,' Hatton said. 'We've just arrived.'

'Who are you?'

'*Vital.*'

The lieutenant grinned. 'She's not very big, is she?' he said.

'I expect she'll be big enough,' Hatton said and realized immediately, as the lieutenant's eyes smiled, that he'd said something rather clever and perhaps rather brave.

'I expect she will,' the lieutenant agreed. 'Been in long?'

'No. Fortunately, there are plenty of people aboard to tell me what to do. Are they bringing the army out?'

'Unofficially, yes. And a beautiful bloody balls-up it is too. We've been at it for days now. Boulogne and Calais have had it and at Calais we're not even trying. They're there to stop Jerry on the western flank and that's what they have to do.'

The idea of being sacrificed for the rest of the army caught at Hatton's breath. It was a noble ideal but he felt it could be very uncomfortable and probably without much future.

'How far have the Germans got?' he asked.

The lieutenant looked up. 'Worry you?'

Hatton swallowed. It worried him a great deal but he tried to pretend it didn't. 'Not so's you'd notice,' he said.

The lieutenant smiled. 'Well played,' he said.

Lije Noble was another who was feeling doubts about his own skill and ability that morning.

He'd spent the night cowering under a hedge with several other men, terrified at the prospect of tanks and wishing to God someone would get a move on and get him away. When he woke at first light, a corporal was giving him a nudge with a boot. As he opened his eyes the silence was uncanny after the remembered tumult of the previous evening and the thought occurred to him that he was dead. For a moment the unreality persisted then the boot jarred again.

'Come on,' the corporal said.

'What's up?'

'Burial party. In the wood.'

Noble accepted the spade that someone handed to him, but as soon as the corporal turned away, he dropped it and slipped round the back of one of the lorries. At the other side a sergeant was standing with an officer.

'Got your explosives, Galpin?' the officer was asking.

'Yes, sir.'

'Right, take your men and head for Bergues. Pick out the bridges that'll have to be blown as we come through, and plant your stuff.'

As he turned away, Noble reached for the haversack containing the brandy and cigars.

'I've got to get back to my unit, Sarge,' he said. 'It's at Bughem near Bergues. Can you give me a lift? Me van went up in the wood there.'

As the lorry roared off, Noble was never so glad to see the back of anywhere as he was of that wood, but as they moved slowly north, dropping men two at a time at the bridges and locks as they passed, he began to feel better. To the south, over Arras, he could see a pall of smoke hanging in the air and farmhouses burning in the area between, with gun flashes coming regularly through the smoke and the occasional glint of a pair of field glasses, which gave him the unnerving feeling that everything he did was being watched by the Germans. He glanced at the sky. A recce plane had appeared above them and he'd learned by this time that recce planes were invariably followed by dive-bombers. He was grateful he wasn't in one of those awful streams of vehicles he'd seen, moving nose to tail at the pace of an active snail.

The sun was just beginning to get up as the lorry slowed to drop the last two men. Beyond the bridge where they stopped was a cornfield and they all climbed out for a smoke. To Noble, it seemed an event of great importance and, after the events of the lasts few days, one that was enormously civilized. He reached for the haversack and, extracting the cigars, offered them round.

The pulsating sound of distant gunfire seemed to drum on the canvas cover of the truck but it was far enough away not to worry them, and they'd just lit up when Noble heard a dull rumbling howl and one of the men they'd dropped, standing by the front of the lorry talking to the driver, swung round, his eyes bulging.

'Fighters!' he screamed.

The air thickened with the howl of engines and Noble dived for the ditch as the cannon shells flashed along the road. As they caught the lorry, there was a tremendous explosion that blew him head over heels into the ditch where he continued to crouch, his arms over his head, listening to the clang of metal dropping around him. As the engines died away he lifted his head. One of the lorry wheels was still bowling along fifty yards away and the road was littered with stones, pulverized earth and pieces of metal, rubber, canvas and wood round a huge scorch mark.

The driver and the man talking to him had disappeared in the explosion and the third sprawled in the road, a shredded mess of flesh and clothing. Sergeant Galpin appeared slowly from the cornfield and studied the corpse. 'Copped it,' he said.

They dragged the body off the road but, because the spade had disappeared too, they were unable to bury it and had to leave it in the long grass. Galpin found a few shreds of torn canvas and draped them over it, then he stood and stared down for a moment or two, as though he were conducting a silent burial service of his own.

As he turned he glanced curiously at Noble who was standing with his mouth open, his eyes glazed as though he were hypnotized. 'I reckon I'd better get back,' he said. 'That last pair we dropped have got a radio.'

Noble watched him go. The sun was blazing hot and, apart from the intermittent sound of gunfire to the south, the countryside immediately around him seemed still empty and alien. His feet ached and, now that the sergeant had left him, he was totally and irrevocably lost.

So was Clarence Sievewright. But there was no feeling of alarm or panic in his heart. He was a placid man who considered himself well fitted by training to deal with emergencies. As a Scout he had once worn badges to prove he was an expert at a thousand and one important things and he felt he was capable of facing anything the war might throw up. His face was round and innocent and he glowed with soap and inner health. Over such smooth features a helmet seemed almost too ferocious.

He had spent the night in a barn which had been comfortable enough, if a little chilly, and that morning he'd gone to the farm nearby to ask for food. It had been deserted, so he'd hunted round the yard and eventually – as he'd expected – found a dozen eggs under a hedge which he'd fried in his mess-tin lid. Afterwards, since Scout Law demanded cleanliness, he'd washed at the pump and brushed his teeth, taking care not to swallow the water because he also knew that it was probably not safe unless boiled, then he'd carefully changed his socks and set off again. Now, five hours later, he was wondering where the British army had got to. He knew it was in retreat and before he'd set off he'd heard it was heading towards the coast. If he walked steadily northwards, he should eventually find it again. He had no compass but as a Scout he knew that if he kept the sun on his back up to midday and on his left after that he'd be heading in the correct direction. Speed and lightness had seemed important, however, and he'd sat down to see what he could discard of his equipment. To his surprise, all he felt able to throw away were two or three paperbacks, a selection of thin socks and a pair of dancing shoes he'd had sent out.

By this time, he'd left the roads and taken to the fields because it had long since occured to him that if the Germans were machine-gunning the roads, the most intelligent thing to do was to avoid them. By mid-morning, he was beginning to feel hungry again but, finding a few potatoes and carrots in a field, he stuffed several in his pack with the intention of cooking them later. Then he found a cow that was bellowing with pain and, realizing it was in need of milking, he swung towards it and with difficulty managed to get the milk flowing.

He extracted more than he needed to make the cow comfortable, then, putting his kit on again, clapped his steel helmet on his head and set off once more with a sense of having done his duty.

When Lieutenant-Commander Hough returned to where Hatton was waiting, his mouth was tight and his face was serious. He wasn't a great deal older than Hatton but he'd been in the war from the first days of September and had already been torpedoed and bombed in the Norwegian campaign.

'Are we going across, sir?' Hatton asked as they fell into step.

'Yes.' Hough didn't seem in a mood to talk and Hatton wondered if he were worried about the bombing. The thought helped him feel more able to handle his own fears.

They picked up the navigating officer and found a taxi back to the harbour. The streets seemed to be full of soldiers. Some of them were heading for the railway station in marching groups, but a few seemed to have escaped and were hanging about outside the pubs. They didn't look like first-class troops.

The harbour was still full of ships as the tender headed out to *Vital*, and along the wall smaller vessels were beginning to gather – hoppers, trawlers, harbour launches and fishing boats. *Daisy* was among them and in her forepeak Kenny Pepper was still waiting patiently. He'd been there all night. During the hours of darkness, he'd sneaked out, desperate for food, and made his way to the galley. Brundrett had been sleeping in his bunk alongside, a fat white shape under the blankets, one fleshy arm hanging to the deck. He was snoring heavily, and Kenny had had no difficulty in extracting half a loaf of bread, a pot of jam, half a pound of butter, a tin of corned beef and a candle. Brundrett's ability to sleep was well known and Kenny, who was still growing and needed more food than Brundrett was inclined to allow him, had often taken advantage of it.

As *Vital*'s tender bumped alongside and its occupants scrambled aboard the ship, Hough called a quick conference to discuss what they were to do. 'It seems we still hold a strip of coast about twenty-five miles long,' he announced. 'From Gravelines to Nieuport. Know it, Pilot?'

The navigating officer nodded. 'Flat, featureless and level, sir. Just a few seaside towns. No piers. No harbour facilities. Sand shelves very slowly to deep water. And all exposed to northerly winds.'

'How about Dunkirk? Anybody know anything about it?'

'A little, sir,' Hatton offered. 'I don't suppose it's much use.'

'Let's hear it, all the same.'

'It's pretty ancient. Grew out of a fishing village. It was a fortress and I think some of it still stands. It's the third port in France and it's got a good modern harbour with seven dock basins.'

'You're better than you think, Hatton. Go on.'

Hatton flushed with pleasure at the praise. 'It has four dry docks, five miles of quays, and three of the canals from the Low Countries feed into it.'

'Good God!' Hough looked startled. 'Where did you get all this lot?'

'I looked it up, sir, while I was waiting for you.'

Hough grinned. 'God be praised for the education and enterprise of the R.N.V.R.,' he said. 'Go on.'

Hatton glanced at his notebook. 'Docks go deep into the town and there's a dredged channel to the sea. It's protected from the tides by long piers and there's a mole that comes out from the oil storage area. There's another from the old fortifications that's over a thousand yards long. If we could have used it, the army could have got away with everything it possesses, but I gather it's not that kind of mole.'

'Charming!' Hough's eyebrows rose. 'Right, Doc, prepare your sick bay for casualties. Purser, we'll need constant hot soup and tea, as well as sandwiches. Not only for our own people but for anybody we might lift. I gather some of 'em haven't eaten for days. Guns' crews, damage and fire control parties will be closed up from the minute we leave harbour. I suspect we're going to be busy.'

It was becoming only too clear to a lot of people that they were going to be busy. Even the commander of the B.E.F. There were no more reserves now and nothing he could do, because the battles that were being fought now were in the hands of his corps, divisions and brigades, and the regiments who were clinging to fragments of village and unnamed stretches of waterway. Slowly, defending its positions desperately, the army was falling back to form a defensive perimeter round the only port left – Dunkirk.

The French were still demanding an attack to the south but there was an air of unreality about the whole idea, because even as it was decided to find out if headquarters could be moved to Cassel the town came under shellfire and almost immediately afterwards a message came from the Belgian king to inform them that he would soon be obliged to surrender. As the new head-quarters was finally set up at Houtkerque nine miles to the north, a telegram arrived from London. '*Sole task,*' it said, '*is to evacuate to England maximum of your forces possible.*'

The end seemed to have come.

Fortunately, the German tank attacks had stopped. With the French army to the south still undestroyed, it was becoming dangerous to allow the wastage to continue, though Jocho Horndorff's unit was still probing forward.

Hard as the campaign had been, they were infinitely better off than the French who had lacked petrol, repair crews, brakes for their cannon, and had the wrong ammunition for their Hotchkiss machine guns, while most of their officers were new from St. Cyr. The British had had the right spirit but hardly any tanks, and whoever had been responsible for their design must have been suffering from a considerable weight on his conscience. The principal influence brought to bear on them had been the cavalry school of thought which had tried to make them as much like horses as possible, so that they were fast and lightly armed and could run away quickly but were useless when brought to battle. The British cavalry regiments had used them with their usual élan, charging like the run-up to the first fence at a race meeting, but this method had changed to others more wary as it was curbed by the diminishing stock of dashing officers and the dearth of tanks. One after another they'd been abandoned with broken tracks or other mechanical defects, and now littered the French countryside, square and ponderous, like garden sheds on wheels and about as flimsy.

The roads in front of Horndorff were jammed with refugees and blocked with broken vehicles but no one got in the way. Horsed carts were dragged off the pavé, cars and vans were driven into the ditches and hedges, their occupants jolting wildly as they bumped over the verge. Men and women pushing barrows and perambulators and bicycles flopped into the grass. Others abandoned their suitcases and packages, leaving them strewn across the road to be chewed to shreds by the tank treads as their owners bolted for safety. There was no shooting but more than one van, moving too slowly, was nudged from the road, and once Horndorff saw a cart slide sideways into a canal, a wheel buckling under it, the horse dragged backwards to the water, screaming with fear. He didn't stop.

When they reached Scheywege they halted and the radio crackled with the news that the British were setting up guns. 'Resistance is stiffening,' the instructions came.

'But of course,' Horndorff growled as he took the report. 'We missed our chance. All right – ' he gestured ahead ' – forward.'

The countryside was featureless now, nothing on its surface to break the monotony but scattered groups of cottages or a level crossing. It was dangerous because there was nothing to hide them except an occasional farmhouse or osier-bed and they moved more warily, Horndorff watching every corner, every barn, every clump of bushes and trees, every low wall where a British battery might be sited.

'Close hatches,' he warned. 'Stand by.'

The radio crackled again and information came that infantry

was held up by a British strongpoint at Zoetsweg and that he was to give help. He stopped the section and, directing two of the tanks to a map reference to the north with instructions to pick him up later, waved his arm again so that the four tanks that were left began to clatter forward once more with the creaking protestation of springs and bogie wheels.

The fields now were quite flat with occasional potato clamps and a lot of dykes, and Horndorff guessed he was approaching the British front line. His eyes were roving round him and just as he caught a movement by a row of clamps in the field to his right the wireless operator started yelling. He shouted down to him to shut up.

'But Herr Major! It's the colonel! He's saying we're to take care because – '

Even as he yelled the warning, Horndorff saw a series of flashes and in the same moment caught a glimpse of the flat steel helmets the British wore.

'Drive, reverse,' he screamed. 'Turret eleven o'clock! One-two-zero-zero – !'

But as the driver heaved on the brakes there was a tremendous crash below him and the tank shuddered and he smelt cordite and smoke. As he looked down, the white questioning faces of the gunner and the operator stared up at him and their lips formed the word, 'Fire!' Then he saw fumes coming from the louvres and, almost at once it seemed, there was a roar of flames and he heard the driver screaming. The inside of the tank turned into a glowing furnace and he scrambled to safety as the hidden guns among the potato clamps began to fire as fast as they could. The gunner followed him but he seemed to panic and began to run in circles. Then as the tank behind stopped dead, there was a muffled thump from inside that lifted the panic-stricken gunner into the ditch. The turret slid off sideways and the screaming that had started died down. Red fountains were playing around them now and Horndorff's mouth was filled with the taste of cordite and he could smell the frightful smell of impending death that went with it. The air was full of lead and noise and he caught a split-second glimpse of tracer curving by in long hot rods that took the breath from his lungs with the vacuum of their passing.

One of the two remaining tanks was trying to bring its gun

to bear but the British shells were still whistling past and he knew
it was only a matter of time before it was hit.

'Get out of it!' he screamed at the fourth and last tank, leap-
ing to his feet and running towards it, determined not to be taken
prisoner. The machine began to slew round on the narrow road,
but there was a dyke on either side and it was difficult, and as he
ran he saw a shell hit the other tank. The whipcrack of the
explosion blew him off his feet and he rolled over the bank of the
ditch, spattered with falling dirt and stones.

Lifting his head, he saw three figures jump out, their clothes
on fire, but a machine gun among the potato clamps rattled and
he heard the bullets chattering against the armour-plate. All three
men went over like shot rabbits, still burning.

The last tank was still trying to turn, moving awkwardly like
a crippled beetle. As it jerked away, he wondered if he could run
after it, but that damned machine gun was still playing across the
open fields and there wasn't a scrap of cover where he could hide.
Then, just as the tank began to roll, one of the shells screaming
over his head hit it on the nearside and he saw the track coiling
like a snake as it curled off the bogies. The tank swung sideways,
and he saw it topple slowly into the dyke.

It hadn't taken Flying Officer Conybeare long to realize that
waiting in Villers-sur-Grandie was going to be a waste of time.
Three hours had elapsed following the telephone call he'd made to
his squadron but there had been no sign of the truck which had
been promised and he'd gradually grown more and more uneasy.

There was an atmosphere of bewilderment and gloom about
the place and when a lorryload of French soldiers had come
hurtling through, pointing backwards and screaming '*Les Allemands*', he'd decided it was time he set off walking. There were
no other soldiers in the village, and now the carts, barrows,
horse-drawn drays and ramshackle old motors had begun to
appear out of backyards and head west, trailing a long column of
men, women and children on foot. The speed of their assembly
had seemed to indicate they'd been ready for take-off for some
time.

At the next village they'd run into another column coming
from the east and the numbers had increased. They hadn't seemed
to regard Conybeare with much affection and it had seemed wiser

not to mingle too closely with them. In the village square the column stopped. No one had attempted to help them and they had slept where they could. Preferring to be where he could make a quick getaway, Conybeare had managed to find a chair in the *Maire*'s office and stayed there until the move west and north started again as soon as the sun had risen. The Germans found them before they'd gone a mile.

When the shooting and the howl of engines had stopped, Conybeare scrambled to his feet and ran along the line of sprawled figures. Men and women were appearing from the ditches, weeping and terrified, some of them cursing and shaking their fists at the disappearing Stukas. Nearby was a woman whose arm had been ripped to shreds by a burst of bullets. Further on were two children sitting in a push chair. One of them was covered with blood and silent. The other was screaming with terror and fighting to get free of the strap that held it in. Conybeare unfastened the buckle and lifted it clear; then as a man took the child from him, he decided he was getting his priorities mixed. He could be more usefully employed elsewhere. He sighed and, turning abruptly, began to head for the fields.

From the point where Conybeare was just making up his mind that a fighter pilot could help more in the air than with rendering first-aid to injured men, women and children who were already surrounded by their families and friends, to the head of the column was just over a mile. Up in front, between a horse that was snorting out its life in bannering bubbles of blood, and an ancient Citroën which seemed to be spouting steam from half a dozen points of the engine, Marie-Josephine Berthelot was on her knees by a dying woman. She had neither morphine nor bandages and the woman's cries were tearing at her heart. From behind, a man offered a brandy flask but in her terror and misery she hardly noticed.

She was weeping softly and the man who'd offered the flask put his hand on her shoulder.

'She's dead,' he said quietly.

Marie-Josephine lifted her face, her cheeks wet with tears, her eyes questioning. 'You are English?'

'No. American.' *And* a goddam fool, Scharroo thought. During the night the Germans had unexpectedly pulled back and when morning had come he'd been shocked to find that during the hours of darkness the fighting had shifted direction and he was now on the wrong side of it.

He squinted at the sky, worried. 'We ought to be moving,' he said. 'That lot were dive-bombers but they didn't drop any bombs. That sounds like they had orders not to damage the road surface, and *that* means German tanks aren't far behind.'

He glanced again at Marie-Josephine. She was small and pretty with soft dark hair and large brown eyes that were circled with the purple shadows all Frenchwomen seemed to have. He put her age at about twenty.

'You alone?' he asked.

'Yes.'

He indicated the suitcase she'd dropped. 'I can carry that for you,' he said. 'Where are you heading?'

Marie-Josephine had recovered her composure now and was looking at Scharroo, stiff-backed, her head up, her small mouth firm, her manner business-like. 'I do not know,' she said. 'I have some relations at La Panne. Perhaps I join them.'

Scharroo nodded. He could stay where he was, he supposed, and wait for the Germans but, though it was no part of his commission, he'd begun to feel that he ought instead to get to Paris. He had a feeling that it would be there that the next big act would take place. There was little doubt that, despite their undefeated armies to the south, the French were unlikely to fight to the death and Paris would soon fall. His job was to be present to see the Germans' triumph. If he could get to La Panne, he thought, he could perhaps get a train from Nieuport to Ypres or along the coast and south via St. Omer. It was chancy but better than hanging about in this empty area of canals and dykes.

'Okay,' he said. 'That'll do me.'

When Conybeare had turned away abruptly and headed into the fields, it had not been an easy decision to make and his mind had been a turmoil of horror and pity.

At the other side of the field, he hit another road full of lorries with which he pushed along for a while, aware of the invisible ring of the enemy growing tighter and harder all the time. Then a truck full of French soldiers came past, insisting on trying to overtake all the other vehicles. There were shouts of 'Wait your turn!' and 'Pull in!' and an officer pulled out his revolver and, jumping on the running board, stuck it in the driver's face. The Frenchman pulled in, but somehow the incident worried Conybeare and, deciding the road would attract attention from the Germans before long, he turned north yet again, keeping the sun behind him as a compass. Eventually, on his left, he saw houses and a church spire and, hungry by this time, he wondered if he could find anything to eat there.

The village appeared to be deserted but he entered it warily, expecting to find the Germans in possession. The fronts of several houses had been blown away and the silence was frightening. Though a few cats stared at him, there was no sign of human life. In a deserted café he helped himself to a bottle of beer from the cold cupboard and, half-starved, wolfed a stale baguette from under the counter and helped himself to cheese and sausage. He was still standing at the bar, tenderly fingering the bruise over his eye, when he heard footsteps in the roadway outside.

At first he thought the approaching man was a parachutist, because he wore overalls and a small round helmet. He was blond, hard-faced and tough, and much bigger than Conybeare who was completely unarmed.

He looked round for a weapon. There was nothing he could use. Then he saw an old hammer-operated shotgun over the bar. He reached for it and, staring into the dusty barrel, saw it hadn't been fired for years, perhaps generations. It was of little value in an emergency but he decided he might manage to do something with it.

The German was only twenty or thirty yards away now, heading straight for the café, and Conybeare slipped behind the door that led to the private quarters. The German's boots clumped on the floor-boards, and Conybeare saw him go behind the counter and take a bottle of beer from the counter. As he took off the cap and reached for a glass, Conybeare stepped out and placed the muzzle of the old shotgun against his neck, feeling like a schoolboy playing a game.

'Hands up,' he said.

As he'd lain in the grass on the banks of the dyke, Jocho Horndorff had suddenly become aware of his tiredness. He had been on the go for a fortnight now and the ambush had been set with deadly precision so that his section had been knocked out with laughable ease.

For a moment he couldn't think what to do. He was alone in front of the army with no means of warning anyone that the British were just ahead. Then he'd spotted houses just to the west and had decided to telephone back to Cambrai or Brussels, which he knew were already in German hands, and get them to pass the message on.

He'd set off walking again, unarmed apart from the pistol at his belt, but the countryside was broken up by dykes and he had to find the little bridges that had been built for cattle to cross, and it was an hour and a half later when he reached the village. There didn't appear to be a soul left in it, except for one or two cats sitting in doorways sunning themselves and a skinny-looking dog which slunk off as he approached.

He began to search for a telephone and found the exchange in a room at the back of the post office, but he had no idea how to work it and when he picked up the headphones there was no sound, as though the wires were down somewhere. He realized he was going to have to start walking again, but the weather was hot and, seeing a bar just down the road he entered it and helped himself to a bottle of beer. He had just opened it when he felt the shotgun muzzle on his neck.

For a moment, as Horndorff froze, Conybeare thought he was going to try to snatch the gun from him but then his hands lifted slowly, still holding the glass and the beer bottle. Keeping the muzzle of the old gun against the German's neck, Conybeare took them from his hands and placed them on a table.

'You are English?' Horndorff said.

'Yes. Do you speak English?'

'I was educated at Oxford.'

'That's a help. What I have at your neck is a shotgun. It's a twelve-bore and if I pull the trigger it'll smear your face across the wall there. Take out your revolver – very slowly – and place it on the table to your left.'

'Who are you?' Horndorff asked.

'I'm a British officer,' Conybeare said, 'and I'm going to pull this trigger in exactly three seconds.'

Horndorff reached for the 9-mm. Luger and, withdrawing it,

laid it on the table. Thankfully, aware that his heart had been pounding enough to choke him, Conybeare picked it up, cocked it, and laid the shotgun down.

'You may turn round,' he said.

When Horndorff turned, he was shocked to see that the shot-gun clearly hadn't been fired in years and probably never would be again and that it was his own Luger that was now pointing at his chest.

'Where are your friends?' Conybeare asked.

'Where are yours?' Horndorff asked.

'I can't tell you. You know that.'

'Neither can I. And you know that, too.'

'Of course. Silly of me to ask.'

Horndorff was recovering from his surprise now. The officer opposite him was very young and, though his uniform was stained and he had an enormous bruise over his eye, he still managed to look like a little boy in his best suit. Horndorff's eyes travelled down until they rested on a pair of manure-stained farm boots.

Conybeare saw him staring. 'French officer got them for me,' he said. 'Lost mine getting out of my machine.'

Horndorff began to smile and Conybeare knew what he was thinking. He'd spent several holidays in Germany before the war and knew they had a different way of measuring a man.

'The British are beaten,' Horndorff said. 'Why don't you throw your hand in?'

Conybeare stiffened. 'They don't seem beaten to me,' he pointed out.

Horndorff shrugged, sure of himself. 'Since we both speak English,' he said cheerfully, 'perhaps we ought to introduce ourselves. I am with the panzers.'

'R.A.F.,' Conybeare said shortly.

'You were shot down?' Horndorff smiled. 'Our pilots are very good, I think.'

Conybeare's face didn't slip. 'Not good enough,' he said. 'Altogether I've killed about eighteen.'

Horndorff was startled by the information but he managed to avoid showing it. 'My dear boy,' he said, 'my friends to the east have more weapons and men than your people have ever dreamed about. *Die Stärke des deutschen Schwerts.* The might of the German sword.'

Conybeare was unmoved.

'Don't call me your "dear boy",' he said in his prickly humour-less way. 'I'm a British officer.'

Horndorff shrugged and, his hands still in the air, he inclined his head a little. 'I beg your pardon,' he said. 'A slip. But it's all rather academic, this capturing, isn't it? After all, my friends will be here soon.'

He'd hoped to frighten Conybeare into letting him go, but as soon as he'd spoken he realized he'd said the wrong thing.

'Then we'd better set off walking towards the British lines, hadn't we?' Conybeare pointed out.

Horndorff was caught by panic. He had no wish to be made a prisoner, especially by this child who with his bruise looked like an infant prize fighter. His hands dropped. 'But this is ridiculous,' he pointed out. 'Our troops are just behind me.'

'Then we mustn't waste time, must we?' Conybeare said. 'And keep your hands up. If they're tired, clasp them on your head. Shall we start walking.'

'Suppose I refuse?'

'Then I shall shoot you.'

'Perhaps you will miss.'

'I don't think so. I was in the R.A.F. pistol team at Bisley in 1938.'

By this time, with Operation Dynamo under way, a senior naval officer had arrived in Dunkirk to take charge. He had formerly been chief staff officer to the first sea lord and had recently been given the command of one of the navy's proudest ships. Early in the afternoon he'd embarked in a destroyer with twelve officers and a hundred and sixty ratings as well as a com-munications staff. They'd been bombed at half-hourly intervals all the way across.

But not by Alfred Stoos.

Junkers 87 D/6980 was still in the hands of the mechanics and the chances of it being repaired continued to be slim.

'For the love of God,' Stoos said furiously. 'You're not making much headway!'

Oberfeldwebel Hamcke was standing on a trestle, watching a mechanic draw out a piston. They both had their heads in the engine space and didn't hear Stoos at first and he had to repeat himself loudly before they turned.

Hamcke watched without a word as the mechanic laid the piston down on the bench and wrapped clean rags round it, then he climbed down, wiping his hands on a ball of waste.

'It's the spares, Herr Leutnant,' he said. 'We're having to go all the way to the frontier to find them.'

'Can't you use a bit of initiative?' Stoos said. 'There must be *something* you can do.'

Hamcke said nothing and Stoos turned away, furious. He was in a desperate mood. The British were gathering near Dunkirk now, as everyone knew, waiting to be shot at like a lot of driven partridges, and there was nothing for him to fly. The fact that Schmesser and Fink had not returned made him all the more eager. Schlegel, in his bland, indifferent way, had said they'd been knocked down by a fighter, and the news only served to make Stoos more contemptuous of Fink as a pilot and of Schmesser as a commander. They wouldn't have been shot down, he suspected, if he'd been there.

He was itching to add to the holocaust in Dunkirk.

There was hardly need. The town had already descended into chaos. The streets were full of rubble and burning vehicles, and dazed French soldiers, too far gone in shock to be able to help themselves, were standing in groups watching as the British began to pour in. Some of the British units had also disintegrated, and had thrown away their equipment and their rifles, but there were still groups with long histories, great traditions or simply good officers who appeared complete with kit and arms, their heads up, marching in step through the ruined streets. The chances of getting them to safety already seemed problematical, however, and it was becoming increasingly obvious to the navy that the only way to do it was to embark them from the open beaches.

Unaware still of what he was facing but conscious that his private life had reached a point of no-return, Alban Tremenheere was waiting on board *Athelstan*. He'd waited all day. Because he was worried about Nell Noone and Number Thirteen, Osborne Road, he'd even slept aboard and now he'd decided it would be a good idea to persuade *Athelstan*'s owner that her place – Tremenheere's too, for that matter – was not in the river at Littlehampton but at Dover. A short period of service away from home, as he'd found out as a young man, was always a good answer to a domestic problem.

He was already behind the times, however, and *Athelstan*'s owner had got the message some time before. Alexander Knevett had inherited money so that, although he was a doctor, he'd never had to work very hard at it. Nothing normally disturbed his wealthy calm, and when Tremenheere arrived at his house that afternoon the sense of urgency he found there puzzled him. There were oilskins, sea-boots, charts, and a kit-bag full of gear standing in the hall, and a maid dressed in black and white holding a yachting cap. Tremenheere, being Tremenheere, pinched her behind. 'What's on then?' he asked.

As he spoke, Knevett himself appeared. 'Who told you?' he asked.

'Who told me what?'

'We were off.'

'Are we?'

'Yes.' Knevett seemed preoccupied. 'You'd better make sure we're in good order.'

Tremenheere's sly face slipped and he turned from the door and began to hurry back to the water's edge. At the boatyard he was surprised to see a crowd outside the gate. It was clearly not just an ordinary crowd. There were men in blue jerseys and peaked caps like himself, and men in naval uniform. In the store, more men were collecting boxes of tinned meat and biscuits and signing for petrol.

'Better sort me out, too,' Tremenheere said. 'Biscuits. Corned beef. Sardines.' He grinned. 'Beer.' Although he was the paid hand he was always careful to make sure he catered for his own tastes as well.

Basil Allerton had been on the road for ever now, it seemed, most of the time on his feet because his sergeant had been taken away from him and his corporal had disappeared with four men to collect rations and had never reappeared.

He was surprised to find he wasn't frightened and he put it down to the behaviour of the ordinary soldiers about him. They were by no means beaten, only bewildered because they'd done nothing but retire without rest, and were ready at any time to turn and fight – anybody, anything, even their friends, they were so angry.

Allerton was still heading for Calais. They'd arrived in France at that port and it seemed sense to head back there because, if nothing else, it was the nearest point to England. Then, however, they ran into three men on bicycles. They wore blue French smocks and looked like peasants, but they were English, old soldiers from the First War employed by the War Graves Commission to care for the vast cemeteries of the 1914–1918 battlefields.

'It's no good going that way,' they said. 'Dunkirk's the only place left.'

The news brought to Allerton a deep secret personal horror that someone had let them down, that somewhere above them in government were men who hadn't cared, and he climbed back into the truck and swung off the road in a more northerly direction. There was a bottle-neck at Neuve Eglise and everywhere there were signs of fierce shelling and bombing. Then, round a corner, came a column of German prisoners guarded by a solitary British soldier with a fixed bayonet.

'You'll not get that lot home, mate,' Rice, Allerton's batman jeered.

The guard, a stunted man with vast boots, made a derisive gesture. 'Awa' and use yer nut,' he said. 'We're takkin' 'em back tae Glasgae tae march 'em up Sauchiehall Street in chains.'

The countryside ahead now was flat with miles of marshy fields that stretched as far as the horizon, all cut up by a network of canals and highways at right angles to each other. Every field was below the level of the canal and each had its own diminutive dyke, and into this empty area the whole of the B.E.F. was pouring. Every road was visible and jammed with transport and troops, great columns of them stretching back to the horizon, all of them drawing towards a single point on the coast : Ambulances, lorries, trucks, Bren gun carriers, artillery columns, everything except tanks, all crawling north over the featureless countryside in the sunshine, their camouflage making them look like slow-moving rivers of mud from some far-off upheaval of the land.

There was shellfire up ahead somewhere and as they drove

towards it Allerton felt his face grow tight, the skin pulled taut and his jaws aching with the clenching of his teeth.

'They've been having a day of prayer for us in England,' Rice was observing conversationally in the back of the truck.

One of the other men chuckled. 'That'll be why the whole bloody thing's falling apart,' he said.

The conversation irritated Allerton. It had once been his pleasure to refer cleverly to guns as slimy tubes of hellish coldness and to soldiering as a low, undignified and hurtful pursuit, but he was beginning to see now that it was more than merely that. It contained a world of grief and pity, and made him shed his light-heartedness and the subdued sense of adventure that had persisted in shoving its way through his intellectual blaséness. That was gone now, to be replaced by grimness and fear and a perpetual mounting weariness of body and spirit. It was a fortnight now since they'd had a decent sleep, and some of the drivers about him had feet that were so swollen they'd taken off their boots and socks and fell asleep every time the column came to a stop at one of the paralysing road blocks.

They had reached a village now, a mere cluster of ugly houses with front gardens facing a series of shabby fields, and a few peasants standing by the roadside. In the fields opposite were anti-aircraft guns which had been blown up by artificers, their split barrels like vast metal flowers, and up ahead Allerton could see the first sign of the coast in a great black cloud hanging low on the horizon, its stormy centre bulging down as though about to swamp the earth.

There was more shelling ahead and he could see the flashes in the growing dusk. The shells were falling near a battery of 25-pounders drawn up in a field. The procession of vehicles came to a stop at once and Allerton and the others left the truck and dived for the open doorway of an abandoned cottage. As the shells exploded, the peasants began to run, one of them a girl, tall and good-looking in a rough country way, and as she ran the breeze caught her thin summer dress and blew it against her hips and large firm breasts. As she passed the doorway where he crouched, another salvo of shells came down and she crumpled and sprawled on her back in the street, screaming in a terrible dry-throated way. Allerton ran out, caught hold of her ankles and began to drag her into the doorway. She made no attempt to help herself and lay as though unconscious while her clothes rode up beyond her stockings, over her strong white thighs and half-way up her body. There was another crash and he flung himself down, falling on top of her, his eyes full of the flash of the explosion, in his ears the clatter of bricks and tiles and the pattering sound of splinters.

Then suddenly there was silence and he lifted his head. As he did so the girl opened her eyes. Her face was dirty and marked with tearstains and her dark hair was dulled with dust. They lay there, their bodies entwined as though they were lovers, but she was staring at him with fear and hatred as though he'd tried to rape her. Mumbling his apologies, Allerton climbed from her and she rose also and without a word disappeared among the rubble.

Supply lorries had been wrecked up ahead, and where two ambulances were blazing in bright orange pyres the wounded were being dragged out and placed on stretchers. One of the drivers had been killed in his cab, half flattened by the blast against the metal, and over the stink of burning diesel there was an awful smell of gunpowder and raw flesh. His comrades had tried to pull him out but had given up in disgust, and what was left hung half out of the open door. Even as the rescue parties worked at the flames, other men were snatching the opportunity to grab tins of peas, potatoes, biscuits, sugar and tea, and even spare parts.

One of the wrecked vehicles was a NAAFI lorry containing supplies for troop canteens, and the manager, a middle-aged civilian, was offering gin and whisky from the damaged cases in the back. 'Come on, lads,' he was shouting. 'Stock up. All you can drink,' and Allerton managed to claim a bottle of whisky which he handed round to what was left of his men.

The convoy still remained stationary but by this time the light had almost gone, and Allerton felt better because the shelling had stopped completely now and he knew they were hidden from the dive-bombers. He was longing for a wash and a decent sleep but the countryside had been so green all day he'd never really believed he was fleeing for his life.

The convoy was still there when it grew dark and, since there was water on either side of them, someone seemed to have decided that any attempt to move would land the lot of them in the dyke. After a while, an artillery officer Allerton knew came past and he offered him a swig of the whisky. The officer was informative but vague.

'Belgians are going to throw in their hand,' he said.

'Thought they would,' Allerton admitted.

'News came through about eleven.'

'How's headquarters taking it?'

The artilleryman considered. 'Not too much panic, considering.'

Allerton offered the whisky again. 'What's the plan?' he asked. 'Have we got one?'

'I thought someone might know what we were doing.'

'Shouldn't think so. I think we're making it up as we go along.'

'What do we do then, when the Germans come? Bite 'em?'

The artilleryman grinned. 'There's one thing,' he said. 'Nobody's disagreeing. We don't know enough to disagree about.' His mood changed and he suddenly looked dog-weary. 'I think the whole bloody thing's a shambles,' he said. 'A present from those bloody people in Parliament who thought an inefficient army was more moral than an efficient one and that it was kinder to shoot with small guns than big ones. That and panic spread by Jerry.'

He held out his cigarette case and they lit up, shielding the flame with their hands.

'I've heard stories,' the artilleryman went on, 'of thousands of tanks, and parachutists disguised as nuns. But *I've* seen none and tank chaps I've spoken to say that these famous panzers aren't all that good, anyway. I think Jerry's won this round with a few motor-cyclists and a lot of bluff.'

Allerton listened to the diatribe patiently. 'Where are we supposed to head for?' he asked.

'Dunkirk, I'm told. But it's a mess. They're bombing it.'

Allerton's artilleryman was dead right. They were.

The streets were a litter of burning rubbish and scattered bricks from tumbled houses, and wrecked vehicles stood in groups on every corner. By the station there were hundreds of French and Belgians but already they were being directed from the shambles to the beaches where the slow process of lifting by ships' boats had now being going on for some time.

It was not yet properly organized, however, and was still painstakingly difficult, and the senior naval officer in the town was by no means satisfied that he was doing all he could. He studied the fragile East Mole carefully. 'It looks strong enough for ships to berth,' he said. 'Let's try. Signal the next one in to have a go.'

The flare of her bows caught by the flames of burning warehouses, the ship berthed, and immediately men started running towards her along the mole, their boots clumping on the boards.

'Signal Dover,' the senior naval officer said.

As men began to scramble across the decks of the first ship alongside, H.M.S. *Vital* was approaching the coast. Darkness had fallen and Dunkirk was shrouded under heavy smoke. The roadsteads were littered with wrecks and to the west oil tanks were blazing. The flames silhouetted the moles and the bridge that was jammed open at the entrace to the basin. Wrecked cranes stood out like crippled storks and, as the smoke lifted, they could see fires in the town itself.

Hatton stared at it with narrowed eyes. Despite his lack of experience, he had imagination and he found his heart was skidding uncomfortably under his shirt. His head turned uneasily as he heard the howl of aeroplane engines and the thud of bombs, but the aircraft were above the smoke and it wasn't possible to see them, though the knowledge that they were there worried him a great deal.

He was still staring fearfully at the town when a signal arrived from Dover. Boats had been swung out on their davits ready for lowering but now, as he read the signal, Hough turned and jerked Hatton out of his worried contemplation of the burning shoreline.

'East Mole, Hatton,' he said. 'Know anything about it?'

It took a moment or two for Hatton to bring himself back to the present. 'Yes, sir,' he said. 'It's just a narrow plankway.'

'Could we get alongside?'

Hatton's mind went back to the few rudiments of shiphandling he'd learnt. 'The tide runs between the piles,' he said. 'It'd be difficult but the piles could be used as mooring posts at a pinch.'

Hough turned to the first lieutenant. 'Have the boats swung back inboard, Number One, and let's have a few of your most athletic chaps handy. They might have to jump ashore to take the ropes. Hatton, it'll be your job to keep these chaps moving. They don't know their arse from their elbow when it comes to ships and they won't have an idea what to do or where to go. See that they're told. And let's have a petty officer on every boarding point. It won't be easy to keep count but we'll try.'

As Hatton left the bridge to take up a position near the point-fives, his eyes swung back to Dunkirk and the huge pall of smoke blotting out the sky. He'd heard that two million gallons of oil were going up and the smoke seemed a mile wide and appeared to rise thousands of feet into the air. To Hatton it looked like the shadow of doom.

Doom didn't seem so far away just then to Private Angelet, of the 121st Regiment, just to the north of Helluin. Among the groups of soldiers trudging along with him there was no concern with the horror over the horizon. They were deep in a horror of their own and the lack of discipline shook Angelet to the core.

There were still refugees among them, despite the darkness, civilians and troops together in a chaos of guns, tanks and military vehicles Most of the civilians were in the last stages of exhaustion by this time, their feet tied around with string and brown paper where their shoes had given out, and covered with mud from flinging themselves in the ditches to hide from the enemy aeroplanes.

Not long before they'd passed the body of a small boy ripped to bloody meat by a shell, and a man who was said to have been shot as a spy. As he seemed to be the owner of a café, it seemed more likely to Angelet that he'd been killed because he wouldn't produce cognac.

The soldiers filled a double row of vehicles that blocked the road and the sight sent a chill through Angelet; then, as they passed a broken-down red-brick château they saw cavalrymen shooting their horses and throwing their arms into the moat.

'What's up?' Chouteau asked.

'The army's cut off,' he was told. The Germans are right behind us.'

Chouteau turned slowly and stared pointedly to the south. 'They're not right behind *us*,' he said.

Angelet swallowed nervously as he listened to the exchange. He still whimpered occasionally but considerably less than he had the previous day. He was slowly getting control of himself, gathering, it seemed, all the loose ends of nerves that made him up, pulling them in one after the other until he seemed to be holding them all in a tight ball in his small and very dirty fist. 'Where will they go?' he asked Chouteau.

'The coast,' Chouteau said. He was tramping stolidly north again, unspeaking, not complaining, not worrying, an old soldier saving his breath for walking.

'What happens then?' Angelet asked.

Chouteau glanced at him. Angelet still looked a child but in the light of the flames he could see there was a subtle something about his eyes that had changed.

'God knows,' he said. 'Perhaps they'll re-arm and re-form us.'

'What if they don't?'

'Then I don't know, *mon brave.*'

There was a long pause in which they could hear only the tramp of boots. Angelet was conscious of an enormous blister on his heel but it was a very small worry considering the way his world had fallen apart. He had a loving family in Marseilles and a girl friend he adored, but he'd long since decided that he was never likely to see any of them again. The whole German army was between them and it made such decisions easy. 'When will our people in the south break through and join up with us again?' he asked.

Chouteau snorted. 'They *won't,*' he said. 'Not with men like Deshayes and Favre.'

'You mean we're defeated?'

'*I'*m not.'

'What are *you* going to do?'

Chouteau shrugged. 'Go on fighting, I suppose. Somewhere. Somehow. This is the third time in seventy years, *mon brave,* that the Germans have driven across France.'

'We beat them last time,' Angelet said stoutly.

Chouteau shrugged. 'Then why are they back again? It was the British and the Americans who saved us then. Make no mistake. That's why I'm going on fighting.'

Angelet considered for a moment. 'I think I will, too,' he said.

When Tremenheere returned to *Athelstan,* Knevett was on board. With him was another man whom Tremenheere knew, a plump man with a red face, whose name was Collings. They made no attempt to lift aboard the boxes of supplies. Tremenheere was the paid hand and as such was expected to do the work. The crisis hadn't changed that.

'We've a couple of hours yet,' Knevett said. 'How long will it take you to sort out your affairs?'

Tremenheere grinned. 'I haven't got any affairs.'

'Fine. We'll need some containers for spare fuel or water. What about that big barrel we got off *Sorcerer* last year? It's at your lodgings, isn't it?'

Tremenheere said nothing because he was none too anxious to face Nell Noone just then and Knevett went on.

'Better get it,' he said. 'We'll remove all unnecessary furnishings, too, while we're at it. Wouldn't want 'em spoiling.'

Tremenheere carried the chairs from the saloon and placed them in the dinghy, with the stool and a box they filled with ice, and everything else he could think of. As he dug out the barrel at Osborne Road, Nell Noone, who was sitting in the dark in the kitchen, listening to the news on the radio, came to the back door to watch.

'I suppose you're pushing off now you've had your fun,' she said.

He decided it might be a good idea to take as many of his belongings as he could with him and she followed him into the house, pulling the curtains to turn on the light, and watching him carefully as he took out a spare shirt, socks and a jersey from the drawer in the kitchen dresser where he kept his possessions.

'Where are you going?' she asked.

'I dunno. Dover, I think.'

'To fetch the soldiers out?'

He said nothing and, as he paused to light his pipe, she went to the cupboard and brought out a block of tobacco. 'You'd better have this,' she said.

He took the tobacco without comment and fished in the drawer again in the hope that he might turn up a forgotten half-crown. There was no money but he found the two medals he'd been given after the last war. They were only campaign medals but he stuffed them in his pocket. They had no value beyond proving his service but he thought someone might ask about it.

Nell Noone was still watching him closely. 'How are you for money?' she asked.

'I've got a bit.'

She fished in her purse and produced a ten-shilling note. 'Better have that. You can give it me back some time. When are you off?'

'He said a couple of hours.'

She giggled and he sighed, knowing what was coming. 'There's just time before you go then,' she said.

It had been a day of disappointment for the admiral at Dover, too, and though the small boats had started moving, it was apparent that until they arrived off the beaches loading would continue to be slow. Less than 10,000 men had been landed in England that day. Fortunately, the battle was not yet lost and the gap where the Belgian army had lain down its arms was already closing. It was nowhere neat and there were still gaping holes, and in the darkness and the confusion units lost touch and commanders lost contact, but the divisions were making their way out of the turmoil and the new front was slowly taking shape as men groped for positions.

Among them, near Helluin, Lance-Corporal Gow lay with a small detachment of men by a bridge over the River Este. Nearby were cows and a manure heap where the flies had bothered them until dark, and in addition, Gow's nose was peeling, his fair northern skin burned by the sun. He and his fellow Guardsmen had driven the Germans back from the Este once already but now, with the cooks and the batmen in the line, they'd been informed that the halt could be only temporary and that the following morning they'd have to pull back again.

'You're to hang on to that bloody bridge, Gow,' his sergeant had told him earnestly. He jabbed at the map he'd handed over. 'They'll come down this road here and try to get behind us, see. There's a field regiment of artillery coming up to help but they won't be here till tomorrow morning and we've got to stay till they arrive. O.K.?'

Gow's expression didn't change. He wasn't given to smiling much.

'When the guns get here,' the sergeant went on, 'they'll cover us so we can pull back, but until then it's up to us. Right?'

'Aye,' Gow said.

He knew exactly what the sergeant meant. One Guardsman was equal to half a dozen infantrymen of the Line, fifteen or sixteen Frenchmen and ten thousand Peruvian field marshals. In the Guards orders were expected to be carried out. Buttons will be polished. Goals will be scored. The Brigade will advance. Berlin will be taken. The bridge will be held. In terms of Guards discipline, the order was extraordinarily simple.

TUESDAY, 28 MAY

Only one thought was in the minds of those who knew anything about it and could see the picture as a whole on that Tuesday morning as Lance-Corporal Gow lay on the banks of the river near Helluin, and that was the consequences of the capitulation of the Belgian army.

The German right hook towards the coast had been met at the last moment by armoured cars and the attack had ground to a halt, and though they'd pushed across the Yser into the streets of Nieuport their bridgehead had been held. Now, as they rushed up their supports, men like Gow, the unquestioning men of Fontenoy and Waterloo and Inkerman, were waiting.

The Este was only a few yards wide where Gow lay, and the bridge was a small stone affair of two arches half hidden by bushes. The position he'd chosen was directly opposite a point where the road curved to approach it and where vehicles moving in either direction had to slow down. The Bren he'd set up was a good solid weapon which could be relied on not to jam, and he felt it ought to be possible to do a lot of damage because a Bren was accurate – almost too accurate, because when they were rushing you it was as well to spray a bit.

As the light increased he settled himself and lit a crumpled Woodbine. 'I'm hungry enough tae eat a mangy pup,' he growled.

Even as he spoke he heard vehicles approaching, and down the curving road opposite he saw a line of lorries moving forward through the mist, led by an open lightweight truck containing an officer, three men and a machine-gun on a mount.

He jerked a hand at the men alongside him and they looked up, duty and courage struggling with uncertainty on their faces to contort them into wooden grimaces. 'Get them fellers in the scout car,' he said. 'I'm after yon lot in the lorries.'

'You'll never get 'em, Jock. Not from here.'

'No,' Gow agreed. 'No' from here. But I will from yon bank. Gi'e us a wee liftie.'

They helped him carry the Bren to the top of a small rise overhanging the river. From there he could cover the road where the lorries were approaching. But it was not hidden by the bushes and left Gow horribly exposed.

'They'll spot you straight away, Jock,' one of the men pointed out.

Gow was occupied in setting up the gun and seemed indifferent. 'They've got two chances,' he said.

He squatted down among the young grass, watching narrow-eyed as the vehicles on the opposite side of the river approached. 'You lot ready?' he called softly.

'Yes.'

'Right, then! Let the buggers have it!'

There was a blast of controlled fire across the narrow river that shattered the windscreen of the truck and lifted the officer over the side, his jaunty cap rolling into the long grass by the approach to the bridge. The driver flopped over the wheel as the vehicle slewed sideways towards the hedge, and the other two men, both wounded, were killed by the second fusillade of shots.

As the Bren roared Gow saw the lorries across the river come to a halt and the figures in the back jumping out. Several of them fell but the rest dived for the roadside and began to return the fire, and he knew it was only a matter of seconds before they started inflicting damage.

He didn't have long to wait, and as his Number Two reached up to pass him a fresh magazine he yelped and fell against Gow, knocking his helmet off. As Gow pulled him into cover and reached for the gun again, he heard a loud elastic twang and one of the lorries across the river seemed to stagger on its wheels and burst into flames. Behind them, two fields away, a battery of 25-pounders was firing over open sights.

It was wonderful to hear the bark of their own heavy weapons for a change and Gow saw another lorry roll off the road, burning. But as he swung the Bren towards it, something exploded in his

head and his long body jerked upright, stiff and straight, then
went down like a felled fir tree in his native Scotland. As he
crashed against the gun, it toppled from the bank and slithered
among the reeds towards the water.

The firing had attracted the men from the position by the
manure heap along the bank and they came up at a crouching
run. The sergeant was with them. 'O.K.,' he said. 'Out you get!'
He turned Gow over. Blood was coming through his hair and
down his forehead over his eyes.

'Poor bugger,' he said. 'Straight through the head.'

Picking up the wounded, they hurried off, keeping their heads
down, leaving behind them Lance-Corporal Gow, his bloody face
turned up to the morning sky.

As Gow had been fighting his little battle, in the office in the
cliffs at Dover the admiral had adjusted his plans again. The
emphasis had shifted back from the beaches to the battered port,
and personnel ships were signalled to approach the flimsy East
Mole. With the setting up of a control system, berthing parties
and a pier-master, and with sailors in the town as guides, the
flow of men, re-directed from the beaches, began to come in and
the destroyers started to arrive.

By this time, Hatton was beginning to consider himself an old
hand at the game. 'Come on,' he kept saying, pushing the weary
soldiers aboard. 'Keep going! Keep going! – '

The soldiers were carrying pets, French cheeses, wine, lace
table-cloths, women's underwear – presents for their families as
though they'd been on a day trip; and since they were well-
organized and in their own units, reporting as though for
manoeuvres, when a worried-looking middle-aged officer with a
smart uniform and a curling moustache pushed forward, Hatton
stopped him.

'Steady on,' he said. 'Which are your men?'

'They're at the other end of the jetty,' a sergeant behind him
said bluntly. 'The bugger's abandoned 'em.'

The officer blushed and thrust past Hatton to disappear into
the press of men on the deck. As Hatton stared after him a
steamer with great paddle boxes and a flat wide deck that had
once plied up Southampton Water began to edge alongside and
ropes were passed across.

'We'll load across you, if you've no objection,' the captain shouted through a megaphone.

Hatton began to direct the men to the wider decks of the paddle-steamer. They were coming along the mole now in large numbers but the stream kept breaking off, as though it were proving difficult in the town to redirect them. Most of them had never in their lives been further to sea than in a pleasure boat and, as it was hard to get them to understand, Hatton soon dropped naval terms. Then, because he was growing a little light-headed with excitement and hunger, he began to behave like a bus conductor during the rush hour.

'Pass down the bus, please,' he kept shouting, and as the call was taken up by the petty officers, the weary faces under the bowl-shaped helmets began to split into grins. The soldiers were unwilling to go below, however, feeling they were safer on deck, and the petty officers began to push angrily to get them out of the way of the guns.

There was a brief lull. They'd been working a long time now and the paddle-steamer alongside seemed almost full. The decks of *Vital* had cleared, however, and the mole looked empty again.

Hough stared along it and examined the town through his glasses. 'Nip into town, Hatton,' he called from the bridge. 'See if you can round up any more.'

Hatton ran down the pier with a petty officer and a couple of sailors. Dunkirk was a wreck and he wasn't anxious to venture too far in case there were fifth columnists waiting to snipe him. The dock area was full of wreckage – a burning train, cranes canted out of true, ambulances punctured with bullets and shell splinters, and scattered brickwork where buildings and walls had been demolished.

Occasionally they came across bodies lying on the cobbles, covered with greatcoats, gas capes or groundsheets, their limbs decently composed, their great boots sticking up in ungainly fashion, and once two men sitting by a wall, killed by blast, a startled look on both the darkening faces. Here and there among the scattered vehicles there was a dead horse or a splintered cart, but there were no civilians and no sign of the town's life.

They rounded up a few groups of soldiers, and then the petty officer found a bicycle which was far too small for him. 'I'll nip round a bit, sir,' he said. 'See if I can find any more.'

Hatton didn't envy him because there were still explosions among the smoke, but he wobbled off and after a few minutes Hatton saw a group of soldiers running towards him.

'This way! Down the mole!'

Eventually, they rounded up about three hundred more men, all filthy, all tired, and some of them hurt, the petty officer bringing them in like a sheepdog with stray lambs.

By this time, the wardroom, small as it was, was crowded with wounded, and the stokers' flats, the petty officers' and ratings' messes were all jammed with men. There were more of them on the stern and along the deck amidships, and they had promptly lolled over and gone to sleep.

His work finished, Hatton reported to the bridge. Hough seemed to be in a good mood. 'Made a good job of that, Hatton,' he said. 'What were you before the war? Conductor on a Number Eleven?'

'No, sir,' Hatton grinned. 'Inspector. Bags of experience.'

It was full daylight by this time and Hough was staring anxiously at the sky. 'Time we left,' he said. He had the megaphone in his hand speaking to the first lieutenant. 'Single up, Number One!' He turned to the bridge of the paddle-steamer. 'We'll pass your lines ashore.'

'Don't worry,' the shout came back. 'We're off, too. We've got 'em sitting in the lavatories.'

Gangways were dragged inboard and the lines were dropped. The water churned as the ferry's paddles thumped and she slowly disappeared astern, and it was as Hatton pushed his way back through the lolling exhausted figures that a man on the point fives called out.

'Sir! Aircraft approaching starboard side!'

The Stukas were screaming down out of the sky already and Hatton's heart leapt as he saw one of them hit and swerve out of its dive. It headed over the town to disappear in a flash of flame and a puff of smoke, and he saw fragments of wing and tail whirring down among the houses. The soldiers cheered and began to fire their rifles, the clatter of shots and the working of breeches audible even above the racket of the guns.

The din was tremendous now and Hatton could see the water of the harbour dotted with splashes as the shell splinters dropped from the sky. The howl of engines filled the air and the muffled crash of bombs seemed to lift the ship out of the water. On the bridge, he could hear Hough shouting above the racket.

'Slow astern port! Hold her there, helmsman! Right – ' he abandoned navalese ' – let her rip! Full ahead both!'

The paddle-steamer was about half a mile ahead of them when Hatton saw a tremendous flash of flame and a cloud of smoke appear on her port side. Almost immediately she began to settle in the water and he could see brown-clad figures jumping overboard. A destroyer was already moving up, its boats lowered and scrambling nets over the side, and *Vital* joined it at full speed, Hough swinging the stern to flatten the water. The boats were dropped and the nets flung down, and Hatton dragged gasping men on board as they climbed up, until he was exhausted and his uniform saturated. Several of them were badly wounded and he couldn't make out how they'd ever managed to swim. As the last living man was dragged from the wreckage the nets were hauled inboard and the boats hooked to the falls. The other destroyer was already moving away.

'All right, Hatton!' Hough shouted down. 'That's it! Can you shove a few more below to clear the guns?'

The hum from the turbines increased and *Vital*'s bow rose as her propellors bit at the water. The vibration that ran through her made her feel like a living animal. A soldier touched Hatton's arm as he passed and indicated the sky. 'They won't be back for a quarter of an hour, mate,' he said. 'I've timed 'em.'

Hatton managed a shaky grin and, wrenching at the peak of his cap, dragged it over one eye. Their arrival in Dover was going to set a few heads turning. 'Excitement over for today,' he agreed.

But it wasn't quite and Hough was staring ahead, frowning.

'Raft, sir,' the wing bridge look-out reported. 'Looks as though it's made of an old door.'

The raft carried a Belgian officer and two grinning French soldiers who'd escaped from Calais, and they stepped aboard carrying their supplies – two tins of biscuits and six demijohns of wine. Also on board the raft was an ancient and very rusty bicycle.

'The bastards were going to pedal across,' Hatton said.

Jocho Horndorff came to wakefulness reluctantly. It still didn't seem possible that he was a prisoner of war and he lay on his back staring bitterly upwards. The night before he'd considered quite cold-bloodedly bolting for the fields but, as he'd halted staring to either side of him, Conybeare's voice had come, quiet but steady.

'Don't,' he'd said.

Horndorff had exploded with anger. 'You will never take me to England,' he had shouted. 'It will be dark soon and you can't stay awake all the time!'

'I've thought of that,' Conybeare had said. He gestured at the vehicles by the side of the road, their engines wrecked. 'I'll find one that'll lock.'

The accommodation he found had turned out to be a wrecked radio-van, its lockers rifled, its sets smashed, its side perforated with bullet holes.

'Fully ventilated,' Conybeare had announced. 'In you get.'

Horndorff had climbed inside, his face red with rage, and had listened savagely to the bolt being driven home.

All night he'd heard the shuffle of boots moving past, with now and then a steady tramp as some unit, still retaining cohesion and discipline, had marched by. It hadn't taken him long to realize there was no way out of his prison.

The shuffle and thud of boots was still going on now as the light increased, then Conybeare's face, his bruised eye black and almost closed by this time, appeared at the small window that separated the rear of the van from the driver's cabin. A portion of sausage and a piece of bread appeared. Horndorff took them sullenly. He was beginning to loathe Conybeare by this time.

'My dear chap,' he said, forcing himself to remain calm, 'You realize that all this is a waste of time. Your troops are surrounded.'

'I expect we'll manage,' Conybeare said. 'And don't call me your "dear chap". I've told you before.'

As he opened the doors, Horndorff's eyes blazed. 'Suppose I refuse to get out?' he asked.

Conybeare raised the Luger and pointed it at a point just to the right of Horndorff's head. Horndorff stared down the muzzle and, when he still didn't move, Conybeare calmly pulled the trigger. At the crash of the explosion, Horndorff flung himself down. The bullet had whacked through the side of the van within a foot of his head.

Horndorff straightened up, hating himself for ducking, hating Conybeare more. There was a strange placidity about him that worried the German who was beginning now to realize that this imperturbable boy was a great deal tougher than he looked.

Soldiers resting by the roadside eyed them as they passed. They'd clearly not yet lost their spirit and they were interested in Horndorff, wondering what sort of man had beaten them, what sort of man had thought out this new and ruthless science of war and collected the machinery to wage it.

'What rat-hole did you get him out of?' one of them grinned.

'He's my prisoner,' Conybeare said. 'I'm taking him to England.'

He accepted all the comments unsmilingly, his smooth young face lacking in humour. When he'd first captured Horndorff it had been as much as anything else a salve to his own pride – to make up for being shot down – but gradually, as time had passed, it had crystallized into an obsession. Now he meant exactly what he said. He was taking Horndorff to England and nothing except death or wounds was going to stop him.

Horndorff tramped on, frowning. 'I think, under the circumstances,' he grated, 'that we ought to introduce ourselves. I am Hans-Joachim Horndorff von Bülowius. My family call me Jocho.'

'Conybeare,' the boy behind him said.

'Your first name?'

'Got three. Don't like any of 'em much. Conybeare'll do.'

Horndorff walked on in silence, snubbed. The fields on either side of them had been flooded and the morning was misty, the vapour hanging in chilly folds over a flat countryside that stretched endlessly towards the north. In the distance he could see a black pall of smoke hanging in the sky.

As his mind churned over means of ridding himself of Conybeare, he saw the men in front of him glancing back, then one of them pointed. Aeroplanes turned in the sky like flies and, as the tramping men began to scatter, Horndorff's heart leapt. Conybeare wouldn't get much response just now if he called for help.

As the soldiers crouched against the steep banks of earth, he could hear the planes above and behind him. He saw spurts of dirt leap from the surface of the road and move rapidly ahead.

But then he realized that with the flooded fields on either side there was nowhere he could run to and, choking on his rage, he turned and, still erect and indifferent to the bullets, walked slowly to the ditch where Conybeare waited patiently, as though he'd known all the time that Horndorff couldn't escape.

'Why do you hate us so, Officer Conybeare?' Horndorff asked bitterly as he crouched down.

Conybeare gestured with the pistol. Further along the bank there was a group of graves; on one of the crude crosses a woman's hat of black straw with artificial flowers and red cherries hung grotesquely. 'That,' he said.

'We didn't want the war,' Horndorff snapped. 'It was forced on us.' He tried to explain. 'In Germany after the last war it was necessary to take whole barrow-loads of marks to buy a loaf of bread. Communism was at our doors. Do you wonder that we turned to Hitler?'

Conybeare didn't know much about the conditions in Germany after the previous war. He'd only just been born, and even now he was still too young to be greatly concerned.

'There must have been others,' he said.

'What others?' Horndorff sneered. 'Wretched people with nothing to offer but theories.'

Conybeare nodded understandingly. 'We had a few of those ourselves,' he admitted.

'This is why Germany chose Hitler. He has *Fingerspitzenge-fühl* – how do you say? – intuition. He did great things for Germany.'

'Like bringing her into a war?'

Horndorff had fallen silent again, faintly depressed. As far as he could see this wretched little boy with the black eye that made him look as though he'd been fighting in the school yard had now actually got him inside the British lines.

'You must let me go,' he said abruptly.

'No.'

'We are both intelligent men.'

'I expect so,' Conybeare shrugged. 'In spite of your being a Nazi.'

'I am not a Nazi,' Horndorff pointed out. 'I have never been a Nazi. I am a German and I believe in my country. We were right to go to war.'

Conybeare's eyes flickered. 'Perhaps you're not *that* intelligent,' he observed.

The day had not started well for a lot of other people besides Horndorff – among them Alfred Stoos, who was on the telephone to command control.

'We need replacements,' he was shouting furiously.

The man at the other end of the line seemed unperturbed. 'You the stores officer?' he demanded.

'No.'

'Commanding officer?'

Stoos choked. Schmesser's successor was Hauptmann Dodtzenrodt and he was flying with Schlegel and the rest of the squadron. Dodtzenrodt had little love for Stoos whom he considered a heartless gong-hunter and, as commanding officer, it gave him a lot of pleasure to leave him on the ground. 'No,' Stoos said. 'He's flying.'

The man on the other end of the telephone was silent for a moment. 'Then who the devil do you think *you* are to make demands?' he said at last. 'You Stuka people have had too much publicity. The 87's not the egg of Columbus.'

As the telephone clicked, Stoos sat staring at it, his face red with rage. Then he snatched up his cap and burst out of the office into the rags of mist. Oberfeldwebel Hamcke saw him coming. 'Oh, Christ,' he said bitterly. 'Here he comes again!'

The day had not started well for the admiral at Dover either. Almost the first news of the day was bad.

'We've lost *Abukir*,' his chief of staff informed him. 'Coming from Ostend, with over two hundred soldiers and refugees.'

'What happened to her?'

'E-boat. Near the North Hinder light.'

There was silence for a moment. This new loss meant that for the first time the German Navy was attempting to interfere directly with the evacuation.

The staff officer, operations, coughed. 'That's not all, I'm afraid, sir.'

'Go on.'

'*Queen of the Channel*. She left Dunkirk at dawn. She had over nine hundred men aboard. She was bombed and sunk by a single aircraft.'

'The admiral frowned. 'What were the losses?'

'Not as bad as might have been expected. The crew and passengers were rescued. There are a few other good omens, too. The French have started to take part. Admiral Abrial assembled a convoy. They lost *Douaisien* to a magnetic mine.'

The admiral rose and walked up and down for a while, his hands in his pockets, his eyes down and thoughtful. 'What destroyers are over there at the moment?' he asked.

'*Mackay, Montrose, Verity, Vital, Worcester* and *Anthony. Codrington, Grenade, Gallant, Jaguar* and *Javelin* are on their way.'

'Good. Good.' The admiral took another turn up and down. 'We mustn't forget the beaches, though. With small boats we might be able to pick up a whole division.'

The admiral's ideas were echoed by the army itself, and those of the army by Basil Allerton. The blaséness which had enabled him at first to regard the war as rather a joke had slipped a little by this time because as he grew more tired he was growing more alarmed, too, not only by the things he'd seen but by the thought that he might even be killed.

They weren't far from the coast now in the poor northern area of France, an ugly place of mean houses of red and yellow brick. To the south the countryside stretched flatly to the horizon in a landscape that looked more Dutch than French, and the road they were on ran along a high embankment above the flat polder land.

Rice and the others were making tea in the kitchen of an abandoned bakery and a few of the little unit's lost sheep had returned during the night. The corporal, they thought, had been captured but, in their cheerful inconsequential way, they didn't appear too worried and were more concerned with the time the water was taking to boil. Like all soldiers, when trouble had come they had simply shifted the responsibiliy to the shoulders of their officers. It seemed to Allerton that they were all taking the situation far too lightly and that he ought to find out what they should do.

Rather unwillingly, he decided to take the truck into the town. All along the road an orgy of destruction was taking place under the vivid blue sky. Engineers were handing out pound blocks of gun cotton and primer detonators to artillery artificers, and showing them how to place them in the breeches of their guns to destroy them. In a big beet field, thousands of vehicles were parked – all of them new – Scammells, diggers, buses, engineering plants, limbers and lorries – and, with a steady, crunching, chopping sound, men were smashing their petrol tanks and cylinders.

A provost officer stepped in front of Allerton's bonnet, waving a revolver. 'In here,' he said brusquely.

'I'm going into Dunkirk,' Allerton protested.

The officer lifted the revolver. 'In here,' he said.

In a fury and still protesting vainly, Allerton drove into the park, but as he left, he found an abandoned motor-bike and, though he'd only ridden one once before, he mounted it and roared off triumphantly into the thinning mist, wobbling wildly and delighted to have thwarted the officious provost officer.

The destruction stretched all the way to Dunkirk, every dyke jammed with wrecked vehicles among the floating straw and the bodies of drowned animals, every road littered with abandoned equipment, caps and helmets. Dunkirk itself was a shock to him. He knew it had been bombed but had never realized how badly. Tall skeletons of buildings were silhouetted against a sword-cut of opal sky, and among the silhouettes fires raged. It was a forbidding spectacle and for a moment Allerton stood in silence staring at it, aware of the awful hammering of noise about him. Then, as he hoisted the motor-cycle on to its stand to ask directions, he heard another sound that rolled in iron waves round the heavens. He dived under a stone seat as the crash of the bombs seemed to lift the ground and hit him in the face with it. Unharmed but shaken, he crawled out and decided that for his own safety he'd better find someone in authority.

The town major's office was a bedlam, with what appeared to be dozens of men all shouting the claims of their units.

'I've got to have the returns,' an officer at a desk was saying. 'I want a nominal roll. I've got to know how many there are.'

'For Christ's sake,' his harassed questioner shouted, 'I don't know myself! Can't we do that when we get to the other side?'

Every now and then, as the aeroplanes returned, everyone stopped, assessed where the bombs were going to fall and then, according to what they'd decided, took cover or remained where they were, flinching at the crashes.

'I want a ship,' an overwrought gunner officer was saying. 'They said there'd be two every four hours. The timetable's not being kept.'

'For Christ's sake,' the man behind the desk said, 'the destroyers are coming over like Number Eleven buses. We just can't get 'em in. The harbour's been destroyed.'

'I *saw* ships,' the gunner snapped. 'Alongside some bloody pier. I've been there. There were destroyers and what looked like a paddle-steamer.'

The man behind the desk looked up, startled. 'Embarking troops?'

'By the hundred.'

'I wish someone would tell *me*! Sergeant Greene, for God's sake, find out what's going on, will you?'

'Just what *is* going on?' Allerton asked the man in front of him.

'There's talk of a stand.'

'What with?' an R.A.S.C. officer behind them demanded. 'Where are the ammunition and supplies? *I've* seen none. We're getting out.'

Allerton wandered outside again, in a state of stupefaction. He hadn't realized the campaign was over. But then he realized that it explained all the destruction of trucks, cars and motor-bikes, all the men burning records and throwing away what clothes they couldn't carry on their backs. When he returned to his men they were all crouching in the doorway of the bakery watching a burning ammunition truck in which charges and shells were exploding above the howl of a jammed horn. Even as he braked, the truck blew up, sending pieces of metal whirring in all directions. The blast knocked him off the motor-bike which continued under its own power into a ditch and disappeared beneath the water. He picked himself up and saw Rice running towards him.

'You stand a good chance of getting killed round here,' he said.

Rice offered him a slice of bully beef and a stale cream bun from the bakery, and Allerton took them without considering the mixture at all odd.

'Are they going to take us back to England, sir?'

'They're trying. There's a rumour that if we get to the beaches the navy's sending in boats to take us off. How long will it take you to get ready?'

Rice grinned. 'We're ready now, sir. We thought you'd find out what to do.'

It startled Allerton that they'd had so much confidence in him, and suddenly he loved their honest ugly faces. When he'd first arrived in France he'd considered himself a cut above the rest of the army and regarded with a certain amount of contempt the rough and ready soldiers whose incoherent statements he'd had to listen to and sometimes had to read. Now, however, amidst the paralysing insanity of bombing, shelling, hostile agents and anarchic bands of French soldiers shooting their officers and holding villages to ransom for food, he found he was taking a different view of them all. The generals in this war actually appeared to know what they were doing, and the regimental officers, N.C.O.s and men suddenly seemed an extraordinary mixture of cheerfulness, humour, blasphemy, piety, gentleness and sheer guts that he could not imagine any other nation in the world producing. For the first time, he felt proud to be among them.

'I think we ought to shove off,' he said. 'It's getting to be rather a dismal party. Form the chaps up.'

Rice gaped. He'd not been on a parade since arriving in France. 'Form them up, sir?' he said. 'There are only nine of us. And we've no N.C.O.'

Allerton shrugged, showing off a little. 'You've just become one, Rice,' he said. 'Will corporal do?'

Clarence Sievewright was also trying to behave like a soldier but even now he was still behaving more like a Boy Scout.

He had once again spent the night entirely alone. In that countryside of flat fields and dykes there were few farms and villages, but eventually he'd found a small brick building and had managed to break the lock with the spike on his jack-knife. There had seemed to be a great deal of rusty iron inside that he took to be farming implements and the fire he'd built wouldn't have warmed a rat, but he'd felt better with food inside him and, making himself comfortable, had bedded down on the floor.

Waking early, he filled his mess-tin from a ditch and cooked the remaining potato and some slices of a beetroot he'd found.

It wasn't much but it helped, and he felt that in the chaos and the confusion he was putting his Scouting knowledge to good use.

He was running short of matches now, and he wasn't really sure that, despite his experience, he could make a fire by rubbing two sticks together. However, in his pack he still had his emergency rations and two large army biscuits he'd found on the road. A tin of them had dropped off a lorry and been crushed to dust by the traffic that followed. Only two of them, projected somehow from the debris to the grass, had survived and he'd pocketed them against the time when he'd no longer have anything to cook.

Having eaten, he once again went through his equipment to decide what to throw out but, concerned that he'd be charged with its loss, decided to keep it all. He felt much happier when he found a discarded French rifle in the grass. There were five rounds in the magazine, and as he might eventually *have* to fight, he shouldered it and set off north once more.

About the time that Sievewright was getting into his stride, Tremenheere was shutting down *Athelstan*'s engines and she lay drifting in the slight swell that was running. Outside Dover harbour, destroyers whooped their way among the crowded vessels and dashed in the direction of the sun, setting the moored boats rolling and curtseying and bouncing against each other in their wash. As fast as they went, others returned out of the glare in ones and twos and groups, tiny dots on the shining surface of the water. There were men on them who'd marched half-way across France; dirty, dishevelled men, their faces black with oil, coal-dust and smoke, their eyes bloodshot with weariness. Some of them were without uniforms, some were without rifles, but for the most part they still managed to wave and even raise a cheer.

Tremenheere watched them pass in a grim, pathetic, heroic stream. Of the little flotilla that had left Littlehampton with *Athelstan* some had fallen out long before they'd even reached Newhaven. More had failed to start that morning. The last of them was just shutting off its spluttering, overheated engine, so that the flotilla fell silent with only the lap of the waves against the hulls and the slap of the halyards against the masts for company.

The silence was broken almost at once when a naval launch, which had met them at Folkestone and led them in, roared to life again and hurried towards them like an excited terrier with a bone in its teeth. An officer was standing on the bridge, a megaphone in his hand. 'Is Doctor Knevett on board?' he was shouting.

Knevett waved and the officer gestured. 'A tender will be picking you up, sir,' he said. 'There's need for you ashore.'

As Knevett received his orders, Hatton's hopes of behaving like a soldier returning from the wars were not being fulfilled.

They'd headed slowly back, steering north-east, MacGillicuddy, the chief engineer, still concerned with his doubtful bearing. Near the Kwinte Buoy they'd been following a small French fishing vessel when it had hit a mine and they'd felt the shock through the whole ship. They'd picked up the stupefied survivors, some of them women, their clothes stripped from their bodies by the explosion. Almost every one of them was suffering from fractures of the legs, pelvis or spine.

'Shock of the deck coming up to hit them,' the doctor said in flat tones. 'Just as if they'd jumped on to concrete from a thirty-foot wall.'

As they'd turned west, an unending stream of vessels had passed them going south – destroyers, personnel carriers, and tugs. There were minesweepers from North Sea and East Coast ports, yard craft, coasters and short-sea traders, Deal beach boats and the *Sues*, the *Three Sisters* and the *Two Brothers*, boats with registrations from the Wash to Poole, some of them still manned by the men who'd stood in peace-time on the harbour walls shouting, 'Any more for the *Skylark*?'

Dover harbour was crowded to capacity, and working *Vital* in through the difficult tidal stream and the press of boats was an intricate feat of seamanship.

'We'll be going alongside at once,' Hough announced. 'Get down there, Hatton, and make sure they don't move until we're alongside. We want no rushing, but make it fast because we're going straight back again.'

There were none of the admiring eyes Hatton had expected. The whole area was a scene of ordered confusion, with loud-hailers squawking as officers demanded permission to leave or moor. The quayside resounded to the cries of red-eyed soldiers begging cigarettes and the barking of the dozens of dogs which had attached themselves to the troops. The only sign of approval was a notice someone had erected, 'Well done, B.E.F.'

'Well done?' a soldier near Hatton said. 'I thought we'd *lost* the bloody battle!'

As the gangplanks were thrust out, a soldier scrambled ashore, kissed the stones of the quayside, and did a little jig. Then the civilian helpers began to clamber on board with stretchers and first-aid equipment, and women began to pass round water bottles and telegram forms, or struggled to help with men covered with fuel oil from sunken ships. 'What was it like?' they asked.

'First-rate,' one irrepressible life-of-the-party said. 'I've learned to swim.'

Some of the older women were in uniform but some were mere girls in summer frocks, who'd been hastily recruited, and their faces were drawn and wet with tears. They all looked hot because there wasn't a breath of wind, not a ripple on the water, not a cloud in the sky, and there were none of the cheering crowds Hatton had expected because the police had cordoned off the docks in case the Luftwaffe attacked.

A group of French-Moroccan soldiers were struggling with half a dozen sailors who were yelling in red-faced fury that the Moroccans had stolen their uniforms, and Hatton saw a woman talking in a low desperate voice to a hawk-featured man in a turban who wanted his arm bandaged because his friend's had been bandaged too.

'But there's nothing wrong with it,' she kept saying. 'It's all right.'

'I should bandage it all the same,' Hatton suggested. 'Saves time.'

More women were working at a mobile canteen with cups borrowed from local catering businesses, handing out food they'd scoured from the town shops. Incredibly they kept their heads, despite the continuous harassment from the men pouring from *Vital*'s lower decks – senior officers mixed with private soldiers, French and Belgian refugees, an alien under arrest, a few German prisoners, even a French postal worker who'd been swept up in the chaos. None of them had time to notice Hatton, and his day was filled with clearing the ship of abandoned equipment as the troops disappeared, and with setting squads of men to clear up the dirt, the fuel oil and the pools of blood.

He was on the quay when a petty officer called down that the deck was clear. As the quayside emptied of men, near the railway lines he saw several rows of stretchers which sweating men were picking up and carrying to ambulances, while women and girls bent over the wounded who remained, fixing labels with names and addresses to their blouses. As he turned to head for the gangway, his eyes rested on one of the girls. She was giving a soldier a mug of tea, holding it for him while he drank because both his hands were bandaged. When she'd finished, she placed a cigarette in his mouth and Hatton leaned forward to light it.

The soldier's eyes looked up at them like a lost dog's. 'Thanks, miss. Thanks, sir.'

As the stretcher disappeared, the girl turned.

'Hello, Nora,' Hatton said.

At first she frowned, then recognition came, but she showed no sign of pleasure or displeasure.

'Oh, Barry!' was all she said.

There was blood on the front of her dress, a line of moist red splashes, and she brushed at them unhappily with her handkerchief. 'They sent me down to get the story,' she said, her voice shaking. 'But there were so many. It seemed to need more than stories.'

Vital's springs were going aboard now and the gangways were being hauled ashore.

'Sir!' One of the sailors called to Hatton.

Her eyes widened and she looked terribly concerned. 'Are you going back?'

'Sir! Mr. Hatton!' The sailor called again and, as Hatton turned, he felt her grasp his hand, then she put her arms round his neck and kissed him impulsively on the mouth.

'Girl friend, Hatton?' Hough asked as he made his way through the grinning sailors to the bridge.

'Old flame, sir. Just happened to be helping here.'

'Enthusiastic for an *old* flame.' The navigating officer said. 'Still a spark in the embers, perhaps.'

As *Vital* headed out to sea again, with her went other ships – and from Ramsgate, Margate, Folkestone, Portsmouth, Sheerness and all the rivers in the south of England as well – mudhoppers, coal barges still thick with black dust, yachts, trawlers stinking of fish, gunboats and Dutch schuits reeking of onions and decorated with geraniums. The crews included old soldiers rejected for the army, men from the isles of Scotland to whom Gaelic came more naturally than English, Chinese stewards, lascars, a few Americans, a nobleman or two, a Dominican friar still in his habit. Not all of them had signed the form which made them naval volunteers for a month. Some wore yachting caps and blazers, others flat caps and jerseys. Some had managed to stow a few rations aboard, others had little but tea, bread and milk. Some didn't even have steel helmets and were seeking out balers and enamel bowls to hold over their heads. Some of their boats weren't even fit for sea and went out still leaking from the long winter lay-up, and in the confusion some carried spare petrol cans filled by mistake with water which stopped their engines as soon as it was emptied into the tanks. Some had charts, some were simply told to steam for the sound of the guns. 'The need to get trained men back to train others is paramount,' they were told. 'Remember that above all.'

As they left, *Athelstan* moved alongside the pier where they'd been moored, and from her deck Tremenheere watched the lifting of the pale, oil-slicked sea, while he sucked at his pipe and drank mugs of strong tea, picking up the news in snatches from ashore. Outside *Athelstan* was an R.N.L.I. lifeboat, and just ahead of her a fishing vessel called *Daisy* which mounted an ancient Lewis. There were two men on her decks, one of them dark and swarthy with a wild wall eye, who was sitting on a hatch-cover finishing a fender he was making from old grass line, the other a large fat man whose white flesh bulged through the holes in his singlet. They were arguing steadily in a stream of obscenity which, even to Tremenheere, who was well used to bad language, was growing boring.

During the afternoon a naval launch came alongside and Tremenheere passed over loaves and tins of bully beef and shoe boxes full of tea and sugar, while the launch's exhausted crew dragged at cigarettes and sank mugs of tea. As the launch left, a man ran down the quay to the fishing boat. The wall-eyed man sitting on the hatch-cover had just finished the fender and he jumped to his feet, holding it in his hand. The man in the singlet had vanished.

'What's up, Gil?'

'We've got to go across, Ern,' the newcomer panted. 'Where's Brundrett?'

'In the engine room. He says the sodden pump's packed up.'

The newcomer glared about him as if he might find the offending Brundrett floating about in mid-air. 'It was all right yesterday,' he shouted.

'Well, it isn't now. It's stripped down.'

The man called Gil looked furious. His face went red and spit flew as he shouted his rage. 'There's nothing wrong with the bloody pump!' he snarled. 'What's he want to strip it down for?'

Tremenheere watched as the two men disappeared. By this time he'd worked out a plan that when it was all over, he'd send a telegram from Dover to say he'd failed to return. There'd be no need to say who it came from, so long as it looked official. Nell Noone would assume it had come from someone in authority and wouldn't ask questions. *Athelstan* was his for the moment and he intended to use her to good advantage.

Knevett had been picked up long since and had disappeared with his medical bag. No one had bothered to pick up Collings and on the jetty he'd turned to glance questioningly at Tremenheere.

'I'm not going ashore, me dear,' Tremenheere said. Ashore was where Nell Noone was.

Collings had drifted off disconsolately, lugging a canvas bag full of the sailing equipment, oilskins and charts he'd brought. His greying hair had hung down in straggling curls because he was a little drunk and had misplaced his yachting cap.

Tremenheere found it later hanging in the lavatory and helped himself to it. It gave him a rakish authority and naval ratings he questioned for news called him 'sir'. It was a new experience which he found he enjoyed and, fishing in his pocket, he took out the two tarnished medals from the other war and pinned them on his chest.

They clinked as he moved and he decided he liked the sound.

The rumble of the firing to the east and south came like the dull roll of thunder on the hot air, and Scharroo moved cautiously to avoid waking Marie-Josephine.

He turned his head to look at her. Her face was desperately

young and unlined, and long curling lashes rested on her pale
cheeks. He wondered who the hell she was and how in God's
name she'd got herself into this mess.

They'd met a group of British soldiers brewing tea by the roadside near Praven and, as they'd stopped to rest their feet, one of
them had offered Marie-Josephine a drink from his mess-tin. She'd
frowned, certain in her straight-laced, stiff-backed way that it was
the British who had brought disaster to France, and she'd taken
the mess-tin unwillingly, her eyes on the soldier's face all the time.
He was a squarely-built youngish man with a rough accent, thick
legs and large strong hands – the product of some northern farm-
land, Scharroo supposed – but there was a dignity and a gentleness about him that puzzled the American. He'd made no attempt
to get Marie-Josephine into conversation, no attempt to take
advantage of the fact that he had something to offer, merely
holding out the tea because he had some and she looked tired.

When Marie-Josephine had finished, she rose and the men's
faces turned as she approached. She was still wearing the cream
coat with the dried blood along the edges, and she looked small,
neat and very feminine, so that they grinned at her appreci-
atively.

'You are very kind,' she said in her stilted English.

'That's all right, miss,' the man who'd offered the tea said. 'It
was spare and you looked a bit like my missis for a minute.'

'Missis? Please?'

Scharroo explained and the soldier gave a shy grin. 'You going
north?' he asked.

Marie-Josephine nodded. 'I wish to go to La Panne.'

The soldier frowned. 'La Panne's no place to go just now,
miss.'

She shrugged. 'Here is no place to stay,' she said, and the
soldiers laughed.

They turned their heads together, muttering, and then the man
who'd offered the tea gestured at the lorry alongside the road.
'We could give you a lift if you keep your heads down,' he said.
'Part of the way, anyway. We've been told to head for the smoke.'
He indicated the dark pall on the horizon.

As they jogged north through the hot afternoon, Marie-
Josephine's head had sagged and finally lolled against Scharroo's
shoulder. They passed Hoegstade where the crowds of marching

men grew thicker, but no one tried to stop the lorry and no one seemed worried when it passed them. At a village near Furnes, the lorry halted and the soldiers climbed out. The place was an extraordinary sight. From every house, from the church steeple, farms, cottages and stables, white flags were hanging, tablecloths, sheets, towels or handkerchiefs. Most of the houses were heavily shuttered and here and there little knots of people stood silently by the road watching, their expressions a mixture of relief that the tide of war was moving on and apprehension of what the arrival of the Germans might bring.

'This is as far as we go, miss,' the soldier who had offered the tea said. 'We've got orders to dump the lorry here.'

Scharroo climbed out and lifted Marie-Josephine down. She was feather-light and slim in his arms and, as he set her on the ground, she held out her hand to the soldier who'd offered them the lift. He stared at it, a little bewildered by the French habit of handshaking, then he wiped his great fist on his trousers and took her small paw.

'I hope you will go home to your missis,' she said solemnly, raising her voice over the grind of engines and the thump of heavy boots.

The soldiers moved off, joining the other men tramping past. There was no order among them, yet there was no disorder. Officers and men were mixed together and different units were intermingled. Many of them had cut branches from trees and were using them as walking sticks and, because they wore their helmets on the backs of their heads and their rifles slung, it looked as though they were on some vast hike.

Through them, ambulances full of wounded threaded their slow way, their sides riddled with bullet holes, their windscreens shattered. Apart from them the only wheeled traffic now consisted of motor-cyclists, French lorries and the transport of regiments moving south towards the rear-guard. The road ran between two unbroken walls of stranded vehicles.

The scale of the destruction was monumental and Scharroo could see it was worrying Marie-Josephine.

He touched her arm and suggested they start walking. She didn't move, remaining motionless, staring at the black cloud hanging over the coast, then her head turned, the big frank eyes wide and worried.

'Walter,' she said. 'I think I am frightened.'

Lije Noble was another who was frightened. He'd been frightened so often in the last few days, in fact, he was now wearing his fear like a clammy second skin.

He was still alone, tramping along among a large group of Frenchmen, when he was stopped at a cross-roads by a British officer staring at a map spread on the bonnet of a car.

'You'll do,' he said to Noble. 'My battery'll be along in a minute. I want you to wait here and direct them down that road there. We were shelled by French 75s by mistake and what's left'll be coming through in dribs and drabs and I can't wait. Okay?'

It wasn't okay at all but he'd climbed into the car and driven off, leaving Noble staring after him indignantly. Most of the men approaching the cross-roads were French and he could see no sign of any British artillery, so he'd grabbed a French corporal and gestured. 'Carry on,' he'd said imperiously and walked off quickly before anyone could ask questions. What happened at the cross-roads, he decided, was somebody else's bun-fight, not Lije Noble's.

He was still brooding on the injustice when he reached a small group of houses by a railway station where there were burned-out Renault tanks, smashed guns and still figures lying sprawled in the fields. One was a British colonel who was said to have been shot in the back by the French for giving them the length of his tongue while trying to halt their retreat. Among the houses there was a Red Cross train on a track running beside the road, and the men from it were rapidly transferring cans of bully beef and biscuits from a string of trucks that lay in a siding nearby. The Red Cross train was pointed north and Noble considered it would be a good idea to join it as a passenger.

The medical officer had no objections but he insisted that Noble throw away his rifle. 'The Geneva Convention expressly forbids firearms,' he said, and Noble was suddenly not quite so sure that his idea was a good one.

'Cut me head off it you like, sir,' he said. 'But don't take me rifle.'

The doctor was adamant and Noble was just wondering what to do when someone shouted, and as he turned he saw an arm pointing at an approaching convoy of tanks.

'Big bastards,' Noble said enthusiastically. 'They'll scare the shit out of Jerry.'

The monsters came on steadily, their turrets traversing slowly like an insect's antennae, dwarfing the drab buildings by the side of the road, and it wasn't until the first one had rumbled past and he saw an open staff car with an officer standing up in it, his grey-gloved hand on the windscreen, that it dawned on Noble he'd seen it all before at the cinema.

'They're Jerries!' he yelled and bolted for the door on the other side of the train just as machine-gun fire shattered the windows and left the medical officer hanging head-down through the broken glass.

There was a huge wheatfield on the far side of the train and he dived into it and didn't stop until he was half-way across. The tanks sent a few shots after him but they didn't worry much and he crossed the rest of the field on hands and knees. At the far side he lifted his head. The train staff were standing with their hands in the air, looking as though they'd been there for centuries, petrified into some strange monument, and though Lije Noble felt sorry for them, he was too busy looking after Lije Noble to dwell on them for long.

Beyond the wheat there was a main road, and he was just on the point of crossing it when another tank swung round the corner, blazing away with a machine-gun so that he had to dive back into the wheat. By the Grace of God he wasn't hit and the tank commander ignored him and rattled on, clearly deciding he wasn't worth rounding up.

Straggling alongside the road was a small village. It was full of abandoned French rifles, packs and helmets, but seemed empty of humans except for two old men standing by a bar.

'Which way must we go?' one of them asked in English.

'Christ knows,' Noble said. 'I wish I did.'

Almost immediately, he heard the tanks again and the old men vanished in a flash. There was a grocery store nearby and Noble dived inside, but then he decided some rotten bastard like Lije Noble might decide to loot it for food, and he shot out again. Further down the street was a carpenter's shop and he decided that there at least he ought to be safe. He plunged inside and slammed the door.

A few minutes later he heard the clatter of treads and

crouched against the wall, panting. The tanks didn't stop but when the noise died down he hadn't the courage to return to the road and, moving on hands and knees, he found a window that looked out on to what appeared to be a farmyard. He forced it open and scrambled through to dive among the haystacks.

By this time he was so edgy he was quite ready to throw his hand in. He was bloody annoyed with the Germans and even more so with the British colonels, brigadiers and generals who'd left him naked and stranded while they mucked about in the immunity of the confusion. Gradually, however, his natural Cockney high spirits took over, and as his sharp slum-dweller's eye roved round looking for the main chance, he found he was filled with an intense curiosity about what would happen next. Because he'd escaped several times already, he was beginning to think he might do so once more.

The light was going as he joined a battery of 25-pounders in a field backed by a clump of trees. The gunners were dragging the guns from their pits and hooking them to trailers, their eyes towards the south where a Scottish regiment was approaching, all battledress and bayonets, led by a piper.

They were grim-faced and staggering with weariness, and it was an unnerving experience to see them passing because, like the gunners, Noble knew that now there was nothing else in front.

'The tanks are just behind us,' the infantrymen said.

'They can't be *that* close,' one of the gunners growled.

'That's what you think,' Noble said with feeling, then three fields away he saw low humps appearing from behind a burning farmhouse and he began to run as the battery started to fire over open sights.

Two or three miles further on he stopped to get his breath. By this time he'd finished his last fag, he was hot and half-starved and, because he'd smoked several of the cigars from the haversack and helped himself to nips of cognac to keep his nerves steady, he also had a raging thirst.

More groups of Frenchmen appeared, also heading north, but Noble gave them a wide berth. Then, as the light began to fade, he passed through a deserted hamlet off the route of the retreat that had been bombed and set on fire. There didn't seem to be a living soul left in it but there was a small farmhouse on the outskirts where he decided to look for food.

It was an old building, ugly, with bleached doors and window sashes, and a chicken scratching in the dirt fled noisily as he approached. There was no wind and the cobbled yard stank of manure. As he cautiously pushed open the door, it reminded him sickeningly of the Kent farms where his parents had taken him as a child when they'd gone hop-picking.

There might even be a bird, he thought, the farmer's daughter, left behind and eager to oblige a man like Kiss of Death Noble, the original Hearts and Flowers Kid, in return for his protection. His jaw hung open with the first pleasurable thoughts he'd had for days as he saw her in his mind's eye lifting soft white fingers to pull the last strap down and let the final garment fall to her ankles. She'd be slender as a wraith, with soft eyes like a gazelle's and pink-tipped breasts, as innocent as a child and just waiting for Lije Noble to show her how to go about things. Despite his numerous amorous adventures, Noble had always been very correct with young girls and had pursued only older experienced women whom he couldn't harm. Yet the idea of possessing an innocent but eager country virgin had always been one of his fantasies, and he was in a soporific daydream compounded of tiredness and a yearning to be safe when, from somewhere inside the house, he heard something metallic like an enamel bowl fall and start to spin.

He froze, the picture vanishing, his heart pounding in his throat. 'Who's there?' It was an English voice and he almost fainted with relief.

The movement came again and he saw a tall figure against the light from a window. It carried a Bren gun and the pouches on its breast contained magazines of ammunition. But the figure moved slowly and awkwardly, and as it passed the window Noble saw its face was covered with blood.

'What happened, mate?' he asked. 'Get you in the head?'

The other man nodded. He was a Guardsman, he saw now, a tall, gingerish-haired man with a bone-white face masked with stubble and sweat-caked dust. His hair was matted with blood that had run across his eyes and dried into hard brown crusts, and as he moved he stumbled badly, his hand in front of him pawing the air.

Noble's mouth hung open in horror and pity. 'You blind, mate?' he whispered.

'I dunno,' the Guardsman said briskly. 'I cannae open ma een.'

Noble came to life with a jerk. There was a pump by the sink and he sloshed water into a tin basin and carried it back to the Guardsman who still clutched the Bren to his chest.

'For God's sake, mate,' Noble said. 'Put your gun down. I can't get at you.'

The Guardsman stiffened. 'I carried this bluidy gun all the way from Belgium,' he said. 'It fell in the water. I had to get it oot.'

Noble stared at the gun. 'That's never been in no water,' he said.

'Aye. I cleaned it. I was taught tae strip and clean one of these things blindfold.'

Noble swallowed again. Having been tempted several times during the day to throw even his rifle away, he was impressed by a devotion that could carry a 23 lb. Bren and full magazines as far as this one had been carried. 'Don't make no difference,' he said. 'I can't clean you up with it sticking up me nostrils.'

The Guardsman laid down the Bren at last, not very willingly, and handed Noble a grubby handkerchief. 'Here,' he said.

After a few minutes scrubbing and with the loss of most of the lashes, they got the eye open and Noble found himself staring into a cold pale-blue eye. The Guardsman gave a relieved sigh. 'How aboot the other?' he said.

After a while that eye opened, too, and the Guardsman's hand went to the top of his head. 'It's all right now,' he said.

It didn't seem to Noble that anything was all right. He was still a long way from his friends and he'd already seen too many men die. 'What are you goin' to do?' he asked.

'Rejoin ma unit.'

'What's that?'

'Coldstream. Senior regiment of the British army. What's yours?'

Noble's reply was received in silence. 'The Royal Welsh I've haird of,' the Guardsman said after a while. 'The Black Watch I know exists. But what the hell is yon bluidy outfit?'

Noble told him and he pondered, a silent six-foot-three, so lean,

Noble thought, a folded pound note would have shown in his pocket. 'What's your name?' he asked.

'Noble. Lije Noble.'

The Guardsman ran his fingers over his chin. 'Mine's Gow. John Gow. Ma mates call me Jock. You can.'

He made the offer as though bestowing an accolade and Noble was flattered. Gow's white granite face seemed to suggest that having friends might be considered effeminate in his circle, and Noble felt he was in the presence of glory and that a little bit of it was reflected on him.

'What are you going to do when you get back to your pals?' he asked.

'Fight, mon. What do you think?'

'With a bonce like that? Even the bloody Brigade of Guards aren't that clever?'

'I always thought they were. And I'll thank you not to swear when you refer to the fucken Brigade of Guards.' The Guardsman seemed to have recovered his aplomb completely, in a way that left Noble slightly awed. 'You got any kit, mon?' he asked. 'Razor? Brush and polish?'

Noble's jaw hung open. 'What for?'

Gow's voice rose. 'To polish ma boots, o' course,' he said.

Noble came to life. 'Listen, *mon fils*,' he said, 'I've lost me kit so often I have to go into bloody battle these days with a retriever.'

Gow frowned. 'That's bad,' he intoned severely. 'Dirty flesh's a serious offence. You can tell a Guardsman anywhere. Not only do we fight better. We look better, too. We're the Coalies. The Lilywhites. The Coldstream. They been working on us for hundreds of years. At Inkerman we picked up rocks when our guns was empty and beat the Russians' heads flat wi' 'em. At Fontenoy we held our volley until one man in three had gone down. And why? Because we're clean, mon. Because we're clean.'

To Noble it didn't seem to follow, but clearly Gow thought it did. He had an unmistakable Guardsman's walk, stiff as a ramrod arrogant with confidence, and he looked the sort of man who, if, he put his mind to it, could destroy a battleship with a jack-knife.

'Och, well,' he said. 'Ah'll have tae save it.' He took a small notebook from his blouse pocket and began to write with a stub of pencil which he held in his big white fist as though it were a sledge-hammer. Noble watched him curiously, wondering what was so important that it had to be entered so precisely and at such a moment. Then Gow put his pencil away and buttoned the blouse pocket carefully. 'Mebbe we'd better find somethin' tae eat,' he said. 'Then we'll try to round up a few of yon bluidy Frogs and see if we cannae make 'em into soldiers.'

Noble stared. His own impression of the Frenchmen he'd seen was that they wouldn't stop for anyone, and he had no wish to be left at the side of the road like the colonel he'd passed, with a bullet through his back.

'Those sods wouldn't stop for anybody,' he said.

'They might. For me.' Gow didn't seem to consider the problem a difficult one but, as he headed for the road, his step was not quite firm. Noble guessed he was still dizzy, and could see his eyes were squinting as though he had a splitting headache. When he swayed on his feet Noble decided it was time he protested.

'Listen, when was it you copped it?'

Gow frowned. 'This morning. Fairst light.'

Noble gestured. 'Eighteen hours ago, mate. Things are changing all the time. You pals are miles away now.'

'Is that a fact?'

'Yes, it is. With that bonce of yours you're in no state to put up a solo rear-guard action.'

'Discipline's the thing, mon.'

'Discipline me arse,' Noble said and Gow stiffened.

'Hae ye no haird how the Scots Guards were on parade when a One-one-oh came down at low level wi' its guns going? Not a heid turned tae see what was goin' on.'

Noble stared at Gow as though he were a prehistoric animal. He held up one finger. 'How many?' he asked.

'Two. No, be Christ, one! Ma een must be a bit bolo still.'

'See what I mean?' Noble grasped Gow's arm, feeling for the first time that he was in command of the situation. 'Could you do with a swallow of brandy, *mon fils*?'

Gow's bony white face turned. 'You got some?'

Noble fished into his side-pack and produced what was left of the bottle.

'Try a swig of that,' he said.

Watching all the drab, dusty, shabby figures filing past, Private Angelet was overwhelmed by an incredible sadness. This was France he was watching pass in front of him. Not the France he'd been brought up to believe in – the France of Louis XIV and Napoleon, not the France of Verdun and the Marne. This was the France of 1870, effete, decadent, its soul eaten by corruption and treachery, defeated, shamed, no longer with the pride to hold up its head.

The men stumbling past were the ruin of an army. Their commanders had thrown in their hands and only occasional units tramped past with their weapons in their hands, their heads up, unshaven like the rest because the French army had never set much store by smartness, but with something in their eyes that showed they were undefeated. Angelet's shy soul reached out to these men as he wished he belonged among them.

'What will happen to France, Chouteau?' he asked.

Sitting alongside him on the bank, cutting slices from a huge sausage he'd found in the last village they'd passed through, Chouteau considered. His hands were working under his greatcoat because if any of the hungry men shuffling past had seen the sausage they'd have demanded a share and in Chouteau's mind the time had come when survival was more important than charity.

He shrugged and slipped a slice to Angelet with a piece of stale bread.

'She will surrender,' he said. 'And they will dig out some useless old fool who's not been involved and get him to ask for terms.'

'And then?'

Chouteau's hands stopped moving under the greatcoat and he sat for a moment, silent, staring in front of him, his expression blank, his eyes empty.

'And then?' he said. 'And then, *mon vieux*, we shall get the S.S. and the torture chambers, and the Germans will march through the Arc de Triomphe and down the Champs Elysées as they did in 1871. They will bring their gauleiters and they will occupy all the best hotels, and the opera will play Wagner instead of Bizet.'

'French people would never permit that.'

Chouteau's hands were still motionless and his eyes were faraway. 'No?' he said. 'Perhaps not you or I. Perhaps not the inhabitants of Belleville and St. Denis and the villages in the

Pas de Calais and the Jura and the South. *They* would fight. But there are also people with apartments in the Avenue Foch who have fat bank accounts and expensive mistresses and spoilt children. *They* will make terms. You and I, *mon brave*, are going to witness the sight of France on her knees.'

He became silent and Angelet stared with him into the road. He thought of the department store where he'd worked, and tried to imagine fat German hausfraus buying the underwear that he used to sell to the midinettes. Then he thought of his girl friend and wondered how she'd face defeat.

Already, on the roads north, he's seen Frenchwomen and girls standing on cross-roads as they'd passed. Their eyes had been full of contempt for the men shuffling northwards and some had already been staring towards that point on the horizon where the Germans would first appear. He was old enough to know that some of them might not even find the Germans unwelcome.

'My God,' he exploded. 'It's too much!'

Chouteau's head turned. 'What, *mon brave*?'

But Angelet had expended his fury, and was back again with his girl friend. On his last leave they'd gone to a hotel. It had been mid-afternoon but, being France, no one had thought it odd. Angelet had not done the paying because the French army didn't allow for such luxuries, and all he could remember about it now was that it had had a big Norman bed and a tin bidet. His girl friend had taken off the bolero jacket she'd been wearing and flung it on a chair, and somehow he'd felt she was completely mistress of the situation.

She'd begun to unfasten the buttons of her dress and as she'd stepped out of it, Angelet had sat on the bed and watched her, shy and entranced. 'How beautiful you are,' he'd said breathlessly, half-blinded by badly-suppressed adoration and dizzy with the sight of something he felt was pure and untouched. Her eyes had been dark and liquid and, even as the excitement ran through his body, he'd felt that she was *too* beautiful for him.

She'd smiled at him, unashamed at her nakedness. 'Well,' she'd said. 'What are you waiting for, imbecile?' And as she'd pushed him back on to the bed, reaching with a sure hand for the buttons of his clothes, he'd realized that, despite what he thought, she was not a virgin.

It hadn't worried him then that he wasn't the first, but he

decided now that she was foolish and in need of love and that without him she'd turn to the first man to offer it to her. And with the Germans everywhere and Frenchmen forced into the shadows where it was safe, she could well be one of the first to fall.

'What will become of us?' he asked 'You and I, Chouteau?'

Chouteau took a deep breath. 'Doubtless the British will let us fight for them as usual,' he said dryly. 'Sometimes, in fact, I wonder which are the worst – the British or the Germans. Neither of them have much regard for France, but at least the British are not Nazis and they will not stop fighting.'

'How *can* they fight? There's nothing to stop the Germans now.'

Chouteau smiled. 'Only the sea, *mon brave*, and that is the best tank trap in the world. Behind it the British will build their armies. Just as they did in 1915. From then, that war was *their* war – until the Americans took it from both of us.'

While they were talking, they hadn't noticed the two khaki figures approaching. The road had emptied for the moment and Chouteau looked up, surprised to see the two Englishmen, one of them small and red-faced with a black pencil-line moustache and a sly expression, holding the arm of a tall, lean, man with a bone-white face streaked with blood which had dried in runnels as it oozed from his stiff matted hair.

'Speak English, *mon fils?*' the small one asked.

'*Un peu*,' Chouteau said. 'A little.'

'Food,' the small man said. 'You have food.'

Chouteau looked up and realized that the little Englishman's sly eyes had noticed something no one else had noticed – the crumbs on his greatcoat. His hand moved slowly towards his rifle.

'So?'

'I've got cognac. My cognac for your food.'

Chouteau stared then he licked his lips. 'I am hungry also,' he said. 'Let us say a little of my food for a little of your cognac.'

As Noble and Gow exchanged food with Chouteau and Angelet, Heinrich-Robert Hinze stood near Mardyck staring at the Channel and feeling as Napoleon and Caesar must have felt when they, too, had stared at its dark waters.

Behind him the battery was constructing gun pits – eighteen

inches deep and sandbagged five feet high in front – and the circular steel platforms had been hoisted from the trailers and were now being embedded in the earth. Already one gun had been mounted, its wheels on the outer rim of the platform so it could easily be slewed round. Trenches had been dug behind in case of counter-fire. Parked nearby were the tractors, the light and heavy trucks from the stores, the trailer racked for ammunition, the officers' mess vehicle, the cook's lorry with the men's mess apparatus and, stacked ready for use, the growing piles of shells and charges.

Hinze drew a deep breath. He could smell the sea and feel the breeze on his face, and beyond the dunes he could see the last of the light on the flat stretch of water to the north. The men behind him were cursing as they always did when there was work to be done but there was no real annoyance. They could all see the end of the war in sight and they all felt they'd soon be home.

He turned and moved back to the lorry where he worked. The major was there. 'I hope to be ready for action at first light tomorrow, he said.

'We shall be, Herr Major.'

'They'll be making a big effort. They'll send in everything they've got.'

'Yes.' Hinze smiled. 'The shooting season will be opening early.'

One of the targets was still waiting in Dover. She seemed to have been forgotten but it didn't worry Tremenheere greatly. There were rations on board, and he was quite content to stay where he was.

All day the boat had bobbed and bumped alongside the pier, the passing ships setting the mat of small craft that surrounded her weaving and dancing. The destroyers were still doing the bulk of the work. They were not built to carry troops and it was incredible that they could carry as many as they did on decks crowded with guns, torpedo tubes and depth charges. But they were experimenting now with larger and larger numbers and were growing so top-heavy that when they swung to enter harbour they heeled at incredible angles. The men aboard held their breath, certain they were going over.

Some of the smaller vessels were limping badly, their decks splintered by bullets and the dead lying sprawled in corners. The cheering and excitement that had existed when *Athelstan* had first arrived had died away as the day wore grimly on.

Watching the women pinning labels to the clothing of the injured with their names, ranks and numbers, their units and their home addresses, Tremenheere had one whisky too many from Knevett's bottle. There was a woman working nearby and as she bent he could see the backs of her thighs, and in the end the salacious thoughts that persisted in running through his head drove him to help her. She was so busy, however, she never even noticed him and in the end he went back in disgust to *Athelstan* and fell asleep in the wheelhouse.

He was awakened by voices and the clatter of feet along the deck, to see it was pitch dark. Leaving the wheelhouse, he saw men in naval uniform aboard the fishing boat, *Daisy*.

'It's no good, mate,' a weary voice said. '*We're* not going.'

There was a little muttering and as the sailors vanished a three-badge man stepped aboard *Athelstan*. 'This one looks all right,' he said. A young stoker appeared, who looked as though he'd just joined up. 'Know anything about this kind of engine?' the three-badge man asked.

'Not a bloody thing,' the stoker said.

'I do, me dear,' Tremenheere interrupted.

The three-badge man became aware of him for the first time. 'Is she your boat, sir?'

'No. And I'm not a "sir", either.'

'Better get ourselves introduced then.' The three-badge man was formal and very proper. 'He's Smudger Smith and the kid just coming aboard's Didcot. Answers to "Diddy". I'm Nobby Clark. I was on survivor's leave when they rounded us up. I was in *Bittern* when she was sunk off Norway and when we got back they sent us on fourteen days' leave. I'd had eight when they recalled me. I'll go and report we're ready.'

WEDNESDAY, 29 MAY

As the clock hands in Dover and in France passed the hour of midnight, the rear-guard was taking up its positions. To the south, soldiers still clung to their strongpoints near Poperinghe and on the mound of Cassel, but they all knew the end was not far away.

The day began with a disaster, and to the offices in the galleries in the cliffs came the news that three destroyers had been lost in the very first hours.

None of this, of course, was known to the men on the beaches where by this time everyone was involved – padres, Pay Corps officers, military attachés and liaison and intelligence groups – all of them doing things they'd never expected to do and trying to do them without panic.

Among them was Basil Allerton. He and his men had just arrived in Dunkirk when the Stukas had turned up, and at the shout of 'Take cover' he had run for shelter to a coal dump near the station. The blast of the exploding bombs had blown him into a pile of coal dust and he'd emerged choking on the grit that filled his eyes, nose and throat.

The beach was one of hard wet sand, with miles of shallow water so that the ships had to stand well out. It had been quiet when they'd arrived, and littered with what seemed to be bodies but had turned out to be greatcoats. The silence had been eerie but now, it seemed, everyone had recovered his breath and the place was one vast inquest on what had gone wrong.

'I suppose they outnumbered us,' one officer was saying doubtfully. 'After all, we seemed to do all right when we came up against 'em. I even heard that when the Durhams went for 'em with the bayonet they ran.'

'The Durhams were lucky,' another officer complained. 'My chaps just had to sit and be plastered with mortars.'

'We could have done with a few of those.' The words came in explosive bursts of disgust. '*And* a few of those blasted sandbags they've stuck round the churches in London. They'd have done better to spend their bloody day of prayer making guns.'

Allerton listened without emotion. He was too tired by this time for emotion and he knew the complaints were the complaints of men who were worried that people would think they'd not done their best. The attitude of the other ranks seemed to be much the same, one of shame that they'd been beaten but full of certainty that it wasn't their fault.

'I'd like to meet that bloke who trotted out all them stories about their tanks being made of papier mâché,' one of them was saying. 'The ones *we* saw weren't.'

There was a bark of laughter, then from somewhere in the darkness, someone started singing, not drunkenly but defiantly. '*Look at the mourners, blooming well crying. Ain't it grand to be blooming well dead?*'

'Shut that bloody man up,' an officer's voice called sharply and someone said 'Dry up, Ted, for Christ's sake,' but the voice went on doggedly. '*Look at the coffin, bloody brass 'andles –*'

Eventually the singing changed to an incredible happy whistling, as though the singer had become absorbed in some job he was doing and had quite forgotten the circumstances; the unbelievable cheerfulness – the same cheerfulness that was still about him despite the defeat and the horror – the one thing that kept Allerton going.

He lit a cigarette. Like everyone else he had dozens of them, looted from NAAFIs or flung from lorries to stop the Germans getting them. The smoke killed the appalling stench coming from inland where he'd seen the bloated carcasses of three dead cows. There was also a dead cavalry horse along the beach. There had been whole groups of them on the sand when he'd first arrived, wheeling and galloping about and squealing in terror as the bombs dropped. One or two of them had been hit and the one along the beach, he'd been told, had been in the sun for three days now.

In his logical intellectual way, he felt he understood what had happened. It had been the unknown they were running away from. Fed by rumour, they didn't know who was pursuing them, or how many, or whether they'd outstrip them. They'd all been caught by the contagion of bewilderment and ignorance, rumour had spread at every halt and no man had had any orders. Their only plan was to reach safety, and if there'd only been someone to shout 'Halt! Do this! Do that!' half their fears would have vanished. It had started with the French and spread to the B.E.F. In the slang of the moment, 'Someone had made a cock of the washing up.'

The thought cheered him and he felt increasingly detached from the battle as hour became indistinguishable from hour. A trial of strength had taken place; the issue had been decided and graves had been scratched in the soil. Now there seemed to be a stalemate and, deciding death in defeat was easier than death in victory because there was no exhilaration in being on the losing side, he found he wasn't afraid.

About him there was even a strange atmosphere of relief. To men who'd been bombed solidly for three weeks and had hardly had a decent night's sleep in all that time, the beaches were a place to rest and they were snatching what they could. Allerton longed to join them and fling himself down but a brigadier, as immaculate as if he'd been on parade at Aldershot, had appointed him to command his particular strip of sand. The men about him were strangers but they were patient and sensible, and their discipline was good. They allowed themselves to be divided into groups of twenty-five, which was roughly what Allerton assumed would fill a boat, and had then tucked themselves out of sight among the dunes. He could hear them instructing newcomers what to do as they arrived.

'You see the beachmaster, mate, and then you take your place in the queue. And don't be in too big a hurry, either, because *we*'re first.'

By this time he had become indifferent to the drone of aeroplanes and the sound of explosions but, with his own men in a different part of the beach, the absence of familiar voices bothered him. Although the boats came again and again, he never saw the faces of the men who manned them and it was a little like living in a vacuum. Every now and then a flare was dropped which showed up the beach in a hard white light and then the bombs came down, most of them falling in the town with vivid green flashes accompained by showers of sparks which reflected on the clouds and on the ripples on the flat surface of the water. Several officers had changed their heavy battledress for light-weight clothes and gym shoes in case they had to take to the sea. Allerton was wearing his best uniform, feeling he might never afford another, and he kept wishing he had the moral courage to strip to his underpants which were a much more sensible garb for swimming the Channel.

Because he was hungry and tired, he was also cold and his feet ached, while the dirt on his body seemed to have a mummifying effect. Several times he was tempted to slip aboard one of the rescue boats in the dark, but he hadn't the courage to step out of turn, and eventually as he became aware that the light was changing, he realized that the sand was not brown but the colour of pearls, flat, wide and striped in black. There were frequent sandbars offshore and a few streams and breakwaters running from the land. Behind, the dunes were half a mile wide in places, heavily contoured and tufted with marram grass and, at that moment, littered with parked vehicles hub-deep in the soft sand and resting at all angles.

As the dawn came, he peered out to sea. The number of boats arriving had grown less in the last hour or so and had finally stopped; as the light increased, it seemed that the navy had dis-appeared. Other men were peering with him, standing in depressed groups in a soaking drizzle that had started, huddled in greatcoats and groundsheets, the water dripping off their steel helmets and laying beads of moisture on their eyebrows and moustaches and the down on their cheeks. Their faces were grey and strained and tense with expectancy. There were thousands of them, helpless, patient, hopeful, simply standing there waiting.

The whole thing seemed unbelievable and he couldn't imagine for a minute that the Luftwaffe would allow them another day to get away with it. His heart sank again as ugly thoughts of captivity filled his mind. With daylight and a clearing sky, he knew the German planes would be back and he tried to shut from his brain the thought of the thousands of casualties that would result.

One of the first casualties of the day was Lije Noble.

A hot night had followed a hot day and he was tired, thirsty and coated with the dust that clogged his nostrils and throat. As he prowled round looking for rations the narrow road vibrated beneath his feet from the distant percussion of bombs and he could see the flicker of anti-aircraft fire in the sky like winking red pin-pricks. Mortar fire thudded to the south and then a thin dry crackling sound came, like a machine-gun or exploding ammunition. Along the horizon there were a dozen fires, all big, one of them a village just across the fields.

In the dirty pink glow he saw a rat crossing the road and because he felt it was time he fired at something, he lifted his rifle and pulled the trigger. The bullet kicked up a spark from the cobbles and went whining across the fields, and immediately the air was filled with flying lead as a nervous patrol fired back.

He dived for the ditch and lay there with his head down. He'd left Gow and the others on the bank of the canal a mile behind him, having driven clean through the German lines during the night in an abandoned French lorry. Noble had been quite prepared to throw in his hand when they'd heard German voices ahead, but Gow had remained quite unperturbed and had collected pieces of farm machinery from a ruined barn and tied them to the stern of the lorry with ropes so that they'd clattered and clinked as they'd driven through the darkness. They'd made enough noise to wake the dead, the bouncing pieces of steel sounding vaguely like tank threads, and in the darkness no one had thought it wise to try to stop them.

As the scattered shooting about him stopped, Noble lifted his head and moved towards the burning village. The traffic had come to a halt outside it because a French corps in trucks held possession of the crossroads and was driving along three abreast, forcing everything else into the ditch. Mile after mile down the road the waiting column grew. Everyone was exhausted and the drivers were dropping asleep in their seats. As the last of the French passed, military policemen began to chase up and down, waking them, officers and men alike, with yells of fury, banging on their steel helmets with the butts of their revolvers. 'Wake up, you bastard! Keep moving! Wake up! Wake up!'

As he watched the crawling procession start again, a shell

screamed over from the east and he heard it explode a hundred yards away. For a moment the darkness was tense as he felt everyone waiting for the next, but the shell seemed to be a stray and nothing more came. But there were flames further ahead and an officer ran along the column shouting for a medical orderly, and Noble decided it was safer to disappear. The next shell might drop on Lije Noble.

He pushed between the vehicles and headed down a side road, and as he entered the village he could see that it was full of both French and British. At the village cemetery, a group of khaki-clad soldiers were forcing the locked gates. With them on the grass was a blanketed figure. 'We've got to bury him somewhere,' one of them was saying anxiously.

In the square a NAAFI canteen had caught fire and Noble joined the soldiers helping themselves to cigarettes. The cash box was just where he expected it to be, under the counter behind a carton of shaving soap, the last thing anyone was interested in just then, and to his delight he saw it was full of franc notes. Cramming them into his pocket, he snatched up as much chocolate and as many tins of fruit as he could carry and headed outside again.

On the outskirts of the village once more, he saw a group of drunken Frenchmen chasing a British soldier and, even as he watched, they started shooting and he decided it was time for him to disappear. The bushes at the side of the road hid him effectively but there were more of the Frenchmen than he'd expected and his detour was a long one. He found himself in a small patch of trees with a notice which said *'Propriété Privée'*, but, since he didn't know what it meant, he pushed on. As he stepped through the undergrowth he felt something against his foot and almost immediately there was the roar of a gun going off and he knew he'd been shot.

For a moment, he lay still, shocked, then he realized the pain wasn't as bad as he thought, and he began to feel himself carefully. His trousers were torn and damp with pin-pricks of blood, but he didn't seem to be badly hurt and it dawned on him he'd tripped off a shotgun which had been set for poachers and then forgotten in the confusion of the battle.

It was a bugger of a war, he decided.

The same kind of thought was filling Tremenheere's mind. It would be all right, he kept telling himself as *Athelstan* chugged steadily on through the darkness. Some big shot would turn up eventually and the thing would sort itself out. In the way it usually did, of course, with the big shots still on top and Alban Tremenheere still on the bottom where he'd always been.

When daylight came it started to drizzle and they seemed to have lost all the other boats that had left Dover with them, but they were still on course and *Athelstan*'s engines were pulling well. They were two miles offshore and the land lay like a silent line along the horizon, just emerging from the night.

'That looks like the place,' Nobby Clark said.

But just then three British destroyers appeared on their quarter and the crash as they opened fire seemed to lift their feet from the decks. They heard the rushing scream of the shells passing overhead and there were several small twinkling flashes on the shore in the very place where they'd been heading.

They turned about without even bothering to discuss it and eventually found themselves off the breakwater at Dunkirk. The sky was overcast and there was a great pall of smoke hanging in it, darkening the sea. It was the funeral pyre of a dying town and they could hear the mutter of battle further inland. All the time, passing them in the opposite direction, boats were going home, singly and in groups, at speed or with spluttering engines, all crammed with that dun mass of troops, every inch of deck and cabin space filled with them.

The pall of smoke had a glow at its base where fires burned among the debris. There were flames everywhere, and wrecks lay in the roads and off the beaches. Deciding the bombers wouldn't waste any more bombs on her, they lay alongside a burning trooper until they could get their bearings. The explosions inside her were nerve-racking and they kept expecting the whole thing to go sky-high, but then Tremenheere managed to pick out the line of surf, and, beyond it, great black masses that sprawled across the sand, stretching from the dunes behind the water's edge like dense forests. At first they puzzled him, then he realized they were men. As they stared a destroyer half a mile away suddenly started firing – whango, whango, whango – and Didcot pointed. 'Up there, Nobby,' he said.

Staring up, Tremenheere saw puff-balls of smoke against the sky as the anti-aircraft shells burst. At first he couldn't see what they were firing at, then he saw an aeroplane among the low cloud and as he stared he heard the scream of a bomb. The sea heaved upwards in vast rumbling explosions that flung spray across the decks and he threw himself down on the safe side of the wheelhouse, his arms clasped round his head.

As the sky cleared, Jocho Horndorff was still Conybeare's prisoner. Surrounded as they were now by men, any attempt to run would have left him riddled with bullets, and his only chance, he knew, was to dodge away in the confusion or the darkness and lie low somewhere until the British had gone.

He'd tried to lull Conybeare into a friendliness he might have taken advantage of, but the night before he'd still been locked in the coalhouse of a half-demolished house, while Conybeare sat with his back to the door. He'd emerged filthy, humiliated, and furious with his captor.

'You realize, of course,' he said harshly, 'that you will never get me to England. You no longer even have an army. It is *ausradiert* – blotted out.'

Conybeare was unperturbed. 'Army's always a bit slow to learn,' he agreed.

Horndorff became silent. They were passing groups of soldiers resting by the roadside but, despite the deathly weariness of their faces, they showed no sign of panic. Up ahead he could see dive-bombers falling out of the sky and dropping their bombs among the flames and smoke, and it dawned on him that if he didn't do something about it soon, before long they'd be dropping them on him.

Batteries of guns were forming up for the rearguard, but there was a complete absence of cover among the beet-fields and he found it hard to accept the cold-blooded heroism of the men digging the gunpits. Immediately the guns started to flash through the dust and smoke, half a dozen observation posts would plot them for counter-fire.

The batteries' trucks were dotted about the field in an attempt to make the bombers think it was one of the vast parking areas that were building up outside the town and in a dry ditch behind the guns, a command post had been set up. Officers and men were digging together, stripped to the waist, indifferent to the incessant flights of bombers that were beginning to appear overhead, thirty at a time, in a monotonous noisy wave of destruction.

As Horndorff watched , the first German shells began to bracket the guns and he saw a truck flower into flame. Immediately, one of the batteries began to fire, rhythmically and slowly as though they were short of shells, then Conybeare jabbed with the pistol and they ran until they were clear, Conybeare awkward in the ugly farm boots.

Just ahead, a mob of men was filling the road at the entrance to a bar situated among a group of shabby red-brick buildings painted with a huge sign, BYRRH. Most of them were French but there was a sprinkling of English, too, and their uniforms were awry and they carried no weapons. They held bottles in their fists and were arguing loudly. As they saw Horndorff the shouting stopped and one of the Frenchmen turned and shook his fist in Horndorff's face.

'*Assassin*,' he screamed, and as the cry was taken up, a man in stained khaki pushed to the front, his thin ugly face twisted in a snarl.

'Bloody murderer !' he said.

Horndorff glanced at Conybeare.

'Keep walking,' Conybeare said.

'*A la lanterne* !' The cry came out of the mob like a flung stone and, though he didn't speak much French, Horndorff knew exactly what it meant.

The English soldier seemed to understand, too. 'That's right,' he said. 'Lynch the bastard !'

Horndorff backed up against one of the buildings, determined not to show how afraid he was, and Conybeare took up a position in front of him. 'This man's my prisoner,' he said. 'I'm taking him to England.'

'Never mind that !' The English soldier's face was full of hate. 'We want him, sonny, and we're having him !'

'This man is my prisoner,' Conybeare repeated. 'I'm taking him to England.' His voice hardened and his good eye flashed. 'And *you* are speaking to a British officer ! Stand to attention and salute ! And don't call me "sonny" !'

The soldier didn't salute but his posture changed. He stood up straighter and began to fasten his unbuttoned blouse.

'Listen —'

'Sir!'

'Okay, okay! Sir! Blokes like him have been shooting kids.'

'This man is my prisoner,' Conybeare said with a persistent patience. He raised the Luger and pointed it directly at the soldier's chest. 'I am taking him with *me*. If anyone tries to stop me, I shall shoot him. Even you.' His voice rose and he began to speak in fluent French. *'Je suis officier britannique. Cet Allemand est mon prisonnier. Je fusillerai l'homme qui lui fait du mal. Entendu?'*

There was a dead silence, then one of the women in the crowd gave a nervous giggle. *'C'est un brave, ça,'* she said.

For a long time the silence continued, then the British soldier jerked at his battledress blouse and turned away. 'Aw, come on,' he said. 'Let the bastard have his bleeding prisoner.'

Sitting by his van in the thinning drizzle, his headphones clamped to his head. Leutnant Hinze could see beyond the dunes towards the sea. There was a dense cloud of smoke that came from the burning oil tanks, and in a strange eddy of currents it had now sunk to the level of the water. Half a dozen ships were manoeuvring towards Dunkirk, just beyond the range of his guns; and in the smoke, he knew, was a large transport. He'd seen her being fired on from Nieuport before the smoke had obscured her, and she'd overshot the harbour entrance in the murk.

He studied the dark cloud intently. His ability to concentrate was one of the reasons for his skill. There had been a sticky moment not long before when a group of destroyers trying to knock out the battery had dropped shells just behind them. In rapid succession a couple of dozen missiles had swished over their heads and burst in the fields a hundred yards away. In the silence which had followed they'd heard a cow which had been hit by a splinter, bellowing in agony.

'Someone go and shoot that animal, please,' Hinze had said politely.

He was still watching the smoke and now, to his delight, he saw the ship emerging from it to the west of the town, closing the range with every yard. She was a big vessel and appeared slowly, as though unaware that she was standing into danger.

'Fresh target,' he instructed.

The gun crews jumped to their positions and the telephone operator wrote down the orders.

'Fresh target . . . HE . . . Charge three . . . Zero five degrees . . . Angle of sight, fifteen minutes elevation . . . Extreme range . . .'

In the quiet morning air he could hear the clang of the breeches.

'Number three gun ready!'

'Number one gun ready!'

'Number two gun ready!'

Hinze kept his eyes glued on the ship. 'Fire!'

As the guns crashed out, a flock of sheep set up a bleating, pigs squealed and he heard chickens cackling, as though every farm for miles had been violently stirred up.

The shells landed just short of the transport and she was obscured for a moment by the splashes.

'Up two degrees,' he ordered as the cases came out, smoking.

The guns roared again and this time the shot went over. Hinze ordered a drop of a hundred metres in range.

'Shot three!'

This time he saw a flash abaft the transport's engine room on the port side and just as she disappeared into the smoke again, he saw her slow down and a huge column of steam appear through her engine room hatches.

With gunners like Hinze, the approaches to Dunkirk were shrinking, and at Dover the admiral was faced with a new decision. Since dawn seven more destroyers had been attacked by aeroplanes and two of them damaged, and to these problems was now added the fact that German guns were being brought to bear even on ships turning by the Kwinte buoy on the last safe route as they closed the coast near Nieuport.

'Is the sweeping of the route by the Ruytingen Pass complete?' he asked.

The commander, minesweeping, shook his head. 'Not yet, sir.'

The admiral stared at the charts, neat, scrupulously tidy like his desk. Then, after a moment's reflection as he tried to translate the thunder and smoke of battle into the rings and arrows of a plan, he brought out the answer like a rabbit from a hat.

'Very well.' He turned to the staff officer, operations, 'send *Jaguar*, *Gallant* and *Grenade* to find out if we can use that route instead of the one by the Kwinte Buoy.' He turned back to the commander, minesweeping. 'And see that the sweeping goes ahead. What about the beaches?'

'*Calcutta*'s back, sir,' the staff officer, operations, said. 'She loaded from drifters. She brought back twelve hundred men. The coasters are bringing them off in similar numbers. Thank God the weather's holding. It'd be terrible if we had a force eight gale.'

Outside Dunkirk, there was firing from time to time, odd snap-shots and an occasional burst of machine-gun fire, but not much else. Shells were screaming overhead in both directions and land-ing in the outskirts of the town. A battery was drawn up in a field on the right, and a barrier manned by military policemen had been thrown across the road by a farm building. By the wall there were a few German prisoners, dishevelled and dirty, and inside the doorway a military police sergeant was writing in a notebook. As Horndorff and Conybeare approached, the cor-poral on the barrier saluted and gestured towards the prisoners.

'Shove him with that lot, sir,' he said. 'We'll have to let 'em go in the end, I reckon, because there'll be no room for them.'

'There'll be room for this one, Corporal,' Conybeare said politely. 'I'm taking him to England.' It was becoming a dogged repetition now.

The corporal stared at him then he turned and shouted. 'Sarge,' he roared. 'We aren't taking no prisoners across, are we?'

The sergeant appeared in the doorway and stamped across to Conybeare whom he saluted punctiliously. 'Shove him with that lot, sir,' he said briskly.

'Not this one, Sergeant. I'm taking him to England.'

'My instructions, sir –'

Conybeare's voice became louder. 'I'm sorry about your instructions, Sergeant,' he said, 'but this man is a panzer leader with the rank of major. I suspect he might be able to help us a great deal.'

It was his manner rather than his words that stopped the ser-geant dead. 'Yeh, I suppose so, sir.'

'Then, thank you, Sergeant, I'll keep him with me.'

The sergeant and the corporal watched them walk away. Then the sergeant glanced at the group of prisoners, back at Cony-beare and Horndorff and finally at the corporal.

'Round the bend,' he said.

As he spoke the dive-bombers they'd been expecting ever since daylight, arrived.

The roads into Dunkirk were crammed with men now. As far as the eye could see across the fields there were long columns all heading north. They came from every direction and seemed to fill the bowl of land with the dust they raised, but then the Stukas fell out of the sky and the columns crumbled and broke for the ditches as the German planes came over.

Dropping to the field at Outreux, the returning machines brought back stories that turned Alfred Stoos' stomach with frustration. As they unfastened their helmets and ran a hand through their flattened hair, the crews were light-headed with tiredness and unable to stop talking.

'They were everywhere,' he heard Schlegel saying. 'There must have been two British divisions and a French army corps all jumbled up together, nose to tail every bit of the way.'

'And the harbour full of ships.' Dodtzenrodt threw down his helmet and lit a cigarette. 'A great raft of them at the end of the mole. *Wie ein gewaltsamer Flussübergang.* They've brought up everything they've got.'

As the crews moved off to snatch a bite of food, Stoos stumbled away across the grass, hardly able to see in his rage.

'Herr Leutnant,' Oberfeldwebel Hamcke replied wearily to his question, 'we're doing our best! We're cannibalizing Oberleutnant Bronowski's machine for spares.'

Stoos's heart leapt. Bronowski had returned the previous evening, wounded by anti-aircraft fire from a destroyer, and had crashed on landing.

'The radio works, Herr Leutnant,' Hamcke explained, 'and we can use the instruments. But we're still short –'

Stoos didn't hear the explanations, only the fact that D/6980 was not yet ready. 'How long?' he demanded.

'Sir – ' Hamcke's eyes were ringed with shadow and his face was dark ' – we've been at it all night!'

'How long?'

'This evening, I hope, sir.'

'This evening? *Gottverdammt!* You know the Führer's words. *Räder müssen rollen fur den Sieg.* Wheels must roll for victory. *Also müssen fliegen die Schwingen.* So must wings fly.'

Hamcke stiffened and his mouth tightened mutinously. 'Herr Leutnant, we can't perform miracles.'

'Midday,' Stoos said.

'Impossible, sir!'

'This afternoon, then.' Stoos swallowed angrily and turned away, his hands clenched so tightly his fingernails dug into his palms. The battle would be over by the time he took any part in it!

Indeed, by the middle of the morning, the rear-guard had already begun to move back. It was under heavy shellfire, and now that the dive-bombers had found them they were making their preparations to pull out when dusk gave them obscurity.

Lance-Corporal Gow was still among them. He'd found a smashed Bren carrier and from the litter of bloody equipment in the rear had produced a bi-pod, spare barrels and magazines, and a few Mills bombs which he'd passed on to Chouteau and Angelet. He was waiting now on the canal bank by the village of Bijghem, near Furnes, where the Guards had set up their strong-points. Another canal converged not far from his position, as well as the roads from Ypres and Nieuport, and Gow was well aware of its importance. With him there were a few men from assorted regiments and the two Frenchmen.

At first light they'd seen moving dots in the fields in the distance which they knew were Germans, but a battery just pulling back past them had opened up and the ground spouted orange flashes. When the smoke had drifted away there were no moving dots, and now the Germans were cautiously waiting for them to leave so they could inch a few yards further forward. Every now and then a rifle banged or the Bren chattered but, after the fighting along the Lys, the Germans were no longer over-keen to try their luck.

Alongside Gow, Angelet crouched over his rifle, his eyelids drooping with weariness; just beyond him, Chouteau, in whose face there was the same enduring look there was in Gow's.

Chouteau saw Gow studying him and grinned. '*Moi, je m'appelle Chouteau,*' he said. '*Gustave Chouteau. La Légion Etrangère.* Foreign Legion. *Comprenez?*'

Gow nodded. 'Me – Gow. Jock Gow. Coldstream Guards.'

'*Les Gardes?*' The Frenchman's eyebrows rose. '*Oh, là là! Comme moi.* Big – great warrior, *n'est-ce pas?*'

Gow's bone-white face cracked and his ginger moustache lifted in what passed with him as a smile. He'd learned very little French because he firmly believed that, to speak to a Guardsman, foreigners ought to learn English, and he produced one of the few French words he knew. '*Oui*,' he said.

He glanced down at his boots. They were scuffed and worn but he'd also found an abandoned side-pack in the wrecked Bren carrier that contained boot-polish, blanco, a button stick and shaving gear and he'd pounced on them as though they were gold. His battered footwear now shone, his belt was clean again and his chin was scraped to the bone. He looked and felt like a Guardsman once more. The wish to be clean sprang simply from a pride in his unit, his home, the one thing that was bringing the B.E.F. to the coast. He gave his boots a rub with his handkerchief, watched by the Frenchman who like most French soldiers was prepared to go as far as cleaning his rifle but no further, then reached out and gave the barrel of the Bren another loving wipe.

'Yon bastards'll learn a thing or two, if they come,' he said, and though Chouteau didn't understand a word of Gow's thick dialect, he knew exactly what he meant.

'*Oui*,' he said. '*Vraiment*.'

Gow was just wishing the Germans would come so he could shoot a few, when he heard Noble's voice behind him. Noble had disappeared the previous night and it had been Gow's firm impression that they'd never see him again. His face was pale and, as he approached, Gow saw he was limping.

'Don't you ever stop fiddling with that bloody gun, Gow?' he asked cheerfully. 'And look at them boots. There must be quarts of spit on 'em!'

Gow frowned. 'It wouldnae do you no harm to polish *your* boots.'

Noble stared at his feet. 'They're all wore out,' he said.

'Nor do y'have a crease in your pants, and no blanco on yer webbing.' Gow's eyes glinted as he snatched the rifle from Noble's hand to squint down the barrel. 'Your bundook's dirty, too,' he announced. 'You could plant potatoes in there, mon, and yon foresight's lousy with spiders and cobwebs and dairty filthy rust.'

Noble stared. Gow took his breath away. He was an elemental force, understanding not much beyond a punch in the teeth, and nothing would ever change him. But Noble was a Cockney, supple, tough and moving with the wind because that was how he survived, and nothing would ever change *him* either.

'I'm not looking forward to a hero's death as a prize for me patriotism,' he said.

'Where've you been, anyway?' Gow asked. 'And for why are ye standing there like a wet hen, mon? Get your heid doon.'

Noble shrugged and, pulling a sandbag forward, produced a handful of army biscuits, a white loaf and a tin of bully beef.

'Bully again,' Gow said. 'It's coming oot o' ma ears.'

'Wait, you ungrateful soldier you,' Noble said and from his blouse he began to bring out sweet biscuits and tins of fruit and chocolate. 'Dessert,' he said. 'Will it do?'

Gow stared at Noble. He was still surprised to see him back. 'Aye,' he said grudgingly. 'It'll do.'

Noble knelt awkwardly and as Chouteau reached out for the loaf he pushed his hand away. 'Less o' that, *mon camarade*,' he said. 'I will *donner une partie à chaque homme*. Savvy?'

Chouteau nodded and nudged Angelet. 'Wake up, *mon vieux*,' he said. 'We're going to eat.'

Gow was studying the loaf. 'Where'd you get it, you bluidy scrounger?' he demanded.

'Where you think? I pinched it. There's Robin Hood, Robin Starch and robbin' bastards. I'm one o' *them*.'

'Where did you get it?'

'I saw this feller –'

'You pinched it? Off one of your comrades?'

Noble was unmoved. 'Listen, *mon fils*,' he said, 'he was belting up the road like he'd got ten legs. *You're* still here, fighting off them nasty rotten 'Uns, aren't you? I thought you needed it more'n he did.'

As they began to eat, tearing at the food like famished wolves, Noble glanced round him, suddenly aware how few of them there were. 'Where's all the rest of the fellers?' he asked.

'What fellers?

Noble looked at Gow in disgust. 'Don't say we're on our own,' he said.

'There's enough.'

Noble snorted. 'Trouble with you, Gow,' he said, 'is that you've got the light of bloody glory in your eye.'

Gow's solemn face cracked a little and he nodded to the distance across the canal. 'Them bastards winnae come out o' yon trees till we let 'em,' he said.

He studied Noble, still puzzled. He'd seen plenty like Noble in the last few days. Some of them had conveniently lost their units, some even their rifles. But, though Noble's rifle and his person were a disgrace even to a Territorial, he was still among those present.

'What did ye do in Civvy Street, Noble?' he asked.

'Nothing.'

'Do all right at it?'

Noble had a feeling that Gow, whom he'd always assumed to be a man without humour, was pulling his leg. 'Yeh. Okay,' he said.

'You a religious mon?'

'No. I don't think it took. Why? What are you gettin' at?'

'I was wondering why you didnae bunk while you had the chance.'

Noble frowned. He wasn't sure himself. It had seemed to start from the moment he'd first seen Gow, blinded but still clutching the Bren. As a Londoner, Noble knew the traditions of the Household Brigade, their calm demeanour, the fact that they had registered, exclusive, privately-built faces which came with training, no matter what sort of features a man joined up with. He'd seen battle pictures of them, wearing red coats and stalking from the fray with long slow strides, every man two yards high, shaved, correctly dressed – even the bloodstained bandages they wore neat – a remnant of a company moving unhurriedly past relieving troops in majestic silence, not a single eye moving from some spot up ahead, as though only they knew how to fight battles. Though in the past he'd considered any man who joined them a bloody fool, he'd also occasionally found himself suffering from a secret envy that he wasn't one of them.

It wasn't just that, though, he knew. There was something about Gow that appealed to him. He was the sort who'd salute an officer on the telephone and he could hardly be called dynamic. Those icy eyes of his sometimes looked like a murderer's and his conversation wouldn't have taxed the resources of a trained parrot, while in behaviour he was about as unlike the unprincipled wide boys with whom Noble had surrounded himself in Civvy Street as a racehorse was from a costermonger's moke. He decided it must be his sheer moral guts.

'I dunno, *mon fils*,' he said slowly. 'Thought you'd need someone to look after you. Quartermaster, sort of. I'm no fighting man, old mate. I'm lines of supply troops. So, okay, I'll supply. You'll not go 'ungry while Lije Noble's around.'

'Right.' Gow gestured. 'Well, now get your heid doon before you get hurt.'

Noble gave him a twisted smile and turned round. The back of his trouser legs and his battledress blouse was torn by tiny holes each of which was stained by a pin-prick of blood.

'I *got* hurt,' he said. 'I bin wounded. I'm the most wounded man in the bleedin' British army, I reckon. Seventy or eighty times I got 'it. Up me nostrils, in me ear'ole, up me backside. You'd better start pickin' 'em out before I get blood poison.'

By this time *Vital* was just completing her third trip, and Hatton was on the point of collapse with tiredness.

The sky was empty as he ran down the mole driving a group of soldiers ahead of him but no one expected it to be empty for long and Hough was watching it anxiously, his face grey with fatigue.

'Good show, Hatton,' he shouted. 'How many does that make?'

Hatton consulted the petty officers. 'Nine hundred and sixty-three, sir. Give or take a few.'

'Good God!' Hough sounded startled. 'The bloody ship'll go to the bottom under the sheer weight. Right. Avast boarding.'

As the gangplanks were hauled aboard and *Vital* began to go astern, Hatton found he was unbelievably thankful to be away. Fear was growing in him with his increasing tiredness and he was itching to be back in the safety of England.

Above him on the bridge, the telegraphs clanged and the ship's propellers stopped as *Vital* swung. A paddle-steamer was slipping inside her to take her place and Hough's head was lifted, his eyes on the sky, as they waited for the steamer to clear their stern. Then, while *Vital* still paused between the narrow sandbanks, the man on the point fives, who seemed to have eyes like a hawk's, shouted. 'Stukas, sir! Port quarter!'

The clouds were clearing now, and as Hatton's eyes lifted he could see patches of blue with small moving specks in them. The guns began to go in a crashing chorus that deafened him, and the aeroplanes began to fall out of the sky, one after the other. Vast eruptions of dirty brown water rose round *Vital*. Then, as she picked up speed, the men on her decks crouching with their heads down against the splinters and bullets, Hatton heard the scream of a shell and saw a fountain of water rise from the sea on the ship's starboard side.

'Six-inch,' Hough said calmly. 'Must be that battery near Gravelines. Let's have smoke, Pilot.'

The navigating officer pressed the plunger and, below deck, Lieutenant MacGillicuddy, standing on his iron grating, still worried sick about the troublesome bearing which was beginning to show signs of growing worse, watched the petty officer in charge adjusting the valves that admitted just too much oil to the furnaces and shut off just too much air to allow complete combustion. The glazed peephole which normally showed a white-hot flame was a gloomy blackness as the oil broke down into greasy hydrocarbons that were snatched up by the draught and poured up through the after funnel. MacGillicuddy studied it dispassionately, not even thinking of the possibility that a shell might rip through the side of the ship and send steam as harsh as red-hot iron blowing through the compartment.

The ship was swinging first one way and then the other, heeling crazily under the weight of the men on her deck. A Stuka dropped down behind her and swept overhead, its guns clattering, then every rifle on board went off with the ship's pom-poms. The bomb seemed to lift the old ship from the sea and Hatton's breath came out in an explosive gasp of fear, but as the column of water the bomb had thrown up collapsed across the deck he felt *Vital* shake herself like a terrier emerging from a pond and continue to pick up speed.

'I wish I'd never come,' some humorist wailed. 'I'm always seasick going to Margate.'

As the bomber pulled up, a patrolling Spitfire from England, at the very range of its petrol, caught it and the ship was pandemonium.

'He's got him! He's on fire!'

A long stream of dark smoke was pouring out of the Stuka now to mingle with the black coil from *Vital*'s funnel, and the aeroplane was racing up the port side of the ship, settling lower and lower all the time. It was only a few hundred yards away, flying below the smoke as though sheltering beneath it, and Hatton could see the pilot struggling with the hood. Then it hit the sea in an enormous splash and as the spray cleared, they saw its tail sticking up, then slowly, as they cheered, it sank out of sight.

'We'll not dally to look for survivors,' Hough said. 'And you can go easy on the wheel now, Quartermaster. We're wearing out the sea.'

His nostrils full of the stink of the belching black smoke, Hatton was still pushing men away in odd corners when MacGillicuddy passed him, thrusting his way through the soldiers.

'That bloody bearing's gone,' he snarled.

The sound of the shell seemed to start miles away over a group of woods to the east. It came from nowhere, starting as a whisper and increasing until it filled the whole air.

'Down,' Scharroo said as he pulled Marie-Josephine towards the ditch.

They were passing what appeared to be the British army head-quarters, situated in a château just behind La Panne. A transit camp had been set up in the surrounding woods and there were soldiers everywhere, melting away as the shell approached. Lorries and pennanted staff cars were parked down the gravelled drive and round the ornamental pond that fronted the building, but they were empty now, their doors still swinging as the drivers bolted for cover. A French horse artillery regiment heading north began to scatter in confusion, charging away in a disorderly line, shouting and yelling, the drivers lashing at the horses, the gunners frantically clinging to the limbers, ammunition trailers, mess carts and waggons. As they tried to swing off the road, one of the horses went down with a crash and they saw it sliding along the ground, its eyes bulging with terror as it was dragged along by the violent forward motion of its companions and the weight of the gun. Then the whole lot piled up in a ghastly, floundering, screaming heap of men, animals, spinning wheels and rolling, bouncing mess kits, just as the shell arrived.

Scharroo had just lifted his head when it exploded in the orna-mental pond with a crash that seemed to strip the flesh from his body. Blocks of stonework flew into the air with a huge spray of water that drifted away on the breeze as the clods of earth and the dead carp whacked down on the lawns and the gravel drive.

Immediately the whole area began to boil again like an ants' nest stirred by a stick. Soldiers appeared from holes in the ground and from behind walls and trees. Abandoned vehicles were re-occupied and began to get under way once more. Limping French artillerymen were trying to drag their horses to their feet and a man hurried past on the road, leading a string of saddled chargers. A military policeman shouted hopelessly at him in English to turn them loose but the Frenchman ignored him and joined the vast trek towards the coast.

The whole countryside had come alive again where a moment before it had seemed empty, and the flow of moving figures re-started, heading like lemmings towards the sea, tramping un-speakingly past the pink and white of the apple blossom and the green of new corn, dragging the last lurching stragglers with them. Some of them were wheeling their wounded in barrows, pride in their unit not allowing them to abandon them, the sergeants chivvying them like sheepdogs. 'Keep the step, lads! It'll help! Keep the step!' Despatch riders so tired they looked like zombies drove up and down the columns and, alongside the road, a group of Frenchmen taking up positions for a final stand were digging slit trenches and covering them with branches from a nearby garden to hide them from the sky.

A group of British cavalrymen appeared from a car park where they'd been dumping soft-skinned vehicles. They formed up in the road and began to march towards La Panne, swinging their arms, in perfect step, their heads up, their kit in excellent con-dition. They looked tired but they were well-disciplined, and a straggler, brushed aside as they tramped past, looked up. 'The 'Dirty Dozen,' he jeered. 'Cavalry: The Manure Collectors.'

A sergeant turned on him at once. 'We're the Supple Twelfth, my lad,' he rapped. 'Quicksilver, and don't you forget it!'

Military police were examining documents but Scharroo's newspaper pass got him through and he was able to vouch that Marie-Josephine had relations in La Panne.

'She says they live in the Rue Isabey and she's trying to reach them,' he said.

'She'll be bloody lucky, mate,' the military policeman muttered.

La Panne had been a favourite haunt of painters for years, a pretty place of parks and gardens, but it had been heavily raided. Houses were burning and there were charred wrecks of cars about the streets, scorching the trees and bushes. A few civilians were in their doorways, jeering at the soldiers, but there were not many and it seemed to Scharroo that he and the girl stood out like sore thumbs.

Dishevelled, exhausted men were resting on the sidewalks among the abandoned vehicles, and they eyed Marie-Josephine curiously, a few even managing a whistle. The sky was full of smoke and the sound of aeroplanes, but they all seemed to be over Dunkirk, and La Panne for the moment was quiet.

Using his press pass, Scharroo got himself inside one of the beach headquarters where a colonel in a gaily coloured forage cap was on the telephone to Dover on a line which was still amazingly uncut.

'Where are our ships?' he was demanding angrily.

'You've got them.' Scharroo could hear the answer quite plainly.

'Have we?' The colonel snorted. 'You'd better come and look for yourself. *I* haven't seen 'em.'

The shelling began to increase and they had to run for shelter. Then Marie-Josephine remembered that the Rue Isabey was on the western outskirts of the town and, rather than go back through the crowded streets, they took a road running behind the sand dunes where there were small hotels and boarding houses, many of them still closed from the winter, their shutters fastened and barred. On the sand in front, thousands of men waited. A few of the more energetic were scratching holes where they could shelter. Thousands more stood in the water cooling their aching feet, their boots in their hands. Two men, preferring not to wait for the navy, had collected barrels and were lashing planks to them to make a raft, absorbed in their task and indifferent to the danger. Nearby an officer, quite drunk, sat in a foxhole, holding an empty wine bottle. Down the beach another, dressed only in shirt and pants, was trying to drag a rubber dinghy ashore for a wounded sergeant whom four of his men were carrying in a blanket.

Indifferent to the noise, soldiers were wrapped in overcoats and even looted eiderdowns, snatching the first real sleep they'd had for three weeks, but queues had also formed near the water's edge in long snake-like columns, and in the shallows tows of whalers and lifeboats were gathering. In front of them, by a Bofors gun, a subaltern was scanning the sky with a pair of glasses and the colonel in the gaily coloured fore-and-aft cap was now arguing with a Territorial officer who was climbing out of a car that he'd driven on to the sand.

'Who's the beachmaster here?' he was demanding.

'You're lucky,' the colonel said. 'I am.'

The Territorial jerked a hand at the car. There were tennis rackets, golf clubs and two trunks in the back seat. 'How do I get that aboard?' he asked.

The colonel gave a bark of laughter. 'You don't. Except over my dead body.'

Where the man in the gay cap worked, the beach was impeccably controlled, and there was even a military policeman directing traffic, but in other parts the crowd seemed to mill about as it pleased.

A stray shell whined over and dropped fifty yards away. The lines dropped flat but the colonel remained upright and didn't even stop directing the columns of men. Then the air seemed to fill with sound again and the lines round the beachmaster began to melt away. He glanced up at the sky and began to walk quickly towards the dunes, not attempting to duck or hurry. Men ran past him, but others simply dropped to the sand and lay on their backs, popping away with their rifles, while others plunged neck-deep in the sea for shelter and stood with only their heads and their helmets above the surface, looking murderously round for something to shoot at.

The howl of engines increased as Scharroo flung Marie-Josephine down and fell on top of her. A bomb landed nearby and he caught the sulphurous smell of the explosive and heard the clatter of tiles landing on the promenade. The air was full of sand and grit and, as he watched, a big ship – the biggest he'd seen so far – was hit amidships and an enormous cloud of smoke burst upwards.

Then three black-painted aeroplanes began to scream along the beach, their guns going, the bullets throwing up the sand in a rippling wave. Their bombs exploded with shattering force but there were few casualties and Scharroo realized that the sand was cushioning the effects of the explosions. Only here and there groups of men ran towards a silent figure caught by the machine guns.

As the din stopped, he became aware of Marie-Josephine moving beneath him. She was face-down, her hair among the marram grass, her head beneath his shoulder, and as she turned over he was aware of the feel of her all the way down his body. Her foot was hard against his ankle, one shin against the muscle of his calf, one knee like a small wedge in the side of his leg. The inside of her thigh was against his and she was staring up at him with unblinking black eyes.

He pulled himself to his feet quickly. 'I guess we should go look for your relations,' he said.

They moved back from the beach into the streets. Food was in everybody's mind and men were wandering among the abandoned vehicles and into gardens and ruined houses in search of something to eat or somewhere to sleep.

They found the Rue Isabey at last and the house they were seeking, a small neat place with a garden and trees. It seemed to be full of men in khaki. Scharroo called to a soldier sitting on the lawn shaving in the sunshine, apparently impervious to the destruction about him. 'Where are the owners?' he asked.

'Owners?' The soldier's head turned. 'I've not seen any owners.'

The bombing Scharroo and Marie-Josephine had watched was the first German reaction to the clearing of the sky and the change of wind.

Field telephones shrilled on the aerodromes the Luftwaffe occupied. Messerschmitt 109s went up to provide top cover against the R.A.F.'s spoiling attacks while 110s and Junkers 87s and 88s were bombed up frantically in the afternoon sunshine and went roaring across the fields, their propeller washes flattening the grass, their crews still adjusting their harness as they lifted into the air.

But not Stoos.

He had reached a point of apoplexy by this time. 'You said this afternoon,' he was screaming at Oberfeldwebel Hamcke.

'Herr Leutnant – ' Hamcke was nearly out of his mind with weariness ' – it's not possible!'

'It *must* be possible! It *must* be done!'

'Sir, if I had another dozen men I couldn't do it before to-morrow now. Hauptmann Dodtzenrodt came back with his petrol tanks punctured and took the men off the job. *He* wants to be in the air, too, Herr Leutnant!'

Stoos saw the possibility of the decoration he'd set his heart on fading rapidly. The war couldn't last much longer. The French were on their knees and the British were being cut to shreds. 'I'll see the captain,' he snarled and, spinning on his heel, stalked off towards the tent that did duty as squadron office.

Hamcke stared after him. 'That man's mad,' he said. 'Stark staring mad! He seems to think they can't win the war without him.'

It was beginning to seem at Dover that they might, however, and the Admiralty had decided that the senior naval officer at Dunkirk was in need of someone offshore to help him.

'The wind's changed, sir,' the staff officer, operations, reported. 'The smoke's blowing the other way and the Germans are giving it all they've got. *Clan MacAlister*'s been hit and she's on fire. They think they'll have to abandon.'

The admiral chewed at his spectacles, then he moved to the fragile iron balcony that jutted from the old casemate in the cliff. The lowering sun was filling the day with golden light, and below him he could see the ships arriving and departing, and the movement of vehicles towards the harbour. It was possible to hear the crash of bombs from across the Channel coming as dull thuds that pressed on the ear.

'They've stepped up the air attacks,' he said.

'That's what the signals say, sir.'

It required no signals for Tremenheere to know that the air attacks had been stepped up. There had been one in operation when they'd arrived and from then on they'd seemed to come every fifteen minutes with ten-minute intervals between them.

'Like bloody clockwork,' Clark observed wonderingly as they headed towards the harbour yet again.

'If the bastards hit us, we'll go up like a bomb,' Smith, the young stoker said nervously. 'All them cans of petrol we've got on board.'

Didcot glanced at Clark. 'Think they'd give us survivors' leave, Nobby?' he asked.

Clark's head turned. 'What for?'

'Well, if we came through that lot, we'd have bloody well survived, wouldn't we?'

Clark shrugged. 'Me,' he said. 'I'm still worrying about me leave from *Bittern*.'

They could see the outline of the town, a desolate huddle of ruined buildings and the stark bones of houses. By the harbour entrance, there were the remains of ships, half-submerged, some of them still burning, but despite the destruction destroyers were still loading against the mole along which, in incredible order, long queues of men plodded, shuffling forward towards safety.

Outside the entrance, minesweepers were at work and all around them on the oily water, small boats moved among the looming bulks of bigger ships. Out at sea, a big vessel was burning, the flames clawing away at her insides and showing through her ports and the holes in her sloping decks. She'd settled low in the water since they'd seen her hit, the sea around her a litter of wreckage, smashed lifeboats, lifebelts, ropes, planks and boxes.

As they went in to the pier they could see the masses of men still on the beaches, stretching to the water's edge, tens of thousands of them, waiting in huddled groups or organized queues that ended in lines of bobbing heads among the surf.

The pier cleared for a moment and Clark took *Athelstan* in quickly. As soon as she bumped alongside, men began to scramble aboard squatting down where they could.

'Didn't you know there was a war on?' one of them asked. 'Where you been?'

'This ain't the first evacuation *I*'ve been in, mate,' Clark retorted. 'What have you lot been doin' to allow a thing like this to happen?'

Some of the soldiers seemed to think the war was over and one or two had clearly given up trying. The rest cheerfully let off their rifles at every plane that came over. The guns started to bang again but Clark seemed impervious to danger.

'How are we getting on?' he demanded.

'Seventy-five below. Sixty-seven on deck.'

Clark turned. 'Jesus, *how many*?' He swung round and pushed the soldiers off the ladder. 'Tell Smudger to handle them gears gently, Alban. She'll be a bit tender.'

They were just going astern beyond the end of the mole when

both engines inexplicably died and Clark swung round, his face alarmed, as Tremenheere dived for the engine room hatch. Smith, the young stoker, was pressing the self-starters in a panic, his eyes bulging with anxiety. Tremenheere thrust him aside and moved between the engines, checking oil pressures and fuel.

As they drifted, a midshipman in charge of another boat, who looked about fifteen, shrieked at them in a high boyish voice and hurled a rope. More by luck than judgment it fell across the deck and Clark made it fast, and a few moments later they were bumping alongside a drifter. As the deck emptied, Clark pushed his head into the cabin. 'All right, you lot. Your turn now.'

A petty officer who was counting the soldiers stared. 'Christ, where did you shove 'em all?' he demanded.

As the last man departed and they began to throw their kit after them, Didcot glanced at the sky.

'Wind's changed,' he observed. 'Dive bombers'll be back.'

The black pall was drifting inshore now, exposing two big paddle-steamers on one side of the mole and two destroyers, two trawlers and a personnel ship on the other. Beyond them there were two more destroyers flying the French tricolour.

'Here they come!' Didcot shouted, and aeroplanes appeared from nowhere, hundreds of them, it seemed, stepped up in flights one above another. *Athelstan*'s engines were still refusing to start, and Tremenheere had just come on deck with the news when a bomb hit the nearest paddle-steamer, and a second hit the mole to send huge lumps of concrete whirring into the water. The paddle-steamer was already listing towards the jetty and men were scrambling over her rails, stretcher cases being hurried towards the other ships without even stopping. Two trawlers were in a sinking condition and one of the French destroyers was on fire, burning so fiercely they could feel the heat across the water. She cleared the harbour under tow, only to sink just beyond the entrance. The second paddle-steamer was just slipping her lines when she too was hit, and sickened by the destruction, Tremenheere saw men stepping into the water to swim ashore. Then, as the drifter on which they'd loaded their passengers moved forward to pick up survivors, another bomb exploded under her stern and she also turned turtle and sank.

As the news of the disaster filtered into the town, Sievewright was following a path alongside a dyke, taking great care to do no damage to standing crops as his Scout training had taught him. Up ahead, he could see the burning pyre of Dunkirk, the dying sun touching the columns of smoke with wisps of blood.

As he was forced back to the road he passed a wrecked house where a dog ran out and jumped up at him. It was only a puppy and seemed eager to make friends.

'Go away, boy,' he said sternly, but the dog ignored the command and, tiring of trying to grab his sleeve, it fell in and trotted happily along behind him. It didn't please him because, like most of the sentimental British, he'd released starving cattle and horses and household pets which had been forgotten by their owners in the panic, and he felt it was taking this one away from its home. Since it ignored him, however, he could do nothing but accept it and be relieved that darkness was approaching.

The darkness that so relieved Sievewright brought worry to Lance-Corporal Gow. As the mist began to curl thick and milky over the canal he was engaged with a penknife and a needle from a 'housewife' in picking the last of the shotgun pellets out of Noble's backside. They were in a cattle shed just behind the bank of the canal, and the work was slow and painful because the carefully-guarded candle gave only a fitful light and Gow had to keep stopping to let Noble recover a little.

Chouteau seemed highly amused. '*Le derrière,*' he observed, '*C'est comme une pelote à épingles.* It is like the cushion of the pins.'

As they bent again, a soldier appeared in the doorway. 'It's the Germans, Jock,' he said.

'Oh, bloody charming,' Noble said. 'And me with me pants down.'

Gow signed him to silence. 'See 'em?' he asked.

The soldier shook his head. 'No. But I heard 'em talking. There was an old boat. I noticed it.'

'Are they coming now?'

'No. It's gone quiet. I think they're waiting till morning.'

Gow frowned. 'They'll get a bluidy surprise, choose when,' he said. He slapped Noble's bare rump. 'Hoist 'em up, laddie. There's trouble.'

Silently, moving cautiously, they had just erected the Bren behind the canal where they could get maximum cover when Angelet appeared. '*Les Allemands?*' he whispered eagerly. 'The Germans?'

'By the bluidy hundred,' Gow murmured.

Noble was lying on the bank, staring nervously into the darkness. War, he felt, was for regular soldiers like Gow and for volunteers who *expected* to be exported overseas. He was a militiaman – and an unwilling one at that – who had only submitted to the call to serve his king because he hadn't realized it also included King's Regulations, Army Council Instructions, regimental orders, company details, commissioned officers, military police, all armed sentries, cooks, canteen managers – and Lance-Corporal Gow. In allowing himself to be caught, he'd made the greatest mistake of his life.

'What do we do now?' he breathed.

Gow pushed a haversack of loose ammunition at him with the spare magazines for the Bren.

'Get filling them,' he breathed.

Noble frowned. 'You know what, *mon fils*,' he whispered. 'I reckon you'll end up as a sodden sergeant-major.'

Gow stared down at him calmly. 'Aye,' he murmured. 'I will.'

The admiral at Dover was also beginning to think about the next morning. A message had just arrived to the effect that Dunkirk harbour was blocked by damaged vessels and that all evacuation from then on would have to take place from the beaches.

There was also another signal on his desk from the Admiralty. '*The rate of loss can no longer be accepted,*' it said. '*All H, I, and J class destroyers must be released.*'

The admiral frowned, unwilling to agree despite the heavy losses of the day. Three destroyers had been sunk and six were out of action, to say nothing of escort vessels, auxiliaries, minesweepers and an armed escort vessel.

'And of course, sir, *Vital*,' the S.O.O. pointed out.

It was Hatton who was sent to the castle with Hough's report and, with things as they were in the town, there were no taxis.

Several times during the return journey he'd found himself thinking of Nora Hart. In its tiredness, his mind was obsessed by the way she'd kissed him and, though he knew it was only a spontaneous gesture springing from the emotion of the moment, he couldn't throw it off. He also wasn't sure that he had the courage to follow it up, however, because she probably still needed a little time to adjust to the fact that Barry Hatton was in circulation again.

The same lieutenant he'd spoken to on his last visit to the castle was still at his desk in the corridor but by now he looked as though he'd been there for ever.

'Who?' he said, and as Hatton stopped before him it was clear he'd quite forgotten his face. '*Vital?* Hang on a minute!' He vanished through a door and when he returned he held it open for Hatton to enter. In his newness to the Service Hatton had no idea of the official title of the man he saw but he was wearing the four rings of a captain.

The captain looked up. He was clearly too old for sea service, but there was a look about him that indicated he'd seen plenty in his time.

'*Vital?*' he said, standing up. 'What's the trouble with her?'

'Shaft-bearing overheating, sir.' Hatton held out Hough's report. 'It's all there.'

The captain took the paper and read it silently, then he laid it down on the desk.

'It's not good enough,' he said.

The fact that not very long before he'd been chasing frightened soldiers through the streets of Dunkirk trying to fill *Vital*, while the captain had been sitting at his desk, seemed to Hatton to demand a protest.

The captain's expression softened. 'How much sea service have you seen, Hatton?' he asked.

'Not much, sir. This is my first ship since I was commissioned. She's a good ship, though, sir. She did well and it was difficult rounding up the men.'

The captain's head jerked round. 'Are you *still* having to round them up?' He pressed a button on his desk and spoke into a microphone. 'I have a chap here, sir, who's just come back. He reports he had to round up men to fill his ship. Would you like to see him?'

The loud-speaker crackled and the captain turned to Hatton. 'Come with me,' he said.

Hatton followed him along the corridor to another office and a man with the rings of a vice-admiral standing by the desk turned as he entered.

'Did you go ashore?' he said without preamble.

'Yes, sir, I did.'

'Tell me about it.'

Hatton did his best, describing the streets and the absence of soldiers, and the way he and his men had constantly had to go into the town.

The admiral looked at the captain. 'It seems to me,' he said, 'that ships' captains don't rate highly enough.'

As Hatton left, the admiral paced up and down once or twice. He knew it was the First Sea Lord's primary duty to protect the sea lanes round Britain and that the destroyers which were vital to that had suffered severe losses. Yet 47,000 men had been brought back to England that day and, without the big modern vessels he was proposing to withdraw, no more than 17,000 could be lifted in the next twenty-four hours.

'We must have the H, I and J ships back,' he said.

THURSDAY, 30 MAY

As Wednesday changed into Thursday, the last of the B.E.F. and what remained of the French First Army arrived inside the Dunkirk perimeter. It was well known at Dover that it couldn't be held for long but in front of it there was no cover whatsoever and a water obstacle every quarter of a mile, as well as flooded fields that formed a daunting tank trap. Nevertheless, a telephone message from La Panne begging for ships raised yet another of those interminable decisions the admiral was having to make. He had calculated that with the fifteen small destroyers he had left, the personnel vessels and the small craft, he ought to be able to lift 43,000 men during the day. But the estimates he'd been given seemed to make it essential that the number should be 55,000 and he still didn't know if the mole was functioning after the previous day's disasters. There had been no bombing since dusk the previous evening, however, and the weather had improved. With a new shift in the wind the smoke cloud from the oil tanks was once more covering the anchorage and fresh small craft were beginning to arrive off the beaches.

It was the sway of the boat that told Kenny Pepper that *Daisy* was at last at sea.

Cautiously he opened the forepeak and put his head out. He couldn't see much and it was raining in a light shower that wet his face. Thinking he was looking in the wrong direction, he turned but, as he did so, he heard the thump of a rubber boot on the deck behind him and was lifted bodily from the forepeak by his collar. His legs were cramped and as he was set on his feet he collapsed to the deck. Looking up, he saw Ernie Williams staring down at him.

'What the bloody hell are *you* doing here?' he said.

'I'm coming with you,' Kenny announced.

Ernie hauled him with dragging feet along the deck to the wheelhouse. Gilbert Williams was holding the wheel. His reaction was exactly the same as his brother's. 'What the bloody hell are *you* doing here?' he demanded.

Kenny repeated his decision. 'I'm coming with you.'

While they were talking, Brundrett climbed out of the engine room and, as he moved forward, his white fleshy body seemed to glow in the darkness. In the faint light from the compass, he looked worried.

'That pump's giving trouble again —' he began. Then he saw Kenny. 'What the bloody hell are *you* doing here?' he asked.

Kenny told him.

Brundrett stared at the two Williamses, then he licked his lips. 'We can't take him with us,' he said.

'Well, we can't chuck him overboard,' Ernie pointed out.

'We'll have to turn back.'

Gilbert's brows went down. 'For Christ's sake,' he said, his voice rising at once to an angry shout. 'After they've fixed the engine? After wasting all that time with it stripped?'

Brundrett licked his lips again. 'The pump's still playing up.'

Gilbert glared. 'Then it'll bloody well have to play up,' he yelled, and Kenny felt at home in the familiarity of raised voices.

As Brundrett turned away, Gilbert stared again at Kenny. 'Think we can put him aboard something going the other way?' he asked.

Ernie looked worried. 'They'll never stop,' he said.

'There's deck boys on the ferries,' Kenny pointed out.

'No, there ain't. They've been took off.'

'Oh!' Kenny hadn't considered that possibility. 'I'll do the cooking,' he offered.

There was a moment's silence. Brundrett's dishes were noted for their absence of taste while Kenny, the only child of a doting widowed mother, had been taught how to make the delicacies he enjoyed.

Ernie looked at his brother. 'He's better than bloody Brundrett,' he said.

Gilbert gnawed at his lower lip, silent for a moment, then he looked about him as though hoping to see the solution to the problem somewhere on the surface of the sea.

'How about bacon and eggs?' he asked.

Kenny grinned. 'Got some eggs?' he asked.

Gilbert stared at him then he grinned, too. 'I'll have four,' he said.

By this time the flames at Dunkirk were so bright they actually removed some of the confusion, but by now Tremenheere was tired to the point of feeling sick and all the thoughts of putting Nell Noone behind him had gone from his mind. At that moment, he'd have been very happy to have been in bed with her and clutching her plump warm body to his.

His brain reeled with the crash of explosions and just outside the harbour the sea was full of men swimming and shouting in the dark where a ship had sunk. Destroyers were picking them up and, in the light of the flames, he felt sure *Athelstan* could be seen clearly by the aeroplanes droning overhead.

He had found water in the carburettors and it had taken him until dark to get the starboard engine going again. Since then they'd been yanking men aboard as fast as they could grab them, pulling till their arms ached and ferrying them to the destroyers, to push them up the scrambling nets until they were drenched with the water that dropped back from their saturated clothing. When they'd emptied all the petrol from the cans they carried they'd decided to head back to Dover and had been on the point of leaving when they'd run into a small cutter drifting in the dark. Going aboard to see if there were wounded below deck, they'd found more full cans in the cabin and had decided to carry on a little longer.

'*Athelstan*'s a big boat,' Clark had said proudly. 'And we've still one engine.'

As they were heading for shore again, however, the thump of the exhaust stopped once more. It happened during a lull in the bombing, and it was eerie and ominous in the silence to be able to hear the putt-putt of other engines and the distant calls of men on the beach.

Didcot leaned over the stern. 'It's a feller,' he said. Peering with him, Tremenheere could just make out a khaki greatcoat and a white bloodless hand protruding from the sleeve.

'Want me to go in after him?' Didcot suggested.

Clark joined them and stared at the water. It was scummy with floating oil. 'Don't be daft, lad,' he said.

While they were wondering what to do, an R.A.F. launch with a naval officer aboard came alongside. 'Go to La Panne,' the officer yelled. 'There are hundreds waiting there.'

'We're not going nowhere, me dear,' Tremenheere yelled back. 'We've got a stiff round the propeller.'

The naval man frowned. 'How many crew do you have?' he asked.

'Four,' Clark shouted. 'Two seaman, two stokers.'

'Right. Let's have one of each. There's a big fishing boat over here with nobody in it.'

The launch moved away with Clark and Smith, to shouts of 'Hope you get your leave, Nobby,' from Didcot. Tremenheere stared after it with a frown, suddenly aware how Clark's experience of war had helped.

'Bloody cheek,' he said nervously. 'And with Jerry coming back, too!'

The thud of the explosions could be heard quite plainly at Outreux where Stoos was still existing in a world of seething frustration. They were responsible, in fact, for bringing him to wakefulness.

He lay for a moment in his blankets, staring with wide-open eyes at the lightening sky beyond the canvas roof of his tent. Then he turned quickly and saw the other beds were empty, their blankets rumpled and draped to the floor.

He sat up with a jerk, aware that his companions had been called for flying and had left without disturbing him. Furiously he swung his legs from the bed and, dragging his clothes on, crossed to the mess-tent. He was in such a hurry he scalded his tongue with coffee, then, cramming bread and good French butter into his mouth, he set off across the field in the dawn light.

A Stuka was standing outside the hangar, its nose towards him, the mechanics screwing the panels into place over the engine. Oberfeldwebel Hamcke was just coming round the tail in the half-light and Stoos grinned at him.

'You did it,' he said.

Hamcke was almost out on his feet with lack of sleep. 'This is 8726, Herr Leutnant,' he said. 'Hauptmann Dodtzenrodt's machine.'

Stoos stared at the aeroplane, his face going red, then his eyes narrowed and his head went down. 'Why hasn't 6980 been brought out?' he snarled.

'Herr Leutnant – '

Stoos's temper, held tight through several days of frustration, boiled over in a shout. 'You're a lout and a slacker!'

Hamcke's eyebrows went down. Sleeplessness and overwork had driven him to the point of hysteria. 'And you're off you're rocker,' he shouted back.

Stoos glared, his eyebrows working, his face flushing darkly with rage, then his arm swung back and, as he lashed out, Hamcke reeled away, spun on his heels and sat down in the dewy grass.

'Oh, Christ,' one of the mechanics said. 'He's hit the sod!'

As Hamcke climbed slowly to his feet, Stoos stared at him, his heart suddenly cold inside his chest as he realized the enormity of what he'd done.

Hamcke straightened up, holding his jaw, 'You god-damned fool, Herr Leutnant,' he said in a low voice.

Then Stoos became aware of Hauptmann Dodtzenrodt behind him, his boots wet with dew. He stiffened and the mechanics working over 8726 quickly bent their heads to the engine. Stoos's mouth worked. There was nothing he could say. Nothing at all.

Dodtzenrodt stared at him coldly. 'I saw exactly what happened, Stoos,' he said. 'You'd better consider yourself under arrest.'

As Dodtzenrodt turned away, Stoos remained standing stiffly, his hands at his side. For a moment, his jaw moved and his eyes glittered, then he came to life and began to walk back towards his tent, his legs moving stiffly as though he were a puppet.

Hamcke watched him go. 'The silly stupid bastard,' he said. 'If he'd only waited! I was going to tell him his machine was ready.'

Lije Noble was with his girl.

From the way she was eyeing him he could see she was in a hurry to get at him and his tongue moved over his lips at the thought. The fact that she was the wife of a sergeant made it all the more enjoyable.

He'd met her in a pub the night he'd arrived in Shrewsbury and, catching her eyes on him, he'd slipped her a message written on the inside of an empty cigarette packet. At that time, he hadn't known her husband had been in the Middle East for eighteen months and that she was dying for a man. She had a neat home and a big bed and throughout his stay in Shrewsbury he'd gone to see her regularly. She was Irish, red-headed and green-eyed to go with her passionate nature; big-breasted, flat-stomached and with the longest, slenderest, most shapely white thighs Lije Noble had ever run his hand along. She was sitting on the edge of the bed now, starkers and looking dead smashing; and she was just yanking off her second shoe, which was the last vestige of clothing on her body, when the picture faded and he realized he'd been dreaming.

'Bugger,' he said.

Then he realized that his backside hurt and it was almost daylight and that the clunk of the shoe hitting the linoleum had come, in fact, from the thump of wood against wood.

He sat up with a jerk, horrified that he'd been asleep, and glanced at his watch. It was a special one he'd 'won' early in the retreat and, with dials for seconds, minutes, hours, days, weeks, it looked like the instrument panel of a Wellington bomber. To his relief he saw he hadn't been asleep more than a few moments and he pulled himself together quickly, looking round sheepishly to see if Gow was watching. In the cold dark of a pre-dawn he was hungry, sleepy, dirty and unenthusiastic.

As he cocked his head, listening, he could hear the slap of water and he looked up quickly. There was no wind and the canal had been silent all night. Then he heard the clunk of wood again and, as his heart pounded with fear, he turned and scrambled down the bank.

'The bastards are moving, Gow,' he said.

Gow sat up. 'Right, mon,' he murmured. 'Tell 'em I'm coming.'

He nudged Chouteau and Angelet into wakefulness and began to thrust Bren magazines at them. Then, moving cautiously, he slid forward to where the gun had been erected and listened to the thump of wood that Noble had heard.

'It's the boat,' Noble whispered. 'They're ferrying the bastards across.'

Gow sniffed the air and laid the spare magazines handy, his movements unwasteful in a way that indicated experience.

'You ever done any fighting before, Gow?' Noble asked.

'Aye. In Palestine.'

'What was it like?'

'Grub was awful. All that Arab stuff.' Gow fished out his notebook and Noble frowned.

'What the 'ell do you keep writing in that thing?' he asked. 'Your will?'

Gow gave him a disapproving stare. 'I'm absent from ma regiment,' he pointed out coldly. 'I'm keeping a record of where I've been.'

They waited silently, Noble wondering if the Germans could hear his heart beating. As the light increased, he realized he could see the opposite bank of the canal and held his breath.

Angelet appeared, moving cautiously. *'Mon sergent,'* he said. *'Il y en a déjà une douzaine à ce côté –'*

Chouteau grinned. 'He say many,' he translated softly. 'Across. *A ce moment.* Already.'

'And a whole batch in the field there,' Noble whispered, gesturing at the thinning mist. 'See 'em?'

Gow nodded. 'We get this lot on this side first,' he suggested. 'Then the boat. Then yon lot. Okay?' He glanced at Chouteau. 'Got it?'

'Mais oui. Bien sûr.'

'Okay, then, let the bastards have it!'

The harsh sound of the Bren opening up tore the silence to shreds. It fired along the bank at the group of Germans on the northern side of the canal and Noble saw blurred figures spinning away. There was a splash as one of them made an agonized backward arc with his body and fell into the water. Then Angelet stood up and pulled the pin from one of the Mills bombs to lob it gently forward. It dropped in the boat among the men pulling frantically back to their own side of the canal. In their panic, and with the din of the Bren firing they didn't notice it. The explosion tore the boat apart, and Noble saw a steel helmet whirr twenty feet up into the air.

Angelet's second bomb finished off a group by the water's edge.

One man had dragged himself to the bank and was struggling up the slope like a crushed beetle, screaming, and as the Bren continued to fire in short careful bursts another man fell on top of him and they both splashed out of sight and didn't reappear. There was only one left on their own side of the bank and as he tried to run Angelet contemptuously killed him with a spade.

Everything was silent again and their nostrils were full of the smell of cordite. Angelet pushed the body from his feet and, standing motionless on the backward slope of the bank, he seemed at first to be crying. Then they realized he was singing softly and Noble gaped as he grasped what the song was.

'*Allons, enfants de la Patrie* – !'

The small cracked voice sounded strange in the vast emptiness of flat fields, but then it seemed to gain confidence and Angelet lifted his head and his voice grew stronger. Eventually, he was standing bolt upright and shouting the anthem at the top of his voice. It was quite spontaneous, springing from the emotions surging through his narrow chest.

'*Marchons, marchons* –!'

The *Marseillaise* was always invigorating, triumphant, impelling, and its clarion call made the blood beat faster. Chouteau's deep voice joined the boy's pipe. Then Noble and another man joined in, even though they didn't know the words, while Gow watched in still, respectful silence. There was only one national anthem Gow ever sang.

As Angelet finished, his head turned. It was almost as though he'd been in a trance of patriotism and, as he realized Chouteau and Noble had been singing with him, he blushed and they saw tears in his eyes.

He shuddered. '*Je veux* – ' he began but Noble gave him a little push, more moved than he'd ever have admitted.

'It's all right, *mon fils*,' he said. 'We got the message.'

In the distance they could hear the thump of bombs and the thudding of guns and the nearer rattling of machine-gun fire, but in their immediate vicinity there was silence. Gow began to pick up the empty magazines. Chouteau worked the bolt of his rifle and pushed another round into the breech. Noble shifted uncomfortably because his behind was hurting. No one spoke, all of them embarrassed by their own emotions.

Angelet stared at them and, as he turned and blew his nose

loudly, Chouteau watched him with eyes that were full of the ancient wisdom of war. He glanced at Gow. *'C'est un grand guerrier, ça,'* he said quietly.

Gow looked puzzled and Chouteau shrugged. *'Soldat,'* he said. *'Il a décidé de se faire tuer en brave, en héros.'* He saw that Gow didn't understand. 'He wish to die like hero,' he said. 'He is much brave, that one.'

Gow nodded.

'Il travaillait dans un grand magasin à Marseille, vous comprenez. Il vendait les vêtements aux dames. Les soutien-gorge. Les culottes de femme.' Chouteau gestured in front of his chest and round his loins. 'He sell to women. This.' His hand waved. 'And k-nickers, you understand.' If Gow had been a laughing type he might have laughed at the Frenchman's expression. Instead he managed a small stiff smile.

'Mais après quatre jours en face de l'ennemi, il a pris son courage à deux mains. He wishes to kill Germans.'

Gow glanced at the boy again and Chouteau grinned. *'Il s'appelle Angelet,'* he went on. *'Angelet. Petit ange.* Litt-el Ayngel. He is called Little Angel. *That* one! *C'est drôle, ça, n'est-ce pas?'*

As Gow and his group fought their little battle along the canal, the evacuation was beginning to get into its swing again. The whole thing was a colossal improvisation. Each destroyer had only two rowing boats, each of which could carry a mere twelve men, and it was taking hours to fill them; but now the powered small vessels were beginning to arrive from England – every kind imaginable, from week-end launches off the upper reaches of the Thames to oyster dredgers and ferry boats from the Isle of Wight, Gosport, Poole and beyond. By the grace of God, the weather continued to hold and the Channel, that most notorious of passages, that scourge of small boats where the tides from the east met the tides from the north in a confusion of broken water in the narrow seas between Dover and Calais, remained calm. It was like a millpond with hardly a ripple on the surface to impede the work of rescue, and only inshore where the waves rolled up on the sand was there any lift to complicate the manoeuvring.

Nevertheless, some men, preferring not to wait, were swimming off the beaches clutching pieces of timber, doors, oars, even inflated inner tubes they'd salvaged from abandoned vehicles. Someone had also had the bright idea of building piers. Three-tonners had been driven as far into the sea as possible at low tide, and behind them a long line of ammunition waggons, Bren gun carriers, anything that was available and would still move, had been wedged nose to stern. Immediately, despite the bombing, engineers scouring the beaches, rounded up planks and ropes and wire and joined the vehicles together in a makeshift jetty so that men could scramble along them and small boats come alongside without danger of going aground.

Some soldiers, their places far back in the queues, were sun-bathing. Others had disintegrated morally and, like all men whose characters crumble in war, they had done so at terrifying speed. The colonel with the gay forage cap Scharroo had seen was arguing at that moment with a hysterical officer who'd rushed the queue and was insisting on taking his place at its head. As dawn had broken the man in the gay cap had splashed in a canvas bath provided by one of the Bofors batteries, watched by unbe-lieving soldiers. Now, tall, blond and unconcerned, he quietly drew his revolver, stuck it in the other officer's stomach and called a military policemen to lead him away. Other men sat among the dunes, unable to accept that the ordered world they'd lived in had collapsed, and were merely waiting in defeat to be captured. For the most past, however, they were prepared only to admit that things were 'a bit dodgy' and regarded their defeat with the air of cynical disillusionment and mocking self-depreca-tion that was the stock-in-trade of British servicemen.

There were all kinds, most of them still clutching their rifles, some with suitcases, artillery theodolites and favourite golf clubs. There were engineers, cavalrymen, tankmen, gunners, infan-trymen, medical men, men who didn't know the first thing about boats and tried to row stern-first or against an anchor some sailor had thrown out before he'd disappeared in the bombing. There were Belgians and Frenchmen from the interior who'd never seen the sea before and failed to understand that human beings crowd-ing into a boat could set it so firmly on the sand nothing on God's earth would move it until they climbed out again. Unlike the island British, they found it hard to accept the queues and worked themselves into a rage of impatience so that the sailors had to beat at frantic hands with boathooks and oars.

There were even a few odd Germans like Jocho Horndorff, watching sullenly as Conybeare spoke to the beachmaster. 'This man is my prisoner,' he was saying, 'and I'm taking him with me. He's a panzer officer and he might be of use to us.'

The beachmaster studied Horndorff. The German's overalls were grimy now with oil and coal dust and soot, and there were streaks of black on his face. He was hungry and tired and strained by the frustration of having Conybeare constantly alongside him; the confident conqueror of three days before had given place to a haggard prisoner.

The beachmaster stared at the small blue-clad figure in the vast ridiculous boots and decided he was a little bomb-happy. 'That bunch in the dunes there,' he said. 'You'll have to wait.'

As they walked up the beach, the Heinkels appeared over the town again, plastering the buildings, the dunes and the sand. The incessant, incredible, perpetual din that left them all voiceless with trying to shout above it, started again. The aeroplanes came in waves, the fighters roaring along the beaches with arrogant indifference to the opposition, the sand rippling ahead of them as their bullets raked the surface. Conybeare threw a spade at Horndorff.

'Dig!' he said.

Horndorff glanced at the sky. Another wave had appeared over the beach now and fighters and dive-bombers were falling out of the heavens one after the other. Their bombs could kill and maim impersonally, indifferent to nationalities or loyalties, and he began to punch at the sand, barely aware of the din and the snake-like rills in the sand as the bullets came. The bursting bombs encouraged him and the hole went quickly into the slope of the dune. Conybeare pointed at a staff car stranded in the sand. Its bonnet had been blown off and lay near them. 'Shove that over the top and pile sand on it,' he said.

Horndorff did as he was told and, under Conybeare's instruction, dragged up a few metal two-pounder shell boxes and arranged them on top and round the entrance to the hole he'd dug.

'Now get inside,' Conybeare said.

Nearby, half a dozen other men were building shelters on the edge of the dunes. Some were modest, some pretentious, and as the aeroplanes disappeared, the man next door looked round. He was a tall officer wearing steel-rimmed spectacles, his face mild and humorous.

'Haven't seen a deck-chair about, have you?' he asked.

'Haven't even seen an attendant,' Conybeare said.

'Sunny for the time of the year.' The other officer gave his shelter a slap with the piece of planking he was using. 'Long time since I went in for this sort of thing. Always used to go to Slapton Sands. Where did you favour?'

'Skegness us. Had a house there.'

Horndorff listened to them in amazement. They seemed quite mad. They all seemed mad. Just down the beach, a soldier with a trumpet was blowing a Germanic dirge which Horndorff recognized as the British national anthem. Judging by the noise, it was the only thing he could play. Not far away, a few soldiers were kicking a ball about.

'Ought to introduce ourselves,' the spectacled officer said to Conybeare. 'Usual when you share sand-castles.'

'My name's Conybeare. R.A.F.'

'York and Lancs. Mine's Wren.' The eyes behind the spectacles beamed. 'I'm building St. Paul's.'

They continued to exchange pleasantries. 'I decided to put my best uniform on,' Wren said. 'Had it made in Lille. Cost nine hundred francs. Big decision.'

'Always difficult,' Conybeare agreed.

'Got my batman to make two piles, one of the stuff I could take, one of the stuff I couldn't. Then we threw 'em both away.'

By the water's edge, two men were tinkering with a small blue speedboat and Wren and Conybeare studied them interestedly, sitting on the sand as though they were taking the air.

'Been at it since dawn,' Wren said. 'Say they're going to have a go in it.'

The bombers came again – 'For what we are about to receive,' Wren said – and the bombs landed on a wrecked ship lying just off the beach.

'They have a go at that every time they come over,' Wren pointed out. 'Luftwaffe must be a bit short-sighted.'

In the dunes just behind them two young soldiers were asleep, clutching each other like children.

'Been there since last night,' Wren observed. 'Bit young for this sort of thing, I suppose.'

As he turned away there was a cheer and they saw that one of the Heinkels was on fire. It swung back above them, trailing smoke, and then, as they watched, it disintegrated in a puff of flame. From the hole in the dunes, Horndorff saw a wing twisting down to splash in the sea and then a single parachute drifting over the beaches above them. He heard a clicking sound and realized that every soldier within a mile was working the bolt of his rifle and lifting it to his shoulder. As he watched, a steady pop-pop-pop started and the figure under the parachute went limp in its harness. As it splashed into the sea, the parachute fell over the body like a shroud.

'Ah, well,' Wren said. He flicked from his uniform flakes of soot that had drifted from the town. 'Not much hope of sunbathing. Too grubby.'

The shelling seemed to be increasing as the daylight grew. Dunkirk was being heavily hit and more buildings on the promenade were blazing, the smoke flattening out over the town.

'Heavy guns,' Wren said. 'Got 'em on the front at Nieuport, I'm told. Business seems quite brisk.'

R.A.M.C. men passed them, carrying a corpse in a blanket. Parties of them were doing the same all over the beach, burying the bodies and carting the wounded off to hospital. The British army was keeping its areas tidy. It was a wonder some sergeant hadn't started whitewashing the pebbles. If it moves salute it, if it doesn't, paint it.

While they watched, a soldier determined to get some fun out of the situation rode past on a black farm-horse. He was wearing a general's cap with its red band, a pyjama jacket and a pair of breeches and polished riding boots from some senior officer's kit.

'Which way did they go?' he was shouting.

'Thataway,' someone yelled back.

It was a ridiculous piece of farce amid the tragedy of thirst and futility and fear, and Horndorff suddenly began to see why it was that people like Conybeare had so much confidence in ultimate victory.

It wasn't quite the same for Allerton.

He'd been released from his duties as beachmaster the previous evening and he'd awakened in the dunes stiff and cold and, now that he had nothing to occupy his mind, with a new sense of worry he hadn't experienced before.

A bunch of north-country soldiers were singing 'I do Like to Be Beside the Seaside' and near them another man was dismantling a radio set for something to do. Two corporals were playing chess, and an officer curled up in a hole was patiently reading Zola in French. It was *La Débâcle*, which to Allerton seemed very fitting. Here and there a rifle was brandished as someone got out of line, but on the whole the affair was one of extraordinarily good manners, as though it simply wasn't done to make a fuss and he was so moved he felt his eyes prick with tears. If this is the British, he thought, they can never beat us.

As the sun rose higher, the beach became hot and the dry sand among the dunes seemed stifling. He rubbed his bristly chin and decided to go for a swim. The planes had gone and the guns had stopped again in a brief respite of heavenly quiet as he headed down the beach, and the unexpected stillness of the air seemed to highlight the strangeness of it all.

As he reached the water's edge he bumped into Temporary Acting-Corporal Rice who was paddling, his spectacles on the end of his nose, his boots hanging round his neck.

'Hello, sir,' Rice said. 'Had a good night?'

'Beds were a bit hard.' Allerton was surprised at the casual manner he was adopting and he decided it must be infectious because everyone else had adopted it too. 'How about you?'

'Lost the other blokes, sir, so I had a prowl round. Thought there might be a night club or two.'

As they were discussing what they ought to do, they saw a small pale blue speedboat lying in deeper water nearby. There was a feather of exhaust smoke at the stern and the man at the wheel waved. 'We've room for a couple more,' he called.

'Where are you heading for?' Allerton shouted.

'England. Care to join us?'

Allerton looked at Rice, then they nodded and they had just started splashing through the shallows when they realized the aeroplanes were back again.

'Gets a bit tiresome, doesn't it?' the man in the boat shouted. 'We'll shove off until it's over. Make sure you're ready.'

As they ran for shelter, they heard the bombs splash into the water and the destroyers' guns begin to bang. As Allerton turned he saw a vast eruption out to sea which caught the sunshine in multi-coloured rainbows of light.

'That was a bloody big bomb,' he said.

'It wasn't a bomb, sir,' Rice muttered. 'It was a mine.'

Allerton couldn't understand his shocked tones until he saw a small pale blue piece of plywood fluttering down out of the waterspout, skidding from side to side like a leaf falling from a tree and catching the light on its wet surface as it fell.

He swallowed with difficulty. 'We'd better go back up the beach,' he suggested.

Rice nodded. 'Perhaps it's our turn, anyway,' he said.

'Yes, perhaps it is. I wish to God someone knew something definite.'

But nobody did, of course, and it was this very confusion that was worrying the admiral in his desperate uncertainty in Dover.

A curtain lay over the evacuation because there was too much distance between him and the beaches, and a dreadful weakness in ship-to-shore signalling that was leading to an immense waste of effort. The establishment of a senior naval officer afloat had brought some order, however, and his hand was at last being seen in the fact that the destroyers were now bringing back a thousand men at a time. The trouble was, there just weren't enough of them.

Nevertheless, at Sheerness the Small Vessels Pool was beginning to work up to full speed, and the motor car engines of week-end yachts and cruisers were being made to turn over after the winter lay-up, while stores and accommodation were being produced for the stream of naval officers and ratings who kept appearing to man them. Rafts small enough to be manhandled but big enough to carry men were being constructed, and shipwrights were busy with ladders to load from the mole or from ships which had grounded in the shallows. Convoy after convoy was pushing out to sea, and from every quarter the numbers grew. London river had long since been swept clear of tugs and all the great towing companies had sent everything they could spare to pull dumb barges. Long-forgotten gunboats, drawing only five feet of water and mounting ancient guns which had been built for river work in China, passed each other in the mist that lay over the Channel, dodging damaged ships that yawed wildly from side to side, unable to manoeuvre. Lifeboats, transporters belonging to furniture removers, firefloats, battleships' boats from Portsmouth, cutters belonging to the 34,000 ton *Nelson*, even the admiral's barge itself, its bright paint dulled to a drab grey; everything that would float and was handy joined them, their names and numbers arriving on the desks of the grateful officers at Dover.

'What about *Vital*?' the admiral asked. 'Is she available yet?'

'Later in the day, sir. They've had a lot of trouble.'

That was putting it mildly. The job had been far more complicated than Lieutenant MacGillicuddy had expected. That near miss as they'd gone astern from the mole had done much more damage than they'd thought. In addition to the trouble with the bearing, they also had leaking steam pipes, sheered bolts, and broken gauge glasses, and everything, both in the engine room and the decks above, had been covered with particles of paint, dust and soot. The damage had all to be cleared before they could get at the oil feed to the overheated bearing which was up against a bulkhead and barely within reach, so that they had to pick out the suspect pipe from a whole array of others, bent double in the stifling engine room at a point where there wasn't even space for them to work side by side.

When they'd finally found the stoppage, they'd realized that whatever was causing it couldn't be cleared with a piece of wire or blown out with compressed air. The message that had gone up to Hough had thrown him into a frenzy of impatience but he'd held on to his temper, knowing that no one could do the job as fast or as well as MacGillicuddy. Struggling to give some form to the sketchy picture of the problems in his mind, he was waiting like a caged tiger in his cabin, while down below in the engine room MacGillicuddy cursed *Vital*'s age and the politicians who'd allowed her to grow rusty with neglect.

'We'll have to saw it out,' he said. 'Bit by bit, till we find what it is.'

'That'll take all day,' the chief E.R.A. pointed out.

'Then it'll have to take all day, won't it?' MacGillicuddy snapped.

They cut the oil feed pipe nine times before they found a piece of cotton waste jammed inside with the consistency of a wooden plug. No one knew how it had got there and certainly no one was likely to own up. They simply removed it and set about brazing the pieces together again.

It was about this time that the message came down from the castle and Hough rang through to the engine room. 'Request from the castle, Chief,' he said. 'They want to know how long we'll be.'

MacGillicuddy drew a deep breath. 'Midnight,' he said.

The reply was received at the castle in icy silence.

The chief of staff tried to sugar the pill. 'One bit of good news, sir. *Vanquisher* reports that the mole's functioning again.'

'Good. Make sure the personnel ships are informed.' The admiral thought for a moment. 'And lift the suspension of sailings. What about the beaches?'

'They've got them working well now, I gather, sir. *Royal Sovereign*'s already completed loading and she's on her way back. Do we know how much longer we've got?'

The admiral frowned. 'A meeting's been called in London. Between the P.M. and the Service Ministers. Gort believes it's possible to hold the perimeter until 1 June. We'll build up a reserve for a final effort up to dawn on that day.'

As hopes in Dover increased, for the small boats navigation grew steadily worse. Several were run down in the confusion and the smoke, and the surface of the water was littered with every kind of wreckage imaginable that had floated up from sunken ships. There were bodies, ropes, planks and upturned boats. There were even floating torpedoes, relics of the previous night's attacks; and, above all, the shallows were full of soldiers trying to be sailors for the first time.

Handling the little boats was growing progressively more difficult as muscles and minds protested, and unexpectedly the wind began to freshen from the north-west to lift an awkward surf; ignoring the queues, tired and anxious soldiers began to push out from all directions. Many of them drowned before they reached safety and here and there it was possible to see exhausted men praying quietly while, in an angle of the dunes, a group of young soldiers were listening to an older man reading from the Book of Common Prayer.

It didn't seem at all odd. Because the sky was so incredibly blue, it didn't even seem real.

All the time the planes rained their bombs down on the scattered boats and men, while batteries like Hinze's bombarded the approaches. Shells now dropped constantly among the crowded shipping and, though most of them exploded in the water, they occasionally hit something. Just offshore, an elderly sloop, her stern blown off, was being towed away by a ship half her size while every tug and fishing boat and launch in the area of the explosion scurried towards her as she settled in a cloud of steam.

By this time everyone was growing hardened to the air raids. Like Scharroo they'd noticed that the bombs did considerably less damage in the soft sand than the noise suggested and they could time their dashes for the dunes to a nicety now. Fortunately, there was no shortage of cigarettes. Most men had at least five hundred from the looted NAAFIs, and some had thousands.

Many arriving on the beaches now had no boots and had marched miles on bleeding feet. Some officers worked themselves to a standstill for the safety of their men. Others concerned themselves only with their own safety. But still they were lifted.

At Dover, the admiral studied the lists, wondering what else he could do. They were still waiting for the final instructions from the meeting in London. When they came they were exactly as he'd thought they'd be.

'Every man possible must be lifted before dawn on 1 June,' he was told. 'French troops must be given equal opportunity of evacuation – not only in their own vessels but also in British ships.'

For a moment the admiral was silent, then he drew a deep breath. 'Then I must have the H, I and J ships back,' he said.

There was a moment's silence at the other end of the telephone. 'We daren't risk any more,' the First Sea Lord pointed out bleakly. 'We must preserve the balance of the fleet against the future.'

'Sir,' the admiral said, 'I have to provide for the present. There are thousands of men still waiting to be picked up. These are the men who'll have to defend this country against invasion, and round whom the new armies will have to be built.'

There was a long silence, then the First Sea Lord spoke again. 'I take your point,' he said. 'I'll see that you get them.'

Unaware of the concern of the admiral for the return of *Vital*, Hatton had unexpectedly found himself free from the war for a while. He was still dog-tired and he still hadn't been to bed; his own job had been easily taken care of and he'd been at the beck and call of every department short of an officer. He'd helped to ammunition and supply ship and been sent about the town on a dozen and one errands, most of them frustrating and bringing only insults because *Vital* was still immobile. In his free moments he'd tried to write a report for Hough to pass on to the castle, but it was constantly interrupted and now he'd been sent ashore again to collect signals and sealed envelopes containing orders. At the castle, however, there was obviously some change of plan in the wind.

'*Vital* might have to go to Southampton,' said the elderly captain. 'There's a move towards Cherbourg and some of our chaps may be going with the French. How long will it be before you're ready?'

'The engine room thinks midnight, sir.'

'Well, there's no hurry then. Can you find something to do for three hours till we know?'

Hatton wasn't certain how to answer and the captain waved him away. 'Surely you can find *something*?' he said. 'Know Dover?'

'Yes, sir.'

'Got a girl here?'

'Yes, sir.'

'Go and have tea with her then. Do you good.' The captain glanced at his watch. 'Three hours. All right?'

Hatton grinned, '*All right*, sir!'

Outside again, he drew a deep breath. The instructions were so unexpected they'd taken his breath away and almost without thinking, he walked to the nearest telephone box. There was a queue of soldiers outside who'd just come from France and were telephoning relatives, and he had to wait for a quarter of an hour. It didn't change his mind. After living through seventy-two hours of tension he needed someone near him whose flesh was soft and unmuscular and who didn't stink of sweat or cordite or salt sea air. To his surprise, Nora Hart's voice sounded much gentler than when he'd last rung her.

'I'm free for a couple of hours,' he said. 'It's official.'
There was a moment's silence and he was terrified she wouldn't respond. Then her voice came again. 'Like to come round?'
Within five minutes he was knocking on her door. She opened it immediately and he felt his nerves relax as he saw the bright chintz in the little flat. She was wearing a yellow-and-white striped blouse and a neat grey skirt, but he noticed that her eyes looked tired. 'Sorry I was a bit short when you rang before,' she said. 'I had someone here.'
'Boy friend?'
'Not really. Man I knew. Just got back.'
Hatton's heart sank. He hadn't thought there might be someone else with the same qualifications of bravery he now had. Jealousy dug at him. 'He must have got back early,' he said.
She smiled, sensing what was going through his mind. 'He's a born survivor.'
She lit a cigarette and handed the packet to him. 'You look good in uniform,' she observed.
'Everybody looks good in uniform.'
They talked for a while, quite easily and with no awkwardness between them to remind him how badly he'd treated her. When he'd left for Fleet Street, she'd written heart-broken letters he hadn't answered and he knew now that he'd been a bastard.
'Shove your legs up on the settee,' she said. 'I expect you've been on them for ages.'
'Ever since I saw you on the docks.'
She lifted his feet up for him. Then she unexpectedly bent and kissed him, gently, in a sisterly manner, her eyes concerned and suddenly warm. 'Was it awful?' she asked.
Hatton shrugged, uncertain how to reply. There had been one dreadful moment on the second trip when his fear had finally taken over and he'd bolted below deck after a machine-gun attack that had left wounded men writhing at his feet. The doctor had seen him but, recognizing exhaustion and shock, had wisely left him alone, and after a while he'd pulled himself together.
'A bit,' he said.
'Different from the newspapers.'
'We're awful liars when we get into print.'

She paused then went on with a rush. 'You know, Barry, you *were* a clot to go to London. We were doing all right, you and I.' He pulled her gently to him. 'I always thought we'd make a go of it,' he said, trying to believe he was telling the truth.

She said nothing, but as his arms went round her she caught her breath. For a second they stayed together, their faces only an inch or two apart, then his fingers slipped under her blouse, and he felt the warm skin in the hollow of her back and the sudden quivering tension of her body.

'You've got a bloody cheek!' she said, but she wasn't angry. 'You buzz off to London and then turn up out of the blue and expect me to fling myself on the floor at your feet. You men always think of us women simply as the matching half of your not so lovely private parts.'

Hatton grinned. ' "Person" they always called it in police courts,' he said. 'Remember? "He exposed his person." '

They began to laugh, and for Hatton it was as though a whole lot of taut strings that held him together were loosening. He kissed her, feeling her against him, as warm and interesting as she'd always been, his hands began to move.

'Do you always do this when you come ashore?' she asked.

'Oddly enough, no.'

'Why now then?'

He couldn't possibly explain that she represented all the things that were missing across the Channel. She represented peace, even England come to that. His hand moved higher up her back and she shuddered. 'I think you're a swine, Barry,' she said, her voice unsteady. 'I was in love with you, you know.'

Her head turned uncertainly as he kissed her throat but she didn't resist as he unbuttoned the blouse and kissed her again. 'Was this what you were after when you rang up?' she asked.

'No. As a matter of fact, it wasn't. The only thing I wanted was to see you again.'

She seemed to ponder for a moment and, as his hand moved again, she put her cheek against his.

'All right,' she said. 'Go on, Barry. It's all right.'

When Hatton woke up, she was standing over him fastening her stockings.

'You said two hours,' she pointed out quietly.

He began to button his shirt and reach for his shoes.

'You know,' she went on. 'You might almost be worth saving.'

'What from?

'You. You used to be a selfish devil but perhaps the war's altering that.'

He was silent, still shocked by the passion of his love-making, the sheer carnality which had been twice as intense because it was such a change from the desperate fear of dying.

Rising, he pulled her to him, and she stood quietly in his arms, allowing him to kiss her.

'Marry me, Nora.'

'You don't have to do that.'

'I mean it.'

'Don't be silly. Are you going back?'

'As soon as we're shipshape.'

She was silent for a moment, her cheeks still smarting from contact with the stubble on his chin. Then she put her arms round his neck and kissed him.

'I'm glad you came,' she said.

She stood by the door as he went down the stairs, and as he stepped into the street, in an excess of stupefied pleasure, he felt he could face anything. Nora was a brick. When he came back next time he'd make it up to her.

In the evening sunshine, Scharroo and Marie-Josephine stood in the dunes. They'd long since abandoned the suitcase they'd carried from Bout-Dassons and Marie-Josephine had stuffed what she needed into the pockets of the stained cream coat.

They'd spent the night in the house in the Rue Isabey. The men inside, with a strange mixture of compassion and awkward gallantry, had even offered to move out.

'No, no,' Marie-Josephine had said. 'You are much tired. If I can perhaps have a little corner. Just to sleep.'

Three men occupying a bed in what had been the maid's room rose without argument and flopped down on the landing among the other sleeping men lying in inert, exhausted heaps, and that morning they'd shared what rations the soldiers had and had then headed back into the town. The three men had moved like automatons back into the maid's bedroom as they'd left.

As they pushed through the crowded streets, the remnants of a Moroccan division appeared, black men who were carrying their boots strung round their necks. They had rifles but no ammunition, and they were clearly terrified. Behind them was a British regiment straight from the fighting, in a pitiful state of exhaustion but far from beaten. They moved like drugged bees and looked ready to drop. One soldier was clearly out of his mind and, instead of wearing his equipment, carried it with his rifle across his outstretched arms. Several men flopped to the ground, but the lonely mind-sick man remained standing, as though crucified, his arms still outstretched, his face empty, and the moving figures heading past him opened as though he were an island and they were water flowing past.

They began to walk out of the town. It wasn't easy because everyone else was walking in and they had to push between the crowding men. Scharroo was hungry now and, though Marie-Josephine didn't complain, he knew she must be growing hungry, too. Shells were dropping in the vast car parks that had been set up. They could see vehicles burning, and before they'd even left the outskirts a sergeant wearing the red-topped cap of the Military Police stopped them.

'Where are you off to?' The sergeant had heard of fifth columnists – indeed he'd been shot at by them more than once – and he was suspicious.

Scharroo explained but the sergeant was unconvinced.

'You can't come this way,' he said.

'We're only trying to leave the town,' Scharroo pointed out.

Probably with the dispositions of the entire B.E.F., the sergeant thought. 'Ain't possible,' he said.

'Look, this is no place for a girl to be.'

'It's no place for me to be. But I'm here.'

'For Christ's sake, man, we didn't ask to be involved in your bloody defeat – !'

The sergeant bristled immediately and Scharroo realized he'd said the wrong thing to one of the touchy islanders.

'*Who's defeated?*'

'For God's sake!' Scharroo said wearily. To someone like himself, standing on the sidelines and able to see the wood without the trees getting in the way, it stuck out a mile.

The sergeant clearly didn't see things the same way. 'Go on, 'op it,' he said.

As they re-entered the town the place was beginning to stink of death. Bodies were along every road and lying everywhere in gardens and houses. In one house, they saw the whole ground floor covered with stretcher cases and nobody looking after them. Marie-Josephine was limping now and they stopped at an abandoned shoe shop where soldiers were changing their worn-out footwear. With their help, Marie-Josephine found a pair of walking shoes and ankle socks.

She was watching Scharroo silently now. Her world had emptied of people who might be able to help her and, just when she'd decided there was nothing left, Scharroo had arrived. He was older than she was – much older, she realized, as old as Monsieur Ambry, whom she'd rejected as a dirty old man – but already in her mind a hundred and one fantasies were taking shape.

'I think I will remain with you, Walter,' she said briskly.

He turned his head quickly but her face was calm and unafraid. It worried him because he had a job to do and the only thing in his mind at that moment was to get out of this madhouse.

'What must we do?' Marie-Josephine asked, like a sergeant awaiting orders.

'Find somewhere we can shelter,' Scharroo said. 'And wait for the Germans to arrive.'

'That would be – *défaitiste*.'

'Who gives a damn?' Scharroo had reached a point of desperation now. 'All we have to do is smile and wave.'

Marie-Josephine's heart tightened with disappointment. She couldn't imagine that any man she admired as she did Scharroo would be prepared for surrender.

'*I* do not smile and wave,' she said. 'Perhaps even I pick up a gun and shoot them.'

Scharroo's head turned quickly but she was quite serious, her small mouth firm, and she went on, her usual business-like manner tempered with a gentle persuasiveness because she wished him to agree with her.

'There are many French soldiers here,' she said, gesturing as though to grasp an explanation from the darkening air. 'They have not *all* been defeated. Some will return and drive away the Germans.'

Scharroo stared at her and she went on earnestly. 'This is not the end of the war,' she insisted.

Scharroo didn't speak. To him it seemed that the war had been over for days. It was just that the defeated wouldn't lie down.

In a way, *Vital's* engine-room crew were an example of this. As Hatton came back on board, while everyone else was conscious of the electrical atmosphere, he was unaware of it. The orders he'd picked up had been very simple. The operations to the south had not even begun to formulate and *Vital's* duty was to continue as before. Hatton's heart had sunk and he was a little subdued, though still in a glow of sentimental nostalgia.

'Sorry to have been so long, sir,' he said to Hough. 'But we nearly got sent to Cherbourg. I suppose they thought we'd got the experience.'

Hough looked at him with loathing as he handed over the orders. He'd been holding on to his patience for so long that by this time the slightest excuse to let off steam was good enough.

'Oh, you do, do you?' he said harshly. 'I'm pleased to hear it.'

Unaware that the outburst was only a safety valve to allow Hough's anger to release itself, Hatton retired, his feelings hurt.

'For God's sake,' he asked the navigating officer, 'what's wrong with the Old Man?'

'Sangus explosivus, old boy.' The navigating officer shrugged. 'Blood pressure. It's been due to spurt out of his ears all day. It'll be all right now.'

It was. Because MacGillicuddy was at last coming to the end of his ordeal. 'Won't be long now,' he said. 'Just the brackets, that's all.'

The circle of faces lit by the naked hand lamp were strained.

'After this lot I'm going to get a job running the boiler house in the barracks at Pompey,' MacGillicuddy said.

Hough's reaction to the news that they could move was not the fury he'd expended on Hatton. It was simply relief. 'Thanks, Chief,' he said.

Hatton had been asleep for just twenty minutes when the

steward woke him. He opened his eyes and glared at his torturer. 'Now what, for God's sake?'

'We're off, sir. You're wanted on the bridge.'

Hatton forced himself to consciousness, his heart sinking. The break they'd had made the thought of going through it again all the worse.

'Thank you,' he said. 'Sorry I was rude, steward.'

'That's all right, sir. We're all getting a bit tired.'

Sievewright was growing tired, too, by this time. In the darkness Dunkirk was no longer a mass of black and grey, topped with inky cloud, but an angry glowing cinder ahead of him. The cloud of smoke was now a glaring fire, and against the ebony of the sky it shone like a bloodshot eye. To the south, a few miles back, long flashes like summer lightning played along the horizon, orange and green in hue, the explosions of British shells mingling with the flashes of the replying German artillery. Every now and then a rocket soared up, bursting with brilliant white light, to report German successes. Their frequency was depressing.

Between the glare of Dunkirk and the lightning to the southeast, great tongues of flame, two or three yards long, leapt through the blackness from the muzzles of the British batteries of the rearguard, lighting up the surrounding area with their flashes and shaking the earth with the thunder of their explosions. There was the constant thump of mortar fire, and every now and then from the sea there was a whitish glow against the sky and then a roar overhead as the navy shelled the Germans miles inland.

A blazing lorry lit the dusk as stragglers drifted past. But they were growing fewer now and their absence worried Sievewright. At the next crossroads, there was a sign, *Dunkerque*, and a converging stream of men – British, Belgian and French – and a group of soldiers round a man lying on the ground.

'Any medical orderlies?' they kept shouting. 'Any medical orderlies?'

No one stopped. In the passing faces was only the strained desire to reach the coast. Sievewright halted unwillingly and the dog, which had followed him all day, sat down alongside him.

'Can I help? Sievewright asked. 'I know a bit about it.'

'Thanks, mate. It's Joe Ferris. His leg's broke. A lorry cut the corner and went over it.'

Sievewright laid down the French rifle. 'Anybody got a light?'

Nobody had and he made them stand back so he could see in the flickering glow of the burning lorry.

'I'll need splints,' he said and indicated a broken fence nearby. 'We'll need two short planks.' His fingers were moving over the stained trousers as he talked and as he touched the injured limb the man moaned.

The soldiers looked down at their friend, their expressions curiously tender. 'Hang on tight, Joe,' one of them said. 'This chap's a medic. He'll fix you up.'

The man on the ground nodded, his face pale, his lips raw where he'd chewed them, and as Sievewright yanked the leg straight he screamed and fainted.

'That's fixed it,' Sievewright said. He looked round for something to bind the splints in place. 'Handkerchiefs?' he asked. Between the lot of them they were able to produce only one red handkerchief.

'No straps?'

They shook their heads. 'We left our kit at Arras.'

Sievewright glanced at his own neat pack alongside the black puppy. 'Take the straps off mine,' he said.

He finished lashing the two planks in place and indicated the broken fence again. Two long poles were wrenched free and, unrolling his overcoat and buttoning it as he'd learned as a Scout, Sievewright thrust the two poles through it; one of the men added his blouse to make a crude stretcher.

As they picked up the injured man and set off – four squat, drab unlovely figures bent under their load, their eyes full of concern, their heads turned inward and downward towards their friend – Sievewright felt very much alone. He had effectively stripped himself of the kit that had been worrying him so much, however, and what was left suddenly seemed very unimportant. Changing into his best boots, he stuffed a spare pair of socks into his pocket; then, removing from his blouse pocket the Book of Common Prayer that his vicar had given him before he left England, he tossed it away and pushed one of the hard biscuits in its place.

Cocooned in his blind faith that the navy would be at the coast to rescue him, he still felt remarkably little anxiety.

Fortunately for Sievewright, a strange paralysis of indecision had gripped the Germans. Troops of Army Groups A and B had moved up, and Fourth Army had been asked to lay on an attack against Bergues. But little headway had been made against the stubborn resistance of men like Lance-Corporal Gow, and guns were brought up instead of armour. No one knew if the Luftwaffe were about to carry out a full-scale attack on the town or not and an irritable officer at Fourth Army H.Q. lifted his voice in bitter complaint on the telephone as he tried to stir the rear echelons to life. 'There's an impression here,' he said, 'that no one's any longer interested in Dunkirk.'

It was just as well and, as darkness fell, the news that came into Dover showed that though it had been a day of tragedy it had been a day of triumph, too. Confusion, exhaustion and the Germans had done everything possible to destroy the B.E.F. but, by this time, it was clear that over 50,000 men had been lifted in twenty-four hours, almost 30,000 of them from the open beaches alone.

It was at that moment that the message arrived from *Vital* that she was ready for sea.

The admiral smiled. It seemed like a good omen.

FRIDAY, 31 MAY

The first hours of the last day of the month were black and still, and for the patrolling destroyers almost impossible. The water was full of small craft and almost any of them might have been E-boats. As fast as they had loaded up and left Dunkirk, more had come in a never-ending procession. Some of the crews, to their indignation, had been given army maps to navigate on; others managed with hasty copies of other people's charts, and they groped their way in, using torches and signalling lamps to find the buoys round which they had to turn, pushing past sunken shapes and drifting wreckage and the mats of floating bodies.

For Hatton it was much worse this time and he was terribly conscious of the metallic creaks about him as *Vital* picked her way forward, the ship's nose a pale wedge on the dark rippling water. Voices were hushed, and across the bows lay the land where, with macabre regularity, the night sky split with dull red and yellow flashes like distant lightning so that he could see the harsh shoulders of buildings.

'Starboard ten!' The quiet order came to his ears along with the uneasy movement of feet on gratings as the ship sidled warily nearer. A listing wreck barred her passage but an urgent command guided her safely round it.

The appalling responsibility didn't seem to worry Hough, and he was standing on the bridge eating a sandwich and calling his instructions through mouthfuls of corned beef. A paddle-mine-sweeper was on the beach just outside the harbour, burning fiercely, while another lay against the mole, its upperworks hanging over at an angle. In the darkness the town seemed to glow with fires.

'Which side do you want the nets, sir?'

Hough pushed his glasses aside and picked up his sandwich again. 'Neither. There are two destroyers off the beaches already. We'll use the mole.'

As they threw their lines ashore, the naval commander who was acting as piermaster scrambled aboard. 'Nice to see you back,' he said.

As the blackness lifted and the greyness of dawn approached, the wind changed again. For days the sea had been as incredibly flat and motionless as a village pond. Men who knew the Channel and its treachery marvelled at the way even the gods seemed to be taking a hand in the struggle, the waves held within such tight bounds that the simplest manoeuvres were possible to frightened or unskilled men in unhandy boats.

But now, first as a stirring of the air, then as an increasing breeze, it began to blow in towards the shore from the north, and in the long shallows the surf rose. It was never heavy but, after five days, it was more than the exhausted men could fight. One after the other the small boats swung round and broached to.

The first to go aground were pushed off but the tide was receding quickly and those which followed were left stranded – all the way from the foot of the mole to La Panne, small lop-sided vessels lying on the drying sand.

Allerton was involved with one of them. When he saw it first it was still drifting, small and clinker-built and with a decked-in bow. A rope hung over the side and there was no sign of anyone on board. Across the stern were the words, *Queen of France*.

'That thing looks as though it's got an outboard engine,' he said to Rice. 'Think we could make it go?'

They stripped and began to swim, but the water was only shoulder-high and they pulled themselves aboard without difficulty.

'It's not an outboard,' Allerton said disappointedly, hanging over the stern. 'It's only some sort of rudder.'

Rice opened a hatch amidships. 'The engine's here, sir. Know anything about 'em?'

They swung at the starting handle but nothing happened and hopelessly they searched the lockers under the stern for tools. Below a hatch in the covered-in bow was a small cabin with a single narrow bunk, with a mattress and a blanket. The *Queen of France* had clearly belonged to someone who'd not been able to spend much on her, and the few pathetic fittings lay on a folded sail under the narrow bunk.

After a while, however, Allerton unearthed a rusty screwdriver and an adjustable spanner also red with rust. They were just about to climb back to the deck when Rice, who had been poking about in the lockers, unearthed a primus stove and a packet of tea. There was also a tin of condensed milk and water in the kettle. As they lit the primus the first raid of the day started and Allerton looked up.

'Might as well stay where we are, sir,' Rice suggested.

'As safe here as anywhere,' Allerton agreed and, despite the racket ashore, they sat together, stark naked, drinking tea, until the noise died and the engines faded.

As they finished they felt the boat bump softly but they paid no attention to it until the kettle fell off the primus and they realized that the cabin was now at an angle. The falling tide had stranded the *Queen of France* solidly on the sand.

Subtly, because of the conditions and without any real instructions from anyone in authority, the evacuation had moved east. Several ships had been hit near the harbour entrance and the others were now trying to avoid the danger and, with nothing to shoot at, Leutnant Hinze and others like him round Mardyck and Gravelines switched to Dunkirk itself; working at extreme range, they managed to bring the loading berths under fire.

To the exhausted men on the beaches, the shelling was a new harassment. There was no food left now, and officers and men were eating from the same tin of bully beef and sharing the same biscuits and the same stale dregs of wine. A constant procession of haggard, unshaven soldiers moved among the abandoned vehicles and through the dead, doleful houses in search of some forgotten tin or loaf or biscuit. A few still bathed in the sooty water to clear their ears and eyes of the grit which had been flung up by the shells and bombs and bullets and drifted by the breeze. A few searched for fresh clothing. One man was washing socks in the shallows and drying them on a string tied to a wrecked ambulance, another was emptying radiators to get enough water to brew tea on a fire made with broken equipment. A few more kicked a ball about, and two despatch riders were racing each other up and down the beach, their eyes always on the sky for the return of the bombers. At the first salvo of shells, at the first sound of aeroplane engines, everything was dropped and there was a rush for the shelter of the dunes.

The sight of the first starving, exhausted soldiers who found their way to *Daisy* had shocked Kenny Pepper. They arrived in small boatloads, stupid with fatigue, so that he stared at them, wondering what had gone wrong, and it was only when he realized that *Daisy* was heeling under the weight of the men hanging on to her sides that he came to life. His reaction was instinctive. *Daisy* was in danger, and in a fury he punched at faces and pounded on helmets and finally grabbed a boathook and went along the side of the boat thrusting at them. 'You get off there,' he shouted. 'Let's have some order!'

It was as they pushed the soldiers aboard a destroyer lying in the roadstead that he heard his first yell of warning that aeroplanes were overhead. He turned to gaze at the lightening sky and suddenly realized he was staring at the enemy. All the numerous bangs and explosions he'd heard ashore hadn't really meant much up to that moment. They'd been impersonal things involved in other men's defeat, but those small glinting shapes above were trying to kill *him*, Kenneth Harry Pepper.

The destroyer's crew started casting off and the coils of the bow rope dropped in loops round Kenny's head. Then the warship began to move ahead at full speed, her wash setting the mat of boats about her rocking violently.

'Let's git out of here,' Gilbert Williams shouted but, even as *Daisy* swung away, the first bombs came down.

'Oh, Christ Jesus God Almighty!' Ernie yelled, his wall eye swinging crazily as though it were loose in its socket.

One of the aeroplanes had come down so low in a screaming dive, it raced between the ships at masthead height. Kenny ducked behind the wheelhouse and swung round on hands and knees towards the ancient Lewis gun. 'Give it 'em, Sy!' he screeched in his high cracked boy's voice.

But it was only when the aeroplanes drew off and the racket died down that he realized he'd heard no answering fire, and Ernie Williams was running along the deck.

'Where's that sodden Brundrett?' he bellowed, snatching at the gun and swinging it round. 'He hasn't even taken the fucken cover off.'

A moment later, Kenny heard him in the engine room. 'It's *your* job,' he was yelling at the top of his voice as he and his brother always did when they were angry. 'You sodden get out there next time and start shooting!'

As he reappeared from the engine room and stamped to the little wheelhouse, his brows went down, his face flushed with anger. 'Said 'e 'adn't realized,' he was shouting. ' 'Adn't realized! Christ! With that row!'

Ten minutes later the aeroplanes were back again and as *Daisy* swung to starboard at full speed under Gilbert's thick hands, Kenny saw a cockle-boat appear directly in front of them, wallowing in the wash of a passing ship. He snatched up the fender Ernie had been making in Dover and ran to the bow with it. It was heavy and Ernie had made it beautifully, taking care to get all the half-hitches even. As the gap between the two boats narrowed, Kenny swung it over the bows to take the shock. The two boats hit with a crash that almost flung him overboard. As he fell on his face on the foredeck, they were all covered with flying pieces of cork and the fender was only a flat bag.

'Nice work, Kenny!' Gilbert stuck his head out of the wheelhouse. 'See you sweep them bits up when you've a minute, mind.' He swung round to the stern. There was no sign of Brundrett at the Lewis again and he yelled to his brother :

'You get on that bleeden gun, Ern!'

As Ernie swung the Lewis, another aeroplane roared over them and Kenny heard the reassuring clack-clack.

'I hit him!' Ernie yelled.

'Nah!' Gilbert shook his head. 'Missed!'

As the aeroplanes disappeared, Gilbert called to Kenny. 'Go and see what's wrong with that fat sod,' he said. 'He must be deaf.'

Going below, Kenny found the engineer-cook half under the engine with a spanner in his hand.

'Giving trouble.' Brundrett had his head in the bilges, but Kenny could see his fat white cheeks quivering and it dawned on him that Brundrett was frightened sick and had chosen the position because it gave him the most protection from the bombs and bullets.

It shocked Kenny that Brundrett could be afraid, because in the stories he read it was only the enemy who ever felt fear, but when the aeroplanes came again and again, tearing at his nerves with the din, he began to see it wasn't all that difficult. The crash of the bombs seemed to strip the flesh from his nerves and leave him shaking. Vast splashes rose in the shallows and he saw ships start to back out from the harbour in a hurry and men scattering like disturbed ants on the beaches as the high fountains of sand rose. There was still no sign of Brundrett and as the aeroplanes came down once more, he saw the bombs falling in uneven lines as though they were about to drop one after another along *Daisy*'s deck. In the sea ahead there was a mat of swimmers where a boat had been hit and he saw a destroyer, taking desperate evasive action, plough through them at full speed, the brown shapes rolling over by the stern as she slewed round to set *Daisy* rocking with her wash.

Gilbert was staring bleakly at the disaster, then he came to life with a start and gave Kenny a shove. Having something to do helped, and as the aeroplanes came down yet again in another numbing attack he saw Ernie swinging the gun round. There were no tracers in the pan and it was impossible to tell where the bullets went.

'Missed the bugger,' Ernie snarled.

In the shallows nearby a cutter was floating empty, its crew blown overboard, and an officer took it over. Crowds of soldiers immediately rushed it and began to clamber over the stern so that the officer had to stand on the foredeck yelling at them to distribute their weight evenly. As it moved towards *Daisy*, it was so low in the water it looked as though it would capsize.

The rattle of rifles and the solid whango-whango-whango of the destroyers' guns came in a deafening chorus that almost lifted *Daisy* from the sea. Then the skipper of the cockle-boat they'd hit yelled that he had engine trouble and asked for a tow, and Kenny made the line fast over the bollard as *Daisy* went ahead.

At that moment there was a tremendous explosion from aft and, as they crouched behind the wheelhouse, a hail of wood splinters and blazing wreckage fell about them, stirring the water and skating through the air to clink and thud on the deck. Lifting their heads as it stopped, they saw there was no sign of the cockle-boat or her crew – just the tow rope trailing in the water astern.

Kenny gaped at it, his mouth slack, then Gilbert Williams swallowed, his adam's apple jerking. 'Get that rope in, kid,' he said in a thick voice. 'Afore it gets round the screw.'

As he pulled in the frayed rope, Kenny realized his hands were trembling. He tried to get a grip on himself, but the trembling persisted and he had to stand for a moment to get over it.

This wasn't at all how he'd expected war to be. The drawings in the magazines he'd read had never shown men being blown to pieces so small that no trace of them could be found, had never shown them run down by their own ships, had indicated nothing of the terror or the weariness of exhausted and wounded men. They'd never explained that blood could stain a deck so that it was impossible to get rid of it with the deck scrubber, or how an injured man screamed when he was flung down by the swing of the boat. They'd never conveyed the stink that was drifting off the stranded ships, a compound of burning wood and burning flesh and putrefaction that filled the nostrils and was almost possible to taste. No, this wasn't a bit how he'd imagined war.

It wasn't how Scharroo had visualized it either.

He and Marie-Josephine had spent the night clutching each other for warmth in a hole in the sand dunes. As daylight came, Scharroo had released himself gently and sat up stiffly. A moment later Marie-Josephine stirred and, as she sat up, too, Scharroo ran a hand over the stubble on his chin and offered her a cigarette. She was dark-eyed with tiredness and her face was pale, but the fastidiousness in her nature drove her to find a comb in her pocket and automatically drag it through her hair.

'It's time we were going,' Scharroo said.

Eddies of breeze were coiling wisps of black smoke down towards the sand, and Scharroo could smell an acrid smell of burning which was touched with the scent of pine trees that he remembered from his youth. Marie-Josephine was peering narrowed-eyed towards the sea and for a while he stood watching her. She'd dropped the stained cream coat to the sand and stood straight and slim and small, the breeze blowing her hair about her face, her thin flowered dress flattened against her figure and legs. He said nothing, enjoying the lull in the bombing, with the luxurious feeling of safety and the sight of a pretty girl among all the misery and terror. He studied her fresh-complexioned face for the hundredth time, the large evasive eyes that were sometimes sullen and sometimes as hard as agate with determination. Behind the gamin there was a rapidly maturing woman who knew exactly what she wanted.

Marie-Josephine was looking worried, however, and at last her problem burst out of her. Her chin lifted and she swung round to face him. 'I think I will go to England,' she said.

Scharroo flung down his cigarette. 'England, for Christ's sake! Why? The war's going to end soon.'

Marie-Josephine shook her head, quite certain in her mind that he was wrong. France had been down before but she'd always recovered and, with true Gallic arrogance, the girl couldn't believe that God would permit such barbarians as the Germans to conquer a nation as cultured, as noble, as intelligent, as gallant as the French.

'I think not,' she said.

She gestured at the wreckage-littered beach. Ships were appearing now and dozens of small boats were moving between them and the patient queues of men like beetles on a pond. 'They do not go to all this trouble if they wish to surrender, I think,' she pointed out.

What she said made sense. Scharroo had never had much time for the British but the effort that was being made to remove their army clearly didn't seem to indicate any immediate intention to give in.

'I do not wish to remain in a defeated country,' Marie-Josephine went on. 'In my town, all was occupied by the Germans in 1914. It is occupied in 1870 also. I do not think I wish to live like that.'

Scharroo frowned. 'For God's sake,' he said. 'If the British go on fighting, the war might go on for years, for ever. You'll never come back.'

She shrugged. She was more peasant than she thought and possessed a peasant's straight-thinking contempt for vacillation. 'Perhaps that is better than to be ruled by Germans. I will encourage someone to take me with them.'

Scharroo stared towards the sea and the hurrying boats. At that moment the destroyers' guns began to fire and he saw small puff-balls of smoke appear in the sky near a group of glittering dots that he knew were aeroplanes.

'By God,' he shouted, as they started to run for the dunes, 'you'll be lucky.'

Luck was what Stoos needed, too, just then.

It was not his idea of military glory to sit in his tent awaiting a court martial. He'd had to wait though the whole of the previous interminable day, watching the machines taking off and landing, their crews strained and silent now with exhaustion. Schultze and von Ahlefeld had failed to return and that morning Dziecielski had returned wounded, his gunner dead in his seat.

'They're shooting us down like rooks,' he'd said as they'd lifted him from the cockpit.

Stoos had spent the morning alone, eating alone, waiting alone. He couldn't drag himself away from the aeroplanes and went to watch every time they took off and landed. In the mess tent he sat in silence, preferring not to answer questions, and no one bothered him as they swallowed their cold hock and French wine and grabbed what food they could cram into their mouths before the next call came.

Dawn had arrived with mist in the fields, so that the trees stood out like ghostly shapes and the stark lines of the Stukas had been softened into blurred bat shapes. His feet in the dewy grass, Stoos stared at the sky. He could hear aeroplanes droning overhead towards the beaches from the German border or further to the south where the knuckled hills of the Somme protruded from the mist.

As he stood with his hands in his pockets, brooding, an engine started up, rising to a scream as the mechanic revved it against the brakes. The sound made Stoos shudder with anticipation, then his shoulders slumped again as he realized it didn't concern him. He lit a cigarette, one of the English ones they'd captured, drew a few puffs and then threw it away. As he did so, he became aware of his gunner, Wunsche, standing behind him.

'Will they let us fly, Herr Leutnant?' he asked.

Stoos shrugged. 'Perhaps. I don't know. I have been grounded.'

As Wunsche vanished, Stoos wandered disconsolately towards the hangar. D/6980 was standing outside, the mist beading the cockpit cover.

Hamcke was by the entrance watching him, and Stoos forced himself to ignore him and walked round the machine, starting at the tail as he'd been taught, checking the fuselage, flaps ailerons and lights. After a while, unable to resist the temptation, he climbed on to the wing and eventually into the cockpit, and sat there, the sun on his neck, deep in thought, thinking of Warsaw and Rotterdam and the roads from Brussels. The dive had never ceased to thrill him.

He became aware of Hamcke standing on the wing alongside him. He was endeavouring to put things right, trying to allow for the fact that, like himself, Stoos was over-tired and affected by the strain of the campaign.

'She's all right now, Herr Leutnant,' he said. 'She's ready for testing.'

Stoos turned his head and eyed Hamcke coldly. 'At the moment, Hamcke,' he said, 'I'm not on the flying roster. As you well know.'

Hamcke flinched as though he'd been struck again and climbed off the wing. 'Well,' he said, 'someone'll have to do it. Everything we've got's going to be needed before we're finished.'

It was a feeling that was echoed by the men on the other side as well, and particularly by the admiral at Dover.

With the news of yet another destroyer lost in the first hours of the morning, came the information that several personnel ships which had left England during the night had vanished entirely in the darkness, and the admiral dared not risk any more of them to crowd the narrows until he knew where they were.

'We'd better suspend sailings until we learn a little more,' he said.

The S.O.O. glanced at a list in his hand. 'Perhaps the position's not as bad as it seems, sir,' he suggested.

The admiral frowned. 'We can't take any chances. What about the French? Are they co-operating?'

'I understand they're arriving on the beaches and the mole in increasing numbers. The formal instruction that they're to be given equal opportunity with our chaps has arrived from London. During the night, though, there was heavy mine-laying from the air and *Vimy* reported seeing a submarine off the Goodwins.'

The admiral made no comment and the S.O.O. went on. 'There's one other thing, sir. These batteries they've set up near Gravelines – Mardyck, it's believed – they're only four miles away now and they have the range of all ships coming out of the harbour area. They've been engaged, of course, but it's not known with how much success.'

The admiral took a turn up and down the room. 'I breakfasted with General Brooke,' he said. 'He thought we'd have to continue for a few more days.'

The S.O.O. raised his eyebrows. 'It'll be difficult, sir.'

'Gort's people seem to think we might manage.' The admiral gestured. 'We'll move what's left of the small craft from Ramsgate to make their main effort after midnight tonight. I think if we proceed on the same lines we've got a fair chance of success.' He paused. 'I hope so,' he ended.

Hatton hoped so, too.

With daylight, his uneasiness had increased. *Vital* was built for speed and was light and fragile. Her side plating was astonishingly thin yet Hough had slammed her against the pier as though she were a tough old ferry reinforced with rubbing strakes.

Among the men now waiting were several stretcher cases. 'Sorry about these chaps,' the piermaster called across to Hatton. 'But we can't get them aboard from the beaches, and orders have been given to leave 'em. After these, you're only to pick up unwounded who'll be able to fight again. There's no room and no time for the others.'

He saw Hatton staring at him, worried by the instructions. 'It's the only intelligent thing to do,' he explained. 'It's bloody awful for them, I know, but we've no alternative.'

He took off his helmet and ran his hand through his hair. He looked exhausted and gratefully accepted the tot of rum Hough's steward brought down for him. 'Look, for God's sake,' he said to Hatton as he left. 'Ask your captain to make a signal to Dover that we can take as many ships in here as they can send. They're *still* going to the beaches and, because of that, so are the men.'

Hatton himself carried the signal to the radio cabin and heard the cheep-cheep of the set as it was sent off. Back on the bridge, Hough was looking worried. The piermaster was right. The supply of men moving along the mole was already dwindling.

'You're the expert, Hatton,' he said. 'Nip along there and see if you can round up any more.'

His flesh crawling, Hatton moved warily into the town. There was a monument at the shore end of the mole where the shells were bursting with terrifying regularity, but the ruined buildings nearby seemed to have emptied and he stood alone on the littered pavé, his feet among the abandoned packs and steel helmets that were strewn among the pulverized bricks and scattered tiles.

'Any more for the *Skylark*?' he yelled.

Three or four men appeared and he directed them to the pier, but no one else came, and he reported back to the ship.

'They must all be on the beach, sir,' he said.

Hough cursed. 'Damnation! All right, let's go. Number One, grab all the boats you can see and get them to feed the troops to us. Nothing's to hold us up. Understand?'

Among the boats *Vital*'s first lieutenant called on the loud hailer was *Daisy*.

The whalers that had been feeding soldiers to her seemed to have disappeared, and in the end Gilbert Williams had decided to go into the shallows himself. All around them were other boats, their engines drumming, their exhausts like pale feathers against the water, and as *Daisy* nosed up to a queue of soldiers, the men surged forward, desperate to get aboard. Several disappeared from sight and failed to reappear. There was no struggle, as though in the extremities of exhaustion there was nothing left to give, and Kenny saw a man he was reaching out for simply sink out of sight, his agonized eyes beneath the helmet vanishing as he made no attempt to save himself.

For a moment, he stared at the ripples on the surface of the water. Then he came to life with a jerk, aware of dozens of hands grasping the side of the boat, clinging desperately to what seemed like a rock in their distress. He reached down and grasped one. With the weight of water in the man's clothes it was impossible to haul him aboard.

Ernie Williams joined him and the man flopped on the deck

like a stranded fish before dragging himself to his knees and crawling aft.

'There's a bunch of wounded on a pier just over there,' an officer pointed out.

The pier was made from lorries and trucks and there was considerable difficulty with the lifting swell and the crowded conditions on *Daisy*'s decks, and Gilbert Williams was beginning to watch the lightening sky nervously. 'Get them fellers aboard,' he kept saying. 'Get 'em aboard quick!'

As they headed towards *Vital*, they passed a group in a rubber dinghy paddling with the butts of their rifles.

'Give us a hand, mate,' one of them croaked. 'We're sinking!'

'You're doing better than you think.' Gilbert shouted back. 'Save your breath for baling.'

'What'll we bale with?'

'What about them things on your 'eads?'

The soldiers stared at each other then, almost to a man, snatched off their steel helmets and began to scoop.

As they neared *Vital*, they passed three large Carley floats, all tied together and all filled to capacity with men standing up to their waists in the water inside. Though *Daisy* was wildly top-heavy this time, they took them aboard.

Alongside *Vital*, however, the wounded couldn't climb the nets, and slings had to be rigged to hoist them to the decks. Hatton climbed down to speak to Gilbert.

'Look,' he said. 'No more of those, old boy.'

Gilbert looked indignant. 'These fellers is 'urt,' he said.

'I can't help it,' Hatton said. 'We can't jeopardize the ship and all the men in her. They've had signals ashore about it. They're being sneaked out by their pals.'

But when *Daisy* returned to the beach for the next trip, there was a soldier waiting with his arm missing, his whole left side swathed in bloody bandages. His face was grey white but he was still incredibly on his feet, supported by two of his friends.

'They said no wounded,' Gilbert mumbled, unable to look them in the face.

'He's not bad hurt,' one of the men supporting the injured soldier said.

'He's lost his sodden arm,' Gilbert hissed, trying not to let the injured man hear.

'For Christ's sake, mate, we'll look after him!'

Gilbert glanced at Kenny and his brother. Then he nodded. 'Go on then,' he said. 'Just the one.'

But the one was the sign for more to appear and when they went out to *Vital* there were six of them, all unable to help themselves. Hough was furious as the slings had to be rigged and Hatton almost fell down the net to board *Daisy*.

'I said no more wounded,' he snapped.

'Christ, I can't turn the poor sods back,' Gilbert said. 'There's hundreds of 'em.'

'Off we go!'

Lieutenant Wren, of the York and Lancaster Regiment, threw down the piece of wood with which he was patting his dug-out and pointed to the beachmaster.

Conybeare banged on the roof of Horndorff's hole with the butt of the Luger. 'Our turn, I think,' he said.

Horndorff crawled out to see the beachmaster waving from the shallows and Wren gazing at his dug-out sadly. 'Sorry to see the back of the old place,' he was saying cheerfully.

Horndorff stared about him. He'd spent the whole of the previous day crouching like a dog in its kennel while Conybeare dragged up a box to block the entrance and squatted outside, holding the Luger and talking idly to Wren. He was furious at the humiliation, and desperately hungry. His lips were dry with the salty wind and the bite of the flying sand.

'Officer Conybeare,' he said bitterly. 'I think you are a cold fish.'

As they headed for the sea the aeroplanes returned, and as the first bombs fell the alarm began to scream.

'I think it's designed to go off *after* the bombs drop,' Wren said.

They splashed into the shallows where a motor boat was waiting. The guns of a destroyer half a mile away began to crash, and the sound was taken up by every ship within reach and every man with a rifle or a machine-gun until the racket was ear-splitting.

'Look lively, you lot,' a man on the foredeck of the motor boat shouted as they struggled towards her.

'Always thought paddling vulgar,' Wren observed as they

waded chest-high in the water. 'Besides, I never did have much time for the seaside this time of the year. August's the month.'

'Who's this bugger?' The sailor on the boat's foredeck was staring at Horndorff.

Conybeare sighed. 'He's my prisoner,' he said. 'I'm taking him to England.'

'We ain't taking prisoners,' the sailor pointed out.

Conybeare frowned. 'I am,' he said.

As the bombing stopped, soldiers began to emerge from their holes and trenches and the cellars of houses, spitting out dust and gritty sand, to form queues once more.

Tired as he was, to Allerton the stink of blood and mutilated flesh seemed stronger than it had ever done. There was no escape from it, and scarcely a breath of wind to dissipate the still more appalling odour of the corpses that had been lying in the town now for days.

He and Rice had found their way back to the queue they'd joined the night before. It was standing in the water now, fixed, immovable, as though nailed there. No one spoke as they tagged on to it, everyone staring silently out to sea, waiting for the next boat. The dead weight of waterlogged boots and sodden clothes seemed to pin Allerton down. His trousers had ballooned out with water and felt as heavy as mercury, so that he was filled with dread that when the time came he'd be unable to move. Just ahead of him, a sergeant and a corporal were supporting a man who was barely tall enough to keep his chin above the water. Every time a swell came they lifted him bodily and, every time, he turned to them and said politely, 'Thanks, Sarge. Thanks, Corp.'

The minutes seemed to tick by like hours and Allerton, who couldn't see much for the men around him, began to be afraid he'd have to stand there half submerged for ever. A leaden depression took hold of him, as heavy as his own waterlogged body. The man in front of him seemed to be asleep standing up and Allerton found that he himself kept starting out of a warm coma that even the chill of the water couldn't penetrate.

Suddenly, he realized a boat had appeared and some wag at the end of the queue, standing neck deep, started to shout – ' 'Urry up, mate, me feet are getting wet!' They all edged warily forward again, the two N.C.O.s in front supporting the small man. 'Come on, short-arse,' the sergeant said. 'Nearly there.'

'Thanks, Sarge. Thanks, Corp. I don't know what I'd have done without you.' The politeness was intense.

As they moved further out, the water began to lap Allerton's chin and the blind urge to reach safety drove him on until his feet just maintained contact with the bottom. Two sailors in tin hats were hoisting the men in front of him out of the water. It was difficult, because the soldiers were so weary they lacked the strength to climb unaided. The sailors didn't spare them.

'Get a move on, you sloppy bastards! Just because you've lost the bloody war there's no need to hang about!'

The sergeant and the corporal pushed the small man up and climbed after him. Then the sleeping man in front of Allerton suddenly slipped away beneath the water. One moment he was there and the next he was gone, and Allerton found that in his weariness he was quite indifferent to his fate. He could just reach the boat with the tips of his fingers but when he tried to pull himself up, the weight of his waterlogged clothes made him as helpless as a sack of lead, and he hung there terrified of being left behind. Then two strong hands reached over and grasped his armpits. Another pair grasped the back of his trousers and before he had time to realize it he was head-first in the bottom of the boat.

On the deck of the destroyer, underneath a gun turret, he found himself with a lot of Frenchmen but then a head popped up out of a hatch in the deck. 'This way, sir,' it said. 'You don't want to be with a lot of French bastards. Come and have a cup of tea.'

The wardroom carpet was covered with treacly black oil, and here and there on the bulkheads were hand and feet marks and smears where grimy uniforms had rubbed. But a Maltese steward gave him a whisky and a sausage sandwich, and as he lay sprawled on a cushioned seat, uncomfortable but without the energy to move, the great burden of responsibility had gone from his shoulders. All the accumulated strain of the last few days had vanished and a sense of luxurious security flooded over him.

Hatton was working near the scrambling nets, shouting instructions through a megaphone to the boats as they came alongside.

Above him on the bridge, he could see Hough anxiously watching the sky, turning his head occasionally as a shell exploded on the beaches. 'How many, Hatton?'

'Damn near a thousand, sir.'

'Just a few more.'

The wind was increasing a little now and Hatton could hear the boats' crews shouting furiously at the soldiers. But no one argued, no one took offence. The soldiers seemed to accept that the job now was up to the navy.

On the bridge, Hough was moving anxiously from one side to the other, watching the floating wreckage and the long coils of floating grass line. Then his eyes flickered to the sky again. The lull had been a long one and he knew they had little time left.

'Hurry 'em along!' he shouted down. 'Keep 'em moving!'

As they hauled the men aboard, one of the petty officers gestured. 'Good God almighty,' he said. 'Now I've seen everything.'

Hatton looked up to see Thames barges passing them, broad-beamed and beautiful, heading towards the shore, their great spritsails soaring to the sky. As they glided past, a hospital ship, the sun on her sides, moved towards the harbour. A flurry of shells from Hinze's battery at Mardyck screamed over to drop near her but she held her speed, heading towards the mole in stately fashion as though it were peacetime and there were nothing to fear. The sight took Hatton's breath away.

'How many, Barry?'

The call from the bridge attracted his attention and he noticed that Hough had got around at last to calling him by his first name and felt vaguely flattered.

'Well over a thousand now, sir.'

Hough was staring at the sky. 'Just this lot then,' he said. 'I don't like the look of things.'

The bus conductor's rigmarole was wearing a little thin by this time but the petty officers and sailors were all using it now – 'Pass down the car, please. No standing on the platform. Plenty of room inside – ' and the weary soldiers seemed to appreciate the joke.

Then, just when he was so absorbed he hardly noticed the guns start in the distance, Hatton heard the klaxon go and heard Hough shouting.

'Get 'em on board, Barry,' he was roaring. 'Jerry's back.'

As the ropes dropped and the last man was dragged from the scrambling net, *Vital* began to pick up speed, a boat still attached by her rope bucking in the wake so that the men in her began to shout with alarm.

'Cut that boat adrift,' Hatton yelled and he saw a sailor reach out, knife in hand.

The sky seemed to be full of aeroplanes now and Hatton's ears throbbed with the din they made. The sea was erupting in great gouts of water that dropped across the decks, drenching the crouching soldiers and the running men in blue, and the guns were yammering in an insane chorus.

Up ahead a mat of small boats was clustered near another ship. At first Hatton thought *Vital* was going to plough through them, but the telegraphs clanged and she began to go astern, the storm of bombs still dropping about her, the brilliant sunshine picking up the lights as the fountains of water dissolved into a rainbow-hued spray. She was just beginning to swing her stern towards the west when there was a crash and a blinding flash, and the ship seemed to leap out of the sea. As she flopped back like a landed fish, vast columns of water collapsed across her, drenching him, and he was surrounded by thundering steam and showers of ancient soot from the funnel.

He had been trying to bring some order into the chaos near the nets and it was this that saved his life. Flung against the torpedo tubes, he clung to them for a moment, his steel helmet awry, while his wits settled back to normal amid the roar of the engine room blowers and the hysterical yapping of one of the dogs that had got on board.

Deciding he'd probably be needed on the bridge, he began to make his way there, but as he reached the ladder, one of the chief petty officers collided with him and they made their way up together, fighting to pass each other in the confusion of the moment.

The bomb had hit B turret which was hanging half over the side with great splashes of blood on the blistered paint. The bridge was an even greater horror. Flying steel splinters had riddled it until it looked like a colander. The navigating officer was lying in a corner, looking as though someone had fired a gigantic shotgun at him, his whole body and face full of red holes all pumping blood. The yeoman was curled up like a foetus, moaning.

The captain, the imperturbable Hough, had been hit by one of the flying splinters and a slice of his skull sheared off as cleanly as if by a knife. His tin hat lay near his head and his brains were oozing bloodily into it.

With daylight Didcot had returned to the gruesome task of clearing the obstruction under *Athelstan*'s stern. Tremenheere had lit his pipe and was staring towards the beach. The sands looked pearly white, the grass waving on the dunes behind. The crowded ranks were still moving in incredible order to the water's edge, and in the shallows boats were being worked laboriously out to tugs and launches, their bows dipping sharply as they reached the surf, their crews pulling fiercely to combat the current.

The smoke from burning buildings was depositing a layer of fine ash and cinders on the water, which was black and greasy with patches of iridescence that marked the grave of a ship or an aircraft. *Athelstan*'s crisp planks were now scarred by hundreds of hobnailed boots, the paintwork was scratched and chipped, and here and there was a smear of blood. The big cabin was full of sand and water, and the cushions were stained with salt. The stove had long since ceased to work and the engine room was like a pigsty. With the habit of years, Tremenheere was wondering how long it would take him to clear it all up again, when Didcot stopped what he was doing and flung up an arm. Almost at once they heard the alarms go on the destroyers.

High in the sky, faint and silvery, like midges in the sun, a group of planes was heading towards them, and the guns opened fire with a crash that nearly split their eardrums, the harsh racket of the pom-poms mingling with the crash of the heavier ack-ack.

As the sky fell in on them and the sea started to heave upwards, Tremenheere flung himself down, the kick of the explosions jarring the deck beneath him. As it jerked he saw Didcot duck and glance round, then go on poking under the stern with the boathook.

Lewis guns from the tugs and the smaller craft and the rattle of rifles from the beaches joined the racket, and the sea was flecked with small plumes of water as the bullets struck its surface and the shell splinters came singing down. Only vaguely,

Tremenheere was aware of the nearby destroyer going astern, the boats alongside her cast adrift. A whaler full of men was passing under her counter and he yelled a warning; but the bronze propellers chewed their way through the wooden boat, and planks and oars leapt out of the churning water along with frantic heads, the screams changing to strangled cries as the men were sucked under.

The dive bombers were coming down in waves now, with a howl of motors that seemed to press *Athelstan* under the sea, below the wreckage of boats and rafts and furnishings and planks. As he lifted his head, he saw Didcot still on the stern, crouching now, flinching at the explosions but still busy with the boathook.

'Get down, you bloody fool!' he yelled.

Didcot was absorbed with his grim task. 'He's coming, Alban,' he yelled back. 'He's coming!'

By this time, deafened, numbed and terrified, Tremenheere was praying with his hands over his head. He hadn't prayed since he was a boy but the din drained all the courage out of him. He glanced up to see an aeroplane with wings like a flat W and wheels that were covered in spats heading straight for him. It looked as though it were going to dive straight through the cabin door, but it lifted above them and he saw a vast bomb just above him, hanging in the air, it seemed, and flung himself down once more.

The 'whump' as it exploded lifted *Athelstan* from the water and sucked all the breath from Tremenheere's body. He was drenched with spray, then suddenly everything was quiet. He lifted his head and looked around. Miraculously the noise seemed to be dying and the aeroplanes were climbing away.

The destroyer was still going astern, heading out of control in a huge circle straight for a paddle-steamer coming out of the harbour, and he gaped at it, wondering what would happen when they met. Then he realized there was no sign of Didcot and he scrambled aft to look for him. The khaki greatcoat with the white hand was still protruding from under the stern but the boathook was floating about twenty feet away and his heart turned over. Then, close to the side of the boat, a slim figure in naval uniform bobbed to the surface. The square collar floating on the water was stained red and from it trailed a scarlet weed. Tremenheere was still gaping at it when the last bomb hit the water and he was flung backwards into the well deck.

There was no pain, only a numbing shock and a feeling of astonishment. He felt himself sliding out of life and it became an obsession to get things in order, so that he suddenly began to worry about Nell Noone. Thought seemed to be drifting away and the darkness he was sinking into was the darkness of the grave. This was the great experience of his life, he thought, yet he was bewildered and dismayed rather than alarmed. As the blackness grew round him he found he didn't care a damn.

Gazing round the shambles on *Vital's* bridge, Hatton wanted to be sick and probably would have been but for the chief petty officer.

'We're still going astern, sir,' he warned. 'And there's a paddle-steamer right aft!'

Hatton swallowed. 'How about the wheel?' he asked in a panic.

'Manned, sir.'

'Right. Stop engines.'

'Stop engines, sir.'

Hatton looked wildly about him, uncertain what to do next. The C.P.O. came to his assistance.

'Slow ahead starboard, sir,' he suggested.

Hatton nodded. 'Thanks, Chief,' he said, passing on the order by the voice pipes. 'I'll need your help. I don't know much about this.'

'O.K. sir. Wheel amidships.'

'Wheel amidships.

'Slow ahead both now, I think, sir.'

'Slow ahead both, Chief. I think we're pulling clear.'

Hatton was standing with his hands on the bridge rail. Ahead of him he could see a personnel ship on fire and he decided he'd better go round it. He felt better now he had something to do, but then, glancing down, he saw his hands were bright red and covered with sticky blood, and he immediately felt sick again.

'Starboard, sir.' The C.P.O.'s calm voice jerked him to his senses. 'Them bloody Stukas is coming down again.'

'Starboard,' Hatton repeated. '*Starboard!*' His voice rose to a shriek and he felt the ship heel. The sea erupted round him and he ducked as it came down on him in spray, fine as rain.

'Dodged the bugger, sir,' the petty officer yelled. 'I think we're clear!'

'Oh, no we're not, Chief,' Hatton said. 'I'm no ship's captain and I don't know what the hell to do. Pass the word for Number One. And let's have another man up here, too.' He was staring about him, trying to watch three manoeuvring ships at once. 'We need another look-out.'

As the C.P.O. vanished to the back of the bridge, for a while Hatton was alone, in command of a badly damaged ship, surrounded by dead and dying men and in charge of all decisions. The voice pipe was shrieking but he daren't take his eye off the litter of wreckage ahead. Then he heard shoes pounding on the ladder and the first lieutenant's shocked voice.

'My God!' he said. Then, 'Well done, Hatton! I've got the con. Answer that pipe and then get the sick bay tiffies up here to clear up the mess. I saw a lot of pongos lying about.'

'Aye aye, sir.' Hatton was aware now of a new prickling feeling of confidence, but he was knocked flying as another officer made his way to the bridge, followed by a petty officer and a rating. Below the bridge was a shambles of twisted steel, torn bodies and the sobbing, swearing shapes of sailors trying to clear things away. When Hatton looked up, the beaches were about half a mile away. Dunkirk was over on his left and half a mile behind him, and it was there that the Stukas caught them for a second time. They came over in tightly-knit packets, black against the pale blue, little dots surrounded by dissolving satellites of ack-ack fire. There was a crash aft and, glancing back, terrified, Hatton saw pieces of metal and wood and human beings hitting the water.

Vital began to settle. Figures burst through the smoke, their heads down, their arms raised against the flames. Hatton was just heading towards the damage when another bomb struck the ship and she began to heel over and the running men began to slide sideways into the flames.

The stern of the ship was terrible now beyond words. Men were being dragged out of the furnace to the comparative safety forward, but the wounded and dying were still lying with the flames licking over them and Hatton's mind was in complete confusion because his experience hadn't fitted him for this sort of horror.

There was another explosion and he felt himself blown across the deck to crash sickeningly against a stanchion. He knew at once that he'd cracked or broken a rib because there was a violent pain in his side and he couldn't straighten up properly. The ships' guns were still going, even with the list that was on her, and then it suddenly dawned on him that *Vital* was rolling right over. He saw the water rise on the port side in a raging torrent and wondered whether he ought to save himself or wait for the order to abandon ship.

Vital was at an angle of forty-five degrees now and he was clutching the stanchion to keep his feet, but then the sea came in a roaring maelstrom and he saw men struggling clear of the swinging stays and falling equipment, and took a deep breath as the water closed over his head.

It was at the first crash that Horndorff realized he'd been given another chance. As he scrambled to his feet, the lights went out and he realized Conybeare had disappeared.

There was a strong smell of petrol and someone shouted, 'For God's sake, don't strike a match.' Then he was fighting his way to the daylight, his strong hands plucking smaller men from his path in his determination to escape. As he reached the deck, he saw a shambles of torn steel and bodies, and splintered bulkheads that were splashed with blood. Sailors were wrenching at corpses, throwing them aside to clear a pathway.

'Over the side,' an officer was shouting, and they began to toss the bodies into the sea as if they'd been so much refuse.

He pushed his way through the struggling men. He was a land animal and knew little about ships, but it didn't take much intelligence to realize that the ship was beginning to settle. The whole of the stern was in flames and he turned round and headed back the way he'd come, determined to survive, determined to get ashore, come what might.

Tearing his helmet off, he hurled it over the side and wrenched at his belt to scramble out of the overalls he wore. As he threw them aside, a sailor bumped into him. He was dragging at the body of a man whose legs had been torn off. 'Give us a hand, mate,' he said, and automatically Horndorff bent to assist.

It was as the body disappeared that Horndorff realized that now no one could tell his nationality, and he was trying to make up his mind what to do next when another bomb hit the ship. As he picked himself up, he found he was sliding sideways and it dawned on him that the ship was heeling over. He was no swimmer but, as he saw men jumping into the sea, he sat down and wrenched off his boots, tossing them away one after the other. He stood up, his trousers flapping against his ankles as the ship began to roll.

A sailor nudged him. 'This way, mate,' he said. 'Or you'll be caught.'

Horndorff followed the sailor over the port rail and, as he slithered down the side of the ship, she disappeared beneath his feet and he was swimming.

The explosion that had freed Horndorff, had knocked Allerton unconscious, and when he came to he found he was being pummelled by boots as men scrambled over him as he lay on the deck. Fighting his way upright, he caught his breath in horror. Bodies were lying one on top of another in a tatter of bloodstained flesh and clothing.

Scrambling over the scattered kit to the deck, he saw that the ship was already heeling over and men were beginning to jump into the sea. Then he realized his face was painful and, putting his hand up, he found it came away covered with blood. Tenderly he felt his mouth and realized he'd lost several teeth.

Bodies were sliding into the scuppers as the ship began to roll, and then he was in the water, fighting his way to the surface through a mass of tangled rope that appeared to come from the ship's falls.

As he bobbed up, spluttering, someone fell on top of him and he was knocked under again, half unconscious. As he came up once more he hit his head on a floating oar and automatically put out his hand and clutched it, hanging over it with his arms on one side, his body on the other, his head almost in the water with exhaustion, pain and misery.

Trapped under the ship, Hatton felt his lungs were going to burst, then the stanchion was torn from his grip and he kicked out. Above him the water grew lighter and he broke to the surface. Not thirty yards away the stern of the ship was sticking up, the propellors still slowly revolving. He could see only one Carley float on the surface of the sea and he began to swim towards it. As he did so a row of splashes appeared and he heard the howl of engines; men swimming just ahead of him sank out of sight and he found himself struggling in water that was red with blood.

He wasn't sure how long he was in the sea, but suddenly he was aware of a whaler with a splintered bow looming over him. A badly wounded soldier near him was pleading for help and he turned to pull him towards the whaler, but by the time they reached it the soldier was dead and Hatton let him go and saw another swimmer push the body aside indifferently as he fought his own way to safety.

As he was dragged over the side, he found himself sprawled by another gasping figure. It was in the remains of its underwear and it was impossible to tell whether it was a soldier or a sailor – only that it was a boy.

'You've no idea how funny you look, sir,' the boy said. 'Just like a nigger minstrel.'

But he didn't laugh and neither did Hatton because laughing, moving, breathing, even thinking, hurt too much.

'Perhaps you'll let my mum know, sir,' the boy whispered. 'She'll want to know.'

Hatton nodded painfully, on his knees trying to catch the whispers. 'Yes,' he said. 'I'll let her know. I'll contact her as soon as we get back.'

But he knew he never would because the boy's identity discs had disappeared, the string burned away in the flames that had scorched his face and charred his body so that he looked bald and black and wet-through at the same time.

How long Tremenheere was unconscious he didn't know. He came round to find himself lying on the well deck of *Athelstan*, staring up at the sky. At first he thought he was dead. But then he realized he could hear the throb of engines about him and the deeper roar of a big ship's blowers somewhere. Remembering that *Athelstan* had been immobilized by a body under the propeller, he decided he just couldn't bring himself to think about it and, climbing to his feet, he stumbled to the private cupboard where Knevett kept his supply of drink. It was locked so he used a marlin spike to break it loose.

It opened with a splintering crash and, reaching inside for the whisky bottle, he wrenched out the cork and, tossing it away, raised the bottle to his mouth. It helped solve a lot of things.

The problem Allerton had to solve was that of getting ashore. Clinging to his oar, he recovered his wits and his strength and, with the will that exists in every man until he dies, he'd started to fight back and kick his way slowly towards the beach.

As he reached the sand, he lay for a long time in the shallows among the floating packs and planks and ropes. Then he realized he was being nudged by the body of a man in the blue trousers and jersey of a sailor, and weakly he pushed it away and struggled to his knees. Staggering to his feet he headed up the beach until the sand became dry beyond the tide line. There the afternoon sun was blissfully warm on his face and he flopped down. Within a moment he was asleep.

For Horndorff it was just as much of an effort. He was a poor swimmer, and, as *Vital* had rolled over more than half a mile from land, even with a splintered spar to assist him it was a long way.

As he drew nearer the beach, he began to feel the tide had turned and that he was drifting out to sea again. In a panic, he let the spar go and tried to head for the shore on his own. But he'd misjudged his own strength and he knew he was going to drown. His flailing arms grew slower and slower, and then he realized that his legs were not moving at all and that he was wallowing half under the water.

He tried again to force movement into his limbs but they were like lead now. Desperately he tried to touch bottom with his feet, but he was still too far from the shallows and he began to sink. His mind full of the cruelty of a fate that allowed him to drown while his comrades won promotion and medals, he at last forced his legs and arms to work again. A man was watching from the beach, but he could hardly see him through the blur of fatigue and aching agony and the glare of the lowering sun.

Slowly he drew towards the surf, but by this time his head was as often under the water as it was above, and as his flailings grew weaker he knew he'd never make it. Suddenly he didn't seem to care, and as his arms and legs came to a halt he lay in the water and allowed himself to sink.

Not very far from where Horndorff was quietly drowning,

Scharroo and Marie-Josephine were still pursuing Marie-Josephine's idea of getting a boat to England. A morning of bombing and shelling had scared the wits out of Scharroo, but Marie-Josephine seemed to have become obsessed by her idea to the point of indifference to danger.

'For God's sake,' Scharroo grated as they spat out grit and clawed the sand from their clothes after the violence of the last terrifying attack, 'you still don't have that crazy idea, do you?'

'But of course!' She looked at him as though startled by the question.

He pointed at the ship lying in the roadstead surrounded by smoke and steam, and at the wreckage where *Vital* had disappeared. 'You see what they're doing to them?'

'Not *all* of them. Some they do not hit. We must ask.'

It seemed that the first essential to getting out of Dunkirk was a permit to board one of the ships but when they found the embarkation office, the man in charge stared at them as though they were mad.

'For *whom*?' he asked.

'Me,' Scharroo said. 'And the girl.'

'And neither of you are English?'

'Right. I'm American. She's –'

The officer interrupted. 'Do you think I've got nothing better to do just now than issue permits to people who want to make day-trips to England.' He flinched as a bomb landed nearby. 'We're trying to evacuate a bloody army.'

They walked slowly back to the beach. Though no one seemed to want them, no one questioned them either. The evacuation was so extraordinary it never seemed to occur to anyone to wonder how they came to be there, and they moved to a pier made of lorries. A naval officer was about to help Marie-Josephine into a boat when he looked up.

'Who the hell are you?' he said.

'She's trying to get to England,' Scharroo said.

'So are a lot of other people. And who are *you*, come to that?'

'Walter Scharroo. American. U.A.P.'

'Sorry. Can't take you.'

'Take her then.' Scharroo was beginning to wish he'd never seen Marie-Josephine by this time.

'She's a civilian. My job's to take *these* chaps back.'

The argument continued as the other soldiers pushed past them. When the boat was full, it pulled away and they were left standing on the pier. The men behind them didn't seem to resent them and Scharroo had the impression that, as far as they were concerned, they could have gone and welcome.

It was late afternoon when they tried again. They'd left it for some time, hoping the climate would change, and by this time they were both hungry. For a long time they moved about the beach, until they found a young officer organizing a fresh queue. Seeing a new point of organization, other soldiers were running to join it and Scharroo grabbed Marie-Josephine's hand and dragged her after them.

As they waited, the officer moved along the line, studying each man. At Scharroo and Marie-Josephine he stopped.

'Where do you think you're going?' he asked.

'To England,' Scharroo said.

'Oh, are you?' The officer looked tired to the point of numbness and his nerves were clearly on edge. 'Who the hell are you, anyway?' he asked.

'Name's Scharroo.'

'British?'

'American.'

'Sorry.'

As he turned away, Scharroo caught his arm. 'The girl's not American.'

The officer turned. His eyes were red-rimmed with lack of sleep and he seemed almost out on his feet.

'British?'

'French.'

'Sorry.'

'For God's sake – ' Scharroo's frustration and anger burst out ' – the goddam French have been fighting for you!'

The officer stared at him coldly. 'I thought we'd been fighting for *them*,' he said.

Scharroo turned away and pushed Marie-Josephine from the queue. 'Come on,' he said. 'The bastards are running so fast you can't see 'em for dust.'

Moving further along the beach, they came to a group of French soldiers arguing loudly. A British soldier watching them sneered.

'The bastards tried to rush the boats,' he said.

The Frenchmen seemed to take a different view, and one of their officers, staring out to sea, his face twisted with bitterness, explained. 'They do not undertand that some of these men have never seen a ship before in their lives,' he said. 'They come from the Jura and the Midi and the Alps and the Dordogne. What do *they* know about climbing into boats?' He gestured angrily. 'One would think their precious boats were made of paper, they are so afraid of them turning over.'

The signal about *Vital*'s end arrived in Dover late in the afternoon.

'It's going to become harder than ever now, sir,' the S.O.O. said. 'Bray Dunes is under shellfire now.'

'What about Gort? Is he off yet?'

'Yes, sir. I understand he's aboard *Hebe*.'

The admiral was silent for a moment. 'Dunkirk thinks it won't be possible to hold the perimeter after midnight on the first,' he said.

'And the evacuation of the rear-guard, sir?'

The admiral looked up. 'Postponed until dawn on the second.'

By this time Hinze's shells were dropping regularly on the beaches. The streams of ships, big and small, kept coming, however, and the wind had diminished a little, the surf had died down again, and the makeshift piers were beginning to pay dividends. As darkness approached, the whole horizon was dotted with small craft, moving in a maze of wreckage and zig-zagging to dodge the explosions. They were manned by every kind of crew imaginable, R.A.S.C. cadets, naval officers, masters of Sea Scout troops, parsons, old men wearing carpet slippers. Tugs pulled crippled ships or tows of small boats full of rescued men to put them aboard the personnel ships. Trawlers jammed men into cabins, fish holds, wheelhouses, and decks, and more were crammed among the coal dust in barges that had only recently been carrying fuel to London power stations.

Among them, *Daisy* chugged steadily backwards and forwards from the beach, Kenny Pepper beyond words at the awe of it all. Despite the noise and weariness, he was impressed by the sheer stark courage about him, and amazed at the admiration and affection he felt for Gilbert and Ernie Williams. From the day they'd taken him under their wing, rough, foul-mouthed, kindly men who'd chivvied and jeered at him, he'd never considered they could be brave but now he'd seen them proving it, and it dawned on him that nobility was something that came to men of all classes.

By this time he'd grown indifferent to things which forty-eight hours before would have turned his heart over, and as they stopped for a moment to draw breath, Gilbert Williams shoved his head out of the wheelhouse.

'Tea, Kenny,' he called. 'Better give old Sy a mugful while you're at it.'

'I was going to.' Brought up on tales of heroism, Kenny was surprised that he could feel compassion for cowardice. 'He can't help it.'

Gilbert nodded. 'Make it quick, son, or them bloody Jerries'll be back afore we've drunk it.'

It was more than likely because it had suddenly occurred to Alfred Stoos that he was sitting on the ground, D/6980 was sitting on the ground and Wunsche was sitting on the ground, and there was work to do.

'She needs testing,' Hamcke had said of D/6980.

Very well, Stoos decided, he would test her.

Allerton had spent most of the day lying on the beach. The sinking of *Vital* had left him drained of energy and he'd sprawled as though dead on the sand. No one had gone near him because they'd assumed he was just another of the drowned silent bodies that littered the shoreline. The tide had fallen away from him and eventually his clothes had dried, but still he hadn't moved. It was only when the tide had returned and the chilly water had lapped at his legs that he awakened.

He had no idea what time it was, or even which day. There was no one about him he knew. Nearby, a soldier was lying on the sand, horribly burned, the only indication that he was alive the slow movements of his hands. There was nothing Allerton could do and he staggered past him towards the dunes. All he wanted was safety – not the safety of England, just the safety of dry land where the sea couldn't snatch him under.

Where he finally sank to the sand again, a man in the coloured forage cap of a cavalry regiment was digging a hole with an empty corned beef tin. He looked up but went on digging, and Allerton went to sleep again. His mind had stopped working. A safety valve had lifted and his brain, as well as his limbs, had gone limp.

When he woke the sun was still shining, but it was low now above the horizon and the cavalryman alongside him lay head-down half-inside his hole. The dry sand, stirred by the breeze, was slipping down in little rivulets from the lip, gradually burying his head and shoulders and disturbing the flies encrusted on the blood on his jacket and the edge of the corned beef can he'd been using.

Then Allerton became aware of the stink again. It was like a slaughterhouse and, scrambling to his feet, he moved out of the dunes and into the town, numbed, stupefied, and devoid of emotion.

Telephone wires hung in dangling loops among the fallen masonry but nearby he could hear laughter and saw a man on a lorry tossing out cartons of cigarettes as he drove post. A machine-gun was chattering away on his left and he heard another answer it, and then a group of light infantrymen in full equipment went by, heading for the beaches in their quick high step, led by a man playing a fife. They were singing.

> Ten men went to walk, walk along the sand dunes.
> Ten men, nine men, eight men, seven men, six men,
> five men, four men, three men, two men, one man
> and his dog walked along the sand dunes.

A group of officers standing in a garden, eating biscuits and bully beef, took pity on him. They were dirty, stained and red-eyed with sleeplessness but they were still part of a unit.

'What happened, old boy?' one of them asked, staring at Allerton's swollen mouth and scarecrow appearance.

'I was on a destroyer,' Allerton explained. 'It was hit by a bomb. What time is it?'

They told him and he rubbed his hand over his features. 'I've lost a day somewhere,' he said.

They gave him a cigarette and a small square of corned beef on a biscuit tasting of diesel oil. 'All we can spare, I'm afraid. Sorry we've nothing to drink. We had a touch of gin but it's all gone now.'

The sun was only just above the horizon now and the Stukas seemed to have disappeared. Groups of soldiers were strolling about the beach, bored with waiting. Offshore, *Vital*'s stern was still sticking out of the water, the bronze propellers catching the sun.

As he lifted his head, Horndorff realized he was lying with his feet still in the water but that his head was clear. At first, because he felt so much at peace with the world and his last thoughts had been concerned with dying, he was certain he was dead. Then he realized where he was and lifted his head to stare into the sun. There were groups of soldiers standing in the water, their boots in their hands, their helmets on the back of their heads. Higher up the beach he could see a lorry blazing and a few men drinking out of tin mugs round a Bofors gun which was cocked towards the sky. Nobody took any notice of him and it occurred to him he was free to go where he liked.

Slowly, still exhausted, he dragged himself on to all fours, chilled despite the sunshine. Then he turned his head and saw Conybeare.

He was sitting down, his figure stretching a long shadow on the sand. He was wearing stockings but had lost the clumsy boots. His tunic with its wings lay alongside him and he looked like a small boy on the beach for the day, but in his hand he still held the Luger and Horndorff was staring straight into the muzzle.

'We nearly didn't make it,' Conybeare said.

Horndorff's eyes blazed and then he realized what Conybeare meant.

'*You* saved me?' he said.

Conybeare nodded. 'Good swimmer,' he said.

'Is there anything you're not good at?' Horndorff asked bitterly.

Conybeare shrugged. 'Good at most things,' he said. 'Got here pretty quickly. Knew what you'd do. Walked up and down the tide line waiting for you.'

Still on his hands and knees, his clothes damp against his big

body, Horndorff stared at Conybeare, his expression full of loathing.

'*You* saved me,' he said. '*You* saved my life?'

'That's right.'

'*Why*?' The word was almost a screech. '*Why*? *Why*?'

Sitting in a garden in the southern suburbs of the town, Sievewright wondered at his own blind faith. He'd long since decided
that too much was happening for him to get involved and had
decided to wait for darkness before attempting to move on.

He'd found the garden at the back of a big house that had
been burnt out. The grass and the flowers were covered with flakes
of soot and fragments of charred wood, but it was surrounded
by a high wall and there were larches and laurel and cedars in it
that had kept the heat of the sun from him. He'd chosen it deliberately because, seeing the black puppy with him, the provost
sergeant on duty outside the town had advised him to get rid of it.

'The bloody place's full of dogs,' he said. 'All going potty with
the bangs. They're having to shoot 'em on the quayside.'

In the time since he'd picked up the animal, Sievewright had
grown attached to it. The idea of seeing it destroyed was just too
much for him, and he sat now with his back to a tree, sharing
his last biscuit with it. It squatted in front of him watching him
as he broke fragments off and passed them across.

He was hungry but in no way dispirited. It was already dark
and soon, with a bit of luck, he told himself, he could go and find
a ship.

Behind Sievewright, at close on midnight, Lance-Corporal Gow
and his little detachment of British and French soldiers were
approaching the town. As they'd moved back after their action by
the canal, they'd picked up an abandoned lorry, but while they
were still crowing their delight it had dawned on them that the
lorry was abandoned because the Germans to the east had somehow managed to filter past; an artillery detachment had expertly
bracketed a bend in the road they were on and were hitting everything that tried to move towards the dumping area on the edge
of the perimeter. In the distance four trucks were burning, and
about them were men of the Wiltshire Regiment trying to make
up their minds how to tackle the problem.

'Well, we cannae stay here,' Gow had pointed out firmly.

Gibbering with fear, trying to screw himself up to the exquisite agony of daring that he'd never have managed without Gow scowling beside him, Noble had driven the lorry at full speed down the road, fully expecting every moment to be his last until, thirty yards from the bend, Gow had screamed at him – 'Brake!' Even as he had slammed the lorry to a standstill, he heard the whistle of shells and saw flashes and mushrooming clouds of dust and smoke in front.

'Now, mon,' Gow screeched. 'Full speed!'

His heart in his mouth, Noble had jammed the accelerator down and they'd gone round the corner on two wheels, their nostrils full of the smell of cordite from the smoke still drifting across it. As they'd headed into the next straight he'd heard the crash of shells behind them, and he'd climbed out by the dumping area on shaking legs.

'Gow,' he'd said. 'I'm frightened. *You* frighten me.'

Now, as they approached the town, the roads were scored with shell-holes and strewn with broken glass, and occasionally in the flames they saw a rat move.

Men were still working in the vast car parks, destroying the vehicles. Occasionally a shell burst and the fragments hissed down, but the work of destruction never stopped. Artificers were attaching 50-yard lengths of signal wire to the trigger levers of their guns. Cordite bags were being taken out of the cartridge cases and their contents scattered, so that if an advancing German – trying for a quiet smoke – tossed away an unwary match, he'd be surrounded in an instant sheet of flame. Men were trudging to the canal with 25-pound shells and loading their last vehicles with dial sights, clinometers and director heads. Only the Bren gunners and the Boyes riflemen kept their weapons.

As Gow and his men tramped past, a gunner picked up a shell, took the fuse cap off and slid it carefully down the muzzle to the breech. Warily, he placed another in the breech with the charge.

'Look out, they're going to press the tit,' a sergeant warned and, as they headed for the ditch, an officer pulled the signal wire attached to the trigger. When they lifted their heads the gun was scrap.

They were all hungry and tired now and Private Angelet was asleep on his feet, putting one foot automatically in front of the other, his eyes open but unconscious of what went on around him. Lije Noble, limping heavily now, also craved sleep but was still uncertain which was worse, being hungry and tired or having Lance-Corporal Gow pounce on him. Only Gow and Chouteau seemed untouched by weariness. For most of the march back, they'd argued in an extraordinary Anglo-French jargon of their own devising which was the better unit, the Foreign Legion or the Brigade of Guards. So far honours seemed to be about even.

Apart from the few gunners trailing behind them the roads to Dunkirk seemed deserted now. Summer lightning flashed along the horizon where guns were still firing, and ahead was only the dreadful beacon of the dying town. The road was strewn with the wreckage of the retreat and occasionally there were stray flashes and explosions.

As they passed through Rosendael, sergeants were calling names in rasping whispers as though the Germans might hear. Skeleton walls like the ruins of some bygone civilization reared on either side of them but the only sound was the crunching of glass under their boots, like the crackling of ice in winter. The darkness was peopled by shapeless muffled figures, and occasionally mysterious shadows appeared in doorways or from round corners – stray inhabitants, a few looters, perhaps an occasional fifth columnist. Names were still being shouted – 'That A Company, 5th Warwicks?' – 'Alf, where are you?' – 'This way, George' – as the British fragments of the rear-guard filtered back. The road was narrow, and a lorry-load of French troops trying to force their way past came within an ace of being shot to pieces as half a dozen tired and furious men had their rifles at the driver's throat in a moment.

As they reached the shelter of the town and began to pick their way through the ruins, the German aircraft came over again and Noble ducked and ran, feeling that the rags of his backside were flapping. Gow remained standing in the roadway, as though wishing he could defy the whole might of the German air force and, from his shelter under the wall of a house, Noble leapt up and took a running dive at him so that they went staggering together from the centre of the road to fall through the hedge into a garden behind.

The bomb hit the house where Noble had been sheltering and he watched the walls bulge outwards and collapse in a balloon-

ing cloud of smoke and dust. The last few slates sliced murderously through the air and the last few bricks came rolling across
the road, bouncing and jumping as though they were alive. Awed
by the near miss, Noble let his head sink wearily to the hard pavé.

Gow pushed at him gently, his voice concerned. 'You hit, mon?'
he asked.

'No,' Noble said. 'Just bloody terrified.'

The admission changed Gow's tone. 'You shoved me,' he
accused. 'Why'd you do that?'

Noble turned his head slowly and looked at Gow's indignant
face in the glow of the flames. 'Because you're bloody soft in the
head,' he exploded. 'Somebody's got to look after you!'

They looked round for Chouteau, but he and Angelet had disappeared. Gow's indignation increased. 'And look what you've
done! Ye've made us lose oor pals!'

Noble stared at him, not understanding him. He'd never
understood him from the moment they'd met.

Gow stood up and stared about him. 'Call his name,' he said.

'I don't know his bloody name! *You* call!'

'I forgot it. Yon French hae such bluidy queer names. What
about yon little feller? Somethin' aboot angels, I think.'

As they moved away they bumped into a soldier stumbling
past with a bottle of wine under his arm. 'Where you get that,
mate?' Noble demanded.

'None of your business.'

Noble swung on the soldier's arm. 'Look, mate – ' he gestured
at Gow ' – I'll get my mate to shove his Bren up your nostril
if you don't cough up.'

The soldier looked at Gow's stark haggard features and glittering eyes. 'Down there.' His arm moved. 'You have to pay.'

Noble patted his back pocket where the takings from the
NAAFI were tucked. 'I can pay,' he said.

As Gow and Noble went in one direction, Allerton was moving
in the other. He didn't feel ill, just incredibly weary and cold
despite the heat of the flames.

By this time the beaches were a bedlam of different tongues,
increasing difficulties and lack of discipline, and the town a madhouse of rumour and counter-rumour, disorder, exhaustion,
growing apprehension and failing communications. No one knew

anything and lives were being lost as orders contradicted each other. It was the debit side of the success.

After a while he met a man wearing a kilt who was either drunk or shocked.

'They said Ah kidnae wear ma kilt,' he was announcing at the top of his voice. ' "Battledress," they said. "Everybody wears battledress." *Battledress*!' he spat. ' "Wee Alec Galt has worn his kilt sin' he joined an' long before," Ah said, "an' he's wearin' it the noo. So up yer, Jock." '

He had a bunch of pamphlets in his hand and he offered one to Allerton. At first Allerton thought they might be instructions on what to do but they were German propaganda leaflets.

'*The Game Is Over*,' he read. '*The Stumps Are Drawn. British Soldiers, your troops are entirely surrounded. Put down your arms.*'

'They must hae known we were short of bum fodder,' the Highlander said.

Passing them now were groups of men who'd got hold of drink. One man was wearing a fur stole. 'Tell Lord Gort,' he shouted, 'that Trooper Forrest of the Yeomanry presents his compliments and tells him he can stick his bloody British army where the monkey sticks its nuts.'

The Highlander looked shocked. 'For Christ's sake, mon,' he said. 'Hae ye no pride?'

'Arseholes to you, you kilted bastard,' the man in the stole said, and the Highlander dropped his pamphlets to the ground and jerked his rifle butt up. The man in the stole was lifted off the ground and lay draped across a hedge.

'That's shown yon bastard!' the Highlander said, carefully picking up his pamphlets and stalking off. 'No bastard insults a Scotsman's kilt.' He turned to Allerton. 'You'll be all right, mate. There are thirty thousand marines coming ashore later the day. This lot's only temporary.'

Allerton watched him stalk off, a stocky figure with a grimy face, wearing his helmet on the back of his head, his kilt swinging as he walked. The man in the fur stole still lay on his back half through the hedge. Several men who had watched the incident crossed the road and pulled him free.

'There's vicious for you,' a high Welsh voice said indignantly. 'His jaw's broke.'

'Serve the bugger right! You can't insult a Highlander's kilt.'

Allerton couldn't see why not. Plenty of people seemed to be doing more than merely insult each other that day.

The corned beef he'd eaten had given him a raging thirst and he moved into a nearby house to find a drink. He tried the tap but nothing came out, and he thought of the lavatory cistern. The water brought life back to him as it went down his cracked throat. Picking his way through streets that had long since become impassable to vehicles, he passed a church that seemed to be surrounded by a rising and falling sound of sighing he could hear even above the explosions. It puzzled him and then, as he saw ambulances, he realized it came from the throats of wounded men.

He went inside and the scene shocked him. It was packed with Frenchman, turbaned Moroccans, British and Belgians. They seemed to be mostly half-conscious but as he recoiled he saw the haggard eyes of one man fixed on him, feverish and piercingly bright. 'Got a fag, mate?' he asked.

The air raids had stopped as Scharroo and Marie-Josephine headed along the beach. Baffled and defeated, Scharroo was aware of Marie-Josephine's honest young eyes on him, all her courage and determination displayed in them.

'If you're so goddam set on going to England,' he said in desperation, 'and if they're only taking the army, then, the hell with it, let's be part of it.'

They began to search the shoreline and eventually they found a pair of trousers, two damp battledress blouses and two steel helmets. Marie-Josephine slipped out of the cream coat without a word and pulled the trousers up round her waist over the flowered dress. As she did so, Scharroo realized she was laughing. Startled that she could manage to find any humour in the situation, he held the battledress blouse for her, pushing the collar of her dress down while she pulled the army jacket round her. Her neck was soft and warm and feminine under her hair, and as the back of his hand touched her throat, she turned silently, and put her arms round him. He pushed her away roughly and struggled into the second battledress himself.

'Let's go see what we can do,' he said.

As they moved along the beach, they could see the pin-pricks of thousands of cigarettes and the occasional flash of a torch in the blackness, and could hear the putt-putt of engines.

An officer was directing men to the boats and they joined the group around him.

'Where do we go?' Scharroo asked.

'What's your unit?'

For a moment, Scharroo was at a loss. 'Well, hell,' he said, trying to remember names he'd heard. 'Royal Durham Light Infantry.'

A torch flashed in his face immediately.

'There's no such bloody regiment,' the officer snapped. 'Do you mean the Durham Light Infantry?'

'Yeah. I guess that's it?'

The torch remained on Scharroo's face. 'Then why did you say "*Royal* Durham Light Infantry". Who the hell *are* you, anyway?' The officer stared, then he turned. 'Sergeant!'

Scharroo grabbed Marie-Josephine's hand and in a moment they were lost in the darkness. The elation he had felt in the Germans' victory had turned to disgust at their methods, yet he could find little to admire in the British and French failure. His lips were cracked by the salty breeze and he found swallowing difficult as he peered into the darkness with eyes that were gritty with tiredness.

'We'd better look for something to eat,' he said gruffly and, swinging his jacket over his shoulder, he began to walk up the beach.

The town was full now of men from the rear-guard, fighting troops trudging through the Place Jean Bart and down the Boulevard Jeanne d'Arc and past the ruins of the church of St. Eloi. They still had excellent discipline but were too tired by this time to do anything more than just put one foot in front of another.

In the rue Gregoire de Tours a baker and the owner of a bar had joined forces, and Scharroo was able to buy a bottle of warm beer and half a loaf of newly baked bread. The charge was monstrous but he didn't argue and took the food to Marie-Josephine who was sitting on the edge of the pavement alongside a man in a navy blue jersey. He was drunk and, even as he approached, Scharroo could smell the rum on his breath.

'I had me own boat,' he was saying loudly. 'And I worked up and down that bloody beach till I was ready to drop. And then they go and run me down with a bloody destroyer. Just like that.' He belched loudly and moved restlessly inside his clothes. 'Ford eight engine she had,' he went on. 'Go for days. Not a nut or a bolt or a piece of wire I didn't know.'

In her prim fashion, Marie-Josephine was embarrassed by the sailor's drunkenness and she finished the food quickly and brushed off the crumbs. 'What must we do?' she asked.

As Scharroo's weary thoughts churned, they heard aeroplane engines again and everybody started to disappear. 'We've got to find shelter,' he said.

Somewhere above them they heard the scream of a bomb starting, faint as a whisper, then growing louder until it filled the air. Pulling Marie-Josephine into the shelter of a big square building, Scharroo crouched with his arms about her. The crash flung them together and, as he felt her cheek against his, he realized it was wet with tears, the first real chink he'd found in her hard little armour. As he stood up, he noticed men running and, guessing they were heading for a shelter, he dragged her after him. He was just in time to see a wooden door in a warehouse slam to, but he flung his weight against it and they fell inside to stumble down a flight of stone steps.

The air was warm and stuffy with the smell of hundreds of bodies. There was a dim light in the distance, and as they moved towards it he saw they were in a cellar. There seemed to be dozens of men there, most of them French, and a lot of bottles circulating. A few people were singing but the smell was one of fear. The moving flames from the candles, sucked and whipped by the eddies of blast, caught the faces and the haze of cigarette smoke, and as they cast their shadows on the brick walls, it seemed to Scharroo like the pictures by Doré for Dante's *Purgatorio*.

They stopped dead, and he saw Marie-Josephine's eyes were large and frightened. The men in front of them were all clearly trying to behave as though they were indifferent, but Scharroo saw their eyes lifting every time the thud of a bomb brought dust from the roof.

'Let's get of here,' he said.

They struggled back towards the door but as Marie-Josephine stumbled along behind him, her helmet fell off. There was a shout and several Frenchmen reached out to grab her. Scharroo swung at them but they came back and one of them seized her round the waist. She started to scream and, as his own arms were held, Scharroo could see her eyes dilated with terror and was certain he was going to see her raped.

Then a small man with a sleek black moustache and side-whiskers brought the butt of his rifle up and Scharroo heard the clop as it caught an unguarded jaw, and a tall white-faced man with dried blood on his face and a bandage under his helmet pushed forward and, plucking the girl aside, shoved the Frenchman away.

'We'd be best oot o' here,' he said.

Scharroo had lost his jacket with his wallet containing his papers, but he didn't attempt to search for it, and as they reached the steps a bomb hit the other end of the building. There was a flash, then the air seemed to be sucked away and, as it came back with clouds of dust and yells, they saw the end of the cellar cave in.

The bombs were still coming down as they stumbled clear and they had just fallen flat on a patch of open land when they saw the corner of the warehouse come down in a thundering cascade of bricks, slates and splintering wood. Several rats bounded across the road, like symbols of doom. Then there was an explosion that rocked the earth and lumps of brick and masonry were hurled hundreds of feet in all directions, and brilliant flashes like magnesium flares illuminated the black heart of the wreathing smoke. When the rain of debris stopped, Scharroo lifted his head. One of the rats was running round in circles in the roadway, its high squeal quite distinct above the din, but there was no sign of life from the ruins of the warehouse.

'There must have been ammunition in there,' Scharroo said.

Marie-Josephine drew a beep breath. 'I do not believe our friends escape,' she whispered.

'I guess not.'

'We must go to the beach.' Marie-Josephine's voice was flat. 'They take us soon, I think. They take everybody in the end.'

It was beginning to seem they might, but in Dover where they were working out the day's totals and balancing them against the losses, the admiral stared bleakly at a map of the coastline. 'There are now only seven and a half miles between the front and the mole,' he pointed out. 'Bray Dunes will be under shellfire now and Malo-les-Bains tomorrow.'

'All the same, sir,' the S.O.O. said encouragingly. 'Sixty-eight thousand men. Twenty-three thousand from the beaches alone. And here's something that'll warm your heart, sir.' He read out from a signal flimsy. 'From captain of *Oriole*, sir. She's a paddle minesweeper, 12th Flotilla. "Submit ref. K.R. and A.I. 1167. Deliberately grounded H.M.S. *Oriole* Belgian coast dawn May 29th on own initiative. Objective speedy evacuation of troops. Refloated dusk same day no apparent damage. Will complete S232 when operations permit meantime am again proceeding Belgian coast and will again run aground if such course seems desirable." '

'Who is it?' the admiral asked. 'Anyone I know?'

'Shouldn't think so, sir. R.N.V.R. type. I gather he decided to use his ship as a pier, and three thousand men passed over her before he finally brought her back with seven hundred of his own.'

The admiral allowed himself a small smile. 'It brightens the day,' he said.

SATURDAY, 1 JUNE

Vital had been hit somewhere before noon and had rolled over shortly afterwards. When the badly burned boy died, and because he could think of nothing else to do, Hatton had found a notebook in his saturated pockets and written down his own name and those of a wounded petty officer, a leading seaman and a medical orderly of the 12th Field Regiment who were the only other occupants of the boat. None of them seemed to think it odd and they gave him their names automatically.

How long they bobbed on the oily water Hatton didn't know because he drifted into sleep and when he finally woke up it was almost dusk and the other three men were silent. The petty officer had died.

It grew darker but he could only guess what time it was because his watch had stopped. To his surprise he found he didn't feel as ill or shocked as he thought he should; merely tired out because it was days since he'd slept properly. Sometime towards midnight a ship loomed up alongside and he became aware that a light was shining down on him.

'Anybody alive down there?' a voice was shouting.

He sat bolt upright, wincing from the pain in his injured ribs. 'Three,' he shouted. 'What ship's that?'

'*Eager.*'

The leading seaman, a middle-aged man who looked as though he ought to have been in Portsmouth with his wife, children and grandchildren, grinned. 'I was in *Eager*, sir,' he said. 'In thirty-six. She's a good ship.'

At that moment to Hatton she was the most wonderful ship in the world.

The destroyer swung, putting one engine astern so that she could make a lee, and they paddled with a broken oar and a plank to her side. Because he felt it was his duty to be last, Hatton insisted on the leading seaman and the medical orderly going first, and as he reached out for the nets he looked back. The petty officer was leaning against the thwarts as though asleep and the boy was lying in the bottom of the boat, grey white now, and quite anonymous. No one had known who he was or what service he'd belonged to, and no one ever would now.

As he was pulled to the deck of *Eager*, Hatton's eyes were stinging and he wasn't sure whether it was because of the fuel oil or the tears. His mouth was filled with a bitter taste that might have been from the salt water he'd swallowed or the bile that came with fear and he felt that when he got back – *if* he got back – he'd seek out Nora Hart and wheel her off to the altar at once. In his exhausted emotional state, at that moment the only thing he felt he needed out of life was a quiet room and Nora Hart in his bed, and the thought of Dover and peace left him feeling weak.

He turned to the petty officer who'd helped him aboard. 'When are we going home?' he asked.

The petty officer's eyebrows rose. 'Home, sir?' he said. 'We're not. We've only just arrived.'

Moving through the town, Noble and Gow picked their way through the ankle-deep sand of the dunes to the gaunt ruins of the promenade. The whole front was a high wall of fire now, roaring with darting tongues of flame, the smoke pouring up in thick folds to disappear into the black sky. Towards the sea the darkness was thick and velvety but it was just possible to see wrecked ships and the shapes of small boats. Nearby, a pier stretched from the beach into the darkness, its piles silhouetted against the glare. Shells burst about its shore end with monotonous regularity.

Along the promenade small groups of men trudged wearily, and guides called out their names – 'A Company, Green Howards' – 'East Yorks, this way' – and a few voices were raised as stragglers tried to find lost units. Then they ran into a line of poilus with fixed bayonets who informed them that from that point on the promenade was reserved for the French. They appeared to think they'd been betrayed by the B.E.F. and Gow was on the point of arguing the matter out when Noble dragged him away.

'You can't fight the whole sodden French army, you mad Scotch bastard,' he said.

Gow didn't appear to agree and seemed, in fact, to feel he might even have a chance of winning, but Noble clung to his arm and dragged him to the beach. The tide was out, and over the wide stretch of sand they could see dark masses which they realized were soldiers. There was no bunching and no pushing, however, and to Noble they seemed much more orderly than many football queues he'd been in.

A new flurry of shells landed on the promenade to bring down showers of masonry and tiles, and a wounded infantryman plucked at Noble's trousers as he passed. As he backed away in horror, Gow dropped on one knee and, with a tenderness Noble hadn't thought him capable of, emptied the last few drops from his water bottle to the dying man's lips. As he rose again, he stared over the beach, his face stiff with grief. 'What a waste,' he said. 'All them lovely fellers.'

The front was now a lurid study in red and black, flames and smoke and darkness mingling in a frightful panorama of destruction, and as they reached the beach Noble became aware at once of the evil atmosphere of blood and mutilated flesh. There was no escape from it and not a breath of air to dissipate it, so that he remembered the stink of the slaughter-house near where he'd lived as a boy and thanked God that the darkness hid the horrors that caused it.

As *Eager* swung towards the harbour, Hatton's heart sank. Despite the shells exploding in the town, the ship sidled expertly to the mole as a paddle-steamer pulled out packed with men. There was no bustle and he saw the naval commander who'd greeted *Vital* still there, still calmly issuing orders, though shells were dropping only fifty yards away now. At every muffled crash Hatton flinched.

'We'll be going out stern first,' he heard a voice above him say. 'So keep an eye on that mast sticking out of the water, Number One.'

Hatton watched numbly, unable to make himself go below. He

was aware now how much store he'd set by the companionship he'd known in *Vital*, and the ship's loss was like losing a limb.

Eager was winching herself in as the paddle-steamer moved astern. A cross-channel ship appeared on her other side as she bumped softly against the piles, but none of the men on the pier showed any impatience, waiting with incredible calm until the business of seamanship was finished and the navy was ready for them. As the gangways slammed into place, the officer on the end of the pier gestured and they began to move forward. They didn't argue or push, the whole dun-coloured column quietly edging forward as its head was swallowed by the two ships.

Eager's crew worked fast, helping limping men aboard with gentleness and compassion. Immediately, the soldiers, seemed to feel their worries were over and fell asleep in grotesque positions, their heads lolling sideways under the heavy helmets. Among them was what appeared to be half the canine population of France, and along the quay Hatton could see a military policeman shooting more dogs as they were brought to him.

The loading was carried out at tremendous speed, the guns' crews in their anti-flash gear and steel helmets like automatons against the reddened sky. Soon, thank God, he thought, they'd be off.

He'd had his injured ribs strapped up but because he felt he could never go below he offered himself to the ship's doctor. The medical orderly who had been in the whaler was working alongside him, too, and they were moving among the men on the deck in the increasing light attending to the injured.

'I think we ought to get some of the worst shock cases into the engine room where it's warmer,' the doctor said. 'Perhaps you'll help.'

The horror of being trapped flooded over Hatton again but the doctor was waiting for his answer and when he saw the medical orderly nod, he felt there was nothing he could do but nod himself.

Conybeare was another who had found fresh transport, though it was a mere pram, no more than ten feet long, and there was only one oar. It had once been used to enable its owner to board a cabin cruiser at Newport in the Isle of Wight and its stern bore the legend *Tender to Opal*.

Horndorff stared at it in the increasing light. 'You are mad, Officer Conybeare,' he said.

Conybeare, who seemed to gain confidence with every minute that Horndorff lost it, grinned. 'I expect so,' he said. 'Had an uncle they had to put away.'

'Put away?'

'Asylum. What do they call it in Germany? Madhouse.'

'*Irrenhaus.* That's where you should be, Officer Conybeare.'

Shells were dropping further along the beach in bright white flashes but Conybeare seemed totally absorbed and it was he who eventually found a second oar. It was different in size from the one they had already but Conybeare didn't seem very worried.

'Come on,' he said. 'We'll pull the boat down to the water's edge.'

'And if I refuse?'

Conybeare shrugged. 'Then I shall shoot you,' he pointed out.

'Perhaps I would be better dead,' Horndorff said bitterly.

Conybeare looked surprised. 'Oh, I shan't *kill* you,' he pointed out. 'Just in the arm or the shoulder. It'll be very painful and you'll still have to go with me.'

His face red with rage, Horndorff took the weight of the boat. As it began to float, Conybeare stood by the stern and gestured with the Luger.

'*I* am to row?' Horndorff said. 'I am a German officer.'

'Well,' Conybeare said patiently, 'I'm a British officer, and one of us has to. And since you are my –'

' – prisoner and you are taking me to England – '

'Exactly.'

With darkness, Sievewright had finally decided the time was ripe to move into Dunkirk. There seemed to be a lull in the bombardment and he thought that now he might safely pass through. He glanced at the dog. It was sitting in front of him, its eyes on his face, and as he realized he'd be unable to take it with him, he decided he must get rid of it.

'Go on,' he said. 'Away!'

The dog grinned and wagged its tail and he tried in French. '*Allez,*' he said '*Allez-vous en.*'

The dog remained where it was and, because he couldn't bear the idea of it wandering the town, starved and terrified by the explosions, he came to the conclusion that it was his duty to shoot it.

He took a deep breath, steeling himself to the job, then he fished into his pocket for the remains of the biscuits. Tossing them to the ground, he waited for the dog to crouch over them then he lifted the French rifle and pulled the trigger.

He hadn't been prepared for the mess a .303 calibre bullet could make of a skull at close range or the way it flung the dog's body away, whirling it round like a scrap of dirty rag to hurl it against a tree, and he had to get up quickly and walk away, his stomach heaving. All the way into the town, he felt nauseated.

Eager was already singling up her lines as he stepped aboard. A petty officer indicated he should go towards the bows, and he moved among the crowded men and found a seat on a coil of heavy mooring rope. There, he sat down, holding his French rifle between his knees and waited. The picture of the dead dog still bothered him but he felt he'd done his duty as he ought.

'Destroyer, Herr Leutnant!' The call came sharply across the chilly morning air. 'Direction oh-eight-three. Range diminishing.'

Hinze took the references and plotted the target on his artillery board, working out the range and angle of sight. Shouting from his position by his truck for the Gun Post Officers, he gave them instructions. 'Fresh target. All guns! Range four-eight-five-zero. Basic direction ... H.E. ... Charge 3 ...'

As the orders were called, the muzzles of the guns swung, moving slowly but with infinite menace.

Eager was still turning and had just picked up speed so that the first salvo fell short and she began to throb like a living animal as she leapt forward in the water, her bows up, her stern nailed to her wash by her screw.

'More two degrees!' The call was passed back among the dunes and Hinze's guns fired again.

In the engine room, Hatton felt the thump of the second salvo as it burst beyond the ship. The shock seemed to hit her seaward flank like a blow with a giant hammer and his heart started to pound sickeningly in his throat.

The job of getting injured men into the engine room had a special terror for him. At the bottom of the long frail ladders, he felt he was working in absolute blindness. The men about him were grim-faced, as aware as he was of the furious anger of steam from split pipes, and he could see one young stoker staring at his gauges with tears in his eyes, his throat full of sobs. No one said anything to him, however, or made any attempt to jar him out of his emotional trance.

He was just returning to the deck when Hinze's third salvo caught the ship. There was a crash below him. He saw flames spring from the boilers, and stokers with their clothes on fire. The lights went out immediately. In the confusion the pumps and electrical machinery stopped and a bank of tubes in Number Three boiler burst in a chaos of heat, scalding steam and water. Immediately he was reminded of *Vital* and, as the ship staggered, he almost fell from the ladder, realizing to his horror that it had come away from the platform so that he had to scramble the last few rungs to safety.

From below, over the roar of the turbines, the awful heat and the ringing crash that had sent a shower of rust flakes down, he could hear a screaming clatter of wrecked machinery and men shouting. As he burst on deck, bent double with the pain in his side, more shots straddled the ship and he heard splinters sing overhead. Ready-use ammunition began to explode and he saw a soldier trying to run along the crowded deck, his trousers burning.

The loud-hailer started. 'The ship has been hit and is down by the stern. Every available man to assemble in the bows.'

The seafaring language seemed to be beyond most of the soldiers and Hatton automatically began to push at them. 'Get forward,' he shouted. 'Up to the bows!'

He grabbed a large pink-faced soldier whose helmet seemed too small for his outsize head. 'Up to the sharp end, man,' he said. 'Quick!'

The soldier stared at him, then he nudged his friend. 'Come on, Fred. I suppose we'd better.'

Unlike the British, the Frenchmen didn't respond and Hatton grabbed their arms, pointing to the bows.

'*Allez*,' he said '*Vite!*'

They seemed to resent his efforts and, as he grabbed the arm of a black soldier wearing a turban, the man evidently thought he was trying to force him off the ship and raised his weapon. For a

H

moment, Hatton was staring down the muzzle. Then a rifle butt jerked up alongside him and the man fell backwards.

Hatton turned to stare at the pink-faced soldier. 'Thanks,' he said.

Hinze was still watching *Eager* through his field glasses, wondering if he could hit her again.

He called for the range and frowned as the answer was called back to him.

'Too far away,' he said. Then, as he glanced at the slope of the dunes, he began to wonder if there would be time to move one of the guns to a rear slope to give it extra elevation. It seemed to be worth trying.

Daisy had just been crossing the entrance to the harbour as *Eager* had appeared.

They'd run all night up and down in front of a large red-brick building, while the remains of a big ship lay smouldering to the east, her decks white-hot with the fires inside her. With the first light, Kenny Pepper had seen more soldiers arriving on the beaches, column after column of them marching through the gaps in the dunes.

Ernie Williams was standing alongside him, staring with him.

'Think we've lost the war, Ern?' he asked.

Ernie rubbed his nose. 'It fucken looks like it,' he said.

Gilbert Williams appeared from where he'd been passing cans of fuel down to the whimpering Brundrett. 'I reckon we ought to be thinking of shoving off,' he said. 'One more run in then we'll go.'

In his heart of hearts Kenny Pepper wasn't sorry, and when the bombs started falling again, his heart was back in his mouth at once and he found himself wishing to God they could go immediately.

The destroyer they'd been feeding was just swinging on to course when the shell hit her and Kenny saw the cloud of steam spring from the hole in her side. As she slowed to a standstill he saw she was already down by the stern and men in khaki were jumping into the sea.

'Stand by,' Gilbert shouted. 'We'll have to pick the buggers up. You ready, Kenny?'

Kenny waved and, as the aeroplanes roared overhead, Ernie sprinted to the gun. 'I'll get one of the bastards *this* time,' he yelled.

His wall eye squinting as he stared along the barrel, he looked ugly and quite inefficient and, after all his earlier lack of success, Kenny didn't for a moment expect him to hit anything.

Scharroo and Marie-Josephine had just returned to the beach when *Eager* was hit.

When dawn came, Scharroo had been sitting on the dunes with Marie-Josephine sleeping alongside him. She had cut her hair with her nail scissors during the night, but she hadn't made a very good job of it and she still looked like a girl with her slender neck inside the wide man's collar of the battledress blouse. With the first light, however, she'd found a long blue scarf that someone had abandoned. Wound round her neck, it gave her a blockier look, and as she stood in front of him, staring towards a ship wallowing just beyond the harbour, he saw something tender and young had gone from her face.

The lines of men still stretched to the water's edge, and as they watched them, wondering which one to join, Scharroo found he was unable to face the humiliation of being turned away again. Glancing at Marie-Josephine, he saw to his surprise that quite clearly she had come to the same decision.

'It doesn't matter,' she said. 'We must decide something else.'

Her determination wearied him. He'd always thought the old races of Europe were worn-out, tired with existing too long, but now he realized they were like a long-distance runner who, past his best as a sprinter, had acquired a great deal of endurance.

He was just about to start arguing again when the first air raid of the day began with waves of machines thousands of feet up, apparently dropping their bombs haphazardly. Then the fighters came in low, roaring along the beach, and as the men began to run he grabbed Marie-Josephine's hand and pulled her to where a shabby grey-painted boat lay on its side on the sand. They flung themselves down behind it as the bullets swept along the beach, whipping up the grit in a travelling wave.

As the racket stopped, Scharroo scrambled to his feet. The flung sand was drifting thick as mist, and new plumes of smoke were rising to flatten out over the town in a dingy grey ceiling that veiled the sun. Men were patiently taking up their positions again as though nothing had happened, and a party of Guardsmen returned to a wrecked barge they'd been unloading. Then he saw that Marie-Josephine was still crouching on all fours, staring at the boat under whose rounded hull they'd sheltered, and he saw her expression change.

It was a small clinker-built vessel with a transom stern, and to Scharroo it looked like a converted ship's lifeboat. The name, *Queen of France*, was painted on its counter.

'*C'est un présage*,' she whispered. '*Un augure.*'

She climbed into the boat, staring over the stern at a strange old-fashioned rudder that looked like a large bucket-shaped claw which opened and shut with a wheel that operated a screw attached to the tiller. There didn't appear to be much wrong with the boat except that its bilges were full of sand and water and it was a hundred yards from the sea, sorry-looking and useless.

'If we push it so – ' Marie-Josephine gestured to indicate the vertical. ' – it will float off at high sea, and there is that man by the bar who knows about motor boats.' She looked at Scharroo, her eyes shining. 'You must fetch him, Walter. He will know what to do.'

As the sun lifted it became clear to Stoos that there wasn't much time left. The affair was almost over. The British were scraping the bottom of the barrel now, using every ship and small boat that could be dredged up from forgotten corners of boatyards and creeks – no matter how forlorn, how tarnished the paintwork, how deep the dirty water gurgling in the bilges. The guns from the east were thudding constantly, and occasionally he could hear other guns in the west – nearer guns – Hinze's guns – banging away at the shipping. The sound stirred in him an almost insane desire to be part of it.

He'd watched Dodtzenrodt and what was left of the squadron take off in the first glimmer of daylight. Dodtzenrodt didn't like him and would do his best to make as much of the incident at the hangar as he could, and, as the machines vanished into the sky, Stoos chewed at his nails. As he approached the hangar, Hamcke watched him warily.

'I shall be testing D/6980,' Stoos said. 'I shall be taking Unteroffizier Wunsche with me.'

Wunsche was just coming out of the mess tent carrying a cup of coffee when Stoos appeared. He was unshaven and his hair was rumpled, as though he'd just awakened.

'We're flying, Wunsche,' Stoos said. 'We're testing 6980.'

When he reached the hangar, D/6980 was waiting with the engine ticking over. Stoos walked round it, checking everything carefully.

'I'll want her bombed up,' he said.

Hamcke seemed to guess what was in his mind. He glanced at the corporal alongside him who also seemed to have caught on. Then he shrugged his shoulders. It wasn't his affair. Sending a man to the armourers' tent, he climbed into the cockpit to switch off the engine. Stoos waited as the bright circle of the propeller slowed down and finally stopped. He could feel the heat from the engine and hear the creaks from the cooling metal. Wunsche was looking distinctly nervous now. He also seemed to realize what was in Stoos's mind and he glanced at Hamcke who sketched another small shrug.

In silence they all watched the bomb trailer approach across the grass and the men work it underneath the machine. 'That's it, Herr Leutnant,' the corporal armourer said, scrambling out. 'It's not fused.'

'Then fuse it.'

Wunsche climbed aboard without speaking and, settling himself behind his guns, moved his hands automatically to check the ammunition. Stoos climbed in after him and fastened his harness. 'Start her up,' he said.

Hamcke waved the ground crew forward. They all looked a little uncertain but they didn't protest.

The Jumo engine burst into an iron-throated howl and they stood back while Stoos worked the throttle. Reaching the holding area, he turned into wind and carefully checked the revolutions and instruments. Then he swung the machine round in a circle and checked the flaps and instruments. As he released the brakes, he saw a group of dots behind him, dropping down towards the aerodrome. It was Dodtzenrodt and the rest of the squadron returning to refuel. It seemed best to go before he could be stopped, and he thrust the throttle open and roared across the ground.

As the machine rose, the headphones crackled and for a moment before he deliberately switched them off he heard –

Dodtzenrodt's voice calling his name. Then, as Outreux passed
beneath him, he turned towards Dunkirk and the ships he intended to make his target.

Hatton was watching the coastline near Mardyck. He knew
where Hinze's shells had come from because he'd watched the
guns firing the previous day, and he suspected they were out of
range only by a matter of yards. His heart was pounding but, as
he turned he saw a big tug, *Gamecock*, bearing down on *Eager*
and could see the men on her stern already preparing the tow-
line.

The air raid siren had gone but Hatton saw the men on the
beaches dispersing for the hundredth time towards the dunes. The
raid was shaping up for one of the heaviest he'd seen so far. A large
force of Junkers 87s supported by 88s, Heinkels, Dorniers and
Messerschmitt fighters, had arrived over the harbour, and the
ship's guns began to fire.

After the first waves the attacks began to move from the harbour to the ships, and every ship in the area, every gun that had
been dragged down for the defence of the beaches, every man
with a rifle or a machine gun, began to retaliate. Just ahead of
Eager a destroyer was turning at full speed in the narrow waters,
and Hatton saw nine bombs fall in a row along her starboard side.
At first he thought she was hit but she continued at speed, heeling
over from the shock of the explosions. As she lifted again her
pom-poms were banging away over the top of a sloop, and as
the aeroplanes swung round in a big arc to head inland, he heard
their machine guns going.

Gamecock was close by *Eager*'s bows now, moving slowly
towards her, the men in the stern waiting to pass the tow-line,
concerned only with their job and apparently unaware of the
drama alongside. The swiftly moving destroyer had slowed down
now and Hatton saw her straddled by a stick of bombs. She was
moving in slow circles, her rudder jammed, and as she did so,
another wave of aircraft came over her and Hatton saw the
bombs fall away.

'She's got it this time,' a man near him shouted.

The bombs hit the destroyer as she turned and she slowed down
at once and began to settle. As tugs approached to take her in
tow, she was hit a third time below the bridge and this time

heeled over and disappeared almost at once. But the sky was
already emptying again and Hatton realized *Eager* had escaped.
By some miracle, the bombers had not noticed her and he could
now see that the heaving line from *Gamecock* was aboard and the
men on the bow were beginning to pull at the heavy tow-rope.

The air raids were just starting again as Hinze's guns began
firing once more, and the one he'd had dragged up the dune was
now flinging its shells the extra five hundred yards he'd been seeking. There had been a lot of guesswork in the operation, but the
roadstead was perfectly visible to everyone and they could watch
the fall of their shots.

The destroyer they'd hit was still motionless but there was a tug
ahead of her now. Through his glasses he could see they'd got the
tow attached, but he knew that to turn her they'd have to pull her
in a wide circle before they could get out of range.

As the destroyer began to move the first shot dropped thirty
yards from her stern and Hinze called out the new elevation.

Horndorff heard the shell that hit *Eager* whistle over his head.
It passed above the pram with a swooshing sound, and as it exploded a vast circle of smoke belched out of the destroyer's after
funnel, followed by clouds of steam.

'Damn,' Conybeare said.

'I think we shall have to head in another direction,' Horndorff
said, not without a grim satisfaction. There was another destroyer not far away, lying stopped, and several tugs were racing
towards her. Small boats were going full throttle to get out of the
way, among them a fishing vessel with a wheelhouse like a box,
and a solitary mast forward where a boy stood holding a rope.
Horndorff stared about him, feeling he'd been granted yet another
stay of execution.

'I think you are running out of ships, Officer Conybeare,' he
pointed out.

Eager had just been moving forward under tow, the water
inside her making the work slow, when Hinze's second shell
had hit her. A great cloud of soot had shot up from the funnel
and dropped across the decks to cover everybody with hot greasy
flecks, and she immediately started to list to port. There was a

frantic and desperate yelling where the splinters had sliced through the crowded men, and Hatton stared about him desperately. The Stukas were coming down one after another now, peeling off at ten thousand feet and dropping with a terrifying snarl of their engines to within a few hundred feet of the water. Another destroyer was hit and he saw the cloud of smoke leap up from her funnel and drift away like a smoke ring blown by a huge cigarette. A tug hurried to her rescue but her inside had fallen out and anchored her to the bottom, and as the tug cast off the tow and prepared to take off the survivors she too was hit. She seemed to disintegrate into small fragments and when the water and the smoke had vanished there was nothing left, not even a few bobbing heads.

In the havoc and thunder of the bombs, Hatton was flinching every time an aircraft came near them. All round *Eager* there were patches of oil where ships had sunk, together with a mat of drifting wreckage, smashed boats, Carley floats, fragments of timber and floating rope. Steam was still coming from the funnel and through the engine room hatches in a vast cloud that he knew would advertise the fact that the ship was damaged to every aircraft within miles.

Stoos's gunner, Wunsche, pointed downwards, and as Stoos saw the slender shape of a destroyer far below him just to the west of the mole he realized at once by the absence of wake that the ship was almost stationary and even appeared to be under tow. She made a perfect target and he could see from the colour of her decks that she was crammed with troops.

He licked his lips, certain he couldn't miss. His eyes didn't waver as he stared through the silvery circle of the propeller. He was only twenty-two years old and quite certain of his destiny.

He could hear voices in his ears as other pilots called out warnings to each other, but he ignored them, his eyes now on only one thing. At the rear of the cockpit, Wunsche crouched over his guns, slight, pale-faced and nervous. He was not a good gunner and Stoos decided he'd have to get rid of him when everything else was sorted out.

He shifted in his seat and glanced behind him. There was another Stuka not far away on roughly the same course, its fixed undercarriage reaching down like the claws of a hovering eagle.

He glanced at the bomb release. The big bomb slung beneath him would soon send the fragile destroyer to the bottom. He was quite unafraid and, settling himself in his harness, pushed the nose down. Immediately the air blossomed with brown shell-bursts. At least they were awake down below, but it wouldn't be long before they were swimming for their lives.

More shells exploded around him but the Stuka flashed through them unharmed, and the engine swelled into a high whine. Behind his goggles Stoos's eyes narrowed with concentration. The destroyer was growing rapidly in size now until it filled the whole of the windscreen, and he could see the brown mass of men crowding the decks suddenly changing to white as faces lifted to watch him. The tracers started, red lines spinning towards him, but he didn't take his eyes off his sighting mark, holding his breath to concentrate more. The machine was rocking but so far nothing had touched him. And then he realized why. There was another Stuka beyond the bows of the destroyer and the fire was being directed at that one instead. As he watched, he saw it lift away and knew that in a moment they would be seeing *him*.

The sky was full of exploding shells now and black with smoke. More tracers curved up and Stoos had to grit his teeth to force himself to keep his eyes on his target. A Stuka coming from the opposite direction burst into fragments that dropped twisting and turning out of the sky, but still the slim line of the destroyer below him grew larger, and filled the whole of his sight as he pulled the release and heaved the Stuka out of its dive.

As the Stuka began to pull away, Kenny saw the bomb fall and Gilbert Williams' voice came in a cracked harsh cry. 'It's going right down the bloody funnel!'

The destroyer leapt out of the water as the explosion tore at her inside, the crash drowning the clatter of the Stuka's machine gun as the aeroplane seemed to hover above them.

'Now,' Gilbert screamed. 'Now, Ernie!'

But Ernie was hanging over the gun, clutching it with whitened knuckles and, as the wild-eyed Kenny watched, he slowly spun away on limp legs, staring bewildered at the drops of blood falling from his open mouth to the deck.

Kenny looked round for Brundrett, but Brundrett was still below in the engine room crouching under the engine and, as the

yellow-bellied machine with its crooked wings and fixed undercarriage began to curve up into the sky, Kenny came to life and
grabbed for the gun. He had no idea how to aim so he simply
pointed it and pulled the trigger.

The crash of the bomb exploding in the bowels of the destroyer
seemed to lift the pram clean out of the sea and Horndorff missed
his stroke and fell flat on his back with his feet in the air. For a
moment he lay there dazed as water and fragments of wood and
steel showered down. Then the waves set up by the explosion
caught them, rocking the boat so violently that he felt sure it was
about to capsize.

When he lifted his head, the destroyer was wallowing, and he
knew she would sink. The tug which had been assisting her had
dropped her tow and was rushing in a wild circle to pick up survivors, while the fishing boat they'd seen was heading quickly
across their stern.

Conybeare was now lifting his head too, and the purple bruise
over his eye seemed to glow with rage. Horndorff began to
wonder if he might take advantage of the confusion and plunge
over the side and, as the memory of that last awful swim deterred
him, he saw that Conybeare was looking like an angry schoolboy.
In any other circumstances he might even have found it within
himself to laugh.

'We're adrift,' Conybeare was yelling. 'You damned idiot!
Fancy letting the oars go!'

Horndorff dragged himself upright, for the first time in days
feeling he'd got the better of his captor.

'*Was sagen Sie nun?*' he said. 'Perhaps you have something
to fit *this* case, Officer Conybeare. I think everybody is too busy
to pay much attention to us.'

He was quite right, and on *Daisy* Kenny Pepper was staring
towards the Stuka he'd shot at, realizing with amazement that it
was faltering in the sky and that its gun had stopped firing.

At first he couldn't believe his eyes. Then he saw a puff of
black smoke break out behind it, and then another which finally
became a steady stream.

'I hit him,' he screamed. 'I hit the bugger, Gilbert!'

He stared upwards, waving and dancing wildly. The Stuka was

turning towards the land now but it was clearly in trouble and the smoke was still pouring from it. He glanced round and saw that the tug, *Gamecock*, had let go its tow and was turning in a tight circle to come up behind them at full speed. Then he saw Gilbert Williams was staring not at the sky but at the deck, and he remembered Ernie. Kenny had never known his father, and since leaving school had found the security he'd needed aboard *Daisy*. The two Williamses had been kind in their rough way and had become like parents to him. As he turned slowly, the only thing he was aware of in his moment of triumph was the sight of the man who'd given him forbidden fags and bottles of beer, who'd taken his side against Brundrett's bullying, now crouched on the deck in a kneeling position, half-leaning against the engine room ventilator, his mouth working slowly, the blood coming out in a thin stream mixed with saliva to form a pool on the deck where his face was pressed.

As the Stuka sagged in the sky with Wunsche dead in his seat Stoos felt a sick feeling of frustration. There'd be no medals for him now.

Even as he thought of it, however, he choked on the smoke pouring into the cockpit and realized his only chance of life was to take to his parachute. The bomber was barely moving forward by this time and he knew that in a moment it would fall off in a stall and then it would be too late.

The Stuka passed him towards the sea in a screaming dive as he fell clear. Then he pulled the ring and felt the jerk of the harness as the parachute opened. A moment later he was swinging safely beneath it.

He watched the aeroplane vanish in a vast spout of foam. It didn't occur to him to feel sorry for Wunsche. Wunsche had only been part of the aeroplane, not a human being, and he'd not been very efficient even at that. Almost without thinking about him, Stoos looked round again for his victim.

At first he thought he'd missed, but then he saw the destroyer surrounded by clouds of steam and smoke and he grinned, delighted, feeling that things would come right after all. He realized he was drifting over the land and felt still better. He wouldn't even get his feet wet. He was only a few hundred feet above the beach now and edging towards the dunes. He saw the

men below move together in bunches and start looking up, and as
he heard the whiplash of bullets it dawned on him they were
trying to kill him.

'No!' he screamed. 'No!'

But by this time he'd dropped another two hundred feet and
the next fusillade tore his inside to shreds. He screamed like a
tortured animal and his arms and legs fell helplessly, a red blur
of pain dimming his view. With glazed eyes he saw the rifles
raised again and, even as he choked in his own blood, a bullet
took out his right eye and another, entering his head beneath the
chin, lifted the top of his skull into the torn remains of his helmet.

The men on the beach watched the parachute drift over the
town, and a sailor – a survivor from an earlier sinking – looked
round at them as they worked the bolts of their rifles.

'Christ,' he said. 'Two hundred of you to kill one sodden Jerry!
No wonder we've lost the war!'

As *Eager* sank lower, the men aboard her were scrambling for
the ships that had appeared alongside. As they filled up and
moved away, a trawler came up on the opposite beam and everyone began to move to the other side of the deck. Standing on the
bow where he'd been sent to help lift the stern out of the water,
Sievewright waited for someone to tell him what to do. Alongside, men who'd been blown overboard were swimming and shouting and as the ship's bows sank lower and lower he wondered if
he should now move to the stern to give more weight there to
lift the bows. Because he'd boarded during the night, he'd seen
little of Dunkirk in the darkness. Because he'd been amidships
when Hinze's first shell had struck, he'd seen nothing of the
shambles aft. Because he'd moved to the bows, he'd seen nothing
of the horror from the second shell or the uproar when Stoos's
bomb had hit. He was still neatly dressed, and was just wondering
if it were still in the tradition to go down with the ship when he
became aware of an officer on the bridge shouting at him above
the din.

'You there! You on the bow! Get into a boat!'

As the head disappeared, he looked round. Someone had
lowered a boat further aft, but, even as he watched, the sailors
cast off and it began to pull away. Then he realized that *Eager*'s
bows were now within a foot of the water. Alongside them a

small abandoned dinghy was bumping against the steel. It had no oars and was quite empty but it seemed a great deal safer than the ship and, as *Eager* settled lower and lower, he stepped off into it. He hadn't even got his feet wet.

'That's it,' Noble shouted above the crash of the bombs. 'She's gone!'

He and Lance-Corporal Gow were standing on the beach staring at the awful butchery of ships. The sun was high now and Lije Noble's mind was beginning to fill with doubts. Gow's back was as stiff as ever, but under his helmet his eyes were narrow in their circles of weariness.

'Mebbe we'll have to swim,' he said.

Noble's head jerked round. During the night he'd found a lieutenant-colonel's greatcoat which he'd put on for warmth but, for all he'd been saluted several times, it hadn't given him a lot of confidence. Gow, on the other hand, behaved as though he were in the Guards Depot at Caterham. As soon as daylight had come, he'd shaved, using the rusty water from the radiator of a wrecked lorry. Then he'd cleaned his belt and polished his boots and given the Bren a run-over before finally adding to the hieroglyphics in his notebook with a calm absorption that terrified Noble with its acceptance of all the horrors around them.

'*Swim?*' he said. 'Swim what? The Channel, for Christ's sake?'

Gow turned slowly and stared at him. He seemed indifferent to the crash of bombs that made Noble flinch. 'Mebbe we could,' he said. He paused. 'There's a raft out yonder,' he said. 'We could use that.'

'I can't swim,' Noble said.

'I can.' Gow sat down on the beach and began to unlace his boots. All about them were hatch covers from sunken ships, broken timbers and oars. 'You can hang on to one of yon,' he said. 'I'll swim behind an' push.'

Noble stared at him as if he were mad but Gow had both his boots off now and was pulling at the grey army socks. His feet were as white and bony as the rest of him. He stood up and calmly took off his ammunition pouches and steel helmet and, laying them down, carefully rested the Bren against them. Then he stripped off his blouse, his trousers and shirt, and stood only in a pair of rather ragged underpants. Watched by Noble, he put on the ammunition pouches and the steel helmet again and picked up the Bren.

'You going on parade like that?' Noble asked wildly.

Gow turned. 'I cannae leave ma gun,' he pointed out coldly.

He'd already found a heavy piece of timber and was dragging it to the water's edge.

'You're bonkers,' Noble bleated, almost collapsing with fear. 'Stone bonkers. When you get to the other side, they'll form you all up to number from the right. The whole bleeding Brigade of Guards. And at the end Lance-Corporal Gow, in his birthday suit with his weapons at the slope.' Like all non-swimmers he was terrified at the thought of being beyond his depth, but with this terrible calm man he knew that unless something happened he soon would be. Then he saw the boat about a hundred yards away, lying on its side on the sand. 'Here,' he said. 'How about that boat there? The tide's coming in and there's a feller aboard.'

Gow studied the boat for a moment. Then he reached for his trousers and shirt and, donning them, began to drag his boots on again.

Noble was already approaching the boat, his feet churning the wet sand. A figure in battledress and steel helmet was bailing furiously, then, as Noble appeared, it straightened up and he saw it was a girl. Recognition came at once. ' 'Ello,' he said. 'Fancy meeting you again!'

Marie-Josephine stared nervously and then she remembered him from the air raid the previous night. 'Good morning,' she said. 'I do not thank you for helping me. It is very gallant.'

No one had ever called Noble gallant before and he was embarrassed. 'Runs in the family,' he said. 'Like wooden legs. What are you up to?'

She gestured towards the shambles at sea. 'I go to England,' she announced.

'In that?'

'But of course.'

'Will it work?'

'My friend goes into the town to find a man who knows about it. *He* will make it go.'

As Scharroo entered the town, the men marching in towards

him had been in heavy fighting. There were a lot of wounded among them, the blood bright on the white of their bandages. These were the last regiments to pull back from the perimeter, proud regiments with long histories, and they still carried their kit and gave a smart eyes right to senior officers as they passed. There was something about them, tired as they were, that stirred Scharroo and he began to see that if he ever reached safety *this* was what he ought to write about.

As he reached the Rue Gregoire de Tours where they'd halted the night before, however, he began to run into other men, without weapons and past hope, standing in odd shabby groups. There was no sign of the man in the blue jersey and he approached a soldier leaning against the wall sucking at a bottle of beer. He was a narrow-faced narrow-shouldered Cockney whose helmet seemed far too big for him, draped about with a ground sheet, small, stunted, his feet in huge boots, the product of underfeeding in some East End slum.

'You seen a guy here?' Scharroo asked. 'Little guy in a blue jersey. I guess he was good and drunk.'

'I wish *I* was good and drunk,' the soldier said. 'I walked all the bloody way from Tournai.'

As they talked, a lorry swung round the corner and began to roar towards them. Heads jerked round to watch as it pulled up. Then tall men in red-covered caps jumped out, and an officer wearing an armband began to gesture with a walking stick. The men in red caps formed up and a sergeant started to shout at the group of stragglers.

'All right, you lot! In threes!'

The red-caps were pulling men into the roadway and one of them grabbed at Scharroo's sleeve. Scharroo snatched his arm away and the policeman made another grab. Again Scharroo snatched his arm away and the officer appeared.

'Get into line,' he snapped.

Scharroo glared. 'I'm not one of your goddam soldiers,' he growled.

'Who the hell are you then?'

'I'm an American citizen. I'm a newspaperman.'

'Wearing a British battledress?'

Scharroo's eyes fell to the blouse he was wearing and then he remembered his jacket was still somewhere in the ruins of the warehouse where he and Marie-Josephine had sheltered the night before.

'My name's Scharroo,' he insisted. 'Walter Scharroo.'

'What sort of name's that? It's not American.'

Scharroo almost laughed in the officer's face. American names covered the whole face of the globe in their origins.

'It could be German and *you* could be a fifth columnist. Where's your pass?'

'I lost it. In an air raid.'

'A good story. Search his pockets, Corporal!'

The corporal pushed Scharroo against a wall and wrenched a brown army pay book from his pocket of the battledress blouse. 'AB64, sir,' he said. 'James Edward McLeod. Corporal. Service Corps.'

'It's not my blouse,' Scharroo said. 'It's one I picked up.'

'Very likely. Hang on to him, Corporal. He might stand investigating.' The officer turned to face the straggling line and, as Scharroo was pushed alongside the little Cockney a tall sergeant with his cap over his nose like a Guardsman stepped forward.

'Right,' he bawled above the din. 'Company – !' Heads lifted automatically, even if not together, and they managed to come to attention. 'Ri-ight – turn !'

As they turned, Scharroo was still standing facing the officer, his face dark with rage. No one took any notice of him.

'Qui-ick – march !'

As the group set off, the little Cockney banged into him. 'Git going, mate,' he growled.

Scharroo tried to step out of line but the sergeant shoved him back and gestured at one of the red-caps. 'Keep an eye on this bastard, Corporal,' he said. 'We don't know who he might turn out to be. Perhaps even Goering.'

The red-cap stepped alongside Scharroo, his hand on his revolver, and the sergeant nodded his approval. Scharroo was being pushed along now by the men behind and on both sides of him, until eventually he was forced to walk with them.

'It's no good, mate,' the little Cockney said. 'If it's inevitable, lie back and enjoy it. Better have a fag. I got hundreds.'

It was a cigarette that finally brought Tremenheere back to life.

When he came round he was lying on the cushions of the wide bunk that Knevett's wife always used. It was stained now with salt water, the cushions stiff with blood, and above it there were several jagged holes through which the daylight showed. As the boat lifted in the swell the sun shone straight into Tremenheere's half-opened eyes and seemed to pierce his brain like a red-hot shaft. He rolled over, groaning, aware of a sickening nausea in his stomach and a splitting ache in his head, and for a long time he lay like that, blinking at the empty whisky bottle rolling about the floor and bumping softly against the lockers.

He felt sure he was dying and his unsteady hand found a cigarette. Slowly it brought him back to life so that eventually he struggled to his feet and staggered on deck. The sun was on the sea, sparkling in a way that knifed through his brain. Just beyond the stern he could see what was left of *Eager* sticking out of the sea. The water between her and *Athelstan* seemed to be a solid mat of corpses, brown and navy blue, rising and falling together in a slow saraband of death as the swell moved past them. There must have been a dozen of them clustered round *Athelstan*'s stern. The one that had caused all the trouble was still jammed underneath with its white bloodless hand protruding from a soaked sleeve and, with it now, another in naval uniform, the square collar floating where the head should have been.

He turned away and vomited into the sea, and as he wiped his streaming eyes he realized he was staring at yet another corpse bobbing in the water below him. He was surrounded by the dead.

'Oh, Jesus!' he said.

For a moment he was unable to make his brain function. Then he tried to shout to some of the boats in the distance. But none of them was near enough to hear and just at that moment the guns of a destroyer began to fire – whango whango whango!

Slowly he pulled himself upright. His intestines felt as though they were being squeezed out through his skull and, as the medals on his chest clinked together, the sound seemed like two great brass gongs clashing in his brain. Then the crash of an explosion somewhere nearby made him jump and his head felt as though it were about to fall from his neck in two halves, like a melon split by a knife.

'Oh, Christ, me dear,' he said aloud. 'Oh, God Jesus Christ!'
He dropped to the deck. The aeroplanes came over again and
the explosions seemed to lift *Athelstan* out of the water. He spent
ten minutes clinging weakly to the wheelhouse and, as the racket
died, climbed to his feet, knowing that he had to do something or
he'd be there all day, surrounded by the mat of corpses.

As he lifted his head, he became aware of a thin voice crying
on the port side and it jerked him to life. A soldier was swimming
towards the boat and Tremenheere could see he was in great pain.
He snatched up a heaving line and threw it. It fell across the
swimming man's head and Tremenheere was able to pull him towards the stern where what was left of Ordinary Seaman
Didcot and the other dead floated. It seemed to take hours to get
him on deck and, as he lay there moaning, the water running
from his soaked clothes, Tremenheere saw blood and realized that
in addition to having two broken legs he'd also been wounded.
How he'd managed to swim at all was incredible.

The soldier was unconscious now, so Tremenheere dragged
him to the cabin and, slowly and with difficulty because he was a
big man, got him on to Mrs. Knevett's bunk. As he did so the
soldier opened his eyes.

'763,' he said. 'Private Bawes, H., Worcesters.' Then his eyes
closed again.

There was still a little water in the tank and Tremenheere made
a mugful of tea. He knew as soon as he reached the cabin with it,
however, that he was too late so he sat down opposite the dead
man and drank it himself.

After a while, he remembered what he'd been about to do when
he'd found Bawes. He picked up the spare boat-hook and, moving
aft, still feeling as though the side of his head was in danger of
falling off, he began to poke in the water. As he shoved, the putty-
coloured horrors under the stern bobbed and danced and turned
over, bloodless hands reaching, dead eyes staring. He had to turn
away and be sick once more, but he knew he could never move
Athelstan while the hampering corpse was still round the screw.
At last he cleared enough space in the water to reach the body
which had caused all the trouble. To his surprise it now came
free at once and lurched to the surface.

Flinging down the boat-hook, he slipped down to the engine
room, only to realize that he'd been wasting his time because it

was lapped by oily black water, the floorboards floating on their rests.

He had just clambered slowly back to the deck when a lone Junkers 88 on its way home dropped its bombs. The first one lifted him off his feet and flung him into the well again with a crash that knocked all the breath from his body. The second and third hit the wreck of the destroyer and the whirring splinters ripped through *Athelstan*'s planking until she looked like a colander.

The day progressed agonizingly in a cacophony of noise. The sun passed its peak and began to sink. The wreckage along the tide line increased, the numbers of the dead bobbing in the wash of the ships grew larger, and the smoke still covered the town like a funeral pall.

Allerton had stood on the empty beach all morning, suddenly indifferent to his chances of reaching safety, watching the noisy tragedy by the mole with narrow-eyed fascination. Not far away, a big transport had been hit abaft the engine room and a huge gout of flame and smoke had reached upwards out of the funnel as she'd begun to sink in a cloud of steam. A destroyer had manoeuvred alongside to put her bow to the transport's fore-castle and soldiers were now scrambling across while naval men dragged more survivors from the sea. By this time the transport had heeled so far over that her forward funnel and mast were in the water, and all the time the German bombers were trying to hit her yet again. Then, as Allerton watched, she turned right over and he could see soldiers running across the keel, still under air attack and with the destroyers' guns crashing away over their heads.

He turned back towards the beach, defeated and unable to absorb any more. His face was swollen and he felt he could hardly place one foot in front of the other. Dunkirk seemed unreal now, a place where army discipline had gone by the board but yet somehow managed to survive. Near him a group of men were wading neck-deep and a man sitting on the sand, his head swathed in bandages, stared silently towards them.

'You on your own?' Allerton asked, and as the man turned his head he saw his face was terribly scarred by burns.

'Yes, mate,' the soldier said calmly. 'It's me eyes. I can't see. Are you an officer?'

'Yes. I am. Can I help you?'

'Nothing you can do for me, sir.'

'I could get you to one of the boats.'

The soldier's head turned. 'Could you do that for me, sir?'

Allerton helped the soldier to his feet and took his hand. The palm was rough and calloused.

'Private Blewitt, sir,' the soldier said. 'East Lancs. I was by one of the lorries, getting wounded out, and when she was hit the petrol exploded in me face.'

He allowed Allerton to lead him down the beach. The nearest queue opened for them to join and Allerton stood with the blind man in the water. No one spoke to them, and Allerton's mind was full of pain and sadness and a new compassion of which he hadn't believed himself capable. Somebody behind him in the line, standing waist deep in the water, was playing *The Londonderry Air* on a mouth-organ with a lilt that he found infinitely moving.

A boat bobbed towards them and one of the men behind Allerton gave him a little push. 'Go on, sir,' he said. 'It's all right.'

Allerton pulled the blind man forward. Blewitt said nothing, patiently allowing himself to be led, and when a floating body bobbed against them another soldier quietly pushed it away.

'It's deep,' the blind man said.

'Nearly there,' Allerton pointed out.

A sailor was reaching out over the bow of the boat and Allerton passed Blewitt's hand to him.

'You'll be all right now,' he said.

'Thanks, mate,' the scarred head turned slowly. 'You're a toff.'

Allerton drew a deep breath and backed away. The man behind him pushed him forward again. 'Go on, sir. You can go in my place.'

'No.' There were tears in Allerton's eyes as he stumbled away through the water. 'It's all right.'

From the mole Scharroo peered over the beaches and the scattered groups of men, at the wreckage along the tide line, the burned-out vehicles and the guns canted up in the sand, the wrecks of aeroplanes and cars. He'd long since stopped arguing with the military policeman who'd marched him away.

Among the men around him now were a lot of Frenchmen squabbling over the contents of a sack of hard biscuits. They were bewildered, not knowing whether to go on the ships or stay with their own country in its hour of disaster. Round their waists most of them wore inner tubes they'd taken from abandoned vehicles, like children on a trip to the seaside.

. The queue began to shuffle forward again and Scharroo moved with it. The little Cockney was still with him, still sucking at a fag. He seemed to have thousands stored about his person and had kept Scharroo supplied ever since they'd left the town. The mole was littered with bloody bandages ripped off by men afraid of being refused permission to board, and from time to time they saw corpses covered with groundsheets or coats, big boots awkwardly protruding. The sun was sinking in a blaze of red now, and Scharroo had a feeling that he'd never see the evening glory again without remembering this day.

'Soon be 'ome,' the little Cockney said. He was subdued now with exhaustion. 'Expect they'll send us to the glasshouse when we arrive.'

'They won't send me,' Scharroo said. 'I'm an American citizen. I tell every sonofabitch who asks but nobody listens. I'm a newspaperman and I have to get some place to file my story.'

'What story?'

Scharroo stared. *'This goddam story.* The biggest defeat the world's ever seen!'

The Cockney looked indignant. *'We're* not defeated,' he said. 'We'll win in the end.' The narrow face became taut. 'You sure you ain't one of them fifth columnists? You're spreading propaganda.'

'Propaganda be damned! I'm a neutral. I'm American!'

'Who's President of the United States then?' The Cockney flung the question at Scharroo as though hoping to catch him unawares.

'Franklin Delano Roosevelt.'

'And what's the capital?'

'Washington.'

'It's New York.'

'Don't be goddam stupid! It's Washington, D.C. And the President lives in the White House. If you like, I'll recite the Declaration of Independence or list the states.'

The Cockney seemed convinced at last. 'You ever been to

Hollywood?' he asked, and there was something in his thin face that indicated he'd spent many delighted hours in cinemas – probably when he was unemployed – watching a brilliant world of which he had no experience himself.

'Once,' Scharroo said.

'Ever meet any of them film stars?'

'One of two. I didn't like 'em much. I guess they were selfish bastards.' The conversation seemed faintly unreal with the bombs crashing not far away and the sky full of smoke and the sound of aeroplanes overhead, but then the whole evacuation had seemed more than slightly unreal from the beginning.

There was a long pause in the loading and some of the weary men sat down and went to sleep, indifferent to the danger, twitching and muttering in private nightmares. The concrete where they now stood was chipped and badly stained with blood. As they moved on again they saw the pier had been cut just ahead. Engineers had laid planks across the gap but they were unsupported and getting across was like doing a tightrope act.

'Fair makes you giddy, don't it?' the Cockney said as they reached the other side. Scharroo said nothing, well aware that there was no going back now. The military policeman seemed to think so, too, because he hadn't bothered to follow and was now walking back along the mole towards the town.

They had almost reached the end of the mole when the aeroplanes reappeared. They came over in waves and the din was tremendous, the crash of the bombs shaking the whole structure. Scharroo wanted to duck and run, but no one else moved and he had to stand where he was. The men about him were patient and silent, sucking at fags, their faces expressionless under the dirt and the lines of strain, and it still puzzled him that they couldn't see that they'd lost the war.

At the end of the mole, he could see a trot of six destroyers all alongside each other, their multiple pom-poms forcing the planes to keep their distance. But a Junkers 88 was roaring crazily along the beach towards them, and the whole queue seemed to subside as men ducked. A naval commander at the end of the pier began to scream. 'Come on,' he was yelling. 'Never mind that! Keep moving!'

Every vessel in the vicinity was firing now, and as the aeroplane roared past, barely masthead high, the rear gunner was so close Scharroo could see his helmeted head and the winking flashes as his gun fired. A few men fell, and he saw one drop with a scream between the ships and the jetty. No one took any notice or attempted to rescue him. 'Come on,' the naval officer kept yelling. 'Faster! Keep coming!'

Then he noticed that the little Cockney was still bowed forward and, as the man in front moved on, he subsided slowly on to his face, his helmet falling off and spinning on its brim like a plate.

'Oh, gawd, mate,' he said as Scharroo bent over him. 'I felt it get me. Right in the spine.'

Scharroo owed him nothing but he felt he couldn't simply leave him there. As he turned him over, however, the soldier gave a harsh scream. 'Oh, Gawd, no!' he said.

The men behind were pressing past them now, stepping over the outstretched legs. One of them, weary to the point of blindness, stumbled against them and the little Cockney let out a yelp of agony.

Scharroo looked up, desperate to do something, and a man in ground sheet and steel helmet stopped alongside him. 'I'm a medical orderly,' he said. 'Seventh Field Ambulance.' He bent over the injured man, asking a few soft questions as he moved his feet. The soldier gave another harsh rasping cry and the medical orderly straightened up and shook his head.

Scharroo bent down. 'It'll be O.K.,' he said. 'He says it'll be O.K. Just lie still. I'll wait here with you.'

He didn't have to wait long and after a while the medical orderly stooped and opened one of the closed eyes.

'You can go now,' he said. Scharroo straightened up and without a word began to move down the pier again with the others, towards a fat flat paddle-steamer lying at the end. The medical orderly removed the dead man's helmet and laid it over his face. Then he too turned and joined the queue.

As the sun sank lower, leaving a bloody trail across the torn land, Allerton moved along the line of the dunes. The experience of leading the blind man to the boats had stirred him enormously, and he'd felt unable to join a queue himself in case there were others. Among the marram grass he'd found several wounded. Three of them were unconscious, but a fourth was only slightly hurt and seemed to be out of his mind. Allerton led him down the beach, listening to his ravings.

As he walked back he found he was moving further and further towards La Panne, finding stragglers, one or two of them drunk, one or two stupid from shell shock, and he sent all of them towards Dunkirk. Then he found he couldn't stop and in his pity he began to move among the injured, trying to find food for them. When an officer came along the beach in a lorry loaded with champagne, offering it to anybody within reach, he took two bottles back to the wounded men.

'I never tasted champagne before, sir,' one of them said. 'And it's me birthday, too.' His face was grey and Allerton knew he'd never see another.

Finding himself near the *Queen of France*, he recognized her at once. Gow was watching the sea creep slowly up the beach with all the flotsam and jetsam of the battle, and seeing Allerton, he immediately came to attention and slammed up a salute as though he were on parade.

'Got it going?' Allerton asked.

'We will,' Noble said from alongside the engine. 'Know anything about 'em?'

'If I did, she wouldn't be here now. And neither would I.'

As Allerton moved away, Noble gazed after him. 'That bloke's had it,' he said shrewdly. 'He's not going to make it.'

Gow began to walk round the boat, marching almost, in a stiff-backed, stiff-legged way as though he were on sentry-go at Buckingham Palace. The Bren lay on the bow where he could get at it, and he'd already used it once or twice against aircraft.

'She's a gey fine boat,' he announced with pride.

Noble was just putting back the engine hatch, watched by Marie-Josephine, when Chouteau appeared. Gow, now standing on the foredeck, saw him first, appearing among the figures drifting aimlessly about the beach in the dusk. Angelet was in his arms and his rifle was slung over his shoulder. He stopped beside the boat and shifted the boy in his grasp. Angelet's face was grey-white and the eyelids over his closed eyes were purple. His head hung limply against Chouteau's chest.

Gow stared anxiously at him. 'The wee boy,' he said. 'Is he deid?'

Chouteau managed a grin. 'No, *mon brave*,' he said. 'He is asleep. He will sleep for a week, I think.' He nodded at the boat. 'What are you going to do with that?'

'Go to England,' Noble said, wiping his greasy hands on his trousers.

'You will take him with you? He wishes to fight. I think he will probably kill many Germans for you.'

'Does he know anything about boats? The bloody valve keeps sticking.'

Chouteau gave a vast shrug. 'But, of course,' he lied. 'He is from Marseilles. Everybody in Marseilles is a sailor.'

He passed Angelet up to Gow who pulled him over the thwarts and laid him in the bottom of the boat. It was a difficult operation but Angelet never moved.

After a while, Marie-Josephine began to study the sea. 'I think the boat begins to float,' she said.

They waded into the dark water and scrambled aboard, Chouteau remaining by the bow, a shadowy figure with the water up to his thighs.

'Come on, mon,' Gow said. 'Get in.'

'Let us be certain that the engine marches first,' Chouteau said.

Noble said a prayer, fumbled for the petrol switch and reached to swing the heavy fly wheel. As the engine started in a low steady chugging, Marie-Josephine flung her arms round his neck and hugged him.

Chouteau pointed to the north. 'That is the direction, *mon vieux*,' he said. 'If by any chance you should miss England you will come eventually to the north pole, and that is still neutral.'

As he put his shoulder against the bow, the boat floated backwards and he walked with it, one hand on the stem, until he was chest-deep in the water.

'Come on, mon,' Gow said anxiously. 'Get aboard.'

Chouteau smiled, then he was gone in the darkness. His voice came over the water. 'This is my country, *mon brave*,' he said. 'I think I will stay behind and slit a few German throats.'

When Tremenheere came round it was dark and he found himself staring at the stars. He couldn't see anything else, but from the motion of the deck beneath him he guessed he was still afloat – even if only just. He could smell burning and the stink of death so he knew he hadn't gone far, and he reckoned that this business of getting himself blown off his feet was coming round just too often. He'd hardly heard a gun fired in anger in the other war, but now it seemed as if the whole German army were aiming at him personally.

His right shoulder was on fire with an excruciating pain and he had to lie still for a while, gathering his courage, before he warily inched his head up.

Then he saw his arm was stuck out at a strange angle and it dawned on him he'd broken his collar bone.

'Oh, Christ, Nell,' he moaned. 'Look what the bastards have done to me !'

As the *Queen of France* headed slowly out to sea in the darkness, it came as a shock to Lije Noble to discover there was more to handling a boat than he'd ever dreamed. There were no brakes for a start, and you couldn't slow down, and when you aimed to pass round the stern of some grounded wreck, you invariably found yourself heading round the bow. He realized eventually that this was the action of the tide setting him along the coast and he began to make allowances to counter the effect, even stopping occasionally to make small experiments with the throttle and the old-fashioned rudder.

By the light of the flames, he could see there was flotsam everywhere – burned, charred and splintered boats, floating grass line, oars, spars, boathooks, planks, doors, rafts, lifebelts, overcoats and battledress blouses. And bodies. There seemed to be hundreds of them bobbing in ones and twos as the ships' washes lifted them, gathering together in little conferences of the dead. 'I wonder who'll answer for this lot,' he said.

'The politicians'll no' take the blame,' Gow observed. 'And keep your een on yon bloody sea. We don't want anything tae go wrong.'

'Leave it to your Uncle Lije,' Noble said. 'I got her going nice and steady now, ain't I ?'

He beamed at Gow in the darkness but at that moment almost as though to prove him wrong, the engine faltered and died.

With night putting a limit to vision the German guns were quieter as Allerton walked back through the town.

Around midnight he found himself by a temporary hospital in a schoolroom. The doctors were working by the light of acetylene lamps and the headlights of trucks now, and there were several Sisters of Mercy and a few exhausted R.A.M.C. men. A soldier bending over a stretcher rose slowly, and from the look on his face Allerton knew that the man at his feet was his friend and that he had died. 'What a bloody war,' he grated.

The place stank of antiseptic, cordite and dirty bodies, and seemed to be full of the bloodshot questioning eyes of the wounded, the sweat and tear-marks still on their grimy faces. A man was quietly dying in a corner, his face shrunken and thin, the skin taut over his cheeks and nose. Somewhere in the shadows another was mooing softly like a cow. Men muttered and groaned in the unquiet dark, and a horrible rattling noise came with deadly monotony. Every few minutes a match flared as someone looked at a pain-filled face where it stood out in stark outline in momentary incandescence. Then, unexpectedly, making Allerton jump, a shell-shocked man leapt up, cursing and shouting, his arms flailing. As he was dragged away, the doctor saw Allerton standing in front of him and assumed he was seeking attention. 'What's happened to your mouth?' he demanded.

'It's all right,' Allerton said. 'That's not why I'm here. I've got some wounded in a garage down the road.'

The doctor's uniform was splashed with blood and he looked exausted. 'I'm busy,' he said. 'There's nothing I can do. I've got two hundred and fifty here and more outside.'

Allerton turned away but the doctor called him back, his voice more gentle. 'How about asking the Sisters of Mercy? They might help.'

Allerton went outside. The garden and the field beyond were full of wounded, dozens and dozens of them, and the Sisters of Mercy moved among them holding hurricane lamps, their bat-winged head-dresses sombre against the light. Several men were burying the dead in a corner, unwashed, unfed, devoid of sleep, scratching themselves as they stared with melancholy faces at the padre intoning the words of the service. Then a spadeful of dirt fell on the blanketed bodies and the mounds of earth round the graves began to disappear.

Allerton stopped one of the Sisters of Mercy, a mere girl with plain pale features and spectacles, her coif marked with red stains. There was something extraordinarily beautiful in her face that came from the spirit and as he explained his wishes, she paused for a moment, spoke to one of the older women, then turned back to Allerton and nodded.

'*Oui*,' she said.

At Dover, they were still trying to assess the losses of the day, balancing them against the numbers brought to safety. The news of the disasters made grim reading.

'*Keith*,' the S.O.O. said, first listing the destroyers, the most precious asset of the Dover command. '*Foudroyant. Basilisk. Eager.* With *Ivanhoe* and *Worcester* damaged.'

He paused and the admiral lifted his head.

'To say nothing,' the S.O.O. went on, 'of the gunboat *Mosquito*, the minesweeper *Skipjack* the tug *St. Abbs. Salamander* and *Prague* also damaged, *Scotia* damaged and sinking, and *Brighton Queen* and the trawler *Jacinta* holed and stranded. Those are the ones we know about.'

He stopped to let the grim list sink in and the admiral frowned, well aware that the slaughter could not go on much longer. Up and down the roadsteads off the coast of France ships were on fire and sinking, and new wrecks littered the sandbanks all the way across the Channel.

'Four destroyers sunk,' he said. 'Four damaged. He stared at a signal which had arrived from the Admiralty in London. '*Discontinuation of the use of destroyers by day off the French coast*,' it directed, and then suggested the suspension of the evacuation at seven o'clock the following morning.

The admiral considered the problem. 'I understand the French have formed a line behind our people,' he said, 'and we're to retire through it.' He picked up a list and studied it. 'We must change the emphasis to night loading, and all small craft must work the beaches up to a mile and a half from the town. The harbour will be served by eight destroyers and seven personnel ships.'

The S.O.O. frowned. 'Some of them have been at it for a full week, sir,' he pointed out.

The admiral was unmoved. 'Then we must put fresh crews aboard. What's the score for today?'

'It's going to be in the region of sixty thousand, sir. Most of those coming in now are French, but we're having difficulty finding them and I understand there's a little difficulty over language. Think we ought to put someone ashore who can speak French?'

The admiral shook his head. 'I think they'll have to manage now,' he said.

SUNDAY, 2 JUNE
AND AFTERWARDS

Everything that would float was approaching the coast now, and odd pockets of men who had failed to get into Dunkirk were still being picked up from beaches outside the town. Small miracles were performed. Men adrift in dinghies made sails with clothing and waterproof capes, and in waterlogged engine rooms engineers stuffed holes with mattresses and stood waist-deep in water to watch their gauges. The Casino and the Kursaal were blazing now, and there were so many wrecks in the fairway by this time that boats were circling them for survivors – and sometimes finding them. Though the patient lines of men still waited along the length of the mole, ships were being hit again and again by shellfire and it was very quickly becoming clear that lifting at that point was too dangerous and the men must be turned about to file back to the beaches.

As the light increased, in the *Queen of France*, Lije Noble began to take off the lid of the engine hatch. Because no one had any matches, they'd been unable to examine it during the night. Now, in the first hours of the day, Noble stared at the old Ford engine and frowned heavily. To Gow, who was no mechanic, it looked merely like a squarish lump of metal with pipes attached.

As they peered at it, Angelet woke. The long black-fringed lashes that many a girl would have given her eye-teeth for, fluttered and his head turned. His eyes fastened on his rifle lying alongside him and he snatched it to him at once and sat up.

'*Où sommes-nous?*' he demanded. Then he saw Gow's face and just beyond him Noble's and he smiled '*Monsieur le Sergent,*' he said. '*Et Monsieur Nobelle.*' He glanced around. '*Où est le caporal?*'

Gow gestured. 'He didnae come,' he said.

Angelet stared, uncomprehending, and Gow turned to Marie-Josephine. 'Better tell him, Miss,' he said. 'You hae the French, I think.'

Marie-Josephine explained and Angelet's big eyes blinked so that they thought he was going to burst into tears. '*Que faisons-nous maintenant?*' he demanded.

'*Nous allons en Angleterre,*' Marie-Josephine said. 'We're going to England.'

'Join the army,' Noble said. 'Fight the Jerries. *Killay les Boches.*'

'Mebbe I could get y'in the Guards,' Gow said stiffly.

Noble was staring at the silent engine again, then he swore and jumped to the petrol tank. There was a stick in the scuppers and he snatched it up and thrust it through the hole. It reappeared barely wet.

'Oh, charming,' he said. 'Bloody charming!' He kicked the side of the boat savagely. 'Sodden old tub! The bloody fuel pipe's come adrift!' He gazed round him at the lifting sea. To a man born and brought up in the busy streets of London, it seemed the emptiest place in the world.

The sun was lifting above the horizon now, laying a golden pathway of sparkles towards them, and Gow squinted into it, frowning heavily, his face tense with concentration.

'There's a big launch yonder,' he said slowly, gesturing with a bony white hand. 'She's drifting and she looks empty, and she has what look like cans o' petrol on her deck. Mebbe we could get her to go.'

Noble lifted his head from where he was trying to attach the fuel lead. 'How do we get to her?' he asked. 'We ain't got no engine.'

Angelet spoke to Marie Josephine who turned to Gow. 'The soldier Angelet say he can swim,' she said. 'He say he will swim to discover if the other boat has the motor which will march.'

Angelet had already stripped off his tunic and trousers and stood stark naked in front of them, slim as a willow wand and just as white. Gow looked at him disapprovingly but Marie-Josephine, being French, didn't seem to find it at all odd.

As he'd said, Angelet was a good swimmer and they watched him pull himself with strong strokes through the water to the big cabin cruiser whose sides were riddled with bullet- and splinter-holes. Hauling himself on board, he disappeared from sight. Eventually he reappeared and began collecting heaving lines and mooring ropes which he tied together. Then, carefully paying them out into the sea, he dived overboard and began to swim back, holding the end. As they dragged him on board, he gasped out his story.

'He say there are two men,' Marie-Josephine translated. 'One is dead and one is broken – ' she touched her shoulder ' – here.'

Angelet had started pulling energetically at the rope and the distance between the two boats was already diminishing. Gow looked at him, frowning.

'F'r God's sake,' he said severely,' 'tell him tae put his troos on.'

As they bumped alongside *Athelstan*, Tremenheere was still lying on the well deck. His face was grey and drawn and he was clutching his arm to his chest. It had taken half the night to get it there.

'Is yon petrol?' Gow asked, indicating the cans on the deck that they had taken from the drifting cutter – years ago now, it seemed.

Tremenheere nodded. 'I tried to tell your mate but he didn't seem to catch on.'

'He's French,' Gow said.

'Oh!' Tremenheere blinked at Angelet's nakedness. 'It didn't show.'

With Gow tearing sheets from the cabin into strips, Marie-Josephine gently secured Tremenheere's arm into position against his body. His face was wet with sweat when she'd finished but he lifted his good arm and re-arranged the medals hanging from his lapel so that they were not obscured by the sling. 'Thanks,' he whispered.

Noble, who was staring into the engine room, turned his head. 'This bugger's not going to get us home,' he said quietly. 'I think she's sinking.'

'Too right she is, me dear,' Tremenheere said weakly. 'She'll go any time.'

'For Christ's sake !' Noble scrambled to his feet in alarm and they hurriedly helped Tremenheere to the *Queen of France* and hefted the petrol cans across. By the time they'd finished, *Athelstan* was down by the bows and seemed to be going faster all the time.'

'Better let go,' Tremenheere whispered, 'or she'll take us with her.'

Noble jumped forward. But the knot he'd tied was no sailor's invention and it wouldn't give.

'There's a knife in my pocket,' Tremenheere said.

It was Gow who snatched it and sliced through the ropes. As they parted with a twang, *Athelstan* rolled over as though she were tired. The stern came up so that they could see the propeller. A length of grass line was twisted round it, jammed by the turning blades until it was as hard as steel.

'I thought there was something,' Tremenheere murmured.

It was as they got going again and swung in a wide sweep towards the east to avoid a mat of wreckage that they saw the figure clinging to the buoy. It was Gow who saw it first.

'Yon feller's alive,' he observed. 'We'd best pick him up.'

'I'm not so bloody sure we can,' Noble said, struggling with the tiller.

'Mon, you just point the nose towards him.' Gow's experience of boat handling was confined to rowing on the Serpentine but to him everything was simple, whether it was driving a car or steering a boat or killing Germans. You just did it.

They tried without success, swinging round the weakly-waving figure, frustrated in their efforts to draw near.

'Go up-tide, me dear,' Tremenheere suggested gently.

This time they were more successful but the boat's bow hit the buoy so hard the figure fell off into the water, and it was Marie-Josephine who snatched up the boathook and held it out. The man just managed to grab it as he drifted past.

'Hatton,' he whispered as they hauled him aboard. 'Sub-lieutenant. *Vital.*'

'You hurt anywhere, mate?' Noble asked.

Hatton raised his eyes to the four faces staring down at him.

They were blurred by his own exhaustion. 'A bit,' he said. 'But not so's you'd notice.'

Gow frowned. 'Ye'll be a wee bit tired, mebbe?' he said and Hatton almost laughed. It seemed to be the understatement of the year.

The *Queen of France* was chugging steadily through the wreckage now, picking her way through the bodies and the floating debris, and they thought they were safe when the aeroplanes came over again.

Gow immediately sprang to the Bren and hoisted it up against the angle of the built-in foredeck, but he got in no more than two or three bursts before the planes swept past towards the shore. As he dropped the gun and peered after them, one of them began to send out puffs of smoke from its starboard engine and curved away in a flat bank, losing height all the time. They saw it crash into the sea about a mile away.

Gow's white face cracked in a bleak smile. 'I got one,' he said.

Since the destroyers and minesweepers had also been banging away and were a lot nearer than Gow, it didn't seem to Lije Noble for a minute that it was Gow who had brought the plane down, but, as he carried the Bren over his shoulder all the way from the frontier, Noble felt he deserved some reward.

'Yes, *mon fils*,' he said in a flat voice. 'Good shot!'

Gow was turning to Marie-Josephine, as though expecting her to add her mead of praise, when she pointed excitedly. Just ahead of them was a small boat with two men in it. They seemed to have no oar and one of the figures started waving. Noble shut off the engine, waiting to see which way the tide was carrying them, then he swung the heavy rudder and manœuvred the boat round.

'I'm getting the hang of this thing now,' he said proudly. 'I reckon I'll transfer to the navy when we get 'ome.'

Glad to see the back of the tiny pram, Horndorff scrambled gratefully to the *Queen of France*. There was a man asleep in the bottom of the boat whom he at first thought dead, and he moved stiffly past him to the bow and sat down. Conybeare followed him, the Luger still tucked into his trouser top.

Noble watched them. The bruise over Conybeare's eye was

every colour of the rainbow now and his eye was almost closed. He looked exactly like the illustrations for *Just William*.

'You any good with one of these things, sir?' Noble asked.

'Not really.' Conybeare said.

Horndorff turned, his eyebrows raised. 'At last,' he said. 'I have found something you cannot do.'

He turned his back and gazed stiffly out to sea and Noble stared at him. 'He all right?' he asked.

'Oh, yes,' Conybeare said. 'He's all right.'

'He looks as though he's got the hump.'

'Yes, he has a bit.'

'Who is he?'

'Friend of mine. Tanks.'

'Not hurt?'

'No,' Conybeare said. 'Bit cross, that's all.'

Horndorff turned and faced the others. 'I am a German officer,' he said slowly, deliberately. 'I am a prisoner of war.'

Noble's jaw dropped. 'I didn't know we'd captured any.'

'You have captured at least one,' Horndorff snapped. 'Officer Conybeare is taking me to England.'

Noble grinned. 'Well,' he said. 'We're a bit short of grub, so if we have to eat each other, we know who to start on first.' He turned back to the business of the boat. 'Hold tight, folks. We'd best be on our way.'

As he spoke, the engine started faltering and he leapt to it at once.

'Now what's up with the bugger?' he screeched.

'Is it running hot?' Tremenheere asked faintly.

'No.'

'Petrol switched on?'

'Yes.'

As Noble spoke, the engine gave a final cough and died.

'Oh, Christ Jesus,' Noble moaned.

Tremenheere lifted himself in the bottom of the boat with difficulty. 'Bring us that can of petrol,' he said.

Gow passed it over, and he unscrewed it one-handed and sniffed. 'Smell's like petrol,' he said. 'Pour a bit out.'

Gow splashed a little of the liquid on to his hand and he stared at it.

'Water, me dear,' he said. 'It's got water in it.'

Horndorff started to smile, and Noble glared at him.

'What's *he* grinning at?' he demanded.

Hordorff looked at Conybeare. 'All to no avail, Officer Cony-beare,' he said. 'You will not get me to England after all. We shall remain here until it is all over and then, when all your ships have gone, the German Navy will come and you will be taken back where we have come from to join the others who have been caught. *Es wird ein deutscher Sieg.* It will be a German victory.'

Tremenheere's soft Cornish drawl interrupted him. He'd been staring about him with interest and now his words came, full of sly pleasure.

'Hard luck, me dear,' he said. 'Not this time. This is a Mevagissey lugger we're in. Or she was once. She's built for large harbours with plenty of sea room and she's rigged for a dipping lug. They take herring, mackerel and pilchards, accord-ing to what comes in, and they're good sea-boats. And I come from Truro way and, if I'm not mistaken, this bloody uncom-fortable pole I'm lying on's the mast.'

Conybeare turned to Horndorff and gave a little smile '*Der Sieg wird bis auf Weiteres verschoben*,' he said. 'Victory will be a little late this year.'

Horndorff's head jerked round. 'You speak German?'

'Had a German governess.'

The German's face darkened. 'Then why did we speak always in English?'

Conybeare shrugged. 'Because you're my prisoner and I'm tak-ing you to England,' he said. 'That's why.'

The big lift was coming to an end. By this time, the destroyer force had been bled to death and the weary admiral had only nine warships left out of the forty he'd handled and only ten out of thirty personnel ships.

The major portion of the B.E.F. had survived, however, all of them wise with the experience of war and possessing the skill to build a new army. With them had come Belgians and French, a few nurses, a few civilians eager to enlist, and God alone knew how many dogs.

The admiral glanced at the signal in his hand. It had come in some hours before. '*To V.A., Dover*,' it said. '*From S.N.O., Dunkirk. B.E.F. evacuated.*'

He stood by the desk, holding it on top of a folder. He looked a little older than he had a week ago and he suddenly realized just how weary he was. He laid the folder down.

'Signal all ships to move away,' he said, 'and instruct the blockships to enter. We must have picked up everybody who's in a position to leave.'

Not quite everybody.

There was still Sievewright.

Eager had been well out in the fairway when she'd sunk, and the dinghy he'd stepped into had been washed away by the surge of water as she'd gone down. The tug that had come roaring down to pick up the survivors had passed him to port and her wake had lifted him further away. As the dinghy had spun round, he'd realized it was drifting.

At first he'd moved further towards the shore but then, as the tide had turned, he'd noticed he was moving out to sea and began to wonder what he should do. As a good Scout, he knew you could live without food, but he also knew that without water his chances were not very good. Sea water brought on madness, and all the rules for survival seemed to include having compasses, hard biscuits, beef extracts, a knife, a rocket, fishing lines for landing fish, something for catching rainwater, and always a sail or a pair of oars. As he stared round the dinghy he saw there was neither sail nor oar – not even a rowlock -- and that all it contained besides himself was a little sea water and some scraps of what looked like bait, which looked so repulsive he couldn't ever imagine being driven to the extremity of wishing to eat them.

He sat down again in the stern and stared back at the land. For once there didn't appear to be anything in his Scout training that covered an emergency of this sort.

The sun was lowering as the French admiral in command of the port moved with his men towards the sea; but as the last retreat began, from the cellars, the ruined houses and the shelters of Malo and Dunkirk, a monstrous army of unarmed men began to converge on the mole, an immense river of refugees and of craven soldiers who'd hidden from the fighting. They snatched the places of the desperate men of the rear-guard who, when the final dawn came, had to stand on the beaches and watch the last of the ships leave without them. A British destroyer, one of the oldest and least beautiful of them all, lifted the final load as German machine guns started firing on her at short range. Behind her, she left only the sacrificed French regiments, their discipline still strong, their bearing still proud, the broken men, the deserters and the wounded.

On one of the last lonely craft moving along the beaches towards the open Channel, its decks crammed with haggard men, Nobby Clark, Royal Navy, late of *Athelstan*, later still of the fishing boat, *Bonny*, and still wondering from time to time about the survivors' leave he hadn't had, stared towards the devastation along the whole ten miles of beach from Dunkirk to La Panne. For the most part during the past week, what with the activity and the noise, he hadn't had much time to stop and think, but now the penny seemed to drop and he became aware of the incredible silence, of the bodies along the tide line and floating in little groups in the calm water, and of the rows of wrecked and abandoned vehicles and guns beyond, like a vast ugly, soundless graveyard in the sunshine. Groups of French soldiers who had fought bravely every inch of the way back stared out to sea along with British gunners of the rear-guard who had blown up their guns and could now only wait despairingly for ships that would never come. Who's going to bring *them* out? he thought. What about the ones left behind? And in the sudden stillness that had come over the battlefield he asked himself, What's it all for? Who's responsible? Since the previous September he had seen some terrible things, but none that had moved him so much as this, and in his exhaustion and the terrible hurt he felt, he seemed broken inside and wanted to sit down on the crowded deck and weep.

On 4 June the sun rose harsh and gaudy, catching the black smoke that still curled up from the blazing oil tanks and drifted along the coast past Gravelines towards Calais.

Along the shore there were still a few small boats looking for men, but nothing else, and the beaches were lonely apart from the wreckage, the immobile dead and the quick mounds of new-filled graves. Above the smoke, the Stukas searched for victims but there were no longer any there. The sea was empty.

When the last ship arrived at Dover, 338,226 men had been brought to England, and they knew it was all over at last. The results were stupendous. Yet there were some who hadn't made it, as they well knew.

Allerton was among them, and as Dunkirk surrendered a padre near him was giving instructions to those who were left. 'Don't be afraid,' he was telling them. 'Just say "*Nicht schiessen — Rotes Kreuz.*" That should do the trick.'

Orders had arrived that one officer and ten men were to be left for every hundred casualties, and that the remainder of the medical staff could leave. As they had prepared to move to the mole, Allerton had noticed a medical orderly standing apart, his head erect, his face stiff.

'You staying?' Allerton asked.

'Yes.'

'I'm sorry.'

'So am I. I've got a nipper I've never seen. I got the telegram the day it all started.'

Allerton said nothing for a moment; then he lifted his head. 'Can't you get someone to take your place?'

The medical orderly turned away, his expression bleak. 'Who'll take *my* place?' he said. 'Here.'

'I will.'

The soldier had just been about to bend over a wounded man and he straightened up again. His face was still expressionless but the dead look in his eyes had gone.

'Better go and fix it,' Allerton said.

There were tears in the orderly's eyes. 'You're a toff, sir,' he said. Allerton shrugged. '*Fais ce que dois, adveigne que pourra. C'est commandé au chevalier.*' Allerton was proud of his erudition but to the medical orderly the words were meaningless.

'What's that mean, sir?' he asked.

Allerton managed a gap-toothed grin. 'It means "*Press on regardless,*" ' he said. ' "*It's a command from the chap on the horse.*" '

Some time during the morning, they heard lorries outside and then the first German entered. He was a corporal and he was wearing a helmet and jackboots.

'*Raus!*' he shouted. '*Alles raus! Schnell! Hände hoch! Der Krieg ist vorbei!*'

As they straightened up from the stretchers and lifted their hands, he gestured with his pistol. 'For you the war is over. England and France are defeated. *Heil Hitler!*'

As his arm shot out in a salute, he was pushed aside. The officer who entered was a tall man, incredibly thin and wearing spectacles. His voice was much quieter and there was no arrogance.

'I'm sorry,' he said. 'But you are now prisoners of the German Reich. The wounded will be properly cared for and all doctors and medical staff will be allowed to continue to attend them.'

It didn't stop the corporal returning when he'd gone and removing their watches and money.

Allerton was not alone.

The dead lay all over the town, in hastily-scraped graves in gardens and parks and among the sand-dunes. They sprawled along the tide line, floated face downwards in the shallows, and lay in the warm yielding soil all the way back to the frontier through the old graveyards of the earlier war, as far south as Beaurains and beyond. They huddled in the ditches, in the fields and in the streets of a hundred small towns and villages, among the wrecked guns and smoking vehicles and all the other detritus of a defeated army. Many more were entombed in the icy hulks of ships beneath the sea.

There were hundreds of them. Lieutenant-Commander Hough, of *Vital* was one, with Lieutenant MacGillicuddy and the rest of the ship's company and the ship's company of *Eager* and many other fine vessels. Even Dr. Knevett, owner of *Athelstan*, was among them, because he'd finally insisted on crossing on the personnel ship, *Scotia*, and she was now lying on her side, a burnt-out wreck. Temporary Acting Corporal Rice hadn't reached safety. Nor had Lieutenant Wren, of the York and Lancs. Captain Deshayes, of Angelet's 121st, hadn't made it either, and despite the efforts he'd made, nor had Private Favre. Neither had Sergeant Galpin, of the Engineers, nor Private Bawes, H., of the Worcesters, now bobbing gently in the cabin of *Athelstan* below the sea, or an unknown Cockney, still lying with his face covered by his helmet where Scharroo had left him on the mole. Or Joe Ferris or wee Alec Galt or Ordinary Seaman Didcot.

On the deck of the last ship to leave, Gilbert Williams was writing his report. It wasn't very official and it wasn't in triplicate. It was in pencil in Gilbert's ungainly hand on a scrap of paper torn from an exercise book and he was finding it hard to write for the tears in his eyes.

'*I wish to report the loss of my boat, Daisy,*' he wrote down. '*I put all my savings into her and now I have got nothing. She was run down by the tug, Gamecock. My brother, E. Williams, is missing, also S. Brundrett and K. Pepper.*'

Even now the water of the Channel was littered with rafts, rubber dinghies, motor tyres and small boats containing determined men who were set on reaching safety. One intrepid warrior of high spirits and great good humour, stripped to the buff and swimming five miles offshore, was picked up by a destroyer as he headed doggedly for England. 'Sure you've got room?' he gasped as they dragged him to the deck. 'I was just getting into my stride.'

A few miles from him was the *Queen of France*, moving northwards under her brown lugsail. There was little wind and she moved sluggishly, but she moved, carrying with her: Private Angelet, of the 121st Regiment; Major Horndorff von Bülowius of the *Spezialdienstabteilung* of the 8th Panzer Division; Flying Officer Conybeare; Lance-Corporal Gow, still clutching the Bren; Private Noble; Sub-Lieutenant Hatton, just beginning to come to life; Marie-Josephine Berthelot; and Alban Kitchener Tremenheere.

They were all tired and stiff and chilled with lack of food and sleep. They stank because they'd had to remain unwashed in a fortnight of blazing heat, and their stained dirty faces were narrow and gaunt with strain. They looked like scarecrows, and they had little to say because a week or more of shouting above the perpetual, din of Dunkirk had left them all croaking like jackdaws.

Horndorff had at last accepted that the war was over for him and was even beginning to feel that the Führer's dream of a conquered Britain might not materialize after all. Private Angelet was wondering how he'd survive in a foreign land. Lance-Corporal Gow was wondering if they'd ever had a Frenchman in the Guards. Private Noble was staring at Gow, deciding that while he, Lije Noble, was a useless bastard, and was going to find himself a dead cushy job, the terrible Gow was going to get himself promoted and was heading for glory – and more than likely death. Sub-Lieutenant Hatton was thinking about Nora Hart and whether he'd ever dare to go to sea again. Marie-Josephine Berthelot was wondering just what would have happened to her if she'd married Monsieur Ambrey as her parents had wished, while Flying Officer Conybeare was considering the possibility of leave and whether any of the girls he knew would accept a date with him. Alban Kitchener Tremenheer's brooding was the deepest of the lot. He *knew* what would happen to *him*. He'd be slapped in an ambulance and taken to a casualty clearing station where someone would ask his name and address and set his broken collar bone. Then they'd pin a label on him and send him home on the train. And with a broken collar bone, he knew there was only one place he could go. He could hardly exist without money and a broken collar bone anywhere else, and Number Thirteen, Osborne Road, Littlehampton, seemed a terrible prospect because Nell Noone would have him, sure as eggs.

As they sat in silence, occupied with their own thoughts and moving to the lift of the boat, Marie-Josephine laid her hand on Conybeare's arm and pointed. He sat up and stared.

'Boat,' he said. 'There's a chap in it, waving.'

It was Clarence Sievewright, and he was growing worried by this time. He was still neat and hardly touched by the war, and as the *Queen of France* bumped alongside, he stepped from one boat to the other without even getting his boots splashed.

'Quite an exciting war,' he said in a masterpiece of understatement.

The others stared at him. 'You don't look as though you've seen so bloody much of it,' Noble said.

Sievewright shook his head. He was a modest man and had no wish to make claims for himself that he knew would never stand up to inspection by this battered collection of human beings.

'No,' he said. 'I've not.'

As they pressed him to tell his story, Horndorff listened in baffled bewilderment. Raised on stern ideals of courage and duty, it seemed to him a matter of shame that a man could pass through such a holocaust as Dunkirk without going out of his way to become directly concerned with it. Yet, with the exception of the silent, bone-white man with the Bren, the other Britishers in the boat, their drawn dirty faces cracked in weary grins, seemed to regard the newcomer not as a figure of shame or even fun, but more as though he had done something remarkably clever. Their own attitude to the war came out in ribald admissions that they had been stupid enough to let themselves be swept up in the drama while Sievewright had all unwittingly shown an old soldier's skill and cunning in avoiding disaster. This self-deprecation was something entirely alien to Horndorff's upbringing, and the protest that broke from his lips at their wry laughter was also his protest at the unfairness of a fate that had allowed him – the expert, a man with years of training behind him – to be taken prisoner by a bunch of reluctant amateurs.

'You English are mad,' he exploded. 'How can you laugh when you have just lost a battle?'

Conybeare shrugged, apparently unmoved at the thought of defeat. 'Long practice,' he said. 'We *always* lose 'em.'

Hatton grinned. 'Everybody expects us to,' he added.

Noble had swung the boat on to course again now. He stared with a professional eye at the dipping bow and then up at the brown lugsail and permitted himself a sly smile, as though victory in war were not a matter of preparation, endurance and bravery so much as of craft and back-street cunning. 'Except one,' he said. 'The one that matters. The last one.'

EPILOGUE

Alban Kitchener Tremenheere was dead right about his future and he did marry Nell Noone. The Littlehampton parish register shows that the wedding took place on 5 November 1940, just seven months before the birth of the first of two sons. As things worked out, he didn't regret marrying Nell as much as he'd expected, and they lived on at Thirteen, Osborne Road, until the 1960s when they followed their children as emigrants to Australia.

James Barry Hatton, however, did *not* marry Nora Hart. Although after it was all over he repeated the proposal he had made she had enough intelligence to know that what had happened between them was only the result of an extraordinary situation and in the end it meant nothing at all. He makes no bones about the affair and admits gratefully that she had more sense than he had. After the war he married the daughter of the managing editor of a Middlesbrough-based newspaper group, and the reference books now show him to be an editor and director himself. Nowadays he sails a little, but he never went to sea again during the war and ended his naval career on the staff of Sir Andrew Cunningham.

Rejecting what he considered the trivialities of his pre-war life for the medicine he studied during his years as a prisoner of war, Basil Allerton became a doctor, and finally a pathologist specializing in leprosy. His base is the Mill Hill Centre, London, from where he regularly journeys all over the world on lecture tours.

Walter Boner Scharroo remained in London throughout the

blitz and his attitude to the British improved even as his attitude to the Germans deteriorated. His broadcasts to America eventually became as famous as those of Quentin Reynolds. When the United States entered the war, he went through the Pacific campaigns as a war correspondent, distinguishing himself with brilliant stories for the *Time-Life* group. He was killed in an aircraft crash in the Philippines in 1950 while on his way to cover the war in Korea.

Hans-Joachim Horndorff von Bülowius married the girl who'd waited for him through five years of victory and defeat and ended up exactly where he expected to end up, as a colonel in the revived German Wehrmacht attached to the NATO forces. According to a recent article on him in *Stern*, he is now retired, influential, and still running the family estates.

Marie-Josephine Berthelot returned to France in 1943 – by parachute – and was in Paris at the time of the Liberation. She was decorated by de Gaulle and the British Government. She never went back to the North, however, and on marriage settled in Nîmes, not far from the Mediterranean.

As a much-decorated wing commander, Rupert Arthur Rokesby Conybeare was shot down on a fighter sweep in 1942 and taken prisoner himself. As one might have expected, he escaped and made his way home through Spain. He retired from the R.A.F. as an air vice-marshal and still a bachelor. Oddly enough he is now an old friend of Jocho Horndorff and godfather to his daughter. When they once appeared together on B.B.C. television in a programme on the anniversary of Dunkirk, they still treated each other with a certain amount of wary caution, as though they both might still expect surprises. Perhaps their friendship isn't all that odd, because both are single-minded, stubborn and professional.

As might also be expected of him, Clarence Sievewright is still with the firm in Luton for which he worked before the war. He no longer keeps up his interest in Scouting and will sometimes sheepishly admit that the stories he tells nowadays of how he fought his way out of France have greatly improved with the telling.

Corporal Gustave Chouteau kept his promise to join the Resistance and remained with them until the fall of Paris. His favourite story – once published with appropriate pictures in

Paris Match – is of how he and Marie-Josephine Berthelot, lying in the gutter alongside each other during the shooting outside Notre Dame when Charles de Gaulle attended the thanksgiving service for the liberation of Paris in August, 1944, discovered they had met briefly once before on the beaches of Dunkirk. To his great regret, he never again met Angelet who, he has since discovered, was killed as a sergeant only a few days before the liberation of the capital while fighting with Leclerc. It would have been pleasant, Chouteau always feels, if Angelet, too, could have been there in the gutter with him and Marie-Josephine Berthelot.

Private Noble, as he will tell you himself without a trace of shame, tried to make very sure that he was never in the front line again. He didn't manage it, however. That touch of glory he'd noticed about Lance-Corporal Gow *had* rubbed off on him and after Dunkirk he was posted as a corporal to North Africa. When Rommel overran the British lines in what he calls the 'Gazala Gallop' of 1942, he and his lines-of-communication comrades found themselves with rifles in their hands. He did better than he expected and, much to his surprise, he ended the war as a sergeant with a medal and a lot of Gow's mannerisms. He hadn't changed a lot underneath, however, and when peace returned he was one of the first to see the opportunities in the sale of ex-Army lorries. He still lives in London – but these days at a rather more high-class address – and is now very respectable and very comfortably off. As one would have expected. He never forgot Gow, and his son bears the name of John Gow Noble.

It turned out he was dead right about Lance-Corporal Gow, too. He was promoted sergeant soon after his return to England and was eventually sent to what he always considered one of the less proud regiments of the British army to knock it into shape after it had been badly cut up in North Africa. It didn't suit him, however, to be part of so ordinary a company, and, according to Noble, who went to a great deal of trouble after the war to find him again, he moved heaven and earth to get back to his own exalted sphere. He was with his own kind when he was killed in Germany in 1945 leading a company of Guardsmen after the death of its commanding officer. Regimental records show he had been recommended for the V.C. but

Coldstreamers who remember him don't seem to find it at all strange that he didn't get it; not even posthumously. 'It was what he was trained for,' they say, 'and they don't chuck those things around in the Guards just for doing your duty.'